Tyrants Rex

Clint Wastling

Stairwell Books

Published by Stairwell Books
70 Barbara Drive
Norwalk
CT 06851 USA

161 Lowther Street
York, YO31 7LZ

www.stairwellbooks.co.uk
@stairwellbooks

ISBN: 978-1-939269-58-4

Printed and bound in the UK by Russell Press
Layout design: Alan Gillott
Edited by Becca Miles
Cover art: Rebecca Macfarland

Also by Clint Wastling

The Geology of Desire

Acknowledgements

I have been helped by many people in writing Tyrants Rex. Firstly my wife, Brenda, who puts up with me vanishing into the study for hours on end and then being asked to read various drafts! I am particularly indebted to Coral for rescuing the original manuscript from the slush pile and suggesting early changes. Becca took over as editor and has been invaluable in her support and taking the novel further. There's a lot of her hard work in these pages and some great debates about the characters within. As always Rose and Alan have provide invaluable friendship and support throughout. As Rose has said, "it's taken a whole village to raise this novel," and I'm eternally grateful to everyone.

Chapter 1: Mycul

The science of landscape enthralled him. From a ship with a shifting horizon and creaking rigging, landscape was something to be savoured.

Mycul looked towards the island that not so much rose but coagulated from oceanic mud. Its cliffs punched above the water leaving a thin ribbon of clay to mark land. "It looks beautiful but don't get left behind," the sailor said. He slapped the youth's back.

"What do you mean?" Mycul pushed strands of black hair from his face revealing his bright blue eyes.

"Dreadful things happen on the Reach of Key."

"Like?"

The sailor came so close Mycul could smell the mix of garlic and rotting gums on his breath. The skin around his eyes was creased with lines interrupted by warty growths. "Mordonts," he whispered, and would say nothing further.

"Mordonts?" Mycul looked more closely at the island hoping they were close enough to catch a glimpse. He remembered the bedtime tales his father had woven into his dreams.

The boson whistled. At the signal, the sailors took up position and began heaving in the sails. "Now you're for it," the sailor cackled, "the Graken tests us all. Those she doesn't like!" He slapped his hands together. Mycul got the meaning.

Still nervous from the ordeal of his first days at sea, Mycul was summoned to the initiation by the captain.

"All new sailors are called to mount the Graken and sit with her rider." The captain pushed Mycul forward and the sailors parted leaving the deck empty.

The rider lowered the Graken's sinuous neck, almost level with the deck. Mycul hesitated but felt the hand of the rider grab his collar and pull him behind on an intricate saddle. The sea monster sprang upright and issued a fierce roar. Mycul nearly toppled backwards and was only saved by his feet catching in the stirrups. He dangled upside down to the roar of laughter from the deck. He felt his life had ended and his humiliation was complete. *Do not fear me, Mycul Zas.* The words inside his head formed like colours. Her name drifted through the hissing of blood in his ears.

1

He saw the horizon tilt as the creature lowered her neck and he regained his seat. The Graken shot upright again. *Mycul Zas!* her fellow Graken shouted until the name lost its meaning in the cacophony of voices. *You must not tell the truth, Mycul. Deny you heard us!* The Graken lowered her neck to the deck and Mycul dismounted.

"Did you hear her voice?" the captain asked, keen to find a replacement rider.

Mycul trembled from his ordeal and lied. The sailors raised a cheer and patted Mycul on the shoulders before lifting him and carrying him round the deck. Only the captain seemed unhappy.

The Duskwalker slowed as they reached the port. The Graken pulled the ship into harbour carefully avoiding other vessels. Mycul knew these creatures towed the largest ships across the sea at great speeds. Their bodies dwarfed the vessels under their control. Above the waves, her slender neck twisted and turned with a solitary rider perched on a saddle behind the Graken's ears. The ship surged forward as the Graken spied its meal at the harbour side. The beast's yellow teeth dripped saliva. Mycul watched. The ship jolted as the head darted forward and grasped the man. He had time to scream before the jaws crunched into the skull. The Graken tossed the head back and swallowed before returning to the body. The blood spurting onto the harbour side excited the creature and it licked the granite blocks before flicking the body into its cavernous mouth.

The Keeper arrived dressed in the purple that marked his authority. "I proclaim this land to be the Reach of Key and subject to the laws of Faires." With this he banged his staff on the ground and the Graken submerged, leaving her rider swimming for the ladders lining the pier.

This was the first time Mycul had seen land for days. His uncle had decided he should see the world: "The farm could wait" he had insisted. The old deck hands had laughed until tears rolled down their cheeks as Mycul told them his story.

That had been his first night on the Duskwalker, a cruel night in which truth unfolded with the contents of his stomach. Slowly it dawned on Mycul how naive he'd been. He hadn't been able to sleep, instead the yawing of the ship induced thoughts of his betrayal and dreams of impossible revenges. He saw it clearly now. Mycul was only weeks from his eighteenth birthday at which age the farm would legally have been his. The Keeper of his village would have held an assembly and proclaimed it. One tap of his staff and his entire village would be obliged to Mycul Zas for land stretching from the hills to the sacred valley. Even mordonts would know of the greatest landowner in the area. Mycul wanted to see the world before he settled down to farm and his uncle had played to that desire. Nevertheless, Mycul also wanted to find out about his father who had vanished all those years ago.

The visit of the scientist a year previously helped Mycul make up his mind. His village didn't usually have important visitors but this man had sought him out. He carefully selected a table and ordered a pitcher of weak beer and fresh bread.

"Are you Mycul Zas?" the young man had asked. The visitor was handsome, his blond hair swept back from his face and he possessed side burns, which arrived at a point half way along his cheek. Mycul had never seen trousers and jacket of so many colours. He counted seven distributed in triangles across the fabric.

"You must be important." Mycul bowed.

The man smiled. "I am Sartesh Andrada, Keeper of the Seventh Law of the Adee. The mordonts told me I'd find you here." The visitor sat and asked Mycul to sit opposite him.

"So what's it like living in Vold Nujun?"

"It's a farming community, so everything has its season."

"And you will own land here?"

"I am a ward of my uncle until my eighteenth birthday, sir. My father disappeared many years ago."

Sartesh thought about this but before he could speak, Mycul interrupted his thoughts:

"How have you talked to mordonts and lived?"

"They are more sinned against than sinning. You've read the history and science of the Adee, so you know the genetic experiments they did."

"Dreadful things and the nightmares they created still live with us," Mycul pulled across the glass and sipped some of his guest's beer. "My father vanished eight years ago. We've never heard from him or found a body."

"Really? Then we have something else in common." Sartesh leaned forward to whisper. "My father also vanished and left me in an uncle's care." The visitor said this in a way which implied they did not get on. "You must travel, my friend," Sartesh concluded. "For your own safety you must travel. Go to The Reach of Key and find out the truth about mordonts. Faires might hate you but it will set you on your journey through life."

Sartesh was tall and possessed the most piercing green eyes that were trained constantly on Mycul.

"I am travelling to Faires Argenta to take supplies of gold to the Protector. I've always loved geology. Here take this, it will help you

3

while away the hours on your journey over the sea." Sartesh passed Mycul a leather-bound text called the *Science of Geomorphology*. Mycul handled it carefully. He flicked through the pages and stopped at one of the pictures. The lithograph showed The Reach of Key.

"What does a mordont look like?"

Sartesh had smiled. "They are fearsome and beautiful. They were the first genetically modified humans and designed to be great warriors." He would not be drawn further. At the farmhouse door, he produced a bottle from his saddlebag.

"Take one drop for the *mal de mare*." Sartesh finally produced a small leather pouch from his pocket. He pressed the object into Mycul's hands and lingered over the touch. Mycul was about to open it but Sartesh stayed his hand. "Carry it with you always. It is loaded and dangerous. The Adee called it a gun: it fires bullets more quickly than an arrow. The Protector of Faires has strictly forbidden their use."

Mycul pushed it back into Sartesh's hands.

"And yet you will have much need of it before we meet again," Sartesh smiled and mounted his horse.

It was only at this point that Mycul had the sense to ask, "How do you know all this?"

"The Ornithon," Sartesh replied.

_*_

Mycul matched the picture in the book Sartesh had given with the vista before him. He watched the Dockers on the quay. His hand searched inside his jacket for the leather pouch. Inside he felt the cold touch of metal and the soft glow of memories stirred in his heart. "Git yourself to the captain now," a sailor said, spitting over the side as he passed.

Mycul responded immediately. Inside the captain's cabin, he noticed the smell – a medicinal concoction of tar and bisphenol. The mariner rubbed his hands in a jar of ointment and massaged his face and cheeks. "The salt dries out my skin. Always has. If I don't use this, I resemble a leper. The men wouldn't be happy. Peeling skin is a bad omen."

Mycul knew how superstitious the sailors were.

"How much do you know of The Reach?"

Mycul opened his mouth to speak then realised it was forbidden to talk of the Adee.

The captain smiled. "Keeping your own council. Good. Whatever happens, don't go up onto the moor at night and beware the mordonts. Still, there's much to keep you in the port. Find yourself someone to lose your virginity to whilst we unload the cargo. Mind you're back on board at second watch tomorrow as we sail with the

4

tide. I've never liked the Reach." The captain looked down at his feet, remembering something painful. When he straightened up, he said, "Take this and go." He handed Mycul a gold sovereign.

Mycul felt the warm metal. "Thanks." He beamed.

"It's not charity, it's superstition. Sailors don't like virgins on-board, besides it's but a fraction of the fee your uncle paid."

"My uncle paid you? Why?" Mycul's worst fears were proven. His smile diminished and was replaced by tightness in his throat and stomach.

He looked at the coin. Mycul knew it was unlucky to have a virgin on a long voyage as the sea gods loved unblemished flesh and would pull ships to their doom to reach them. Mycul didn't believe in folk tales but he knew it was unwise to upset your peers when hundreds of miles of ocean separate you from land.

As the ropes were cast ashore, flags above caught the breeze. One pennant proclaimed *Zhedhelion Barkbada Uita*! Mycul fed the coin into the lining of his uniform and pinned it in place. He patted it and smiled.

The boson whistled. At the signal the crew took up position and began heaving in the sails. The Graken resurfaced, looked around and let out a shriek.

-*-

Seawater was swilled over the quay to remove the sacrificial blood before Mycul was allowed to walk along the pier. The locals seemed friendly enough. They said *hello* or *good day* as the mood took them and without exception, they wore the grey of the proletariat. Mycul walked a little unsteadily until his balance adjusted to land and he began the incline from the wharf to town. His collar chafed at his neck and a curious excitement buzzed within his body.

He made for the whorehouse and was surprised to find it a well-kept building with a host of colourful flowers in the garden. He picked a pink and placed it in his lapel.

"Good morning, sir. And what brings you to Madam Messalina's?"

He whispered in the woman's ear, taking in her lavender perfume as he did.

"You have good currency?"

"What might I get for half a sovereign?" Mycul fingered the coin in its hiding place.

"We're quiet today, so you can have…" the madam whispered and Mycul felt his colour rise at the possible choices.

"Half in advance."

Mycul pulled the coin free. Madam Messalina laughed and handed over the change.

"Never pay in advance and never trust a stranger. Those were the two things my mama taught me." Madam Messalina clapped her hands and took him through the fly screen and into a gaudy room. He took in the rich reds, mauves and violets of the décor and savoured the exotic scents. The curtains at the back of the room fluttered and a procession of people emerged. First, a naked woman with pendulous breasts and a care-worn face stepped into the light; she was followed by a youth who was possessed of fine physique. He had the look of a Mennedic warrior about him. A man with rippling muscles was next: he stared defiantly at Mycul, then licked his lips and smiled. The fourth out was a pale waif of a girl, perhaps sixteen, and last a black skinned woman with sultry brown eyes, firm breasts and a slender waist.

"Take your time, young man." Messalina led him forward and let him touch those on offer. "All my whores are clean and perform their best. They enjoy their work."

Mycul toured the five again. The young girl wouldn't look him in the eye but Mycul saw the joy in the man's sultry brown eyes. He stood in front of him for a moment.

"Cydar is very versatile. The younger is Stazman if he's more your type."

Messalina brushed her hand through her hair.

"Do the women have names?" Mycul asked shyly.

"Petu has been here as long as I, Varga is very popular and here is Orlando."

Mycul could not decide who might sate pleasure the best. The madam swished away a fly. Decisively he tapped the black woman on the shoulder. "She's beautiful isn't she? Orlando is yours."

Mycul was escorted through the curtain into a room full of cushions and flowers. The perfume filled his head and intoxicated him as he undressed. The cushions absorbed his body and the woman's scent aroused his desires. "Let's share a drink?" The woman poured two glasses and began stroking his skin.

The next thing Mycul remembered was waking on a plain bed in a darkened room. Orlando fanned herself as she watched him from a cane chair. "You were good."

Mycul pulled a sheet over his naked body.

Orlando laughed.

"You rode me like a bull. I cannot say that of every man I meet."

"Thanks." He lay back. He wanted to be alone at that moment. He felt exhausted and his skin was clammy as though sweat had drenched every surface and dried.

"Are you ready for your bath?" She stood and waited.

"A bath? Yes."

Orlando opened the door and revealed a tiled alcove containing a deep bath like a pool. "You must hurry or Messalina will charge you more."

Mycul stood for a moment and as the door closed, he allowed the towel to fall. He stepped into the pool. He expected cold, but the water was warm, sulphurous and – like the tiles – tinged blue. Mycul smiled as he submerged himself and held his breath. He picked up the soap and washed. Orlando entered the room a few seconds later. Her skin glistened with sweat and she sat at the edge of the pool before entering the water. "Here, do my back," she smiled and passed over the soap.

Mycul obliged, running his fingers over her dark skin and kissing her between the shoulders. She giggled and scolded him. She turned and held him at arm's length. "There's more to being a man than this," and her finger traced a line from his navel downward. "You must go now but leave the balance of payment with Madam."

Mycul emerged from the water and dried. He dressed, fastening the collar with a simple pin. The material felt itchy again. He paid Messalina and walked out onto the street.

He was disorientated. He had walked uphill to the town in daylight and now the ship was lit by innumerable lamps and the sun setting as a slender crescent on the horizon, casting wave after wave of colour into the encroaching darkness. He ran down the hill feeling rejuvenated.

"Not so fast!" The familiar voice brought him to a halt. Mycul looked around. The Captain pulled him into the shadows between two buildings as a group of people climbed the hill. "I cannot save you now, but be at the wharf at first light and the Graken will do the rest."

"What do you mean?"

The captain looked around nervously. "You've been sold to the geneticists."

"The geneticists? I thought they were banned." Mycul's stomach wound tighter.

"It's common practice to get rid of someone. The gold piece I gave you was part of the payment your uncle gave me. You've been betrayed."

"Betrayed?" Mycul's throat went dry.

"The pleasure you so recently spilt at the whore house will already be in the laboratory and now they need you to finish their experiments."

Mycul remembered to breathe. His heart pounded and he had to force himself not to run out into the street. When he turned back the captain had slipped away down the alley.

There was a shout. A man with a brand signalled and pointed. There could be no doubt that Mycul was discovered. He ran uphill, leaving the road and the town for bracken and crumbling granite. At first Mycul made good progress but as he reached the island's summit he slowed, tripping over boulders in the dark. He decided to lay low between the great rocks, found a narrow crevice and slowly edged his way in. He recovered his breath as the sounds of pursuit rose. He could feel the warmth of their breath around him but slowly the noises faded and became silent. He smelt the sweat of one of his pursuers. Though he'd never seen one before, the way it moved and sniffed it must have been a carniver.

He waited until the only thing he could hear was the sea crash on the shore. Slowly he extricated himself from the chasm; he picked his way carefully through the rocks until he regained the road. The blow was unexpected and knocked him sideways. The carniver rolled him over and pinioned him. He stared up into the cruel, red eyes. The putrid breath of the creature enveloped him and he felt saliva drip down his face.

"Me na da ger dra," the woman's voice intoned. "He'll not hurt you, his fangs have been removed. I've never hurt any of the souls I've sent into the Experiment."

The creature backed off allowing Mycul to sit up. He wiped his face. "Somehow that doesn't sound reassuring."

The woman helped him to his feet. "You're shaking."

"You've upset me. I thought I was going to die."

She examined him, circling him once.

"Clean with the vaguely sulphurous smell of the island. I'd say you set your fate on passing sperm to one of Messalina's whores. It's the DNA they're after. If you were well educated in the ways of the Adee, you'd know. The men are coming back."

"Any chance of bribing you?"

The lady laughed. "I like a sense of humour in a man. I'll give you one chance. If you've studied geology you'd know that waves find a line of weakness. The contact between two different types of rock will provide that."

Mycul tried to search her face but the moon went behind a cloud and she was cast once more in shadow. Mycul took a deep breath. "Might I know your name? After all, I may give you such a sporting chance in the future."

The lady laughed. She beckoned the approaching party. The carniver sat on its haunches ready to spring. "Just ask for Tahoola."

"I will. I'll be sure to do that." Mycul waited. He smelt the man before he saw him. The blow left him rolling in pain.

"You've cost us our bonus."

Mycul was cuffed then beaten and dragged unceremoniously toward the Tor that crowned the Reach of Key. He looked back only once and thought he could see the ship in the moonlit harbour. Silently he vowed revenge on his uncle, the captain and Tahoola.

The man smote his staff on the rock. It rang out and a door opened. Two people wearing white coats and boots emerged. Their faces were covered by tall hats from which hung gauze to conceal their faces. "Welcome, Mycul Zas. I hope you're going to help us study the human genome and become one of the Keeper's spies." The smaller of the two protected humans walked forward and Mycul was injected with a liquid that made the world fade away.

He came to with a dull ache in his arms. He tried to move them but found that something metallic restrained him. He panicked but as his sight regained focus, he managed to bring it under control. The room was pristine, banks of instruments glowed in a multitude of colours. He saw the two people dressed in white and remembered.

"Ah! Mycul, you're back with us." The woman moved toward him and placed a device against his arm. "Heart rate 89, blood pressure normal, body temperature 37.4." The machines came alive at this information. "You'll have to forgive my husband. All this isn't necessary but he enjoys old fashioned methods of restraint."

"Professor Ulia is quite right. She does the intricate work requiring intelligence, I merely provide the specimens for her table."

"I'll leave you in his capable hands." The woman took up a clipboard and left the room. As the doors slid open Mycul clearly heard a cacophony of animals.

"Don't worry, they're my monsters and soon you'll be one of them. Of course the chains aren't necessary but as Professor Ulia implied, pleasure is a rare commodity here. Your DNA matched the mordonts. Do you have any idea why?"

Mycul shook his head.

The man smiled and took a scalpel from a tray. He slit open Mycul's shirt to reveal his chest. "Are you sure you've no idea?"

Mycul shook his head and struggled against the chains.

"Good, I thought you might be too easy a conquest. How are you connected to the mordonts?"

"I don't know. That's the truth." Mycul took another breath and tried to calm himself.

"You will tell me." The doctor slipped the scalpel along a rib and peeled away the flesh. He smiled cruelly as Mycul screamed. "I've been here a long time. I desire the open air but I have a duty to perform, I must keep the mordonts alive and improve their genetics so they become better soldiers. I am the proud creator of some of these creatures."

Mycul looked away as the scalpel roamed his body. Another layer of skin was peeled back. He didn't hear anything more as pain became everything. It filled his soul until he passed out. He was revived. Mycul regained focus on the laboratory.

The geneticist stopped and produced another instrument shaped like a pen; it emitted a light that warmed and sutured the wounds. A thin red line was all that remained. "Yes, I have the cure for pain."

Mycul tried to swallow. When he spoke, his voice didn't sound right inside his head. "My father disappeared some eight years ago. His body was never found." Mycul remembered the dreadful uncertainty of those long ago days.

"There, it's so easy to please me." The man unfettered Mycul's left hand and passed over a drink. "It's a rehydrating agent with something to calm the pain."

Mycul drank until the glass was empty. He watched the man consult the bank of lights. He realised this place was a legacy from the Adee.

"Before they were wiped out they'd started experimenting on human-animal embryos, splicing genes and creating hybrids. In places like this carnivers were manufactured and mordonts too. Their work was too important to lose, we were ordered to continue and continue we have for thousands of years and tens of generations!" The man was proud of his heritage and achievements. He consulted a book. "Yes, 25th October in the second year of our Protector Ceelan the Dark, a farmer from Vold Nujun. Gene implantation via a virus host. My records are infallible."

"Is he still alive?" Mycul asked.

The scientist smiled. "Yes, after a fashion."

"I've heard about you. Dr Ambrose."

The man was taken aback.

"How?"

"My friend Sartesh Andrada, Keeper of the Seventh Law, told me mordonts were more sinned against than sinning. I didn't realise they were the creation of the Adee until now. Slicing up human genes and altering them by insertion of other DNA. What did they hope to create?" Mycul asked.

"You are well read and perhaps wasted as fodder for my perverted pleasures." He opened a cupboard and took out a white suit and a pink collar. He placed it against a machine and briefly it lit up. He clasped the cold metal round Mycul's neck. "Let me demonstrate." He pressed several buttons. The layers of pain built in every nerve of Mycul's body.

"Don't even think about not following instructions. A pleasure delayed is a pleasure enhanced, I always say." He took the scalpel and removed Mycul's remaining clothes. He stood back and looked at the young man. Mycul recognised the same sadistic streak his uncle possessed.

Dr Ambrose led Mycul naked down the hall to a darkened room.

"Your rest area. Shower and dress and wait outside the lab for instructions."

Mycul looked at the dials on the wall. He turned one and moved quickly to avoid the torrent of cold water. He slowly turned the other. He smiled as he entered the wall of warm water then gritted his teeth as it touched the recent scars. He looked down at the thin red line. Someone would pay for this, but for now he had only one thought: how to escape. He dried himself and put on the white one-piece suit. He waited outside the lab; he could hear the man and woman arguing. The woman left the lab and paused momentarily to look at Mycul.

"Don't get in my way!"

She turned the control dial for the collar up to maximum. Mycul fell screaming to the floor. She laughed and walked off. He noticed that the further she went, the pain diminished. Mycul leaned against the wall and caught his breath. The cold rock eased his pain. The cold rock. He remembered what Tahoola had told him. The contact between two rocks. He looked at the corridor tunnelled through this weakness. He paced toward the door until he dared go no further. He turned – just in time, as the man came out of the lab.

"I've a job for you. You can culture your own DNA." He showed the slides gently swaying in the warm broth. "When all the chromosomes have developed, collect me from room twenty two."

"You would trust me to do this?"

"Yes. If they don't develop properly the consequences will be the return of agony. I'm going to splice a sample of your DNA back using a virus to invade every cell. The telomeres will accept the new genes and replicate, slowly changing you into a mordont."

"That doesn't sound too appealing."

"No, but if it goes wrong you'll become one of these." The doctor pressed a button and keyed in a code. Mycul memorised the numbers. The bank of computers slid into the wall and revealed a glass enclosure. Professor Ulia was giving out food. Mycul searched amongst the shadows. Grotesque beings emerged, all with some human features left but others were so deformed their bodies could not move correctly. Mycul felt he might be sick. "Horrific."

The man smiled. "All my own work. It would be a shame if you joined them. These are part of the Protector's great experiment: genetically modified humans. Ceelan wants to create perfectly intelligent and resourceful fighting machines using Adee science."

Mycul thought this morally repugnant but said nothing.

The man smiled. "My wife and I are the final gene masters."

"Did you make all the mordonts?" He felt sick again but despite his anger and hatred, Mycul turned on the charm.

The man laughed. "Not I! We aren't able to experiment on that scale any more. The Adee created living things in their image. It was their greatest conceit. Graken, faeries, carnivers and the hated mordonts. Each was suited to its task, a mix of human and animal DNA to replace extinct creatures. When their society broke down their creatures bred wild upon our Earth and in the seas," Dr Ambrose continued.

"So much was created through science during the Adee. They had different values to us." He pressed the button. The bank of computers began sliding back in place. Mycul remembered Tahoola's suggestion and saw where hard granitic rock abutted slate and shale. All the fissile metamorphic rock had been eroded or removed to create a great gash that was a continuation of the corridor. The female scientist continued providing food; as she'd left the laboratory, Mycul realised there must be another way in.

"Why do you keep them alive?"

"They remind me I'm fallible, and that there's a fine line between torture and murder. I don't expect you to understand that."

"You could explain it to me."

"Not tonight. It's late and you have your work to do. After that, you're free to retire."

"You trust me to move freely?"

"Try to harm me."

12

Mycul stood dumbfounded. After a third encouragement, he lifted his fist and punched the man. Before the blow connected an intense light blinded him and waves of noise surged through his brain. The man smiled. "I think we're safe, don't you? Try to escape and the same thing happens." Dr Ambrose yawned and left the laboratory.

Mycul was alone with the developing slides. He waited and eventually plucked up courage to check the room. Finding his possessions, he searched for the gun. It was still in the leather holster. He checked the corridor. It was empty. He pressed the button on the computer and closed his eyes, trying to remember the code. There was a click and the bank of computers slid to one side. The enclosure was in darkness.

Mycul stood at the glass and stared in. He felt he was being watched but could see no movement. The walls of the lab betrayed no light source; at home, gas lamps had been the norm but here with all this Adee technology perhaps he just had to speak and things would happen. "Light," he said. There was no change. He made his way round the enclosure.

The voice was nothing more than a whisper. "The silver plate."

Mycul saw the object and pushed against it. Slowly the lights brightened. Mycul pressed himself to the wall. He bit the back of his arm in fear and revulsion but the eye that stared back did not hold malice. There was some aspect of the face he recognised from a long time ago. He walked forward. The eye followed his progress –

The one eye which was human. The other half of the monster was bovine and in its face contours of each creature amalgamated.

"Don't look at me." The creature shrank back into the shadows.

Mycul recognised something in what remained of the face. "Who are you?" Mycul looked again, and despite the deformity there was something human left.

The creature returned to the shadows.

"Don't leave me. I need help if I'm to escape."

"Why should I help a human?"

"Because you are human still and you would destroy this entirely if you could."

The creature almost bellowed as though words eluded it. "Tell me your name then, human." The creature ventured into the light once more.

"Mycul Zas."

The creature sucked at the deformed flaps which passed for lips. Mycul studied the creature. "How long have you been here?"

"You know already."

"What is your name?"

"Cevennes." The mordont tried hard to pronounce the name.

"Father?"

"If you think something human is left, I was your father. I remember the rolling hills of Vold Nujun, the photograph preserved in the inn."

Mycul felt his heart race and he felt light headed. There was an unbearable silence. A door opened somewhere. Mycul approached the mordont. Half of the face was indeed his father, the other resembled a bull. His body was likewise deformed half bull, the rest human. From the centre of his head a single white horn gleamed. Mycul held the creature in his arms and felt tears roll down his cheeks.

"Mycul. Mycul. I never wanted you to see me like this. I must get you away from here."

"The weakness in the rock."

"Yes, it leads outside but passes by the failed creatures. The perversions of Ulia's experimentation, perhaps we could do something?" The amorphous human retreated. "We all possess the collar. There'll be so much pain."

"It will pass."

"You will see many hideous things before we meet the mordonts."

"There can be nothing more hideous than Professor Ulia and Dr Ambrose."

The light in the room faded. The creatures from the geneticist's menagerie were asleep. He saw the contorted features, the pain etched into every line and sinew. Even in sleep, some whimpered. The stale air became cooler and the sounds of animals louder. Footsteps from behind gathered pace and suddenly an excruciating pain burst into Mycul's body. He stopped and tried to breathe. His father clutched at his neck then his body contorted and the animal emerged as he overcame the pain for the sake of his son.

Cevennes carried Mycul and took him until he could hear the sounds of waves and the wind sighing through trees. Here in the glade above the cliffs Mycul was set down. As the light broke above the horizon, his pain eased. All around him were the sounds of moving creatures. "Do not show any fear, my son. These are my brothers and sisters, the mordonts. We all need your help to escape this island, to find our way in Faires and make our homes."

"You'll be hunted down and killed!"

"Possibly, but some will survive and be free --just getting the chance is better than serving Professor Ulia."

A huge creature moved forward. Mycul became frightened and his body tensed. The mordont had the body of a muscular man but his skin was mottled like the hide of a bull. The smell of animal was overpowering. Mycul saw his face was human, but the horns that protruded were large and sharp and behind these, the creature began again. Mycul wondered which part of the creature would be dominant. He smelt the hot rancid breath of the mordont as it moved closer and raised his hands. Each finger resembled a miniature hoof. It gripped Mycul's collar and tore it apart. Mycul fell. He took deep breaths. He picked up the two parts and threw them over the cliff.

"Thank you." he said, bowing to the creature.

The mordont bared his teeth and swayed his head before liberating his father.

"The human part is fighting the animal for dominance. Soon the animal will win. That's why those evil people experiment. They want to know why some people succumb immediately to their gene implants but in others it goes wrong and they finish like me, a lingering death."

"Are all mordonts humans who've been altered?"

"Some. Others were born to that condition as their ancestors were made by the Adee. Maybe that was part of the vile experiment as well, seeing if reproduction was still possible."

Mycul shook his head. He looked around at the assembled creatures, their human bodies mottled, contorted into bovine contours with the men displaying great pairs of horns and the women huge breasts inflated with milk or pendulous and creased. He felt pity for them and for himself. Mycul sensed the creatures becoming nervous.

"We have been followed." Mycul's father looked back at the cave and saw Dr Ambrose had appeared. He was carrying a weapon and several collars. Professor Ulia emerged a few seconds later carrying a gun and several vials of liquid.

"We will not be slaves again." Mycul's father took up a large branch.

Mycul warned, "Those guns bore holes in flesh before killing."

"We must do something!" Mycul's father summoned the mordonts. There was a cacophony of bellowing and they spread out around the cave entrance. Several creatures moved behind the gene splicers and sealed off their retreat.

The doctor and his wife walked forward with menace. The collars clanged together like bells. Professor Ulia took aim and shot a mordont in the leg, then smiled and shot the felled creature in the other leg before placing a collar round its neck. Dr Ambrose took aim and shot a creature at point blank. The contents of her brain arced across the rocks.

Mycul unpacked the gun and aimed it. He squeezed the trigger. The bullet hit Professor Ulia in the forehead. For a moment she walked on and then blood oozed through the hole. Dr Ambrose rushed forward firing his gun wildly. A mordont selflessly stood in front of Mycul and took several hits. The man still ran. The mordont who'd removed Mycul's collar ran towards the man. The gun clicked but did not fire.

Realising his defenses were down the mordonts surged and before the scientist could retreat, he was pulled from the entrance and torn apart by the angry herd. His screams were muffled by the bellowing mordonts who trod what remained of Dr Ambrose's body into the earth leaving the soil viscous and red.

The mordonts now surrounded the cave entrance and uttered a deep discordant sound, it echoed round the hollow chamber. After a moment of silence, they carried their dead and took them to the edge of the cliff before launching them into the churning sea below.

When this was finished, Mycul looked around the assembled mordonts, their gaze fixed on him. They had indeed been more sinned against than sinning.

"Thank you my friends. Now I owe you all a debt." Mycul sat down and sighed. His father, Cevennes, had a human face from this angle, and the face he remembered caught the sunlight.

"Sooner or later I'll be like him." His father pointed to the lead mordont. "That's the problem of all those who play god, they don't foresee the consequences. No one knows how long it takes for the entire human DNA to be transformed in to a mordont. Our leader was once Pregul Andrada. He claims to be from the village of Bretan. Look at him now; he's so completely animal he doesn't remember how to speak. Some of the others were born mordont. They're formidable fighters. Tough, agile, resourceful: that much of the plan worked."

"Pregul Andrada, the father of Sartesh?" Mycul asked. The lead mordont bent low until his eyes were level with Mycul's and his horns scraped along the skin of his cheeks. Mycul placed his hand between the creature's horns. "It was Sartesh Andrada who visited and persuaded me to find the truth about mordonts on The Reach of Key." Mycul looked at the menagerie milling without purpose. "I'm going back into the lab. I want to see if there's something that can reverse this dreadful mutant strain."

Cevennes stood swaying. "All mordonts know there is a cure. Its name is Calufras."

Chapter 2: Calufras

Above the waves pounding the cliff, the vibrations fed through to every living thing upon the land. The power of the sea was tremendous but Mycul realised that the power of Calufras was more important. He had searched the database in the laboratory. The entry stated: *It isn't known how it works but it has a proven efficacy in arresting genetic change. Calufras is worth more than gold and that metal is so rare since the Adee depleted our lands of resources, that we mine their rubbish for a single ounce. Calufras can only be obtained in Deidar Mela, the place of healing.*

The Keepers of the Seven Laws knew how the Adee lived and how they died. Like the Fall of the Roman Empire, there wasn't one single cause, just a gradual weakening. There had been an epidemic; there had been genetic experiments; and the madness of burning poisonous fuels. Mycul only knew these things through his friendship with Sartesh. According to the histories, Calufras was unknown until after the Adee.

"We will find this drug in Deidar Mela," Mycul said to his father.

"Then we must travel all the way across Faires and into the highlands to consult the healers. I know there are some mordonts who will not want a cure. They are too far gone or else were born to the condition."

Mycul looked at the creature who had been Sartesh's father. There were others likewise too altered, with the human aspect now subservient to the animal. "I don't know how well Calufras works. Does anyone? I couldn't find any information about that in the lab."

"You wouldn't. Dr Ambrose was only interested in eugenics." Spittle ran down the working side of his father's mouth.

"Perhaps I should talk to the mordonts and ask them what they want to do." Mycul took a deep breath. His father shrugged.

"My friends!" Mycul shouted. Most of the creatures stopped and listened. "I will take any who want to go to the place of healing called Deidar Mela but to get there we have to find a ship and cross the sea. It is my hope that any who wants and needs it will receive Calufras."

A mix of words and bellowing struck up. Most mordonts began leaving the glade where the fight had ended. Pregul Andrada bent down his head and sniffed Mycul. The horns almost encircled the young man's head. Mycul looked in his eyes.

"I will tell Sartesh everything and bring him back to meet you."

The creature raised its bovine head and bellowed into the morning sky before making his way into the woodland. If Mycul added his father, there were only seven mordonts who wanted to leave. They were the most grotesque and misshapen creatures, still possibly half human. They needed hope and Mycul provided that hope. If only he could find them a ship.

_-*-_

Standing now at the top of the cliff, Mycul looked out to sea. The aquamarine ocean rippled under a gentle breeze, seagulls yelled and the scent of salt and pine surrounded him. No matter how hard he thought or listened, the voice of the Graken was gone. Mycul heard the crash of waves on the rocks below.

"There'll be other ships, my son." The smell of mordont hung in the air. "And when they come, there is a revenge I've plotted for many a year." Both father and son looked at the curving horizon. "But without Calufras, I will forget and become a beast."

Mycul nodded. "I understand. Once we've disembarked from a ship, how many days walking is this place of healing?"

"It's on the borders of Faires, in the highlands, so ten possibly."

"That's a long journey."Mycul realised he was exhausted by the morning's events but with renewed enthusiasm said, "If that's what it takes."

"Deidar Mela. The valley of healing. They claim to have lived there unmolested since the time of the Adee."

"That's where the Child is to be born," Mycul said.

"The stuff of myth."

"The material of hope," Mycul suggested, but his father did not reply. He sat and dangled his feet over the cliff edge and imagined the song of the Graken, its high-pitched notes flowing through the air. He had to admit defeat. He didn't know how to call the beast. "Cevennes was the name you went by in the past," Mycul said.

"Sometimes I say my name to remember what I was but you are the first to call me by it in years."

The other six mordonts rested, ate leaves and provisions of meat from their stores. In the shade their dappled bodies were camouflaged. Sounds interrupted Mycul's thoughts, which he realised were human voices getting nearer. A group entered the clearing. He stood.

"What has happened here?" Mycul recognised the voice. It was Tahoola. She brought the carniver to heel and it bared what remained of its fangs, trying to lunge at the young man. The group talked urgently amongst themselves. "We have come for our payment for supplying people to the experiment."

"You're too late," Mycul said. "Professor Ulia and Doctor Ambrose are dead." He pointed to the bloodstains on the grass.

"You will have incurred the Protector's wrath for killing her geneticists. Ceelan is not a forgiving person," Tahoola said.

"You know her?" Mycul asked.

"I did." Tahoola changed the subject. "Well, dead or alive there must be gold in there somewhere to pay their obligations."

"I've been inside but found nothing."

"For men, things are always difficult to find," Tahoola winked. "Women are generally much better."

"Tahoola? You gave me some good advice and I used it well. I don't think your team would be too pleased if they knew who had provided the information in the first place." Mycul gestured for her to pass and try. He smiled and gave a little bow.

Tahoola reigned in the carniver. "I believe you're right. Perhaps this line of business has lost its profit margin. I've always fancied a military uniform." She took out a knife, and with a quick movement, the blade severed the carniver's carotid artery and windpipe. For a moment the anguished face looked human as blood pulsed from the wound, then the creature collapsed.

"Maybe being your friend is a dangerous occupation," Mycul observed.

"Being my enemy is more dangerous," Tahoola smiled, as she lifted the young man's chin and looked into his eyes.

Mycul felt his knees tremble. He wanted to say something but took a moment too long to reply as Tahoola strode off.

"I believe you'd look good in black and gold."

Tahoola turned and smiled and Mycul saw for the first time she had beautiful grey eyes. Tahoola shouted for her team to follow. "One good turn deserves another," she said.

"I hope we will meet again."

Tahoola saluted before entering the dark corridor.

Cevennes followed them a little way into the mouth of the cave but he would go no further. "She's planning something, that one, she doesn't ring true." The mordonts gathered their possessions and moved out of the clearing.

"She helped me, so she can't be all bad," Mycul replied.

"She's a very beautiful lady but did you see the colour of her eyes? Mutant!" his father spluttered, and the word made him stop. Perhaps he realised the implication as Mycul had only ever heard it used as a derogatory term for mordonts before.

The group began the slow descent towards the town. Ahead, trees gave way to moorland and he recognised the rocks where he'd been discovered the previous night. The mordonts marched ahead at speeds Mycul would only be able to match by running.

Vibrations fed through the ground. A blast of air and dust rolled from the tunnel. Debris rose into the air and scattered like hail onto the earth behind them. There was a long silence in which mordonts stared back at the settling dust. A figure emerged with its body contorted in pain. The person slipped to their knees and stared towards the creatures, then fell head first onto the grass.

Mycul ran to see who had been hurt, and if anyone else was going to emerge. The dishevelled nature of the person made them difficult to identify but turning the body over, it was obviously Tahoola.

"You might as well kill her now," his father said. "What use will a woman be without a right hand?" She was still breathing. Mycul tore a strip of material from his shirt and wrapped it round her forearm. The tourniquet stemmed the flow of blood.

"She needs more medical help than I can provide. Can we carry her to the village?"

A couple of mordonts raised her between them and set off at a run; Mycul lagged behind unable to match their pace. He felt a sense of relief on nearing the houses of the port. The locals pushed themselves against the walls to avoid the creatures: the mordonts ran until a line of soldiers barred their way.

The Keeper stood in front and held out his hand. "Brothers. What can we do for you?"

The mordonts waited, with Tahoola semi-conscious and groaning.

"I need a doctor to tend Tahoola's wounds," Mycul struggled to say, gasping.

"There are no doctors on the island. You'd be better off praying." The Keeper buttoned up his long purple jacket. "But there is the healer, he lives at the second house below the whores. Ah! I believe you are acquainted with them. Do not delay, I doubt she'll last long but at least he will ease the pain of her parting."

The soldiers stood to attention and drew their spears up. They stared at the deformed creatures carrying the woman. Mycul snapped his fingers and they followed him downhill. He did not wait on ceremony but barged through the door.

"Are you the healer?" he demanded.

"I might be."

"If you are then save this woman."

"Ah! Saving. Sometimes I do that well and with others I fail. Either way I need money."

"Either way you'll be rewarded, more so if she lives." Mycul looked around the room.

"Is she something to you?" The healer gave a wry smile.

"A person who is better alive than dead. Make a good job; she wants to join the army."

"With one hand?" the healer asked incredulously. "I've never heard of a soldier with one hand, and any amputation will be above the wrist. The shock might kill her, but so too might keeping the hand when infection sets in. It is a dilemma. I'm glad I don't have to make the decision."

"Take every action necessary to save her life."

"Her life? Very well but there's a cost in gold." The healer began arranging tools around the table.

Mycul felt his heart race and acid churn in his stomach. Tahoola was brought in and laid on the pine table. The healer prised open her mouth and added a few drops of liquid onto her tongue. She recoiled but quickly stilled and her breathing steadied.

First a tourniquet was applied. The healer then washed and scrubbed what remained of the appendage. Slowly he poured a saline solution over the surfaces. He picked up a knife. His hand shook a little as if remembering something horrific. The healer took a deep breath and his hand steadied before the knife cut through remaining flesh, leaving a flap of skin.

Mycul watched although he felt sick as the stench of a tormented body rose. The healer carefully tied the ends of major vessels and cauterised them. A smell of cooking flesh emanated. He picked up the saw and began to rasp through bone until what remained of the hand dropped to the table. Skin was then sewn across the bone and sinew.

"There, it's the best I can do. The patient has lost a lot of blood and there's also shock to consider." The healer tended some of the minor cuts and abrasions. He moved carefully and methodically over her body before ringing a bell for the patient to be removed to a bed.

"The cost is ten reals of gold. Mind the coin must have the Protector's head on it. I do not deal in Mennedic gold. It doesn't leave the impression of your teeth."

"I will organise for you to receive the fee. And the cost of looking after her?" Mycul asked.

"Another real a week for after care." The healer threw the remains of the severed hand into the fire. He then poured sawdust on the table. "Well?"

"Thank you. My servant will be along in an hour or so with the gold." Mycul breathed deeply from the fresh air outside the building. Cevennes pulled Mycul to one side. "Where will we get gold?"

"Protecting the town?"

"No, we don't want the army after us. We need a legitimate way of finding the money."

"I have an idea," Mycul said.

"Why do I think I might grow to hate that phrase?" his father replied.

Mycul smiled in a way only the naivety of youth can muster. "One thing is certain: I need a drink to take the taste of blood away. And I need to sleep."

"But first you need to acquire gold." Mycul's father swayed and snorted like a bull. He closed his eyes and focussed.

"My plan is to use the whores' house. To blackmail them into a bargain. But to do that, I'll need the help of your friends." Mycul looked up at the lanterns in the windows of the brothel.

"There are only a few mordonts who will follow instructions but I'll ask them."

Mycul sat at the side of the road. He picked up a pebble and flicked it across the street. A second joined it.

Cevennes nodded. "They are ready."

"Enter the building on my whistle."

Mycul's father moved up the hill with the mordonts. He looked back and observed his son, doing what he might have done to collect his thoughts before acting.

Mycul entered the brothel. The lavender perfume was overpowering. He looked around, and could hear Madam Messalina laughing, her charm bracelets jingle, then saw her gold jacket before her bulk appeared in the office doorway. She was momentarily startled.

"Hello," Mycul smiled as best he could.

"You've come back for seconds?" Messalina asked.

"Not quite, I've come back for a loan of twenty gold reals."

Messalina laughed. "I love a good joke."

"I'm not joking. I wonder what arrangements you had with the gene splicers on the hill. It seems many of your customers ended up in experiments."

"What an accusation."

Mycul whistled. The mordonts filed in.

"What is it, Madam?" Orlando asked, as she entered, tying up her gown. She stopped and stared, then added, "I told you no good would come of your arrangement with Tahoola and her gang." She walked up to several creatures and gave a nervous sigh. Looking at what remained of their faces, she saw in them the humans they once were.

"Well, what's your proposition?" Messalina asked.

"A loan of 20 gold reals will pay for Tahoola's surgery and nursing. The rest we'll use to get passage off The Reach of Key."

Messalina did not respond. One of the mordonts strode towards her. Mycul held out his hand to stop the creature. "We are civilised people and mordonts are more sinned against than sinning."

"Well put like that, how could I not agree." Messalina left the room and returned with the coins. Mycul checked each one for the Protector's head.

"A loan, mind," Messalina said.

"A loan," Mycul confirmed. "And as I've had a really bad day, you can throw in a bed and a bath."

"I think given the smell, it'll be the other way round," as she clapped her hands and her workforce returned. Messalina whispered orders and people scurried away. Mycul nodded and the mordonts filed out, braying and snorting as they went. Mycul was left staring into the face of a youth no older than himself but shorter and thinner: the Mennedic.

"Come with me." The youth held open a door. He was possessed of a fine physique. Mycul noticed the way his eyes followed him, as a glass bath slowly filled with water. Other attendants brought in a large tub of hot water. Soap was scattered over the surface and stirred vigorously until it foamed and reflected the blues from the glass below. "You can undress now." Mycul hesitated. "I've been doing this work since I was twelve; nothing you have will surprise me. Nothing you ask for or do could be a first."

"I wasn't going to ask for anything, except this bath and a bed to sleep on."

The youth smiled. "Are you going to leave the island?"

"Yes, when I can work out how to call the Graken." Mycul took off his jacket and shirt; his limbs felt cold and stiff. He continued undressing.

"Would you take me as well?"

"Are you free to go?"

"No, I'm a slave like the others but I'd like to make something of myself as a free man."

Mycul slipped into the water. He took a deep breath and submerged. He stayed under for as long as he could, breaking the surface and sending water and bubbles over the floor.

"That's right, make it more difficult for me."

"I'm sorry," Mycul said. "I'll help you clean up."

"Why would you want to do that?"

"Because I've been worse than a slave, I've lost my freedom and inheritance through not standing up for myself. That's not going to happen anymore. You want to come with us, then you shall! I've always hated the idea of one human owning another. I believe everyone is equal."

"Ah! The great experiment of Faires."

Mycul slid under the water; as he surfaced warm hands began massaging his shoulders and neck. He felt the tension drain away. Mycul emerged from the water and walked into the waiting towel. He dried himself slowly then lay down on the bed and without any hesitation fell into a deep sleep.

In the morning, light streamed in through the shutters catching a million particles of dust spiralling through the air. He turned over and found the youth sleeping on a chair. Mycul tried to sit up. He groaned with the pain. He rolled over on his side and sat up using the edge of the bed.

"You were tired."

"Exhausted!" Mycul stood and walked slowly round the room. His aching muscles eased. "Do you have a name?"

"Stazman. There is nothing more you need to know."

"I am Mycul Zas, I have nothing to hide." He held out his hand, the youth grabbed his elbow. Mycul mirrored this. "A Mennedic."

Stazman produced a knife and threatened Mycul. "Do you have something against Mennedics?"

"Yes, as your knife is against my heart."

Stazman hesitated allowing Mycul to grab the knife and overpower him. That done Mycul passed the knife back.

"There has to be trust or there is nothing."

"I understand. I am Stazman Zem."

Mycul nodded. "Now I must consult with a seer and find how to contact the Graken."

Stazman laughed. He placed two fingers on Mycul's shoulder. "Here and here are the creature's marks. You are hers and she is yours. Hold them and sing her name."

"How do you know that?"

"I wasn't born a slave," Stazman said aggressively.

24

Mycul pulled back the shutters, held his shoulder and sang. His voice carried across the air and vanished into the silver of the early morning sun. He sang until his voice was hoarse.

"A beautiful tune. It reminds me of one of mother's lullabies but tell me, how will the Graken hear it?"

Mycul thought about this. He imagined the molecules of oxygen and nitrogen taking the sound vibrations through particle after particle until the tune was no more and the call nothing but a slight disturbance amongst the atoms themselves.

He looked at the view of the harbour, its ships mostly under sail except one pulled by a Graken. He wondered how many prisoners were needed each day around the world to feed these creatures. It was an impossible figure to calculate. As his eyes ranged over the town, he remembered Tahoola. He pulled on his boots and straightened his clothes. The coins clinked in his pocket. He touched the purse before setting off down the hill.

The healer's house stood with its doors and windows open. The healer was scrubbing the wooden floor and preparing for the new day.

"How's your patient?"

The healer turned slowly to face him. He possessed a black eye and bruised nose.

"Surely that wasn't…?"

"Think again, Mycul." Tahoola strode out onto the veranda. The stump still oozed blood through the bandages.

"She must have the constitution of an ox!" The healer leaned the brush against the weatherboards. "I only asked her for sex."

Mycul sniggered then saw the mood on Tahoola's face and resisted any further comment. "I didn't think you'd make it."

"Didn't you? Well it shows how little you know me." Tahoola sat down. Her face betrayed her pain but she took a deep breath and steadied her resolve. "When you leave this island, I'm going with you." Tahoola looked at the amputated limb.

"Is all as it should be after your operation?"

The healer shrugged his shoulders and picked up the brush.

Mycul turned back to Tahoola.

"We are going in search of Calufras, not gold, not adventure. In fact, I'm hoping to avoid adventure altogether," Mycul confessed.

Tahoola smiled. "Why ruin things?" Her head nodded against her chest, and the healer pressed his hand to her brow.

"The drug I gave her has knocked her out. I'll get a blanket."

"Here," Mycul said, and the healer turned back. "I think you deserve this." Mycul clattered eleven gold reals into the healer's hand and his eyes lit up in astonishment.

"I never thought I'd see so much gold." He dashed inside, no doubt to hide his earnings. Mycul looked at Tahoola as she slept. Her short-cropped hair possessed the finest of gold colours and her face, though streaked with dirt, was graceful. He flicked a stray hair back in place.

Chapter 3: Nag-Nag Naroon

"Everyone knows the world is flat and was created on the 7th September, four thousand two hundred years ago." Nag-Nag wiped slaver from his beard and replaced it with the froth from his beer. His cheery red face boasted weather beaten skin tanned and wrinkled from years of work. His hands were large and possessed as many fine black hairs as his face.

"Tell us about Gorangoth and the Pass to Great Menne, Nag-Nag." There was a chorus of approval and several empty tankards banged in unison on the benches.

Mycul hadn't seen a storyteller for a long time: there weren't that many visitors to his home village. He sat quietly with his tankard of ale.

Nag-Nag waited for the room to fall silent. His eyes shone like those of a young lover as he quietly let his voice narrate the tale. "I am the only man to survive meeting Gorangoth the Golden. Yes and I will tell you how I did it. It was at the high pass into Menne, I was armed only with my sword and brandished it as the giant Gorangoth appeared. He placed his hands on his hips and laughed. It was so deep and strong leaves were blown from the trees. I'm not afraid to say I felt my legs shake and I wanted to run away. But I'm a brave man…"

There were several heckles.

"…so I stood my ground. I realised a sword would be useless and cast it to the ground. I have but one skill in life and that is to tell tales, so that is what I did. I said, *Great Gorangoth, the brave, the feared, I beg you to let me pass into Great Menne. I am but a humble storyteller.* The giant replied, *A storyteller!* His voice shook the ground like an earthquake and the birds tumbled from their nests but I Nag-Nag Naroon stood my ground, I bowed and began the tale of the Child and how his coming is foretold and how he will be killed by his only friend on the summit of Alqaf Nul. The giant stood in silence. I was fearful I had roused his anger but at the end of the tale, he wiped a tear from his eye and said, *Beautiful.* That is how I got past the giant where many had failed before." Nag-Nag took another great gulp of beer.

"Now if you want to hear more, you must pay a little coin. I have a thirst and a hunger." Coins tumbled onto the table and the storyteller smiled. "You are good customers and you deserve the best."

There was a chorus of voices. "Tell us about the time of kings and princes." "Tell us about the fall of Adee."

"Tell us about the Ornithon," Mycul asked, then realised he'd broken some taboo when everyone fell silent. It was too late to go back, so he persisted. "The Ornithon. I need to know the story as I've a mind to find it for myself." Mycul pulled up a seat opposite Nag-Nag. The smell of the old man's coat was a powerful mix of horse and sweat that must have been ingrained. Mycul spun a gold real on the table. Its sides reflected the light from the fire and the greed in people's eyes.

"And why would you need the Ornithon?"

Mycul took a deep breath. "There are some things a storyteller shouldn't know and that is one of them. Will you tell me the tale?" Mycul's hand covered the coin before Nag-Nag could reach it. "Or have you forgotten it?"

Nag-Nag smiled and stroked his beard. "I'd sell my grandmother for a real of gold."

"You already have!" the barman quipped.

"Are you the youth who released the mordonts? Are you Mycul Zas?" Nag-Nag asked. Mycul nodded.

"Then I can tell you because it's foretold by the Ornithon itself. Remember you must be careful what you wish for as you might just get it."

"I understand," Mycul said.

"The Ornithon is one of the last remnants of the Adee. It is a solid glass tower which speaks to some who visit and yet not all. It is concealed and yet the only building standing. It calculates the future from your past and shows many wonderful things, some which will happen, and others that only might happen.

"Manhedreth used it five times to foretell whom he would marry, though he didn't need the Ornithon to know that all five wives would die by his hand. He did not hear the stone sing *Zhedhelion barkbada uita, Pengal, pace Yderiphon*. He did not hear its voice, he saw only what he wanted to see, his riches growing, his power growing until the greed of Warmonger Lazlo was aroused and the Emperor dealt a cruel fate. His flesh was served at the coronation banquet for all to feast on." Nag-Nag made a revolting sucking sound with his lips and teeth.

"But where is the Ornithon?"

"If I knew that I'd be a rich man." Nag-Nag finished his beer and slammed the tankard on the table. He waited.

Mycul wasn't convinced. "Bring us a pitcher of beer," Mycul shouted to the barman.

Nag-Nag smiled. "I need free transport from this place. Those are my terms for giving you any information."

"Then you'd better tell me now before someone has a mind to silence you," Mycul threatened.

Nag-Nag smiled. "It is impossible to silence me or my tales," he replied then touched his nose. Nag-Nag passed a folded piece of paper over the table and exchanged it by sleight of hand for the gold coin. Mycul briefly touched Nag-Nag's hand and felt the cold smooth glasslike quality of his skin. Everyone looked at Mycul. He surveyed the room with his piercing blue eyes. He tried to remember every face.

"Tell us about the Child," someone asked. "Tell us the prophecies of his coming," and the chorus of voices rose and Nag-Nag took a deep draft from his beer before silencing the crowd and continuing.

Mycul stood and moved to the fire. He felt chilled but despite his sudden discomfort he listened to the story woven by Nag-Nag. He almost fancied he could see the people acting out his words against the backdrop of Nofa Flows.

Only when the storyteller had finished did it occur to Mycul to unfold the paper and read what was written. It was blank. Mycul was about to skim it into the fire when he saw the watermark. It was a picture of a building standing proud above cliffs. These rocks were one homogeneous unit and possessed the unique feature of an arch. Mycul studied the picture by the light of the fire and then placed the paper in the pocket closest to his heart. He felt a mild elation. Things were going well today.

"…and that is how the Child will be killed, without pity, naked and alone at the summit of Alquaf Nul by the hand of one who should have protected him. Zhedhelion Barkbada Uita."

The audience quietly intoned the words in the old language. Several dabbed their eyes and talked in hushed tones; Mycul finished his drink and waited for Nag-Nag's signal. The storyteller stood and moved toward him. "My good friend Mycul," he continued at just a whisper, "you must never again ask about the Ornithon in public. Our Protector, Ceelan the Dark would kill anyone who searches for it. In Menne, just to mention the name is death."

"We are not in Menne but Faires, where all are equal and there is free speech."

"Just as well for us both, young Mycul. I once found the place but I never went in. I have been told it is marvellous and frightening in the way it reads your thoughts, your desires then extrapolates them. It's very easy to be side-tracked."

"I want to know where to find Calufras and that was my best shot."

"Calufras! Why, you don't need the Ornithon to tell you that. It grows wild and free on the hillsides of Deidar Mela."

Mycul encouraged the man to continue, so asked, "But to get there you need to pass Gorangoth the Golden."

"No, the valley of healing is south west of that country. It is high in the mountains and impenetrably cold in winter."

Mycul thought about this. "If I had a boat and took you with us, would we sail north, south, east or west?"

Nag-Nag touched his nose and smiled. "For that I'd need to be on-board and well treated."

"Everything comes at a price," Mycul said.

"Ah! Everything indeed comes at a price, even your friendship with Sartesh Andrada." Nag-Nag scratched his stubble and picked out a louse, cracking it between his fingers.

"How do you know? You said you never consulted the Ornithon."

Nag-Nag smiled. "But the lady I went with was very keen to talk and left me there as a token of her visit. Perhaps you will make a good student after all."

Mycul realised the stratagem and bought the storyteller another drink. Of course, he was certain that Nag-Nag being on the island was no coincidence. He must have seen something to his advantage linked to either Mycul or Sartesh. "Are you thinking of retiring soon?" Mycul asked when the man's face emerged from the tankard of ale.

"Retiring? What would a retired storyteller do?"

"Presumably anything if he had money." Mycul observed the man and sipped his drink. "Perhaps your luck will change."

"Perhaps it will," Nag-Nag replied his expression inscrutable.

Mycul realised he would get no more information so he finished his drink, made his goodnights and joined Cevennes outside. The cool clear air and calm sea allowed them a view to the horizon. The waters were empty and there was no sign of a Graken. "Are you disappointed?"

"No. I've found us another passenger. All we need is a ship," Mycul replied.

"I meant to ask this earlier but what makes you think the captain will let us on board?"

"That much is simple. I am a Graken rider. I hear their voices."

"But that means I will lose you to the sea."

Mycul held his shoulder. "That doesn't necessarily follow."

They both looked out across the vast ocean and waited for some sign. The Reach of Key rose from the bay towards its granite core. The fields and town that made it famous were based on the clay, which eroded into in the sea metres at a time, creating an ever-shifting pattern of coastline.

Stazman came running down the hill. "Mycul! Mycul!" He was pointing frantically but too much out of breath to speak. Father and son followed the outstretched finger to a dot on the horizon.

"You must have much better sight than me." Mycul strained but the dot didn't resolve into anything.

"It's a Graken pulling a great ship."

"There are many Graken."

"Hold your shoulder and greet it. You'll soon know," Stazman held his sides and breathed deeply.

"How many Graken riders have you known?"

"They are lonely men," Stazman said, "they have needs like any other. My most pressing need is getting off the Reach of Key."

Mycul held his shoulder again and thought of the Graken's tune. The reply felled him. The noise broke like an earthquake in his head and when it finished the silence was a moment of calm.

"I guess that was your answer." Stazman hugged Mycul. "Thanks."

"How many people have you promised a place on board?" Mycul's father struggled with the human words.

"There's Stazman, Tahoola of course and Nag-Nag Naroon as well as you and six other mordonts. I don't think the captain will be too happy. His crew might desert him."

"mordonts can do the work of four men. That is why we were genetically altered, to become The Protector's secret army. However, this soldier is focussing all his energies on revenge."

"As am I!" Mycul led the way down to the harbour. The ship moved towards the port at great speed and Mycul could see the garrison had been thrown into confusion by the unexpected arrival. In fact, a crowd of onlookers was already forming as if sensing something special was happening.

Mycul waited on the pier. As the ship pulled into port, he knelt down and bowed his head. He waited, not daring to look up. First he heard the roar of the great beast then he felt drops of saliva fall on his head. The creature exhaled and bathed him in a putrid odour of fish and flesh. He held his breath and waited for the tongue to wrap itself around his neck and head. He had been accepted and inside his mind the creature planted its name. Mycul stood up. Although there was a round of applause from the crowd, he noticed that only the Graken's rider smiled.

The captain swung down and took strides towards Mycul. His face was set with anger. "For over a day the creature has dragged us here, costing me extra fees in delays!"

"And I have been waiting. You carelessly left me behind."

"That was the intention."

"Yes, I remember. Would it be impertinent of me to ask how much my uncle paid you?" Mycul's blue eyes flashed anger as he spoke.

"It would."

"Nevertheless, I'd appreciate an honest answer." Mycul waited.

"You were fodder for Dr Ambrose's experiment as your uncle instructed and you do not need to know more."

Mycul noted how the captain's skin was peeling over his cheeks and forehead. He walked round him once before whispering to the Graken. She bent down her head and roared.

"Would you like to reconsider?"

"No," the Captain replied.

"I want the thirty gold reals my uncle gave you and the fee Tahoola paid."

"A miserly sum not worth considering."

"You will give me all thirty gold pieces," Mycul insisted.

"I cannot."

The Graken roared and sniffed around the captain.

"I gave you one for your pleasure," the captain whimpered. "You may take the balance."

"Thank you, I will. Now, about your new passengers. Myself, my father Cevennes…"

"But he's a mordont!" the captain exclaimed.

"Yes, thanks to people like you who betray humans, but he comes with us and so do six other mordonts. Finally there's the storyteller Nag-Nag Naroon, and Tahoola."

"I'll lose half my crew. Don't you know it's bad luck to carry mordonts on a ship?"

Mycul smiled again. "Why don't you tell them that. They're right behind you."

On cue, a mordont bellowed out her name. Mycul could just make out the human consonants. They all followed suit. Mycul's father even spelt his name, "C-e-v-e-n-n-e-s."

The Captain bowed, put his foot back in the rope harness and signalled to be winched back on board. There was a long silence followed by raised voices and much swearing amongst the sailors.

Mycul took a deep breath and swallowed as the Keeper walked towards the group, resplendent in his purple uniform. "I cannot let you take Stazman from this island, he is an indentured slave belonging to Madam Messalina. The legal implications are too grave to consider."

Mycul searched the crowd and picked out the madam in her long turquoise coat and turban. He walked over to Messalina. "Madam, your servant."

"Good day, young man."

"Did you hear my conversation with the captain? I will be able to repay you by nightfall."

"I am indebted to your honesty," she replied. "I didn't expect such prompt repayment," she added, fanning herself. "I can't let you take Stazman, however. He's very popular and I'd lose a lot of money."

"Then perhaps I might borrow him for the journey?"

"I'm not certain." Messalina turned and consulted Orlando.

"I think if we let him go for a month, a further five gold pieces might be appropriate," Orlando calculated.

"But what if he is killed or kidnapped?" Messalina seemed genuinely concerned.

"Then a fine will be imposed payable with interest?" The Keeper intervened.

Messalina nodded agreement.

"The gold is needed now my good captain," Mycul shouted. A few minutes later a strongbox and key were lowered to the wharf. Mycul untied the rope and unlocked the box. He repaid the loan to Messalina and added the five extra coins.

"You could get to Menne by airship for the amount you have there," Madam Messalina observed, her jewellery clanking as coins slid into her concealed purse.

"I'll need these funds for our journey. Inns and food always have a price."

"Everything has a price," Messalina said knowingly. She held out her hand.

Mycul looked at Stazaman then took the woman's hand. Messalina had a firm grip. She pulled him towards her until he was enveloped in her odour of violets.

"Beware Stazman Zem," she said. Without adding any explanation Messalina turned and walked back up the hill, followed by her sex workers.

"I'm never coming back here," Stazman said.

Mycul looked at the youth annoyed that he spoke openly in front of witnesses. "That's your decision but I won't break my word. You'll need to make certain you earn enough to buy your freedom outright and settle the matter with the Keeper."

The Keeper acknowledged this and bowed.

"Where am I going to get money like that?" Stazman asked.

"By selling your soul."

"Mycul, don't. Never make that sort of joke," his father chided.

"I was being honest."

Stazman looked aghast. He followed Mycul towards the gangway that had been lowered onto the dockside. "You do know she let me go too easily?"

"Madam Messalina?"

"She's up to something," Stazman concluded.

"Like what?" Mycul watched the mordonts coming on board. Their eyes betrayed their animal fear of being on water, which the human side struggled to counter.

"I know the lady well, she's avaricious so she must be getting money from someone else." Stazman stood proudly, his roughly cut blond hair shimmering in the sun.

Mycul thought about this. There could only be one other person who might pay her and that was Ceelan, the Protector of Faires. This realisation alarmed Mycul. If the Protector was involved, her assassins would be close by to ensure her bidding was executed. "So do you know something I don't?" Mycul asked.

"I know a lot of things but now isn't the time to reveal them."

"If you endanger anyone…" Mycul let the threat hang.

Stazman stared at him. The youth took a deep breath as though he might have thought better of saying something.

Mycul wondered if he was doing the right thing, taking this slave from the island. He went over to his father, who was standing by the mast. The Graken's cry saturated the air around them as her rider spurred her into action. The boat lurched forwards and a wave broke over her prow. Slowly the port diminished and the contours of the island flattened and vanished into a thin line on the horizon before finally being lost to view.

Chapter 4: The Ornithon

Seven mordonts and four humans all shared the same quarters. Mycul insisted on the equality. A gentle breeze from the big windows at the back of the ship kept the room cool, yet there wasn't enough light to read. The Duskwalker was moving freely across the open sea. Mycul unfolded the piece of paper he had been given by Nag-Nag and tried to decipher it.

"The air is putrid down here." Nag-Nag's face contorted at the odours. "Might I suggest we venture onto the deck?"

"I'll just check on our patient," Mycul said.

Tahoola had been placed in a captain's bed nearer the window. She had gained a little colour to her cheeks whilst her hair appeared to have prematurely greyed. Her calmer demeanour hinted at the possibility of recovery. Stazman remained by her side as if she were a new customer, ensuring her nursing and medications were administered.

Mycul followed the storyteller out onto the deck. He watched the mordonts work hard preparing the ropes and rigging for the voyage. He saluted his father.

The Graken roared and lurched sideways. Mycul was thrown to the deck. He felt the wind of an arrow glance behind his head. His father was not so lucky, taking a hit through his neck. Cevennes stood transfixed. Mycul thought he'd screamed out a warning but it was too late.

Everything seemed to happen in slow motion. He embraced his father who was struggling for breath and beginning to drown in his own blood. He helped him to the ground. Blood seeped through his mouth and he gargled alarmingly. The alarm bells sounded and sailors began running to their stations. A second arrow penetrated Cevennes' ribs and pierced his heart. Blood seeped then pulsed through the wound. His father's eyes pleaded but there was nothing Mycul could do. Mycul struggled to stop panicking. His stomach wound up into a knot and he swung himself over the railings, spewing relentlessly. Nag-Nag swung the harpoon round and fired. The rope unravelled from the deck. A few seconds later, there was a scream.

"Haul her in!" Nag-Nag shouted. "Pull away, don't kill her."

"Her? Her? How sure are you?"

"Very. All the Protector's assassins are female. All trained at the same school in Faires. We'll see what this one is made from."

Cevennes's eyes dulled and Mycul closed them. Blood seeped and congealed. He was dead. Mycul propped up his father.

"From beyond death he'll see this assassin suffer!" Mycul shouted.

"Let's hope we get her on board alive," Nag-Nag smiled. "I always thought pleasure and pain made good bed fellows."

The assassin was hauled aboard. Her screams killed all other sounds.

"Tell us everything you know," Nag-Nag smiled and ran the edge of his blade across her face. The blade scored a second line on the way back. "A quick death is assured if you speak truthfully."

The storyteller sliced into flesh again. The assassin whimpered but refused to speak. Mycul stepped forward and stayed Nag-Nag's hand.

"I am the Protector's to do with as she sees fit. Kill me and you will incur her wrath! Torture me and I'll die knowing I never failed Ceelan."

Mycul wanted this murderer to suffer. He felt the anger concentrate at the point of his knife. He ripped open her jerkin and for a moment hesitated.

"Are we not civilised?" Tahoola's voice was weak and quivering with emotion. She surveyed the scene. "No one deserves this!" She moved forward and plunged her dagger into the woman's heart. She pulled it out again and wiped the blade on the assassin's cloak.

"I am sorry for your loss, Mycul. Feed her to the Graken and bury your father at sea. It is honourable and the gods will provide."

"It's revenge I want!" Mycul's anger made him louder.

"Then it's the Protector of Faires you need to destroy," Tahoola said and placed her hand on Stazman's shoulder. He guided her back to the cabin.

Both bodies were committed to the deep. The first, Cevennes, was weighted down with lead and fed gently into the waves with a prayer of thanks for his life. The second was thrown overboard naked and fed to the Graken.

Mycul was greatly troubled. He'd let revenge rule the last few months of his life. He understood this desire concerning his uncle and also the anger but was alarmed at his ability to condone torture. The shock of his father's death and what he had so nearly allowed to happen had him pacing the decks until a sailor offered him rum. After the tankard was drained, he found a kind of sleep.

Mycul woke neither rested nor sober. His mouth tasted like a vat of vinegar and his breath stank. He looked at himself in a mirror feeling remorse and detached in his bereavement. Either revenge or his temper would finish him if he didn't control both. Yet without revenge how would he assuage his father's murder?

There was no sign of land and the relative motion of the horizon made Mycul feel sick. He threw up over the edge of the ship and rested on the rail feeling sorry for himself. His legs shook. There were seabirds wheeling behind the ship looking for fish churned up in its wake. The weak warmth in the sun spoke of autumn and the freshness in the air made his lungs feel cold and clean.

Mycul tottered over to the vat of water and pushed his head into it. He rinsed out his mouth and for a moment felt better. He took a drop of Sartesh's potion and returned to the side of the ship.

He felt an arm extend around his shoulder. It was Tahoola. "I also know guilt," she said looking directly into Mycul's eyes.

He looked down at the waves running alongside the ship. "What I was going to do was truly awful."

"It's when you stop feeling like this you should worry. I have regrets as well," she sighed.

"About the accident which caused you to lose your hand?"

Tahoola nodded.

"Was it an accident?"

Tahoola shook her head. "It was a necessary evil. I wanted to destroy my past and my gang. They would never accept me retiring. I was short sighted and went about it in the wrong way."

Mycul understood what she was telling him. "So you were trying to protect yourself?"

"Yes, I was trying to save myself but I overdid the charge. I'll have to live with the consequences," she looked to the distant horizon.

Mycul studied her. He realised Tahoola was beautiful and had a complex personality. If he could avoid the hormonal surge of being attracted to her, he might find out more.

"I must go back and rest," Tahoola said. "It will be a long time before I am fit enough to join the army."

"Do you still think you'll be able to?"

Tahoola pulled Mycul's sword from its scabbard with her remaining hand. She did some fancy manoeuvres and returned it to him.

"Fortunately I am left handed," she smiled, and held up the bandaged stub of her right hand.

"But will you be able to fight?"

"I'll learn. Believe me, I will learn. Now escort me below."

Mycul guided her towards the steps and descended in front of her. He ensured she reached the safety of her bed and arranged her pillow. "You should rest or at the very least relax."

Tahoola sat up and looked out to sea. Again he saw how beautiful she was, her grey hair and eyes, the slant of her eyebrows, how her fringe fell across her right cheek. "How old are you?" he asked.

Tahoola smiled. "Your senior by many years, Mycul Zas."

Mycul flushed with embarrassment, as if she'd read his thoughts.

"An older woman might be good for you," she teased.

"Do you like reading?" He clumsily changed the subject. "If you do I will lend you the Geology of Faires."

Tahoola laughed. "Not the greatest romantic hook. Now if you had the history of the Adee or the Times of Kings, I might be interested."

"Are you keen on such stories? I have a battered copy in my bag."

"With taste like that we might end up being good friends," Tahoola suggested.

Mycul felt a strange response rise through his body. Seeking to hide this he went to his possessions and rifled through his bag before pulling out a battered edition of the book in question. As he crossed the room, Mycul felt the yaw of the ship. He sat by Tahoola and began reading the tale of Manhedreth and his six wives but realised after a couple of minutes that the patient's eyes were closed. Mycul put the book down at the side of her bed. He looked at the woman and the way her fine grey hair cascaded about her face and neck. He thought she was beautiful. Desire stirred within him, which he fought to control; and then he remembered what his father had said about *mutants*.

Stazman ran his hand across the book cover, feeling the smooth vellum. "I love the stories of the kings. One of Manhedreth's wives is still alive."

"The corruption and stupidity of royalty fills me with hatred. I know Faires must always be a republic."

"So you persist in the idea that all people are born equal?" Stazman asked.

"I will never be dissuaded from it," Mycul said and ran his hand through Stazman's hair. The youth gave him an odd look. The ship pitched and the sound of a wave hitting the deck echoed round the room.

Stazman pushed his blond hair behind his ears. "We're running into a storm." They heard the rigging creak.

Mycul looked out of the rear windows and saw the blue sky being obscured by cloud. There was no land to be seen. He hoped the bearings Nag-Nag had given proved to be good. He wanted to get back on land and yet when he thought about it, he had a connection to the creature towing the ship. Ever since he'd ridden the Graken, when he concentrated he could see the world through her eyes.

From this vantage, he saw the pencil thin line of the coast over to the west and how they were running parallel to this. When the Graken looked back, he saw the ship from above. He could see Nag-Nag talking to the Captain. The body language was all wrong. They talked like old friends, mirroring each other's actions. Mycul opened his eyes on his current position and felt the Graken observe the inside of the cabin through him. The creature dwelt a long time on Stazman and Tahoola.

As Mycul walked along the corridor, his nausea returned. He hurriedly climbed the ladder and as he opened the hatch, seawater washed over him. He gained the deck and gripping a rope found purchase on the next set of steps leading to the wheel.

Neither Nag-Nag nor the Captain greeted him. The Captain looked a little dishevelled as if he'd hurriedly dressed.

Mycul decided it wasn't wise to inform people of his ability. The two older men exchanged glances. Nag-Nag showed a little concern. Mycul closed his eyes and saw the world again as the sea monster did. He asked what the great lady of the sea had heard. The Graken's voice broke softly.

They are thinking to make a profit at the Ornithon, then ransom you to the Protector of Faires!

Mycul forced a laugh.

There is nowhere out of earshot for a Graken, the creature said within him. *You are learning quickly Mycul Zas, but you must learn faster still to stay one-step ahead and alive. One of these men is a traitor and will try to kill you. I feel the malevolence but cannot pinpoint the source. If only I had time before we reached the Ornithon.*

Mycul thanked the creature and looked up at her graceful form. Every day he found the Graken more beautiful. As if she heard, the creature bellowed out over the tempest and he felt the boat accelerate through the waves.

I will look up your future in the Ornithon, Mycul offered.

No, you must destroy it.

Why? He was incredulous the creature could ask him to do this.

The future is not ours to know. This was all the Graken would say. The creature pulled the ship closer to the cliffs, trying to gain some shelter from the gale. Through the driving rain, Mycul could make out the headland composed of pure white rock, which had eroded into an arch. On top of the arch stood a pyramid of dark material.

"We'll have to get to the port on the southern side and walk," the Captain said tersely. He brought out his whip and lashed several sailors.

The cliffs were frighteningly close, rising sheer for some three hundred feet. Mycul observed the changing textures of the rock. What at first appeared homogeneous was made from layers of white rock, each with different textures and hues. The guano of perilously perched seabirds caused some of this, yet other changes were wrought by the action of the sea on softer sediments. The arch on which the Ornithon stood was one such area.

The vision of the future was lost in a haze of rain and spume and the ship now veered west and hugged the coast. A small port was just discernible where the chalk abruptly stopped. A solitary light burnt on a tower.

The Graken slowed, surveying the port for a berth. A bell sounded and the long arm of a jetty engulfed the craft and gave some shelter from the storm. The ship came alongside the wharf and the workers secured the ropes and made the vessel safe. A prisoner was duly dispatched from the dockside prison. He cowered naked before the beast. The Graken responded immediately, tossing the entire body into the air and swallowing the man whole.

"I hope I shall not have the honour of transporting you again," the Captain said.

Mycul held out his hand; it was not taken.

"I'm afraid whilst you are pulled by this Graken, I will always have need of you. You will stand ready at my service."

The Captain spat with the wind and cursed under his breath. The party collected their possessions and steadied themselves against the howling gale.

Mycul still felt the motion of the ship even on dry land. He walked along the stone jetty and knelt down. He incanted the Graken's name and thanked her for the journey. She placed her tongue on his cheek. Her breath smelt of blood and fish which Mycul found not entirely unpleasant this time.

Young Mycul. Farewell for now. Remember my advice. Destroy the Ornithon. Do not let anyone else see your future. The creature lifted her long graceful neck and her rider struggled to stay in control. *Beware the traitor in your midst.*

The ship was made ready for the storm with ropes. The Graken was released and cast one glance back at the party on the jetty. The six remaining mordonts, Nag-Nag Naroon, Stazman and Tahoola all waited, as if Mycul was now in charge.

"Well?" Tahoola asked.

"Well," Mycul replied, "we wait until the morning. We have enough for an inn and a warm meal."

"And ale?" Nag-Nag hoped.

"And ale," Mycul added as he wiped water from his face. They walked down the deserted street until they found a large inn to welcome them.

The fire roared and crackled as more wood was piled onto it. The room was large and the wooden tables around the outside were unoccupied. Workers lined up at the bar talking in hushed tones, except for one woman who drew her blue cloak around her and pretended not to notice the visitors. The innkeeper flicked dust from the bar. "Welcome to Pem. The last island of the Reach of Key," he stated.

Mycul was taken aback. "I thought this was the mainland."

The innkeeper smiled. "No that's a half day further by boat and a lot longer if you swim." Several workers laughed.

"In truth we might once have been part of the mainland. Several cities of the Adee are nothing but rubble at the bottom of the sea. Fishing boats trawl up items like these," he said then stood back and revealed the shelf of assorted objects: a glass vase, a plate decorated for the year 2000, and a mug.

The innkeeper filled a jug of ale and handed over four tankards. Mycul passed over some coins and the landlord pushed back his change. Out of the corner of his eye, Mycul saw a young woman observing him. "My piece de resistance is…" The barman gave a mock fanfare and placed a picture on the bar. The image was encased in a light clear material. It showed a busy street scene with people and wheeled carriages. "People used to drive themselves to places. Imagine all that travel?"

"Automobiles," Mycul added remembering the name for the self-propelling vehicles of the Adee. "They had engines and used fuel in the same way that a fire uses wood to burn."

"Amazing!" The innkeeper leaned over the bar. "You must be well educated."

"The best Vold Nujun has to offer," Mycul joked. "Also I am friends with the Keeper of the Seventh Law."

"And no doubt you are here to try your luck with the Ornithon."

Mycul smiled. "Might be, might not be. Is it important?"

"It's your business," the innkeeper laughed, sending ripples across his apron. He wiped his hands and served a woman at the bar before whispering to the woman in the blue cloak.

The group took a table by the fire and shared the drink. The beer was fresh and light unlike the heavy liquid offered on the ship. Tahoola turned to stare into the fire. She looked deep in thought. Mycul watched. Her fine hair was now almost all grey, as if the shock from the accident had changed its hue. Her eyes had always been grey but her skin glowed with the reflected warmth of the fire.

"Well everyone knows what we're here for, so I don't suppose there's any harm in plying my trade," Nag-Nag said as he finished the tankard, burped and wandered over to the bar.

"What is Mennes like?" Mycul asked, hoping to start a conversation.

Stazman took a sip and warmed his hands before replying. "The country is mountainous and people live in scattered villages for the most part. The old Adee capital still stands in Karlize but the ruins were being cleared for Warmonger Lazlo's new fortress and town. The men are warriors, shaving their bodies to better show the tattoos of their families. The Mordocki make a point of speaking in the accent of the ancients."

"But you have no accent or tattoo," Mycul said.

"Shows a man doesn't listen as well as a woman," Tahoola quipped.

Stazman continued, "I was enslaved before I was of age. But when I return I will have the trisos emblazoned on my sword arm and chest. As for accent, well, I've been away a long time."

"So you only go with us to the valley of Deidar Mela?"

Stazman became grave. "I need to kill the woman who did this to me."

"The woman?" Tahoola asked.

"Barser De Sotto. I've imagined many cruel ways to despatch her and one day I'll find the opportunity."

"You'll need an army," Tahoola said. "She married Lazlo a few months ago. I'm surprised you haven't heard."

"We don't hear anything from Mennes on the Reach of Key."

"I wouldn't say that too loud or there'll be one less," Tahoola said and downed her drink and banged the tankard on the bench. They each looked at each other.

"Another jug of ale, landlord!" Stazman shouted.

Mycul observed the reaction in the room. No one stirred except the woman in the blue cloak. Mycul nudged Nag-Nag who in turn attracted Tahoola's attention.

Tahoola replied. "Perhaps she is an assassin like the one you wanted to torture."

Mycul looked at the stranger. She realised she had been seen and moved away from the bar.

"No," Nag-Nag said, "she has the demeanour of someone used to ordering people about, someone who's fallen on hard times, given the patching in her cloak."

"You've obviously all got better observational skills than I." Mycul watched what the woman was doing.

"No, we just interpret what we are seeing with greater enlightenment. When a young man sees something, sex clouds his vision, that makes him vulnerable," Tahoola said. She seemed to possess more energy now.

Mycul struggled to understand this statement and there wasn't a chance to ask as Stazman returned from the bar with two more jugs of ale. His face was alive with enthusiasm. "I've just found out this inn has a pool of volcanic water in the cellar. A bath house! Who'll join me?"

Nag-Nag turned away. "I don't bathe."

"I've noticed!" Tahoola said, barely concealing her contempt.

"Mycul! Looks like you're the lucky man."

Mycul looked around the room.

"Go on, you know you want to," Tahoola said trying to keep a straight face.

"That's settled then. Pay the man," Stazman ordered.

Mycul set several coins on the table, which the innkeeper wasted no time in collecting.

"We'll have to wait until dawn before taking the cliff path. Hopefully the Ornithon will be revealed to us. It would be nice to face our futures free from dirt and grime."

Stazman downed his tankard of ale and stood waiting for Mycul to do likewise. Mycul took his time.

"Maybe he's having second thoughts," Tahoola joked.

"If he isn't back by suppertime we'll know what's stuck where!" Nag-Nag laughed until he coughed, but his red face disappeared into the tankard when he realised no one else found his comment funny.

Mycul and Stazman followed the innkeeper down a wide flight of stone steps. The air became warmer and more humid and the walls were covered in fine fungal growths. When they reached the basement the stone gave way to tiles of the deepest azure. Into these were set four large pools of the deepest blue with water creating a permanent mist around the floor. Three of the pools were already occupied. "You've paid enough for one hour. You may leave your clothes on the shelf here, so they won't get damp." The innkeeper walked away.

Stazman ripped off his clothes and stuffed them in an untidy heap in the corner. Mycul was much slower and more methodical, folding everything neatly and stowing any coins deep within the pile. He stood naked and waited. Stazman already sat with water up to his neck.

"Come in! It's beautiful. It's like being caressed by many delicate fingers."

Mycul stepped into the water and slowly slid into its cleansing heat. Stazman was right. He smiled and closed his eyes. Immediately he thought of Orlando.

Stazman moved closer.

"I've a question for you," Mycul said. "I often see you and Tahoola talking, sometimes you break off when I come near."

Stazman looked at the man who had released him from Madam Messalina.

"We are both grateful to you. We've both been given a second chance courtesy of you."

"The problem with having a second chance is making something of it," Mycul said.

Stazman dived beneath the water surfacing next to him. "Precisely what Tahoola said." They lay soaking in the warmth of the room.

"This is no good," Mycul said, parting the mist and swimming to the far corner of the pool.

"I thought it was very good," Stazman admitted. "And there's the added advantage of making Tahoola jealous."

Mycul's expression changed. "Why would this make her jealous?"

Stazman stopped. "You must be nearly my age and yet you don't read people well. I'm just playing around, trying to find out what kind of man you are. It's impossible for you to appreciate what it feels like to be free after eight years of slavery."

"I hope never to find out." Mycul flicked water into his friend's eyes and the two wrestled and writhed through the water, trying to gain supremacy and air. They acquiesced and again sat calmly in the bath only this time taking more notice of what was going on around them. The long thin legs of a woman towered over them. Mycul looked up from her toes to her green eyes then they dwelt again on her fine delta of pubic hair. She stepped daintily into the water and slid under, emerging with her breasts concealed.

"I feel I am safe here," she stated. "You two seem too interested in each other to attack a defenseless lady."

"This is Stazman and I am Mycul."

"I know. I am Ra'an De Sotto."

Stazman froze at the name, his face fixed in anger.

"Any relation to the witch Barser?"

The woman laughed, "I am her sister. But do not draw your dagger yet. Oh! I see you haven't one," she joked, "but I might well be useful to you if you let me join you on your mission to the Ornithon."

"Nag-Nag warned me not to mention it. You overheard my request?" Mycul was distracted by the contours of her porcelain skin as it curved towards her nipples.

"I might know the names of all the Protector's assassins for instance." The woman slid back in the water. She opened her legs and surveyed the two men. Mycul felt his cock stiffen.

"Wouldn't that mean you were an assassin yourself?" Stazman ventured.

The woman thought about this. "I am nobody's fool. I would be killed as soon as I entered Mennes, like yourself, Stazman Zas, Prince of Catherine. There is a price on your head."

Stazman's mouth opened wide in astonishment. Mycul kicked him in the shin to bring him back to his senses. "To give me that title would mean my three brothers are dead."

Ra'an nodded. "Two certainly, at the hands of my sister, the third has been missing a long time. Catherine is a changed place, since your exile. It is a state where one cannot breathe a word of dissent without fearing summary execution. It is a country where a child's word outweighs an adult's in any court. The whole population lives in fear. Stazman, we have to put the country right."

"We?"

"You and I."

"It wasn't part of my plan," Stazman said.

Ra'an smiled and ran her fingers though Stazman's blond hair. "When we have seen the future in the Ornithon and you wear the tattoo of the trisos on your chest and arm, you'll want power so badly, you'll do anything."

"Anything?" Stazman's voice tightened with nerves.

"Anything." Ra'an was obviously enjoying herself. "What you need to do is find the opposition leaders and get them on your side."

"Then we all need to play for the same side," Mycul said, trying to take in the implications of everything Ra'an had uttered. "Who is the assassin in our midst?"

Ra'an smiled, leaned towards Mycul and whispered. He went pale despite the heat and looked around.

"Tahoola? Are you certain?"

She nodded and climbed slowly from the water. A towel was wrapped around her and she picked up her clothes and walked away.

Mycul looked at the youth opposite him with his scruffy hair and ochre eyes shining from beneath his fringe. "I have rescued a Prince of Catherine. Do you think there might be a reward for that?"

Stazman laughed. "Barser will only pay if the reward is severed from my neck. Perhaps the Ornithon will reveal all."

"When were you going to tell me this vital piece of information?" Mycul asked.

"When the time was right," Stazman said. "I won't expect you to bow, yet."

"Don't worry, I won't," Mycul said looking at his companion. He didn't like secrets. "So we'll set off alone at first light, just you and I and see what this remnant of the Adee has to tell us."

"But first," Stazman said, "we have much to do." He climbed out of the water and Mycul followed. Attendants wrapped towels around them and drained the water. "I've never considered how to take over a country before."

"I don't think that's our priority. Remember that no one does anything without the thought of a reward." Mycul dried and dressed.

"Does that include you, Mycul?"

"No, my energies are focussed on something else," he replied before looking across the room trying to discern where Ra'an went.

"Revenge perhaps?"

"Revenge," Mycul replied.

Chapter 5: The Story Teller of Pem

"Upon the purple mountain lives a man
Whose ways are wondrous strange to me.
Upon the purple mountain lives a man,
Who guards the only path to Great Menne."

Nag-Nag had just completed his story of Gorangoth and how he, alone amongst men, had been granted access to Great Menne.

"Of course it's not entirely true," Stazman conceded, "but it's a good story."

"It is surely a geographic truth. There is only one path into Menne. But we are going to Deidar Mela, so it's west to the mountains for us after The Ornithon!"

The sun had risen, a weak gold over the now calm sea. The white cliffs stood as a resolute barrier and as they walked along the coast, they started to climb. The windswept trees, always to their left were contorted into such shapes it was easy to see why locals believed in dryads and faeries. The shadows of the couple stretched far into the undergrowth as the sun rose higher and feeble warmth penetrated the layers of their garments.

Mycul and Stazman had dressed before first light and set off without a guide or mordonts. It was Mycul's intention to outmanoeuvre everyone before he destroyed the Ornithon. There were more questions than answers but the most important was: should he consult the oracle at all? He smiled. He knew his decision.

The cliffs rose higher still, leaving the sea crashing against rocks far below. The little port was rendered insignificant by distance and the long coastline behind it stretched pencil thin due west until it blended with the sea. Looking south it was easy to think of Pem as an island but to the north the rising barrier of chalk hills gave the place the feel of something larger and perhaps once part of a whole.

"What might the Ornithon tell a Prince of Catherine?" Stazman asked.

"That he is a man like any other and their equal," Mycul opined.

"Surely you don't believe that?" Stazman seemed horrified at the idea.

"Stazman, until you were taken from the Reach of Key, you were a sex slave doing whatever your clients paid for. Now on the word of an assassin you're a prince!" Mycul smiled. "Don't you think there might be an element of fantasy here?"

"A life can be incredible," Stazman said in his defense.

"It can also be mundane and the better for it. Remember the curse, wish upon your enemies that they live in interesting times."

"Ah! You would deprive me of hope," Stazman ran along the path a little way.

Mycul shouted, "Just be true to yourself or you'll end up very unhappy." The path began to curve to the left. A long way behind, Mycul saw the rest of the party, the mordonts leading as their great strides covered the greater ground. He looked out over the sea and thought of his father and sighed.

When his gaze returned to the path ahead, he could not see Stazman. He turned a corner and still nothing. He shouted and he felt his heart beat faster with the effort and fear. He had a premonition of danger and forged ahead. Round the next bend he could see the path rise and for a great distance it was empty. Mycul stood and turned round slowly. He peered over the edge of the cliffs and he searched the perimeter of the woods; that was when he saw the yellow inserts of Stazman's jacket.

He moved closer and found Stazman crouched and observing something, enraptured. He too knelt and peered through the autumnal briars. The creature was small, not much larger than Mycul's hand, and naked. At first it appeared to be a child but as it turned there could be no mistaking the nature of a full-grown male. Stazman reached out and the creature froze. "I will not harm you," he said and inched closer.

Mycul watched. He could see the problem. The male's wing was pinioned by the thorn of a briar. He swept a mass of black curly hair from his face. "Can you really fly?" Stazman asked.

"I'd have cut my wings off years ago if I could not!" The creature sounded angry.

"You are fastened tight."

"Let me help." Mycul drew a knife and passed it round to his friend. "Cut off the thorn and we'll tend the man on the path."

"The man?" The creature almost laughed then winced in pain.

"You are a man, though admittedly I've never seen one in miniature, with wings."

"We were created like all the other creatures to fill the void left when animals became extinct."

"You were produced by the genetics of the Adee," Mycul said.

48

"I have not heard that but we pollinate flowers now bees have been wiped out."

Stazman held the creature gently as he cut away the thorn.

The faerie continued. "Our skin is dark, our hair is thick and dark to show the pollen, and our reward is nectar."

"Whatever you were formed for, you are beautiful," Stazman added.

They assisted the man through the briars and out onto the path. The curled limb of the thorn was cut through and fed back through the small hole in the faerie's wing. Mycul and Stazman stood back. "You are free to go," Mycul said.

Stazman watched the faerie stretch his wings and gently flap them. His eyes followed the creature as it hovered. The creature's soft dark skin absorbed the sunlight and radiated warmth and the wings now moved so quickly the colour bars became a solid line.

"I thank you. I hope we will meet again, Stazman Zem, and for your help I give you one piece of advice. The Ornithon is guarded by those so small they are insignificant but together they become greater than any." The creature waved farewell and flew towards the woods. It stopped above the largest oak, turned and waved. Stazman had to be dragged away.

"His magic captivated you," Mycul suggested.

"No, it was his beauty."

Mycul looked back. Tahoola and the other members of the group were almost upon them. The mordonts arrived first, their skin glistening with sweat and their horns dirty from foraging. Nag-Nag and Tahoola arrived a moment later. The woman sat down and recovered her breath. She took a swig of the painkiller. "My hand, I feel my hand. I feel the cold and yet it isn't there. I woke up imagining it had regrown but when I looked down…"

Mycul heard the despair in her voice. "Perhaps in Deidar Mela?"

She looked at Mycul. "Perhaps," Tahoola said. Her grey eyes narrowed, "but I will not be viewing my future in The Ornithon. I'd prefer not to know."

"We've been warned that the Ornithon is guarded," Stazman said. He was still gazing at the oak tree as if he had lost a great love. "I saw a…"

Mycul kicked him and whispered. "I don't think it wise to say you've just seen a faerie. At the very least there'll be a few ribald jokes!"

Stazman invented a lie, "It is a legend in Menne that something small guards the Ornithon and yet together they become greater than any army."

"We must be cautious." Tahoola stood and began climbing the path.

"It seems you forgot our bargain," Ra'an de Sotto said then jumped down from the branch where she had been waiting. She wrapped her blue travelling cloak around her. "Well met, Tahoola."

"Well met, sister. How fares the Protector?"

"Last time we met, Ceelan was still the most beautiful woman I've seen and she remained very angry with you."

Tahoola smiled as if remembering something.

The sound of waves breaking was punctuated by the cry of seagulls. The party walked towards the arch of rock they had seen from the ship. The obelisk of the Ornithon appeared ahead. Nag-Nag broke ranks and began to jog towards the strange glass prism. He turned back and smiled. "Isn't it the most beautiful sight?"

He faced it again, then shook his leg and scratched his back. Nag-Nag screamed and took a step or two back towards the group. The soil around him erupted and millions of ants emerged, crawling over his body and completely covering his face. His eyes briefly opened then burst. As he screamed countless insects entered his mouth. Nag-Nag's form dissolved. His left hand emerged imploring help before it was stripped of flesh and muscle. The bones hung a second longer before they were also devoured. The soil ceased moving and all that remained where the storyteller had been were two cubes of glass.

Mycul walked forward and picked them up. He studied the ground. He felt vibrations emerge from below and ran back to the group. The attack ceased.

"I'll go second, Mycul. I can wait to find out my future!" Tahoola backed away.

Stazman was pale and trembling. He turned and was violently sick. Mycul went over to comfort him, resisting his own urge to gag.

"I worked on a farm for nearly eighteen years. We always used oil and camphor to keep insects at bay," Mycul said, but these things weren't available.

"You try first," Ra'an said and sat on a rock.

"What about lining a path with fire then running for your life? It's perhaps a hundred yards to the door," Stazman said, then peered carefully toward the archway.

"There'll probably be more guards we cannot see."

Mycul studied the obelisk then he headed off. He covered all the ground between the party and the best vantage point above the bay before he returned.

"This is not the entrance, there is another way." Mycul led them all to the top of a path meandering down to a cove. Etched into the cliff further round the bay was a slender path made from many hundreds of steps with direct access to the obelisk door.

They climbed down into the bay. Here the chalk was covered in a green slime which made keeping balance difficult. The carved steps had the appearance of a ladder and Mycul began climbing.

Tahoola took one look and walked away. The mordonts huddled together and bellowed; they were too large to attempt the climb. Stazman gingerly began the ascent but slipped on the tenth step and fell winded on the rocks of the beach. When Mycul looked down again only Ra'an was behind him. The move nearly cost him his life, his legs slipped from under him and he hung suspended by his arms. He desperately searched for purchase with his feet. He wondered how he might climb back down again.

With determination, Mycul scaled the many uneven steps and regained the top of the cliff. In the distance he saw where Nag-Nag Naroon had disintegrated but looming a little to his left was the door of the Ornithon.

Mycul stood on the bare chalk path. He panicked as the ground either side heaved like the swell of waves and ants began to climb over each other in their quest for flesh. They could not cross the path. Mycul ran quickly to the door and stopped at the threshold. The door was inscribed with Adee words. "If only Sartesh was here," he thought.

And then, he was. The impossibility of hearing the voice of his friend Sartesh made Mycul turn several times. The voice was muffled as though wrapped in something. He listened again. "Mycul Zas, if you want my help, just look in the cubes."

Mycul searched his pockets and withdrew the cubes. He clearly saw Sartesh within the material. "You have acquired Ornithon cubes, they are used to communicate across great distances. Also, whilst you have them, the nanobots won't harm you."

"Nanobots?" Mycul tapped his head to make certain he wasn't imagining the voice and image.

"Mechanical ants. They are vicious and relentless. Be warned, once you've seen your future within the Ornithon, you are connected. I'm not certain I understand how that works. Now hold the cube to the door and let me see the words."

There was a long period of silence followed. "It's a quote from an old Adee novel called The Lord of the Rings: *Speak friend and enter.*"

"I'm sorry Sartesh, I don't follow that."

"Friend, say the word friend!"

Mycul did and the door slid open.

"The person who built this had a sense of humour," Sartesh added.

"Thanks," Mycul said then realised the cubes were solid white shapes once more. He looked at the patterns on the tiles. Each was a separate letter of the alphabet, repeated in a cunning pattern. He picked up some pebbles from the path and threw them onto the floor.

"You'll be glad I'm here," Ra'an said. "I love these puzzles. There's one similar in the Palace of the Protector." She took in the pattern. "You must walk to spell out the secret word."

Mycul looked around the entrance.

"I don't suppose you know what that is?"

Ra'an shook her head. When she looked at him again, Mycul saw she also had feline grey eyes. Perhaps the same gene was shared by all assassins. Mycul picked up more pebbles and gently skimmed them onto a few letters.

"I have it!" He stepped on the first tile, the letter A.

"You've confounded me; I thought it would be Zhedhelion Barkbada Uita!"

"No!" Mycul cast another pebble. "This was created by the Adee and for all their faults they had one great motto: all are created equal."

"You're sure?"

Mycul pointed at the pattern the pebbles made on the tiles. Half the motto was spelt out. He covered the rest of the ground and gained a central island. Above him was the pinnacle of the obelisk. He stood and waited. Nothing happened.

Ra'an joined him on the island. "What happens next?"

Mycul shrugged.

"I am Mycul Zas." Nothing happened.

"Perhaps we should retrace our steps?" Ra'an peered around and suddenly stopped. "Look at the walls." The layers of glass that made up the obelisk were beginning to glow and radiate colours. First reds, then yellows and through the spectrum until they began to mix and form an intense white radiance that bathed both of them until it was so bright they could no longer open their eyes.

"Mycul Zas," a female voice affirmed, "welcome to the Ornithon. Welcome to your future!" People emerged from the light. The first was Sartesh Andrada. He wore a gold embossed leather gilet over a thick white jumper. Over his shoulder he carried a cylindrical weapon which when fired made a fearful noise. Sartesh's dark green eyes made his face look pale. The image held out his hand and balanced on the palm, Mycul beheld Ornithon cubes.

Tahoola appeared, the stub of her right arm now covered with leather and possessing fingers which she could move. She wore the uniform of a gen of the army. The older woman who next appeared wore black. Her body split open on the impact of something metallic. She fell and joined many bodies on the floor. Later, Tahoola and Sartesh appeared to stand at the top of the sacred mountain of Alquaf Nul, holding out a child to be blessed by the rays of the rising sun.

Further visions disturbed these scenes. A great noise hurt his ears before Mycul watched a battle in which the fleet of Faires drawn by their graken were victorious over the navy of Mennes. Hypnotic colours obscured these images, replacing them with Mycul standing on the prow of the flagship surrounded by cheering sailors.

The Ornithon began delivering images faster: Mycul waiting outside his old farm holding the severed head of his uncle. The Protector of Faires standing beautiful and proud in her throne room with an assassin poised behind a purple curtain. Now Sartesh appeared crowned as king of an unknown land. He sat motionless in front of a purple flag. Mycul stared at it and the material unfurled to reveal a yellow reversed Z emblazoned in the corner. Next Mycul saw himself and Stazman on opposing sides during a land battle. They engaged in a sword fight until both, by some quirk of fate, fell on each other's weapons and died embracing each other.

Mycul closed his eyes hoping the pain in his head would subside.

The lights diminished and an older woman emerged dressed entirely in black. Her outfit possessed a high collar decorated with a lion's head and woven through her hair were tiny jewelled skulls. The mists cleared and a younger lady appeared by her side.

"We have free will, Mycul. Do not believe all you see in the Ornithon, it can deceive just as other human creations."

Mycul stared at the younger woman, taking in every contour of her face and body. Her shoulders were bare and her pale skin contrasted with jewellery made from jet which hung from her neck. The outfit began royally with fox fur decorating a basque fitted over a dress of grey embroidered with interwoven black flowers. Their eyes met and the lady smiled. Mycul felt himself grinning back.

The older woman stood apart. Mycul realised he had just seen someone similar die.

"I am the Necromancer and you will meet my daughter Alleyya soon. Mycul Zas, it is vital you carry out your task." Their images disappeared.

The voice who welcomed them warned, "The Ornithon has been violated."

A loud crack ruptured the tiles sending millions of nanobots into the room. Ra'an screamed. Mycul dragged her to the door. In his head he shouted for the Graken.

I am always with you, little one. My brothers will also attend.

Mycul ran as waves of insects followed and gained on them, pursuing them to the cliff edge. Mycul looked down. "There is only one thing to do." He felt his head burst with the song of the graken, not one but many creatures close by.

"I hope you aren't going to say, jump! I didn't see my death in the images presented," Ra'an said.

"Did you see the same as me?"

"I saw myself as queen of Catherine and more besides."

Mycul looked behind at the seething wall of unnatural insects. "Well your majesty, ants or water?" He took Ra'an's hand and together they launched themselves off the cliff. The air screamed past them and the waves churned below. The air sped by so quickly Mycul could not open his eyes. He smelt the presence of a Graken, felt the warm damp of its mouth as the creature caught him. He opened his eyes to see Ra'an was also safe.

She slapped him across the face. He rubbed his cheek after struggling back upright. "You could have killed me! And now we're about to be swallowed by a ravenous sea monster," Ra'an said.

"This Graken has risked much to rescue us. You should thank him." The rank air within the creature's mouth was replaced by fresh as its jaws opened and the pair were disgorged onto the strand. It was from here they had begun their climb. He looked up and saw the pinnacle of the Ornithon fall. His friends stood amazed as the creatures continued to knock great chunks of rock from the cliff until the headland cracked and the entire arch slid into the ocean. The boiling waves took a long time to settle.

You are unharmed? the Graken queried.

I am fine. My thanks to you and your brothers, I hope one day to return the favour. Mycul thought out his reply and realised all the Graken could hear him. They lined up across the bay and all bowed. Mycul returned the gesture. *I don't understand why you chose me,* he questioned.

The female voice replied, *It is a gift. You have done well and should rest. It is a long journey to Deidar Mela and I cannot help you there. You will feel sad without my voice inside your head and no matter where you are you will always yearn for the sea but you must be strong.*

I will try my best. That's all I can do, Mycul replied. The party watched the Graken turn and submerge. Larger waves broke on the shore a few minutes later and rocks ceased tumbling revealing a new set of contours for the cliffs.

-*-

The group returned to the inn, their mood sombre. Mycul stayed at the bar and drank a tankard of ale. The mordonts sat unobtrusively in a corner, barely tolerated by the proprietor.

"How do you put up with them?" the landlord asked, stroking his bearded face.

Mycul raised his sad eyes. "It's simple, my father was turned into one and I might have become one had I not been helped by Tahoola."

"The one-armed lady. She's a tough individual."

"They must build assassins in that way," Mycul said.

"Assassin? It's not often we get those in here and now we have two. Doesn't that strike you as an odd coincidence?"

Mycul looked the man fully in the eyes and tried to think of an answer.

"I'll tell you what it means, young man, the Protector of Faires has heard of you and that's either very, very good or…"

"Very, very dead," Mycul said then gulped the rest of his beer.

The landlord took the tankard and washed it. "Your friend has ordered another bath. Will you join him?"

Mycul's first thought was to decline but eventually he flicked a coin across the bar and went down the steps into the phosphorescent glow of the subterranean bath house. He piled his clothes tidily on the shelf and slipped into the tub. The heat eased Mycul's aching limbs and the hot water bubbled reassuringly blue and pushed a thin mist over the tiled floor. He stretched his arms out and let the heat penetrate every fibre of his muscles. He breathed the air scented with rosemary and eucalyptus.

Stazman slipped in next to him. "You haven't said what you saw in the Ornithon."

Mycul put his arm around his friend. "You were there at the start and at the end."

"So we're always together?" Stazman asked.

"We even die together," Mycul said and changed the subject. "When will you get the tattoos done?"

"Shh! I've already been told I look like Mennedic, if I sport tattoos I'll be murdered as one."

Mycul thought about the final embrace and the fatal blow delivered by Stazman.

"Tahoola was playing with those glass cubes. She got the shock of her life. They talk! You can clearly see Nag-Nag's head delivering all his best stories."

"So that's what he meant," Mycul mused.

"She made us all laugh by saying they were even better than the real thing. At least now we don't have to smell him as he tells tales!" Stazman laughed again at the joke before realising his friend hadn't found this funny.

Stazman turned Mycul round and began massaging his shoulders with sweet smelling oil. Slowly Mycul relaxed and he felt the cares of the world lift. "You were right; he did give off an odour." Mycul decided to omit hearing Sartesh in the cubes. "Let's see them work! I just hope they're not from the Adee or we'll all end in trouble."

"I think trouble is following us. Destroying the Ornithon will soon get back to the Protector," Stazman replied. He poured more oil and continued his work.

"And which of our assassins will be the messenger?"

Chapter 6: A Knife in the Night

"What's the point in being an attractive woman if the only men in the party have no time for you?" Tahoola joked as Mycul and Stazman cantered ahead of the group again.

Mycul gave an appropriate gesture. The mordonts who were following at a discreet distance concerned him. He couldn't form a bond with them as he had done with his father. Increasingly they were distant, and perhaps the animal DNA was taking an irreversible hold on them.

Mycul took his feet out of the stirrups and swung down from the horse. The animal moved to the roadside and began eating. Mycul walked back to the mordonts. They had no leader, so he asked them to gather round. He felt intimidated by their size and overpowered by their smell. He had to remind himself they were still in part human and that they were relying on him to find Calufras. It was an obligation and a duty. "I am going to take you to Deidar Mela. It is what I promised my father and it's what he would have wanted me to do. More importantly it's what I want for you, if you still desire a cure," Mycul said.

"I am Leeman, Mycul Zas and you have my trust. You released us from purgatory. It is still my wish and the wish of the other mordonts to find Calufras. We want to hold on to our human selves, so please take us there." The mordont closed his eyes. His hair had been replaced by the shiny black hide of a bull and his horns descended from huge growths in front of his ears. "Once I was like you. How old would you say I am?"

"Perhaps thirty," Mycul replied. The mordont had a muscled physique with several deep scars where he had been caught by the horns of another bull.

"Would you believe twenty-two? The pain of the virus spreading through your body is indescribable; the changing of cells that were once human brings more agony as you see yourself shed each layer of humanity. That is why we who remember crave Calufras. If it brings a month's relief it would be worth a year's trekking," Leeman said.

"I so nearly shared your fate but Dr Ambrose was more interested in torturing me and that gave me a chance to escape."

"You were lucky."

"Very and for that reason I will do my best to see you get to Deidar Mela. It is four or five days walk from Crilce and perhaps ten from Faires. We must find a ship bound for one of these ports."

"Do not venture to Faires. We will be killed there or worse, recruited into Ceelan's army," Leeman said then scraped the ground and snorted.

Mycul stroked the hide on Leeman's back then patted it until the dust swam in the air. He noticed Leeman's feet were swelling to form hooves.

Leeman looked down. "It's been happening all morning and has made the wearing of shoes impossible." His eyes betrayed the suffering.

"How long will it take to be irreversibly a mordont?"

"Another month perhaps. So anything you can do to speed our journey would be appreciated."

"Anything?"

The mordont nodded.

Mycul returned to his horse and mounted. He dug the creature with his spurs and cantered to Stazman.

"You treat them too well," Stazman stated. The look of beauty in Stazman's face took on a darker quality. "They are only mordonts."

"They were once like you and I. Leeman is of similar age to us and would like to regain his humanity. Have you lost yours?"

Stazman thought about this. "It was wrong to create them," he said in conclusion.

Mycul held his friend's shoulder. "It was wrong, but now they're alive, don't they have the same rights as you and I?"

Stazman reflected on this but said nothing. Something in the way he held himself told Mycul he didn't agree with this sentiment.

The road slowly descended the chalk heights and kept the broad sweep of the bay to their left. The second port on Pem was ten miles or so due west and apparently couldn't be missed. In the sunshine of an autumn day that was probably right but the clouds gathered and first fine drizzle, then mist descended. No one felt like talking.

The path narrowed as tree branches reached over the road, causing drops to land on the cloaks of the travellers. The road split. Mycul took a few minutes to go down each route. When he returned, he consulted the map the innkeeper had drawn. "We should take the right fork."

"I don't think so." Ra'an was adamant the way lay downhill. "I've been here before, on a mission. The top road turns inland to a small village."

Mycul peered downhill into the bank of fog. He was uncertain. "Well," he said eventually. "We will have to defer to your greater knowledge."

"Yes, you will," Ra'an replied.

The road was well made and through the mist Mycul thought he could hear singing. The melody was rich and mesmerising. Through the grim weather, a brightness approached. Mycul would not have been surprised to see some creature bearing a lantern but it was a gnarled old woman wrapped in many dirty and decaying shawls.

"Who passes my house?" she asked.

"Friends," Mycul said. He yelled in pain and fell from his horse. Blood shot from a wound in his thigh. He looked up for help and found the party had been set upon by thieves. Even the mordonts were being lassoed and corralled. He thought there might be five instead of six but a blow knocked him out.

When Mycul began to hear sounds, his head ached and the pain in his leg was a searing burn. He tried to move his arms: they were numb. His vision shimmered into focus. He realised his arms were tightly bound. He looked down and saw his wound had been cauterised but the skin still glowed an angry red from the burn. His clothes had been taken and he stood transfixed, lashed to two poles. He looked around and found no sign of anyone else. A group of people gathered, each bearing a rusty sword and a bow slung over their shoulder. They all appeared to be old, or at least what could be seen of their grimy faces were weather beaten and creased.

"Mycul Zas, well met."

"Forgive me if I don't shake hands," Mycul joked and received a blow from someone nearby.

"Here we preserve our meat in salt water. You will be lifted into the sea and near drowned before you are filleted and preserved in that vat of brine. It usually takes several hours to kill you, plenty of time for you to reflect on your life and make peace with your maker."

Mycul searched for help. Several of the group lifted the poles and he was carried face down into the sea. Here a special socket had been created in the rock and the poles sat upright, facing the incoming tide. The robbers retreated, leaving Mycul naked and alone as the sea slowly covered his feet, then ankles. He shivered with the cold. He remembered the Graken and called out for help. The tide had risen to his knees and he hoped it might be enough. *We are too far Mycul. Trust to yourself*, the faint voice said.

Mycul twisted his hands but the rope cut into his skin and the salt spray stung the wounds. The water rose quickly and the cold penetrated. He wondered how long he had before he was filleted. The mist closed around him and Mycul could barely make out the rocks ahead. He was able to move his feet a little more now they were used to the cold water. The waves lapped around his knees and made an uncomfortable journey higher. His skin ran with goose pimples and his teeth began chattering with the mix of cold and fear.

"You said I was made by the Adee and not by god, is that true?"

The faerie hovered just in front of Mycul's face. He felt the cool breeze from his wings.

"As far as I know, that is the truth. Dreadful experiments were carried out by people thousands of years ago and all that you see around you is their work."

"Why would they do that?" The man's head was cocked to one side.

"They killed off most of the animals on the planet through greed then repopulated it with things part human when food webs failed. Only farm animals remain as they were in Adee times."

"How do you know this?"

"Sartesh Andrada." Mycul wondered how long this questioning would go on when he heard voices wading through the water. They sounded confused.

"If you're going to rescue me, now would be a good time!"

The faerie moved round the back and suddenly Mycul's hands were free.

"I cannot swim, but you might borrow my blade to free your feet."

"Here!" The captors sounded close.

Mycul leaned and cut twice. He fell forward. The splash alerted his captors and they ran through the water. Mycul swam out to sea then turned left and followed the faerie back to land. He pulled himself up on the beach. He tried to stand but there was no circulation in his feet and legs. With great effort, he pulled himself to the cliff and waited.

The winged creature hovered.

"You must move and then rescue your friends," the faerie said.

"But I'm naked."

"Naked?" The faerie didn't appear to understand the word. "Without the covers you wear over your skin?" He flew off and returned several minutes later with breeches and shoes. "It was all I could carry."

"I owe you my life. You are a worthy friend."

"Friend? Is that good, being a friend?"

"That's very good," Mycul said as he dressed. He walked a few paces, steadying himself against the cliff. His steps were ungainly but he managed to coax the circulation back.

"The only way is up," the faerie helpfully said.

"Or another swim." Mycul didn't fancy more cold water but when he looked up at the cliff towering many feet above him, he knew swimming was the only sensible choice. He shivereded as he went back into the water. He swam back across the bay and reached the furthest edge of the sand.

He cautiously walked ashore and let the water drain from his trousers and shoes. He listened. The voices were further down the beach and he fancied he could see a torch as the mist had an orange glow. The faerie whispered the disposition of the enemy.

Mycul stole into the encampment and retrieved his sword, a bow and some arrows. He carefully investigated the huts. They were all empty. The prison, which held his companions, was more makeshift, consisting of two wicker fences running parallel and concealing the poles to which all the party were tied. The guards were wrapped up in dirty and ragged clothes. Mycul tossed a rock in their direction. They became alert and peered into the mist, then one gave silent signals to the other. The guard approached.

Mycul threaded an arrow, pulled the string taut and waited. The arrow whizzed through the air and caught its target through the heart. The second and third guard came rushing on Mycul's position. He launched another arrow that winged one assailant, causing the other to scream in alarm.

Mycul engaged him in combat, parrying blow after blow until he rolled to one side and thrust his sword firmly into the thief's stomach. His assailant's intestines unravelled onto the ground and almost fell on Mycul. The injured guard hurtled towards Mycul who with a single blow severed his arm from his shoulder. The sounds of the attackers running up from the beach made Mycul move with haste. He released Stazman and Leeman.

The main group of robbers was upon them but Leeman used his greater strength to overpower several whilst Mycul freed the remaining captives.

Tahoola picked up a dead man's sword and entered the fray. The conclusion was swift. The thieves realised the greater strength of their erstwhile prisoners and ran into the forest.

The party searched the huts for their belongings and found most items, before hurrying back up the trail towards the main road. Of

Madam Messalina's gold, there were only the two pieces left: those Mycul had placed into the hem of his trousers.

Exhausted and afraid, the group made their way up the hill. As the mist lifted, they saw dismembered bodies impaled in the branches of trees. The crows flew off as they approached.

Much later, their heavy hearts lifted as they saw the lights of a village. It bore no name sign and the inn was a ramshackle affair, but once inside the patron was welcoming enough until she saw the mordonts.

"They'll have to feed and bed in the stables," she insisted.

Not wanting any trouble, Mycul acquiesced. In truth, he was exhausted and tackling the landlady's views would have to wait. "We were attacked by outlaws. I think they intended eating us."

"Cannibals only a few hours from here!" exclaimed the landlady. She yanked off her apron and despite her frame ran out of the pub. She returned with their Keeper, dressed in the purple of his office. He heaved himself through the door and twisted the fine ends of his curling moustache.

"Good evening," said the keeper, "Mistress Merryweather says you were attacked on Pem." The Keeper wiped his brow with a silk handkerchief and sat down at a large circular table. "What an awful thing to have happened and only a few miles from here."

Tahoola held out her hand to restrain Mycul, deliberately sitting herself opposite the official. "Good evening, sir," Tahoola offered.

The Keeper looked at Tahoola's figure and smiled.

"At the point where the road splits, we mistakenly took the low road rather than the high." Tahoola reached out and touched the back of the man's hand. He was instantly engaged. "We were very quickly set upon by a group of at least ten men and women who overpowered us."

"Well, first thing tomorrow, I will set off with the garrison and flush these miserable creatures out. There is no place for them on Pem."

Tahoola gushingly thanked the official, sat, and shared a drink with him. The mood lightened further when the landlady went back into the kitchen and began shifting great pans of steaming food. The smell enveloped them all but not everyone was hungry. Mycul again downed two tankards of ale in quick succession.

"Alcohol will only ease your conscience temporarily," Tahoola said, leaving the Keeper to his fine wine. "I find living with mine, however uncomfortable, is the best way forward."

Mycul tried to work it out. "Ra'an intended us harm. I don't understand why she revealed herself now."

Tahoola thought about this. "It might be as simple as orders from Ceelan. It might be that she had another assignment given. Either way, none of us would trust her now."

"But she is still at liberty to cause havoc," Mycul said.

"Indeed," Tahoola grunted, and leaned against the bar. "You have the advantage that I trained as an assassin."

"Are you sure you didn't become one?"

Tahoola smiled. "Would I tell you if I had?"

Mycul thought about this. "I'm going to err on the side of caution and trust you."

Tahoola leaned across and almost planted a kiss on his lips. "Never trust an assassin who offers a kiss," she said before returning to the Keeper.

Mistress Merryweather came over. "I'm about to serve food but just to let you know, your creatures are safe and comfortable in the stables. For yourselves though, I'm afraid I've just the one room left. It's at the back and there are four pallets for beds. You'll get a good night and be woken early when I light the fires to cook breakfast."

Mycul smiled, thinking he would rather sleep with the mordonts. Their suffering had reduced their human qualities but not obscured them. They were truly more sinned against than sinning.

He gazed at Tahoola who rested her right arm on the table. Despite the grime, she possessed an inner beauty which troubled Mycul. He stood up and walked out of the inn. He didn't feel like eating. He walked out into the courtyard, then into the street. The houses and cottages in the village were mostly in darkness; a few chimneys pushed out smoke. Mycul stood and looked up at the navy blue sky. The evening star was bright and a new moon had risen beside it.

He thought about how many other people might have stood and watched just such a pattern in the sky. How many tonight, how many yesterday or thousands of years ago when the Adee ruled the Earth? Mycul folded his hands under his armpits for warmth; there would be a keen frost that night.

Low in the southeast the hunter appeared with his sword and belt made from stars. Mycul resolved to talk to Sartesh about borrowing a device for magnifying the stars. Surely not everything the Adee did was evil and corrupt? This was a dangerous thought; people had been branded with the 'S' of sedition for voicing such opinions. With a final look at the sky, Mycul saw a star wander from north to south.

He returned in doors and took to his pallet bed. Sleep eluded him and when the gentle snoring of his friends began, he made to slip out of the room, intent on the cool night air.

There was a cry. Mycul turned and saw a knife flash in the moonlight. It descended once more into his empty bed.

"Who's there?" he shouted and ran into the room, his voice waking the others. Mycul stood in front of his assailant. He clearly saw Ra'an. "Are you going to kill me?" he asked.

Ra'an lunged at him. "If I don't, a carniver will."

"But you'd like the glory and more importantly, the reward," Mycul said as he dodged the blade.

Ra'an flashed a grin. Stazman drew his sword and Tahoola also. Seeing she was outnumbered, Ra'an fled. Mycul followed her and jumped the stairs, landing heavily on the flags of the ground floor in an effort to outpace her. He ran, grateful that the thin light which builds before dawn aided his pursuit.

Ra'an had made for a large barn at the end of the village. Mycul redoubled his efforts but before he could reach the building, a great sphere of red rose from behind it. It made a roar like a caged beast and Mycul flung himself down, not knowing what was going to happen. The sphere rose and now he saw the thing for what it was: a craft for taking to the air. Ra'an was climbing unsteadily into a basket suspended from the balloon. A man was operating a burning jet and as a flame shot into the balloon, the roaring happened again. Ra'an was lost to them, already too high for anything to reach save an arrow.

Tahoola and Stazman caught up with him "That's the work of the Protector of Faires. Who else could afford such a contraption?" Tahoola hissed.

"I have never seen one before," Mycul admitted.

"It is the work of the Adee and not to be trusted," Tahoola said firmly.

"But to ride in the air like that, to see the world below…" The romantic look in Stazman's eyes showed what he was imagining.

"And then there's you," Tahoola chided, "what sort of guard would let Ra'an attempt to murder Mycul?"

"I didn't trust her but I had no proof," Stazman said unhappily.

"I don't suppose we've seen the last of her," Mycul said. "And I guess that just answered my nagging question as to who is in the Protector's employ." Mycul then turned his attention to Tahoola. "Although it would be nice if you told us why you left the Protector's service?"

Tahoola sighed. "If we are to be friends there can be no secrets between us, though I warn you, you may not think so highly of me thereafter."

"Okay. After a decent breakfast, the revelations." He gave a jokey drum roll. Tahoola raised an eyebrow.

As they walked back to the inn Stazman asked, "Why did Ra'an choose now to show her hand? After all, she had our confidence until we were captured."

"I think I have an answer." Tahoola pushed open the door and added, "The ambush was planned in advance, using one of these." She pointed at the cubes. "They communicate with one another. I've seen the Protector use them."

"I spoke to Sartesh through them at the Ornithon," Mycul said then rubbed his wrists where the ropes had burnt. The skin was still red and raw.

Mistress Merrymore appeared. "Is everything alright?"

"It is now," Tahoola said. "I don't suppose you have a preparation for rope burns, do you?"

Mistress Merrymore noticed Mycul's wounds. "I have a cream which I'll bring over after you've eaten your breakfast."

A large wooden tray arrived with tankards of ale, plates of bacon, cheese, butter and bread. Everyone ate heartily, except Mycul. He couldn't bring himself to eat the bacon. The cooked pink flesh reminded him of what so nearly happened to them all. Stazman leaned over and skewered the rashers with his fork. "Waste not, want not," he said.

Chapter 7: The Protector's Assassin

Tahoola sat back in her chair. A fire burned in a large hearth lending her pale features an orange glow. She surveyed the two men. They were vastly different, Mycul's tall dark build set against the smaller, pale frame of Stazman.

"We know one thing about Ra'an: everything was well planned. She was hardly out of our presence and we didn't expect to stay here."

Stazman toyed with the rind of bacon left on his plate. "She could only have planned this desparate attempt on Mycul's life if she also planned our capture."

Everyone thought about this. It was Mycul who pointed out how persuasive Ra'an had been about taking the lower road. "Also I didn't free her, she freed herself."

"Or she was never really tied; we weren't in a position to check." Tahoola thought about what had happened. "It would take quite a lot of money to bribe a tribe of cannibals and also to arrange the balloon flight. There was a well-organised mind at work here, obviously not a male. Sorry boys. Also, I hate to say this but only the Protector's assassins are allowed to use the Ornithon cubes."

Mycul realised the truth immediately. Ra'an must also have a cube. He took one out of his pocket. Tahoola stayed his hand. Mycul took a deep breath. "You have proved yourself more than once but despite that I think it's time you explained to us about being an assassin."

Tahoola finished her drink. "I have been sworn to secrecy but as I have already broken one vow, never to leave the Protector's service, another will not hurt," she said.

Mycul stretched his feet on the chair next to him and leaned back onto Stazman.

"I have known nothing of life except being an assassin. We are taken from our foster-families at the age of eight and never allowed to see them again. The trauma of guilt and hatred this generates is channelled into our studies. The way of fighting, the sisterhood, becomes everything. We deny ourselves all except service to the Protector. She is very beautiful and graceful, six-foot-tall with cropped black hair. Her smile is radiant and her anger the most frightening thing I've beheld. I loved her like my mother, like my best friend. I would have served her forever except..." Tahoola surveyed her audience and looked around the room to ensure there were no eavesdroppers. "...for the man I loved. He was the Keeper of the Seventh Law." Tahoola smiled as she saw Mycul register this fact. He opened his mouth but she waved her finger, "Nallor Dhze. He was my lover and also the man who taught Sartesh everything about the Seventh Law. I would scale the walls to meet Nallor, I would organise hunting expeditions to places where he mapped rocks.

"Of course, it was impossible to keep our love secret. His letters were found in my belongings. I remember the way the Protector smiled when she spoke to me of her disappointment. I remember the way her kiss felt like poison. The Protector exacted her revenge. She ordered me to assassinate Nallor or be executed."

"What did you do?" Stazman asked, enthralled by the story.

"My life was more important to me than my lover's. At nineteen, you still think selfishly, so I dispatched him with a trisos," she said and wiped away a tear. "The Protector heaped gifts on me. This gold band, and other presents of such great value they are safely stowed. Using the trisos was a tour de force. It created the impression there was a Mennedic plot on Faires. In reality I had betrayed my lover and myself. You can only imagine how I felt."

"Worse was to come," she continued, "Not only was Nallor dead but Mennedics were rounded up and executed without trial. I was back in Ceelan's favour. It was a dreadful victory. I hated myself with a fury that hasn't abated. I had become corrupted by the act."

Stazman's hand was on his dagger but Mycul stayed him from drawing the weapon. "You killed Mennedics for no reason?" His anger turned his face crimson.

"I did not! It was the Protector who sentenced them. I am not proud of my part in events but I cannot undo the past. However I might do something to help you in the future."

"I will never be able to trust you," Stazman said.

"I understand," Tahoola replied. "I will have to earn that trust back – if I can."

"How did you escape her service?" Stazman played with his hair then sat up straight to listen more attentively. "The punishment for deserting is to be pursued by carnivers until devoured."

Tahoola said, "I left on the first ship from Faires. Its cargo of bounty hunters suited me well. No questions were asked. I have worked in the profession for five years and killed four carnivers. The fifth I tamed to be my guide; the one whose throat I cut before the blast on the Reach of Key."

"Are there any more carnivers after you?"

Tahoola nodded. "Whilst Ceelan is Protector of Faires, there will always be a carniver searching for my DNA."

Mycul laughed nervously. "Then I guess we have something in common, as Ra'an suggested one would pursue me," he sighed, realising the enormity of the task they faced. "So, in order to ensure our safety, we must not only find Calufras but make Stazman Prince of Catherine. With his principality as a base we might survive long enough to overthrow the Protector of Faires."

Tahoola placed her stub on the table. "Put like that it sounds some considerable task. The important thing is, shall we try to achieve our goals or just walk away?"

"Never! We must succeed!" Stazman cried.

Mycul looked at Stazman. "So long as we get them all in the right order."

"If we can believe what Ra'an said about the death of your brothers," Tahoola added.

"I've learned something from you both. The future doesn't just happen; you have to make it happen," Stazman said.

Mycul thought about this. He wondered what Ra'an might have seen in the Ornithon and how her future and his might intertwine. "What do you mean you have to make it happen?" Mycul asked.

"That now you know my potential, you could ensure I become Prince of Catherine."

"And could you see how we might become implacable enemies?" Mycul remembered the scene form the Ornithon.

"No, that's impossible!" Stazman put his arm around his friend. Mycul did likewise with Tahoola. He wondered about Stazman and himself falling on each other's sword. Was it a potential reality or a metaphor? Yet he knew what he'd seen. It was impossible not to reflect on how events might unfold to such an end.

"We should visit the Keeper before he rides out with the garrison," Mycul said. "Perhaps we should introduce him to the mordonts so he knows what the Protector gets up to?"

"You're getting the idea," Tahoola said.

The Keeper was unimpressed with the story of geneticists on the Reach of Key. He glanced at his desk, then looked up at each of them.

"I'll have no truck with mordonts. You leave me in a dilemma. I don't think you'll find a boat to let you leave Pem."

Tahoola smiled.

"We need only try, perhaps with your permission?"

"My influence is not so great out here. We are a long way from Ceelan's powerbase." The Keeper dabbed his forehead with a violet handkerchief. "Besides, my carriage is ordered and I will take the garrison out to the bay and find your cannibals. There will be no survivors." The Keeper returned to his paperwork, ignoring the trio. They took the opportunity to leave his office. At the door they heard him say:

"I wish you a safe and speedy journey but do not associate yourselves with mordonts for too long."

"Thank you for your advice. We must use daylight wisely if we're to make the mainland," Mycul said.

The nine remaining members of the group set off towards Pem's second port and a boat to Crilce. Getting to the mainland was the most important part of their immediate plans, and would only be possible if they could find a captain to take them.

The road was busy with people returning from market. They moved to the opposite side of the road and hurried along when they saw the mordonts. Leeman barely concealed his anger and bellowed.

The port was full of sailing ships but there was no sign of any ship pulled by Graken. Dockers loaded carts and took them off to warehouses.

"We'll need a lot of money to bribe a captain."

"Or we could steal one and sail it ourselves."

"Let's try something legal first," Mycul said.

All afternoon Mycul and Tahoola tried every ship in port. Not a single captain could be persuaded to take both humans and mordonts to the mainland. It seemed mordonts had been outlawed by the Protector just a month before and demoted to non-citizens. Mycul returned to Leeman to tell him.

"You have a choice. Leave us on Pem, or steal a vessel. Decide." Leeman pushed himself back into the shadows of the store where the mordonts were hiding.

Mycul entered the building and looked at the despondent creatures, all of whom seemed even less human.

Stazman pushed in, his uneven blond hair stuck down by sweat on his forehead. "It seems the Keeper sent word ahead and we were expected."

"So, it's theft or a long stay on Pem," Tahoola added.

Mycul sat down on a large crate. "Neither are attractive propositions," he replied. Silence pervaded the room as each pondered what could be done. The mordonts shifted restlessly. Leeman tried to calm them but their desire for Calufras, and anger at being reduced to non-citizens could not be assuaged.

Eventually Tahoola broke into their thoughts. "You are sitting on the answer."

Mycul looked at her in disbelief. She came over and kicked the crate. "You can read; they are packed with porcelain bound for Crilce. Surely, such a container might be large enough for a mordont? We could hide the porcelain under the straw."

"But we don't know when this stuff is to be loaded. Nor if there is air within a crate to keep a mordont alive."

"We must try. Empty the first," Tahoola said. She lifted a crow bar from the wall and tossed it to Stazman. He prised off the lid. The fine china mugs and plates in plain white were evidently meant for the cheaper end of the market. The wares were removed, passed hand to hand, and hidden beneath the hayrick. Leeman ventured into the empty container. The lid was fixed.

"There is enough air and I can see out through the poorly joined planks," the mordont said, "Though it is stuffy. Our smell might betray us."

"Or your weight," Mycul said. "When did the next transport leave for Crilce?"

"High tide tonight, according to the chart," Stazman replied.

They repeated the process until all the mordonts were stowed away. The three humans hid themselves when they heard voices. The dockers hauled the crates onto low carts and affixed the seals of loading. A crane hoisted each in turn into the hold of a ship called the Surfrider.

The captain remembered Tahoola.

"The one-armed woman is back. Here, give us a hand, dear!" He laughed at his joke and Tahoola smiled falsely. "Sure, I'll take you humans to Crilce. I am glad you've come to your senses. It won't be long before all mordonts are rounded up and destroyed, you mark my words. The Protector is in no mood to tolerate genetic deviants. She's had soldiers capturing and killing faerie folk as well."

"Don't you think they've been harmed enough?" Mycul asked.

The captain gave him a strange look. "I wouldn't go repeating that opinion on the mainland."

Mycul offered the last piece of gold and the captain snatched it from Mycul's open hand.

"Come into my office and I'll sign the necessary papers."

"We are very grateful," Tahoola purred. Mycul thought she might lean forward and kiss the officer but she saw the way he looked at Stazman and pushed him forward.

The cargo was safely stowed in the hold. Mycul gazed at the crates and hoped the mordonts were coping in the confined space. There was nothing he could do.

The ship headed out of the port just after high tide. The weather forecast was for a stiff southerly breeze with showers and the mares-tail clouds were evidence of a change. They skidded across a weak blue sky whilst the Surfrider sailed across the strait towards the mainland.

The captain busied himself at the wheel and in the chart room behind, leaving the three travellers to take the air on deck and relax. "Ra'an will go back to the Protector. Within three days there will be a decision on what to do with us," Tahoola said and Mycul took her meaning well enough.

She placed her hand on the rail. The breeze blew back her hair and revealed the fey shape of her ears for the first time. "Maybe not even as long as that. The Protector has Ornithon cubes for talking over distances. They are a little like those cubes of yours except that what you see exists a long way off."

"These must do the same. I spoke to Sartesh via them. Maybe that will give us some advantage? One thing's for certain, we'll have to think of alternatives and a faster approach on Deidar Mela. I have one idea – you might consider it foolish but it will be fast," Mycul said. He patted Stazman's shoulder. "Are you keen on flying?"

"You wouldn't be thinking of stealing an assassin's airship?" Tahoola looked aghast then realised that was exactly what he was thinking. "The depots are too well guarded."

"But you're an assassin and we are your friends," Mycul reminded her.

"And we're playing for high stakes now," Stazman volunteered.

Tahoola thought about the depot at Crilce and how it might be attacked. Finally, she realised the fatal flaw in the plan. "Airships take a long time to inflate, Mycul."

"Then on what signal are they prepared?"

"An assassin's," Tahoola said.

"Good, then we need a strategy."

The three of them talked for over an hour, until a working plan had emerged. The sun was now setting and flocks of seagulls followed the wake of the ship. The skies darkened and the promised shower sent heavy drops pounding on the deck. The rain turned to hail and the sailors worked hard to brush the accumulation away and keep the gangways clear. The sinking sun shone golden rays from the west and a rainbow appeared.

"Perhaps the rainbow is a good omen," Tahoola said.

"Let's hope no one is alert to terrorist threats in the state of Faires."

"Well, they soon will be," Stazman said. He let the breeze blow his hair across his face. He pushed it back. "What's the punishment if we're caught?"

Tahoola whispered in his ear. Stazman went pale and then swayed unsteadily before going into a faint.

Mycul caught him and gently lowered him to the ground. The captain appeared, clicked his fingers and a bucket was brought. He unceremoniously tipped the seawater over Stazman. The youth struggled for breath, coughed and came to his senses. Sailors around them laughed.

"What did the lady ask him?" one remarked. Another provided an answer with an appropriate gesture. Bawdier lines followed. For the first time Mycul realised that others saw Stazman differently.

They spent a restless night in the communal sleeping area. Sailors dressed and left for watch and were replaced by their tired and bedraggled compatriots. No one else made comments about Stazman but the damage was done. Every time Mycul woke, he turned in his hammock and saw Stazman's eyes staring.

By the first light of dawn, Stazman got up and left for the deck. He looked drawn and ill at ease. Mycul closed his eyes and let the gentle rocking of the ship send him back to sleep.

_*_

When Mycul awoke, he felt completely refreshed. Sunlight streamed in through the porthole and showed dust motes cascading. He stood, stretched and realised the ship was calm and quiet. He ran up onto the deck. Instead of sea, layers of sandstone rose ahead and were capped by a signal station with a great fire sending flames and smoke into the sky.

"Welcome to Crilce," the captain said. "You slept better than your friend," he pointed out Stazman, who was talking to Tahoola. "Now, she's a remarkable lady, if I didn't know better I'd say she was an assassin. They have a look about them, it must be in the genes. I hope for your sake you're on the same side!"

It was a joke but Mycul couldn't bring himself to laugh. "Do we need papers to disembark?"

"The tickets I prepared will need to be cancelled at the Keeper's lodge up the hill."

Mycul thanked him for the safe crossing and gingerly took the gangplank to dry land. Already the crates were being unloaded. Mycul followed one cart to a large wharf side warehouse, where he helped Leeman out. The mordont stretched and flexed his back and shoulders. He tried to speak but no words came, only an animal grunt.

Chapter 8: Flight to Deidar Mela

The noise and klaxons told of an emergency. Some people were running away from the port and soldiers were running towards it, swords drawn. Mycul and Leeman ran towards the Surfrider. In the midst of the chaos, they saw a crate had fallen from the crane and split open. The mordont within was dead. The other four were surrounded by troops and Stazman was about to swing down on a hawser. Tahoola took the longer way, her sword already drawn. Mycul could see her calculate the disposition of the enemy.

He looked around for a vantage point and found it was already taken by a woman dressed in white. She observed proceedings through a monocular and spoke to a man at her side. The Keeper appeared on the same balcony, instantly recognisable in his purple. He looked flustered and kept nervously twisting his moustache and bowing in deference. Mycul guessed the woman was someone important, but with no time to spare, rushed towards his friends.

Tahoola sliced through the soldiers sent against her until they held back. Stazman was holding his own against his opponents. The superior strength of the barely-human mordonts gave the advantage. Mycul rushed to their aide, facing off against half their assailants. Physically he was no match for so many and he could see Stazman was tiring as well. Only Tahoola was making progress. Leeman waded into the midst of the soldiers, knocking heads together and throwing men out of the fight and into the sea. Mycul realised archers were lining up on the balcony.

"Have you got a plan B?" he shouted at Tahoola.

Tahoola almost dropped her sword.

"The Protector, here!" she visibly gulped. "Yes, all of us make a run for it, towards her. The balcony marks the assassin's depot. If I'm not mistaken we'll find an airship and could make our escape."

Mycul parried several blows from an opponent. Tahoola ungraciously stuck the soldier through the heart and withdrew, sending spumes of blood over Mycul.

"Thanks," he said wiping the liquid from his face.

"Three, two, one, run!" Tahoola shouted the words at the top of her voice. The sound continued for many seconds, until her face went purple from the effort. They all ran. Eight people took off towards the assassin's depot as a second mordont was killed. They dashed from sunlight to deep shade where the overhanging buildings provided protection from the archers.

"Where to now?"

"In here," Tahoola said and pushed against a door, leading into a courtyard. An airship was standing ready: a basket and cylindrical balloon tethered to the ground which harnessed the energies of faerie creatures.

"Time for you to work your charm, Stazman," Mycul said as Stazman approached the winged creatures. He spoke in an animated fashion and then listened carefully to the reply.

"Cut the ropes," Stazman called over his shoulder, "and they'll take us to Deidar Mela, where we must release them. From there we must make our own way into the valley of healing."

Mycul had sliced through the retaining ropes and already the craft was hovering above the ground. It threatened to climb higher but Tahoola held on to the edge so the mordonts could gain the basket. Their eyes were filled with fear but the human need to escape prevailed. Their weight pulled the gondola back down. Stazman leapt in and pulled the chord to the burner. A flame shot into the silk of the craft and it rose again. Tahoola was pulled into the basket.

"Come on, Mycul!" several of the party shouted. He hadn't realised how quickly it would ascend. He grabbed a dangling rope and swung off the ground, then climbed with agility towards the basket. With a dull thud, an arrow penetrated his shoulder. He grappled with his right hand but could not gain purchase. He fell with a cry.

His friends watched helplessly from the craft. Mycul spun the end of the rope round his foot and held on. He was tugged feet first into the air with a yelp, his face mere inches from the ground. Stazman pulled the cord that fed the burner. The craft rose and was tugged toward the middle of the courtyard by faerie folk.

The Protector entered the courtyard. She walked towards Mycul. His head was now level with hers as he dangled from the craft. Ceelan smiled. He saw her upside down, and stared at her white boots, skirt, jacket, pearls, and elaborate, white hat and half veil protecting a face of serene beauty. She smiled and her jet-black eyes lit with an inner fire.

"You must be the insignificant one," the Protector said.

Mycul pulled her close with his free hand and kissed her. "You are very beautiful," he said. The rising balloon jerked him out of reach. "I'm certain you'll see me again," Mycul called as he was pulled higher.

"I doubt it," the Protector smiled as she stood observing events. "There is nowhere in my country where my presence is not felt."

"I'll trust in a miracle and will hope for another kiss before I die."

"How charming of you. I might even oblige-- if you survive."

The craft rose into the air and the Protector stayed her archers from firing. Those in the gondola grabbed fistfuls of rope and pulledwith all their might to bring Mycul aboard. When he fell into the basket, they realised the extent of his injuries but could not explain the fixed smile on his face which endured despite his pain.

_-*-_

A long time ago, the Adee made great advances in surgery and the relief of pain. All their knowledge is now contained in Deidar Mela. It possesses an expertise recognised by all, harbouring great healers and free thinkers; a true Sanctuary.

The ground beneath the gondola became more rugged; the burner needed to be on for longer to ride the peaks of each successive hill.

Mycul had long since lost consciousness. His skin burnt with an inner fire.

"The arrow was poisoned, it's a common enough assassin trick and explains why the Protector stayed her hand," Tahoola said. She cooled Mycul's forehead with a dampened a piece of cloth.. "Our best hope is getting him to Deidar Mela quickly. The Protector knows where we are going and why."

Tahoola looked at the bleak landscape below them. "It's not what I expected: great scars in the landscape where so much rock has been removed the hills no longer exist. This surely must have been the work of the Adee."

Stazman joined her and looked over the edge, and felt the basket shift slightly under their weight. "You mean there's an antidote?"

Tahoola patted his cheek. "If anything can be done to save him or ease his passing then we are going to the right place."

Great forests of ash gave way to oaks; as time passed these became smaller and more gnarled, as though the harsh climate stunted their growth. Even so, each peak had been gouged almost away, leaving strange scars and precipitous cliffs. They glided over a stone statue of flowers erupting from a corpse.

"The border of Deidar Mela," Leeman cried and gave thanks.

"I don't understand why they took so much from the Earth and returned so little," Stazman said.

"We would have to become Keepers to know of such things," Tahoola replied pulling her coat tight about her.

"It is simpler in Catherine as everything Adee is banned. We decided to start anew, that's why I had no complaint about Mycul destroying the Ornithon."

"I'm not so certain he has. Damaged it perhaps but if the cubes still work, something of it remains," Tahoola said. She turned her attention to the steep sided valley below. "Once something is destroyed, its knowledge, good or bad is destroyed forever. How can we learn from a history we do not know?"

"But surely we are truly free at that moment and depend entirely on ourselves and our sense of right and wrong. That's when we'll create Yderiphon," Stazman said.

Tahoola pointed to a complex of buildings rising from the valley ahead. The towers were supported by great buttresses, above which lancet windows showed. Several towers possessed beacon fires which were tended by soldiers.

Stazman let out some of the hot air and the craft slowed and descended. The great hall possessed such large windows the rays of the setting sun could be seen in panes of multi-coloured glass. Already a party of priests appeared below them. Several stretchers were ready, so as the gondola descended, they prepared Mycul.

"We only need one," Stazman shouted to the waiting priests.

The basket scraped along the ground, rucking up tussocks of grass and revealing the rock below the thin soil.

"Welcome to Deidar Mela. Welcome to Sanctuary. Here all are equal in accordance with the rules of the Adee. You have injured to tend?"

"Several," Tahoola shouted as she jumped over the edge, "but one is life threatening. He's been poisoned by an assassin's arrow."

The priest raised an eyebrow. "An assassin's arrow? How long ago?" He clicked his fingers and the acolytes picked up Mycul and placed him on the stretcher before carrying him into the building. "And the others?"

"Mordonts in search of Calufras." Tahoola pointed out the creatures disembarking the craft.

Again the priest raised an eyebrow. "More sinned against than sinning. The Protector would rid the land of those who are not genetically perfect humans. Here we celebrate all that is diverse whether created by the Adee or the geneticists of the Protectors."

Tahoola gave a nod.

Stazman took out a knife and cut through the ropes enslaving each faerie. They flew into the air and circled, gathering around Stazman. His eyes lit with wonder.

"My people owe you their thanks. We never forget a friend." A faerie woman bowed her head, as did her friends.

Stazman also bowed.

The group flew off in the direction of the setting sun and the jagged peaks that marked the boundary of this country.

"The Protector is going to be so mad with you!" Tahoola joked.

"Angrier with me or you?"

Tahoola thought about this and whispered the answer.

"You are welcome to stay in the guest rooms," the priest said.

"We have no money," Tahoola answered.

"Then you are welcome to stay and work for your keep. My acolyte will show you the lodgings."

The great hall was a mixed dormitory and dining room with great fires at either end. The dais in the centre hinted at some hierarchy in Deidar Mela. Behind it, niches in the walls contained all manner of statuary. Faerie with their graceful wings, mordonts armed and ready for battle, carnivers devouring their prey, graken pulling ships, Protectors in their finery and Keepers possessed of their keys. All these were preserved in a hard stone made from crystals of a pink rock. As they stood admiring the statues they heard a voice raised.

"Yes! I'm talking to you lot." The woman rubbed her hands on a grubby apron. "Boy!" the woman shouted. "You can help me prepare the food. Woman, go to the wood yard, our fires are hungry for fuel."

Tahoola acknowledged the instruction and went back outside.

_*_

Tahoola came in to take over nursing Mycul, just before the moon set. "They have given him an antidote to the poison. It is slowly clearing from his system," said Stazman, as he ran his fingers through the long dark strands of hair. "His wounds are knitting closed and the dislocation has been put right. Once the arrow wound has scabbed they will start physiotherapy in a heated pool they call a life pod."

"It sounds as though he is in the right place but what do they charge?" Tahoola asked, as she felt Mycul's forehead.

"The cost? There is the problem. They have a fixed fee. The DNA of every patient. They extract it and use it in their own experiments. It seems the Protector isn't the only one intent on corrupting the human genome to repopulate the Earth."

Tahoola stared. "So there will be more creatures like mordonts, carnivers, and faeries: more monsters?"

"It seems humans are the worst monsters of all. There are those animals which survived the fall of the Adee: the wererats, wolverine, and sabre toothed-cat, all carnivores preying on surviving livestock and human kind.

"Sometimes I smell mice. I hate the creatures but there must be many of them and bats, I loathe bats." Stazman stopped talking and returned to his patient. He looked longingly at his friend. "I worry about him. I wonder what he really wants. I know it isn't me."

"It isn't me either," Tahoola said. She stood and looked out of the window. "Have you seen anything of our mordont friends?"

Stazman shook his head and joined her looking out at the mountains of Mennes with their snow-capped peaks. A long way to the north was the province of Catherine. It would already be winter there, its passes impenetrable until the thaw of spring. Outside, the leaves were silvered by moonlight and frost. The fields were barren, ploughed ready for the coming of spring.

"What do you want to do? It seems we have reached a turning point. Do we stay together or go our separate ways?" Tahoola caught sight of several cows being led into the slaughterhouse. Men were beating the frightened animals with sticks as they were corralled into the building.

"Whatever you decide I will stay with Mycul," Stazman said and sat next to him on the bed.

"It's my guess that his future lies with the sea and the Graken," Tahoola said, turning away, "and mine is with the army."

"Whose?"

Tahoola stopped abruptly. "You know I'd never thought about that. It can't be Faires, the Protector would kill me."

"It couldn't be Menne as you're from Faires. How about Catherine?"

"Use friends with influence?"

Stazman smiled. "You get the idea, however to possess the influence I need to get to Catherine."

"A gen of Catherine. Is the uniform nice?"

Stazman laughed. "It is if you like black!"

"Once I am certain Mycul is recovered I'll make a final decision," she smiled; and just for a moment Stazman thought she looked fey.

"Well, I can't leave until then either. Somehow our futures do seem to be woven together," Stazman replied.

_-*-_

The nights drew in and the soil froze. Patches of swampy ground became passable and great carts lumbered along the roads bringing all manner of goods in to store.

It was a week later when the priest came running across the frost smeared grass. He leaned against Stazman and paused whilst he recovered his breath which condensed and cascaded in the still air.

"Your friend is awake now and requesting food. This is a very good sign." The priest sniffed the air as if sensing something before he escorted them back to Mycul's room. A dark-skinned man stood and bowed to them. "The healing of Deidar Mela has been successful," he said.

Mycul was sat up in bed and he opened his arms to both. "Do not get too comfortable here, we must leave soon even if it is the chilliest of winters," he said and awaited their response.

Stazman embraced his friend and Tahoola kissed Mycul on the cheek. "We were so worried," she added.

"My dreams have been of the Graken, and of me becoming the admiral of a great fleet," Mycul said and held out his hand. It was cupped by the man with jet black hair and black skin who had been waiting by his bedside.

"Who is this?" Tahoola asked.

"You've met, but you haven't, if that makes any sense. It's what we came here for," Mycul added enigmatically.

Tahoola and Stazman both looked at the man before them.

"I am Leeman," the man said.

"The mordont?" Stazman asked with incredulity.

"More sinned against than sinning. Even I daren't hope for such a reversal from Calufras," Leeman added.

"But you are still mordont?" Stazman looked as though he didn't quite understand.

"I am still mordont. If I don't take the drug, I will revert, it was explained to me. The drug interferes with cell replication." The man sensed something in Stazman's demeanour. "I was human first. I'm not second or third generation of creature."

Stazman stood uneasily and didn't take Leeman's hand.

"I've been told I might walk on the balcony tomorrow, are there any offers?"

"Of course!" Stazman embraced his friend. "I'll collect you after washing up!"

"A prince doing the washing up!" Mycul joked.

"A prince," the waiting priest declared, his tone nervously higher. "A prince of where?"

"We are all equal," Mycul reminded the priest.

"Catherine," Stazman smiled at the prospect of undeserved preferential treatment.

"My lord, can you forgive our lack of hospitality?"

"I still have no money, ever since the robbery on Pem."

"But surely you would send the gift on your return home?"

"Of course I would," Stazman said, enjoying the priest's obsequious behaviour. "And I would thank you in any dispatches."

Tahoola whispered in the youth's ear. "Can you put in a good word for me? I'm fed up of fetching and carrying."

Stazman smiled. That night all four companions enjoyed a meal in front of the fire with Mycul, whilst condensation froze against the glass and the moon and stars shone down.

Chapter 9: The Key is Turned

The priests had never known a frost to arrive so early and be so severe. The ground was still solid three weeks later and horses took everything at a walking pace so it was slow work travelling and filling the stores with all manner of produce.

They were also busy bottling jams and conserves and preserving fruit in flavoured alcohols. The guests had been treated with generosity and Stazman's standing had been enhanced by a visit from one of Catherine's envoys. The woman had been deferential and any doubts she had were kept behind her inscrutable façade. The ambassador confirmed Ra'an's news that his brothers had been murdered and one had been missing for over a year. Barser de Sotto had made herself Protector of Catherine after their demise and the province was subdued except for a group led by the Necromancer.

"Every one of The Necromancer's followers vanished. It was as if the Earth swallowed them," the ambassador said. She was either unwilling or unable to provide any more details.

"So you are in post due to the good word of Barser?" Stazman seemed to grasp the politics well.

"I paid a substantial bribe to receive this post in Deidar Mela. It helped me get my family out of the country, should there be any difficulties," the envoy replied, loosening the scarf round her neck, revealing fine lines of age.

"Could you see your way to a little duplicity?" Stazman stood with his back to the fire. The Gothic arch behind him rose from a corbel carved with musicians.

"I am an ambassador, that's what I'm employed to do!"

"Perhaps," Stazman added, "I could ask you to mention me in your report to Barser?"

"You have no need to ask. She'll be delighted at news of you," the ambassador smiled. "You must let me know if you need money, fine clothes, and so on during your stay."

"Yes indeed, how thoughtful. Could you organise it?" Stazman asked. "You might also add that we've made the acquaintance of her sister, Ra'an."

The ambassador nodded. She was mentally totting up the reward she might acquire on presenting such news.

The night skies shone with the five planets, myriad stars and the Milky Way. The moon waxed and waned on its cycle and with each passing night Mycul regained his strength. Inevitably, discussions turned toward their next task.

Tahoola sat Mycul down and stood behind the ornate oak chair. "We need to get to Catherine very soon or winter will prevent or delay our plans," she said. "Even so there are no guarentees we won't be murdered on the way. Barser won't want a Zem in charge of Catherine."

Mycul stroked her hand. "I'd never really worked out what happens next but I know you want to become a gen. It will be a hard task but I know you will succeed."

"Thanks," Tahoola said and her whole attitude spoke of pride and perseverance.

"I wish you well. I have already decided to return to the sea. It is as my Graken said, the longing grows with every day."

"Catherine has a coastline, would you travel with us that far?" Stazman asked.

"And perhaps the mordonts will remain as our companions," Mycul said watching his friend's reaction.

Stazman took a sharp intake of breath and managed to stay calm. "They should stay here where they can work and remain human."

"I will follow you, Mycul," Leeman announced, "but not my companions. They wish to remain in Deidar Mela. For hard work they will receive the Calufras needed to stay human."

"We will buy you a supply," Mycul promised.

The priests took an interest in what Leeman said and talked amongst themselves. Someone broke open a pack of cards and began dealing. Their laughter stole into the dark corners of the room where even an assassin might hide.

Mycul thought of Ra'an and her lithe body stepping into the warm waters of his bath. Her image then morphed into the Protector's smiling face bearing down for a kiss. As he thought about her, he felt her mind seek him out, thoughts magnified across some distance. His musings ended as a log broke into the roaring cinders and scattered dancing embers into the air. He heard her voice, *I am coming for you, insignificant one.* Mycul looked around the room, expecting to see her glide gracefully across the floor. He stood and went over to the head priest, and the woman gestured with her fingers before whispering.

Mycul strode to the windows. He peered out and saw firebrands flickering through the glass.

He opened the window. "We are betrayed! Ceelan is here!" The group looked at him with incredulity. "We must make use of the full moon and fly! The only escape route is north to Mennes and the Pass of Gorangoth the Golden."

They quickly gathered their few belongings, mounted their horses and galloped across the frozen earth. When Mycul cast a glance back he saw troops had surrounded the gothic splendour of Deidar Mela. The night shone with stars and the cold penetrated. They slowed to a trot and finally a walk as the trees became denser. By dawn the horses were exhausted and everyone was in need of food and warmth.

"We'll walk for a while." Mycul dismounted, picked up the reins and led his horse. The late autumn sun shone silver through the trees and the leaves floated to the ground. Golds and reds in such number were stirred from the branches by a soft breeze. The confetti of leaves denoting an autumn day continued unabated as they walked through the forest. Mycul fancied he could hear a simple melody in their fall.

He looked around at his travelling companions. None of them were immune from the beauty in this entropy and the spell it wove around them.

The spell was invisible but the webs were not. It funnelled their journey and glistened with drops of water suspended like tears. Mycul closed his eyes and only with difficulty opened them. He realised they were trapped but it was too late to respond. The travellers were standing in a clearing and even in the early morning light the finest of gossamer webs could be seen woven from tree to tree. It only remained for their captors to show.

Mycul waited. He tried to move his arms. He felt his fingers respond but not his limbs. He looked between the trees and above. Slowly the creatures revealed themselves. Genetic experiments had much to answer for in creating monsters but here that mission surpassed the stuff of nightmares. Perhaps parts of the head were human but the eight eyes were black as any spiders and their limbs articulated like arachnids. They slowly and gracefully descended from the trees.

Stazman panicked and struggled to be free from his bonds. This brought the creatures scuttling to him. They surrounded him and one pointed her elegant finger before a needle emerged and pinioned him, its venom pumping into his body. Their spinets began their work in cocooning Mycul's friend.

Mycul thought fire might be their only means of escape and wondered how it could be achieved when many flaming arrows whizzed by, filling the clearing. Smoke and an acrid smell hit Mycul's nostrils. The creatures clicked and screamed. His senses became alive once more but still he could not move. He could only watch the ensuing carnage as the hideous creatures were destroyed without mercy by the assassins. It was only a matter of time before he received some similar fate.

_-*-_

"I never expected you to get so far," Ra'an said, cutting a fingernail with the blade of her knife. "Of course, what I saw in the Ornithon had a different emphasis."

Mycul didn't feel like talking but for some reason he remembered her stepping into the bath at Pem. His body kicked back into life.

"I didn't tell you at the time but it was my second visit to the Ornithon. It was I who accompanied the Protector on her last visit. She was very pleased with her predicted future."

"Did it show my execution?" Mycul asked.

Ra'an nodded. She seemed surprised by his candour. "And yet you did what you thought was right?" For a long time she contemplated this idea.

The Protector dismounted from a grey horse. Her outfit was a stunning combination of cream and faun. She might be attending some great event in Faires and yet for all its beauty there was a certain functionality about her clothing: the trousers for riding, the long, split jacket and pill-box hat. She appeared to glide across the clearing toward her captives.

"You have served me well, Ra'an," she said and kissed her on the forehead. "Ah! Insignificant one, at last we meet properly. Tahoola, lovely to have you back in my power. Stazman Zas, my sister thinks you are dead, you soon will be. You will be left here to the mercies of those creatures who survived."

Stazman struggled.

"Tahoola, you know the punishment for desertion, it will be carried out in front of all the dignitaries of Faires after," here she stretched out a finger and lifted Mycul's chin, "a very special execution. What fun we will have watching you die, insignificant one. I'll invite everyone, especially your dear uncle. I like to ensure someone has a happy ending, in fact I always like to ensure that's me!" She searched in his jacket pocket for the gun and withdrew it. She caressed the cold metal before placing it in her pocket.

Mycul felt his legs weaken. He was placed on a horse and bound tightly to the saddle. Tahoola was strapped to the rear of the Protector's horse so she could stumble behind. Mycul felt tears roll cold down his cheek and he became despondent. He looked behind at Stazman, left alone in the clearing. He thought he saw the eyes of many creatures bear down upon him.

"Goodbye," he whispered, then repeated it louder and louder until Stazman responded.

"Touching," the Protector said. "He might last an hour before the creatures return and devour him. Personally, I hope the queen will use his body to house her next egg."

Mycul felt sick at the thought. He struggled to turn round but already the clearing was too far behind. The Protector brushed a gloved hand over his cheek.

"You are handsome. If I had a weakness for men, it would be someone of dark complexion like yourself."

"You would disappoint me if you had any weakness," Mycul replied.

The Protector laughed and spurred her horse to a trot, pulling Tahoola relentlessly in her wake.

Chapter 10: The Mordocki Revolver

Mycul had never seen Faires. He brooded over how misfortune was bringing him to this place. His mood reflected in his face and demeanour. The rings under his eyes were dark from lack of sleep, fear and anger. His hair was matted and a shadow formed around his lips and chin. He had prayed to several gods over the last few days but they had all been found wanting.

He thought of Stazman alone in the wood, waiting to be devoured by the human-like spiders. He remembered the look of fear on his friend's face. His anguish remained when he closed his eyes and the thought of what the Protector had promised to do to him prevented any sleep.

At the end of the first day, Tahoola had been tied onto a horse in the manner he had but Mycul had been transferred to a prison van, pulled by four horses. Perhaps there was still a glimmer of hope for her but his captors delighted in telling him what would happen to Mycul Zas as though he no longer existed as a person.

He was certain seven days had gone by when Faires appeared in the distance. The City was seen from a viewpoint at the summit of an escarpment. The sandstone bluff below them was almost vertical, its layers composed of many shades of red like his blood which would be spilt.

"I often come up here, Mycul. I love riding out and surveying my kingdom. I'm delighted you could share this moment with me," Ceelan said.

Mycul beheld the radiant beauty of the Protector. Today she was dressed in a purple gown designed for side-saddle and a flowing purple coat lined with yellow satin. "The colours of Yderiphon," Mycul remarked.

The Protector smiled. "How clever of you. Tomorrow. Ah! Tomorrow, alas, your last day on earth. You'll be taken from the prison and tied to a cross. There my executioners will attend to you. They always start with the testicles. It seems fitting that the part which creates mere humans like yourself should begin the agony. Next, they will remove the flesh and muscles from your ribs before the cutting begins. You will be boxed, Mycul Zas, limbs cut from your body and placed neatly in a casket. I imagine the pain will go on for a very long time. It is a cruel fate and one I had to look up in the annals of the Adee. I hope you're impressed at the attention I lavish upon you."

"Couldn't you find clemency and cut the torture short?"

"Clemency. That's not a word in my vocabulary. Please don't lose the will to live now, where would the fun be in that?" The Protector gracefully walked along the ridge to a vantage point. All the assassins attended on her. Mycul tried the bars on the cage and he felt tears rise as the futility of his situation became clear.

One assassin remained assigned to him. Mycul took a deep breath and found himself crying again. His guard was draped in a long cloak and hood. Her cross bow hung from her saddle. Her large leather boots were etched with a Mennedic design of a dragon eating its tail. Mycul thought he saw the bottom of leather breaches similarly engraved but dismissed the idea. "Tomorrow sounds very unpleasant, Mycul Zas." The voice was deep and possessed an accent from the north.

Mycul didn't respond.

"What would you do to be saved?" the voice cruelly asked.

Mycul took more notice of the assassin. The face was still hidden in the shadow of the hood. From between the folds of the cloak he spied a large gun etched with gold. For the first time in many days, Mycul managed to think there was hope. "Sartesh?" he whispered.

"Get back into the corner!" Sartesh said. The shot was loud. Birds screeched into the air and the assassins' horses shied, reared and bolted. The door hung ajar and Sartesh pulled Mycul onto his saddle, turned his horse and spurred the beast onward.

"I hope you've got some back up?" Mycul said, looking behind and seeing the assassins regroup and catch their horses.

Sartesh said nothing. His horse galloped along the escarpment then drew to a halt.

"They are gaining on us!" Mycul observed with trepidation.

"Good. I like a challenge," Sartesh's vowels still had a Mennedic drawl. The horse picked its way carefully down the bank, the assassins cantering behind and ready to draw their bows. The lead group turned the corner. A series of explosions showered rocks on them. Several were dismounted, creating confusion. The final explosion blocked the way entirely. Sartesh threw back the cloak and laughed.

"Still good for a probably ex-Keeper of the Seventh Law."

"You know too much of the Adee. It will be the death of you! But for now I'm so grateful I could kiss you."

"Don't let me stop you!" Sartesh said and laughed again, his gold ear rings flashed in the sunlight. The horse galloped into the cover of woods. "Now we must really use the knowledge of the Adee and fly!"

"No, we must go back and rescue Tahoola," Mycul said.

"Tahoola? The assassin who murdered Nallor Dhze? She can rot in hell."

Mycul remembered the conversation. "I don't think it's that simple but now isn't the time for an argument!"

Sartesh dismounted in the Mennedic fashion and immediately faerie folk emerged from the forest to look after the horse. Sartesh whispered something to their leader and for a moment Mycul could read the winged creature's emotion. He wondered how Sartesh had engendered such gratitude.

Sartesh led Mycul across the clearing. The downward march of the forest was halted abruptly as though an invisible boundary held back the trees. Sartesh stood for a moment before speaking. "I wondered that too and being a geologist I brought an augur to find out why. It's a change in rock from sandstone to a very old igneous rock somehow intruded into the layers of sediment. No time for mapping it now though."

With a flourish, he pulled the tarpaulin off a great winged contraption. Mycul observed the meticulous preparations. He touched the surface of the craft and found it to be made from canvas and the frame light enough for one hand to lift. Sartesh turned the propeller and the engine burst into life.

"This one act has given me away," Sartesh said. "The sound of an engine hasn't been heard here for many thousands of years and only the Protector will know its meaning. Get in, put on the glasses and fasten that belt."

The engine produced a sound so intense and a smell so repugnant that Mycul thought he might choke. The forces on his body pinioned him into the seat and his stomach lurched. Finally, the roar subsided and Mycul realised they were airborne and the plane turned revealing the vast expanse of the forest below. The land fell away and in the distance Mycul could see the long causeway which linked Faires to land and the great white walls that kept the sea at bay.

He looked back to the escarpment and saw almost as dots what remained of the party who had been his captors, then he looked forwards at Sartesh. The man's blond hair was swept back by the breeze and his thin face contoured by side burns which extended as thin lines on his cheeks. He wore a gold embossed gilet over a thick white jumper. He was still smiling as they flew over the wild grasslands and the terrain again became hilly.

"The Lithage Hills." Sartesh pointed below.

Mycul was beginning to enjoy the experience of being airborne, but not the turns. Below mutant grasslands choked any remaining trees with outcrops of rock marking the peaks. The sparkling blue sea was now indistinguishable from horizon.

The plane banked and in the distance a range of mountains capped by clouds rolled into view. They travelled west before Sartesh brought the plane down with skill in a wide valley dwarfed by its desolate and scarred sides. "Welcome to my home, the gold mine of the Protector. This is her source of power and bought at a great price to her people," Sartesh noted.

"Her people? I thought we were all equal citizens?"

Sartesh slapped him on the back and laughed. "Food, drink and a bath," Sartesh held up his hand, "and then we'll discuss your complaints."

"They're not complaints. It's a matter of life, death and my morality. I have left one innocent person to die, I will not let another," Mycul explained.

"Ah! Morality, you do not hear that word associated with gold. I had forgot about it. You will have many questions and I will answer any I can, but first food, drink and a bath."

"Why not all three at once?" Mycul suggested.

_-*-_

Sartesh and Mycul sat at either end of a large circular bath. Its waters reflected the green tiles and wall paintings depicted animals and humans in a sylvan setting. There was very little steam as the room itself was heated and the floor tiles almost too hot to walk on in places. A flagon of ale, bread and cheese were placed between them on a floating tray.

"Thanks for saving me."

"No problem, just don't make a habit of crossing Ceelan's path." Sartesh broke off some bread and began chewing.

"Sound advice!" Mycul ate heartily, then sat back and relaxed in the water. "But you have crossed Ceelan in saving me."

Sartesh smiled, "Go on, tell me all about Tahoola, it's eating away at you."

Mycul observed his rescuer's green eyes and muscled torso. He drained his tankard of beer. "Tahoola was acting on orders when she killed Nallor. She was his lover and Ceelan gave her a choice: her life or his," Mycul explained.

"Is that supposed to make me feel better? Nallor was the man who rescued me and brought me up as his own. He was my guardian for ten years. If I rescue Tahoola it would only be to have the pleasure of killing her myself!"

Mycul broke off more bread and chewed it as if considering his next words. "When I saw the Ornithon, two scenes concerned me. In one, Stazman and I fight to the death and fall upon each other's swords. That future is no longer possible as Stazman was left to the spider creatures in the forest." Mycul dipped his head under the water, emerging and combing his black locks away from his face.

Sartesh steadied the tray. "I wouldn't be so quick to dismiss your companion as dead. I took the place of an assassin called Ra'an who unexpectedly left the Protector's services. She doubled back to rescue him and was more than happy I impersonated her. Her lack of loyalty surprised me but I don't believe she thought me capable of passing myself off as an assassin."

"So the Ornithon's predictions can come true?"

"You might have to go back and study them further," Sartesh said.

Mycul smiled. "I had the place destroyed."

"Destroyed? The Ornithon destroyed." Sartesh leaned forward in the bath and sent a ripple shimmering over the edge of the tray.

"The Graken commanded me to do it! In fact I couldn't have done it without their help," Mycul said, worried he'd offended his host.

"So none of us have a future now?" Sartesh laughed again. This time Mycul joined in.

"The other possible future was a scene in which you and Tahoola marry and have a child."

"Me marry? I'm not the sort of guy to marry!" Sartesh was incredulous.

"I wouldn't be so quick to dismiss the Ornithon's predictions."

"You have much to learn, Mycul. When I visited the place, I saw you executed by being cut up alive. That's probably not going to happen now." Sartesh drained the tankard and poured another generous helping. The older man licked his finger and scored a point. "So I must rescue my sworn enemy for the sake of an unborn child?"

"Not just any child, the Child, the one who has been prophesised."

Sartesh shook his head. "No, Mycul: that is going too far. Let me put another idea out there. The images we see are those someone wants us to see in order to either avert events or draw us toward them," Sartesh surmised.

"How could they do that?"

Sartesh shrugged. "If they had a plan?" He ate the last of the cheese and drained a tankard before standing and emerging from the bath. Mycul followed, noticing the scarring that etched his rescuer's back. He turned his friend around and studied Sartesh. He traced his fingers round his nipples. An uneasy silence was broken by Sartesh: "Careful, I might enjoy the attention."

"But that can't be right," Mycul said.

Sartesh didn't realise the object of his friend's concern.

"You have nipples!"

"Of course, doesn't everyone?" He looked across at Mycul and saw he did not. "Surely…" It slowly dawned on Sartesh that he might be different.

"Only the female of the species has them." Mycul said with certainty.

"Oh! That sounds bad." Sartesh said. "You're having me on just to cover up for the fact that you haven't got them!"

Mycul shook his head. "I'll prove it to you someday."

"I've always thought it was a sexually antagonistic trait."

"What does that mean?" Mycul didn't understand.

"Adee science states it's a waste of the male body's resources. It means there's a genetic difference between us," Sarteh explained.

They dressed in silence. Sartesh found Mycul leather boots, clean trousers and a fine leather gilet. They almost looked like brothers as they stood next to each other but Sartesh was the more resplendent with gold patterns woven into the hide.

 Sartesh produced a sample bottle. "Would you mind?"

Mycul remembered Dr Ambrose and went pale.

"It's not obligatory; I'd just like to know why we're genetically different. It might be important."

"How do you do it?" Mycul asked.

A swab was waved. "Open wide," Sartesh said and gently took a layer of skin from Mycul's cheek and placed the resultant smear in the bottle. They went down many stairs to a lab.

"I don't have the technology here, so it'll take a while to develop." The machine appeared to be automatic and powered by a series of copper wires. Mycul touched one and recoiled. It felt as though he'd been bitten.

"Electricity. Try not to touch." Sartesh ran the sample. "People think I'm an inventor but I'm not. I'm a reinventor of useful items from the time of the Adee."

"As Keeper, you have access to documents I could never hope to see."

Sartesh took out the plates. The series of blue lines matched each other perfectly except a faint additional line in Mycul's DNA profile.

"There!" Sartesh pointed. "That's the area I'll have to look at." Fired with energy and enthusiasm he regained the stairs and took them two at a time. "This way if you want to see your room." He held the door open to reveal a small but tidy room with a bed and desk. The wall was lined with books. "Help yourself. I've got some alterations to make to the aircraft and then tomorrow, if the weather is fine, we'll be ready to rescue your friend," Sartesh said.

Mycul took a step into the room and turned round. "Thanks. I owe you!"

Sartesh placed a hand on his shoulder. "Friendship has its own rewards."

Outside Sartesh checked the plane and made some adjustments to the aircraft. He placed great floats over the wheels and on the edges of the wings and screwed them tight. Fuel was pumped from a rusty looking tank. After this was done, Sartesh tugged a green canvas cover over the craft to aid camouflage.

It was all sorted just as the bell sounded for the end of the shift in the mine. Bedraggled people emerged from the cavern and made their way towards a series of huts. They were watched all the way by carnivers. Sartesh sighed. He tried to look after his workers but it was difficult. The Protector had her spies and informants everywhere.

He went over to check how much gold had been produced. Amounts were getting smaller each day. Soon they'd be better off mining Adee rubbish heaps. Indeed, he already had such plans.

_-*-_

When Mycul came down for breakfast, he found Sartesh reading a manual as he cleaned and primed a gun. The smell of the oil was strong. "Are they Adee?" Mycul pointed.

"They have been recreated from their blue prints. A lot of work went into reconstructing these evil mechanisms," Sartesh said.

"So why do it?"

"I like to stay one step ahead."

"Even when it's illegal?"

Sartesh nodded. He washed his hands and pulled a pan of beans from the hob. He shared them and cut large wedges of bread. They ate heartily.

"The Protector must know what you are doing?"

"Yes, she tolerates my work because it benefits her," Sartesh explained.

Mycul used a fingernail to clean between his teeth.

After they had cleared away, Sartesh pulled out a map and showed it to Mycul. "We will fly in daylight to this point then wait until darkness. I need to talk to some friends; their aid will be indispensable."

"So, you will help me rescue Tahoola?" Mycul asked.

Sartesh nodded. "Against my better judgement but I don't want to overlook any possibilities." He went over to a large chest and returned with two black cloaks and a large case. This he opened to reveal two guns.

"I know what you're thinking, two bullets and we're done. These are not guns, they are revolvers and the barrels hold seven bullets. I borrowed them from the Mordocki some years ago. Beautiful, aren't they?"

Mycul picked one up and inspected it. The balance was perfect as he took aim. The barrel was fine steel with a blue tint but the trigger and grip were etched with runes the Mordocki used in their brutal rituals. "I'm surprised they let these go."

"It wasn't done willingly, I can tell you," Sartesh nudged his friend.

They walked out into the autumn sunshine. There was a chill in the air. The cover was removed and the plane stood ready. Sartesh primed the engine then turned the propeller. It fired first time and the fumes misted the air around them. Sartesh gave his friend a leg up into the cockpit then passed the cloaks and gun box. "Put on the glasses and fasten the harness. It's going to be a bumpy landing!"

The noise was tremendous as the plane taxied along the grass and gained speed. It bounced several times then soared above the valley. The plane banked and followed the Lithage Hills until they diminished into undulations and the coastal plain dominated their view.

Mycul saw the empty sea below and watched the patterns of waves and the colours. He thought of his Graken and strained to hear her voice. The aircraft followed the coastline until the buildings of Faires Argenta were discernible in the distance.

The plane lost height and the engine growled and whined until with a great jolt and bang the plane landed on the sea. Bits of debris floated away. Despite this, Sartesh brought the craft up onto the beach and secured it like a boat.

"This is the point of no return. You and I will already have carnivers sniffing us out and programmed to kill. Once we rescue Tahoola, if we can, we will all be outlawed, with a price on our heads," Sartesh said.

"It must be done. I'm already dead in the eyes of the law. You're not having second thoughts are you?"

"I have a good life as Keeper of the Seventh Law: a great salary and I am one of a handful of influential people to whom Ceelan will listen.

Perhaps I have made a mistake?" Sartesh looked away and patted the machine as though it might have feelings.

"Surely you might have a better life being crowned Emperor of Menne?"

"You saw that too? Was I alive or dead?"

"Very much alive."

"That's good. Well, we'd better get on." Sartesh looked at the distant city. "About a mile would you say? We'll wait until dusk," he said before climbing the low cliff. He returned with a smile some minutes later. "They agreed," he announced without further explanation.

Mycul looked out to sea as though he'd heard something.

Sartesh stopped and watched. Mycul knelt down in the sand and let the grains fall through his fingers. He lowered his head and waited.

The great sea monster broke surface offshore and used its flippers to haul itself onto land. The creature lowered its head and for a moment Sartesh thought his friend would be devoured but very gently, the creature's tongue flicked out and caressed his face and neck. They were communicating. Sartesh stepped back and waited. All the time he rested the revolver over his shoulder. The creature turned its attention to him next, sniffing the air and letting its tongue take in his odour.

"All hail the Emperor of Menne,
All hail the once and future king,
All hail Sartesh Andrada."

Sartesh bowed. "I am pleased to make your acquaintance too, Cyrene Queen of the Graken. I take it Mycul is the chosen one."

"He is my link. It is said a Graken dies when her rider dies but this is not true. I have lived a hundred and ninety years on this planet, daughter of the altered ones, and seen seven riders but Mycul is born to lead, not ride, he hears us all. It was I who ordered your beloved Ornithon destroyed," the Graken said.

"I fear you destroyed but one part. You did what you thought was for the best and I admit I'd become besotted with the future rather than living in the present. Events don't just happen, you have to do something. That's why I rescued Mycul," Sartesh confided.

The Graken bowed her head. "I am grateful you did." She resumed her communication with Mycul before turning and pushing great waves of sand and water towards them as she slipped back into the ocean.

"Did that conversation help?" Sartesh asked, wondering what sort of plan they might need to come up with.

"More of an insurance policy. Plans I leave to you."

Sartesh drew a diagram on the beach. "I had a plan but it was long term. I thought who might want to be Protector of Faires and the answer I worked out was the Keeper of the First Law, Gurdon. He's waited a long time and, well, he can't become leader before our current Protector dies. Get a rat to catch a rat I say."

"So you haven't got a plan then?" Mycul sat down.

"I'll think of one," Sartesh said.

"Reassuring," Mycul replied with sarcasm. He wrapped the coat around him and closed his eyes.

The sun set and the tide turned as the beach was consumed by deep shadow. They began walking along the strand and reached the city as darkness was complete save for the light from the waning moon which illuminated a slender path across the sea. The waves lapped calmly on the shore and the temperature began to fall. Mycul shivered despite the layers he was wearing. Sartesh continued to stride out but stopped abruptly.

The lights of the city were crowded before them. They climbed up onto the causeway which joined the city to the mainland. There were more and more people, some promenading from the city in their finery and others hurrying home. Guards were stationed at intervals with their silver armour reflecting the moonlight.

"Plan B," Sartesh whispered. "We use the aqueduct taking fresh water into the Protector's palace and I'll use this hypodermic dart on any guards."

"Does it kill silently?"

"No, it puts them into a deep sleep. It looks less suspicious. My only problem will be finding your friend. I'm not familiar with the Protector's dungeons and if I were Ceelan, I'd use Tahoola as bait. See, I told you we should have stayed at my place and left her."

"She's going to be your wife, not mine," Mycul said.

"Please don't say that too loudly, I've reputation to uphold."

Mycul began to guess at what that might be but said nothing. He followed Sartesh through streets lit up by glass spheres of light that seemed to levitate. He wondered how they might work but before he could ask they climbed up onto an aqueduct. Water trickled along its path toward the palace.

Sartesh and Mycul negotiated the maintenance route alongside. The edge was low and the drop became precipitous. Sartesh picked his way along the path as though he knew it well. It descended to the roofline, then it meandered through a garden filled with aromatic plants and where drainage channels bisected the main flow.

The entrance to the Protector's palace appeared, its white marble dome punctuated by a dark shadow where the tunnel began. Water gurgled through a steel grill which hung securely in place. Sartesh tested it. The gate didn't yield. He took a set of keys from his gilet and fiddled in the dark. After what seemed ages, there was a click. The gate squealed open on rusty hinges. Both climbed through, and Sartesh secured the gate once more.

Sartesh put his finger to his lips and pointed upward. They walked along the water course feeling the cold penetrate their feet and ankles. The way was illuminated by flickering torches. The first guard was already asleep, an empty flagon of drink next to him.

Sartesh signalled there were two guards ahead.

"Distract them." He pulled a hypodermic syringe from his belt.

Mycul picked up a pebble and tossed it to land by a guard. The woman snapped alert. The second guard pulled a firebrand from the wall and peered into the darkness. Mycul dropped a second pebble by their feet. Sartesh was already behind them. The needle entered the neck of the first. He folded onto the floor but the woman was vigilant and faced Sartesh.

"Why Keeper…"

Mycul knocked her senseless with the butt of his revolver. Sartesh gave him a look. "Isn't that what it's for?" Mycul asked.

Sartesh quickly reminded him of the need for silence. They walked along the edge, trying to be quiet in their footfall. Eventually, the water spilt through an opening too small for them to follow.

Sartesh guided his friend up a flight of stairs. The passageway opened above an internal courtyard. Below, several women bathed, one instantly recognisable as Tahoola with her missing right hand. Sartesh shrugged his shoulders but Mycul leaned over the edge taking in all the sights and the perfumes. The courtyard was lit by a chandelier holding perhaps thirty candles. The rope securing it led to their passage and then hung limply down the wall. Sartesh stood and calculated the arc.

He pointed. Mycul shook his head. Sartesh pointed again, making his purpose clear. Again Mycul shook his head.

"She trusts you," he hissed and lifted the rope until the end sat neatly coiled on the floor. "You have one minute to collect her and get back up here. See the doorway below. Always right."

"How do you know the women's area so well?"

Sartesh raised his eyes and pushed his friend forwards. Mycul took hold of the rope and pulled it slightly before leaping from the parapet.

He swung out and shimmied down the rope to the floor. He gave a little bow before Tahoola.

She covered herself with a towel and ran for her clothes, shrugging into them as Mycul fended off two assassins. Tahoola despatched both by skimming a pair of trisos.

They gained the passageway, turning several right corners to some stairs, but were pursued. Sartesh took the revolver from his shoulder holster and took aim. He knew the noise would bring all the palace guards so he waited. Tahoola appeared first. She came to an abrupt halt as he trained the gun on her.

"Duck!" He pulled the trigger and fired. The bullet hit an assassin in the middle of her forehead. She fell back down the stairs.

"Do that again and I'll kill you!" Tahoola warned.

"Next time the bullet is for you," Sartesh snapped.

Mycul picked himself up.

"I didn't need rescuing, everything was under control," Tahoola shouted, her complexion red with anger. "Ceelan had forgiven me. I might even have had the chance to kill her. Now I'll have to go with you or we'll all die horribly."

"There's still a chance of that happening! Follow me." Sartesh ran through the water but instead of taking the way they'd come he ran up a set of spiral stairs until the three of them emerged on the highest tower of the palace. He sealed off the door. Beyond it, shouts and stomping feet could be heard.

"We're safe here," he said breathlessly.

Tahoola looked down.

"Any more bright ideas?"

"No," he admitted, "but I did have the foresight to ask a few friends to help."

A group of faerie folk slid down the roof and gathered before them.

"All hail the once and future king.
All hail the emperor of Menne,
All hail Sartesh Andrada."

Mycul found himself smiling. He remembered Stazman's fascination with these creatures. These females were beautiful and much smaller in stature than Tahoola but possessed of gossamer fine wings which folded and stretched. As fists and weapons began to pound on the door, two of these folk gripped each escapee and lifted them from the floor. They slowly flew over the roof tops of Faires toward the waiting aircraft.

Cyrene lay coiled in the shallow water. *I do not usually stand guard but this device appeared unprotected and the weakest link in your escape.*

Mycul bowed and gave his thanks to the Graken. She slid gracefully back into the sea, then turned and appeared to watch as Sartesh started the plane. It skimmed over the water and passed the Graken. The extra weight meant it took a long time before the craft became airborne and once in the air it struggled to lift above the waves. Sartesh revved the engine and great spumes of black smoke engulfed the passengers before Sartesh banked left and skirted treetops.

Perhaps two hours later they landed. It was uncomfortable with the aircraft lilting to one side and bouncing before coming to a halt in front of the mine buildings. Sartesh jumped down and helped the others out, then he began investigating the airplane. He shook his head. "Two days' work."

He ushered Tahoola and Mycul into the house. "To make the most of our advantage we should leave at first light. I had hoped to avoid using horses but needs must!" Sartesh busied himself removing rucksacks from a cupboard.

He collected the Mordocki revolvers and placed them carefully in their box. "Do you still have that gun I gave you?"

Mycul shook his head remembering the Protector had taken it. "But, I do have these," he said, and held out the cubes containing the stories of Nag-Nag Naroon.

Sartesh picked one up. The image of Nag-Nag evaporated and was replaced by a swirling blue.

"Ah! Sartesh Andrada, I'd expected better. You killed one of my assassins, you know the price for that?"

"Carnivers." Sartesh replied.

"Indeed. It's standard procedure. One for each of you. Ah! You've acquired another Ornithon cube," the Protector said.

"Just a little something I picked up," Sartesh replied.

"I hope you didn't pick up the attractive young man who went with them." The clouds cleared and they saw the Protector was immaculately dressed in black silk and leather, the outfit that left her shoulders bare and revealed her perfect skin.

"You know my weaknesses well," Sartesh joked.

"And still wearing those Mennedic rings I gave you?"

"They remind me of your beauty," Sartesh said and held up the purple and yellow bands. "Still, it's good to know we can keep in touch when required."

"Don't worry on that score, Sartesh, I'll be close at hand and eventually I'll find you. We've all seen the future in the Ornithon, that's why these cubes still work. The Ornithon gives us an advantage but it also means everything is predetermined. Let me leave you with this question: if the future is predetermined, who is in control?"

The cube swirled with an opaque blue cloud and the image was gone.

"You and the Protector seem to have a history," Mycul observed.

Sartesh ignored his friend. "We leave at dawn for the land of Great Menne."

"Menne, why?" Mycul asked.

"To fulfil our future."

"We don't have one, it's all predetermined."

"I'll prove that our future is entirely in our own hands, if it kills me!"

"It might just do that if I don't get a say," Tahoola said. She dragged her finger over surfaces and then snarled as she brushed off the dust.

"Can you think of anywhere carnivers can't get to?" Sartesh asked.

"No," Tahoola replied, "they chase their programmed DNA until they rip their victims apart... or they are killed."

Chapter 11: The Necromancer's Daughter

"I don't think the Mordocki will take kindly to seeing you again," Tahoola tried on a leather cap over her stub. She winced with the pain.

"They'd be delighted. I think they'd kill me very slowly then cook my brains before using my skull as a drinking vessel."

"So how did you come by those revolvers?"

"Whenever something goes wrong in my life there's always a woman at the heart of it. A group of Mordocki warriors set upon me as I was prospecting for metals in the borderlands. They were impressed by the range of metal ores I'd found and persuaded me to tell them how I knew where to look. I told them about the geology of their land. How a great formation of molten granite had been punched through layers of rock and slowly cooled a long way underground. The cooling granite and fractured rock were filled by geothermal liquids rich in metals which over millions of years had crystallised."

Sartesh picked up various samples from the shelf behind them. "This is sphalerite, the ore of zinc and these cubic crystals are the ore of lead but gold is always found pure. The orange lines written through this sample are gold."

Tahoola lifted the sample. "It's heavy."

"Dense," Sartesh corrected.

She looked carefully at the fine lines weaving through the sample. "It almost looks like the Earth is writing to us."

"I never thought of it like that before," Sartesh said then remembered who he was talking to.

Mycul picked up the sample and turned it in his hand. He saw the thin veins of gold meandering through the rock. "Are you sure it isn't writing?" He passed it back to Sartesh. "You cannot see it?"

Sartesh looked. "You are seeing things not there. It's like reading constellations in the stars. They are seen only from this perspective but elsewhere, their shapes distort and new patterns form."

"How can you know that?"

Sartesh pulled two large photographs from a drawer and beckoned them to compare the images.

"They are both of stars," Tahoola said dismissively.

Mycul nodded agreement.

Sartesh pointed out several stars of different colour. "These are the same but one image is from here and the other from Mars."

"Now I know you are being stupid," Tahoola said incredulous at this suggestion.

Mycul studied them again. "Did the Adee walk on Mars?" Mycul looked as though he hadn't slept much with his wild black hair.

"I think they might even have built towns there," Sartesh said. He looked at his friend. "I have a sleeping potion which will knock you out. You look exhausted."

"It's contemplating my own demise. It brings everything into perspective."

Sartesh placed his arm around Mycul's shoulders.

"Can I keep this sample?" Tahoola asked then realised what she had done.

"I am postponing killing you because of Mycul."

Tahoola smiled. "You might try of course. I was ordered to kill Nallor Dhze or be killed. It was a dilemma I solved without considering the morality. Besides, I've been in Faires long enough to know you aren't above murder."

Sartesh went bright red.

Mycul stared at his friend. "What do you mean, Tahoola?"

"There were rumours, nothing more. I'm sure they were just rumours," Tahoola smiled, threw the sample in the air and caught it again.

"Faires is full of rumours. I'll show you to your rooms," Sartesh said, nervously twisting the yellow and purple rings given him by the Protector.

-*-

The leather holster was engraved with an interlace design of a dragon, fastened to a belt more plainly decorated. Sartesh knelt before Tahoola and fastened the buckle before giving her the gun.

"With this type of pistol you must fire the bullet and reload. Aim at the leather bottles." Mycul held out the gun and squeezed the trigger. He stumbled backwards and the shot hit the rock some three or four feet above his target. Tahoola aimed along her arm and fired. The bottle rocked, disgorged its contents and fell.

"Place the bullets in the chamber, so," Sartesh demonstrated. He held the pistol as an extension of his arm, aimed and fired. He knocked off the remaining two bottles. "Never hesitate to use them before a sword or crossbow. They are much faster and sometimes the noise alone might frighten the enemy."

102

"But they are forbidden, Sartesh. The culture of the Adee is forbidden to all except the Keepers and the penalty is death."

Sartesh smiled.

"Then it's just as well that I am one of the Keepers. Moreover, we will be entering a section of the country where the Mordocki Warriors live. They are the best gunsmiths of all and have no foibles about using Adee weapons."

Sartesh showed them how to disassemble the gun. "Once you have fired a weapon it must be cleaned," he said, and demonstrated. "Tedious but essential to avoid misfiring."

The bell sounded for the next shift of miners. Mycul led the packhorses from their stables and ensured their harnesses were fastened. Sartesh strode out of the camp leaving Mycul to lead the animals. Tahoola picked up her bag and slung it across the last horse, causing it to shy and whinny.

Their long haul uphill on horse back was rewarded by a great vista, a wide vale dotted with farmsteads and a patchwork of fields. In the distance, a range of mountains rose and their snow-capped peaks faded into the cloud building ominously in the north. Stretched before them was the valley of Nofa Flows and the villages in which both Mycul and Sartesh grew up. Sartesh peered into the distance for some time.

"We have both suffered greatly at the hands of our uncles," Mycul said and placed a hand of support on his friend's shoulder. He saw the last great valley of Faires stretch many miles before him with a river meandering through its heart. He wondered how many thousands of years this view might have remained the same.

"You've not explained how you came by the Mordocki revolvers," Tahoola reminded him.

"I'd mounted my horse and was leaving their village when this girl emerged from the crowd and said, *There's the man who talked to me without having a licence.* As you know the Mordocki place the word of a child above the word of an adult. I have never understood that, it seems a reversal of logic. There were gasps of horror and I was pulled from the horse and thrown into a hole in the ground under their dining hall."

"An oubliette," Tahoola added helpfully. "Did you talk to her?"

Sartesh gave his wry smile. "You know my type, Tahoola: tall, dark, radiant blue eyes. No, I didn't ask her anything. It was a set up."

"What's the sentence?" Mycul was fanning himself to calm the high colour of his embarrassment.

"Hanging."

"They do that for everything, don't they?"

Sartesh nodded. "Anyway I wasn't going to hang around. The walls of the prison were damp but I noticed that quartz pebbles protruded from the conglomerate and that the sandy matrix was soft. I eased several crystals out and began carving handholds into the rock. I climbed to my escape. I thought I would take a souvenir of my visit. So we will need to avoid all Mordocki in Mennes. Do you know how difficult that is?"

"Impossible," said Tahoola.

"So I'm going to affect a disguise. A Mennedic warrior perhaps, I'll try and sort it and see what you think."

"They don't have gold ear rings," Tahoola reminded him.

There was a long silence. Mycul realised Sartesh had vanished. The couple continued to descend the hill. The trees stood devoid of leaves but the briars possessed leaves of red and gold to hide their thorns, which ripped at their skin as they passed.

Fir trees provided shade and reminded Mycul of the fearful day they had left Stazman to his fate. He wondered if his friend was still alive and then unaccountably he found himself wondering how the Prince of Catherine would get on with Sartesh. His reverie continued.

"Me na da ger dra," the guttural voice demanded as the dark figure slipped to the ground ahead of them. Mycul rushed forwards and drew his gun but the Mennedic warrior tapped it from his hand with a sword.

The tip of the blade held Mycul transfixed.

Tahoola laughed and applauded. The warrior sheathed his sword and gave a bow.

"Sartesh, I could have killed you!" he saw it was his companion. On closer inspection he saw the nipples. Sartesh wore the tattoos of a mordont's head over his chest and the word 'warrior' on his arm. A leather belt fastened a shield to his back. His trousers were low cut and revealed that he had shaved his body all over. The boots were the same as he remembered from his rescue, etched with a dragon in gold.

"Okay," Tahoola said, "I can see that I'm wrong, you make an attractive warrior even down to the platted beard on your chin. That's my only suggestion, shorten it. You look too young for the platted filial."

Sartesh pushed his head to one side. It was his weakness for wearing gold and he knew Tahoola was right.

"I guess that means we aren't going to Bretan?" Mycul said.

Sartesh shook his head.

"Could we go to Vold Nujun? I've a score to settle."

Again Sartesh shook his head. "Revenge will have to wait, young Mycul. We go to the heights of Menne and the Pass of Gorangoth. There's seven days walking ahead. I suppose that will be enough time for me to get used to being semi naked. It feels cold, I can tell you. And whilst it's early winter here…"

"We've been to Deidar Mela. We've experienced highland weather."

"And we all need to be hardy to survive the Pass of Gorangoth. Think of the next seven days as an investment in staying alive." Mycul drove the horses onward as Sartesh said this.

"Think of all the fetching and carrying a Mennedic slave might do for us before reach our destination," Tahoola joked then realised her promise to Stazman.

Sartesh ran ahead for a while before vanishing into the woods. Whatever he was doing he moved silently.

By the time the party began to lose the light, clouds had gathered and a fine mist descended. Low cloud enveloped them all. In the distance a dirigible could be heard. The sound grew louder and filled the air with vibrations. Sartesh returned and signalled for them all to leave the road. The airship circled overhead then moved away over the valley towards the village of Bretan.

"The Protector is looking for us," Tahoola said. "You can bet carnivers aren't far behind."

"We'll make our way across the valley, sticking to hedgerows and coppices for cover," Sartesh suggested.

"Or better still use the road all night and rest by day. We'll not have a new moon for a few more days."

It was agreed that they would walk through the hours of darkness despite the growing number of orange eyes that watched from the undergrowth. The drone of the airship returned. This time its gondola was lit and a searchlight picked out soldiers forming a search party.

"Bury all the provisions. It's time to mount up and fly!"

"Leave them by the wayside; there'll be nothing left of them in a few minutes. Those eyes watching us are wererats," Sartesh said.

All the essential materials were transferred to their packs; everything else was left. The three mounted up and cantered away. The searchlights picked out the hoard of wererats screaming and tumbling over the remains of their provisions.

The earth muffled some of the noise from their hooves but quickly the horses tired and the party were forced to dismount and walk. The darkness lifted in shades of grey and low cloud, from which a fine rain developed. "The weather has saved us, even if we feel miserable," Tahoola said, wiping rain from her face.

They had a short rest. As they now had no food they quickly continued on their way. The airship was still hunting; now it was weaving through the low cloud, its form picked out by the ethereal orange glow cast from the lanterns.

"Remind me why we didn't fly?" Mycul asked.

"Our combined weight, the lack of fuel and the time for essential repairs all seemed valid reasons," Sartesh replied knowledgably.

A high-pitched noise was followed by the unmistakeable voice of the Protector over some contraption. "I know you are down there, Mycul Zas, no one escapes my justice and my troops are closing in on you. Give yourself up and I might spare you some of the worst pain." The screeching noise happened again as the airship turned and headed away.

"The motivational approach," Tahoola said and stood. She twisted round searching their surroundings. "It's clear. We need a plan."

"Fortunately I have one, but you won't like it," Sartesh said. The lights from the airship were faint now and the engine noise receded enough for the bird song of dawn to be heard. The crack of branches in the undergrowth set everyone on edge. Sartesh continued, "We have no choice but to take the old Adee route under the mountains."

"A tunnel?" Tahoola thought about this. "What about over the top?"

Sartesh pointed upward. "Then we have to deal with daylight. I know what the Adee did in tunnels towards the end. They stuffed them full of radioactive waste. They even hid the worst excesses of their genetic experiments. But we need to get over the border without being captured."

Mycul opened his hands in submission. "We have no choice." A long silence ensued. The clanking and grunts of soldiers could clearly be heard coming closer, and the party moved off with stealth. Mycul signalled for them to regroup. "I've had this nagging doubt about tunnels and I wondered about making for the coast and taking a ship for Menne. It has the advantage of wrong-footing the Protector."

"All the ports will be watched," Tahoola said, listening intently to sounds in the distance.

"I agree, we have come too far not to take the most direct route," Sartesh said, and pulled the sword from its sheath. He stood in silence, then signalled the others to move into the undergrowth. He sniffed the air.

"Well boys, what have we got here? A Mennedic warrior. Let's have some fun." The soldiers encircled Sartesh and drew their weapons.

"Zhedhelion Barkbada Uita!" Sartesh engaged with some fancy sword play. Several soldiers applauded and Sartesh used the opportunity to swing and sever the commander's head. The body stood upright as though nothing had happened, then blood spurted high into the air and the force knocked the cadaver over. Tahoola and Mycul slit the throats of two others leaving just the one. This final grunt turned to evaluate her enemies. Sartesh skimmed a trisos, which transfixed her.

"Shame, she was quite attractive," Sartesh said as her gurgles diminished. He retrieved the weapon and cleaned it on the grass. The bodies were quickly consumed by wererats.

"Tunnels!" Mycul said and set off at a run to round up the horses.

Sartesh and Tahoola followed. Slowly the low cloud lifted as the rain became heavier and the path oozed mud. They dismounted and jogged alongside their horses. Ahead the mountains grew in stature but were still days away. Mycul's heart beat so fast he thought he would die. He stumbled with exhaustion. Sartesh signalled left and they descended into an old quarry.

No one said anything. Each sipped water and lay on the wet earth until their breathing calmed and heart rate diminished. The horses became unsettled and Mycul tied up their reins.

"What type of rock is this?" Mycul asked as he returned.

Sartesh looked around, picked up a piece of the material and ground it between his fingers. He sniffed the residue. "Oil shale."

"We must continue," Tahoola said, "the soldiers are at least the match for us. I hope you have the revolvers, Sartesh."

"Why?" he asked producing one from his belt.

Tahoola looked around and sniffed, her grey eyes widened. She held up two fingers then signalled. The carniver leapt upon her. Its fangs were bared ready for the kill and talons emerged from its fingers. Sartesh took aim and shot. The sound was muffled by the shale but crows were startled by it. Tahoola rolled on top of her killer and slit its body open. Inside was a cube covered in blood and entrails but recognisable as a piece of the Ornithon. The three now stood back to back and waited. They felt another carniver was nearby circling its prey. The roar came from behind. Tahoola dispatched a wererat frightened into attack and as Mycul turned to see what was happening, the carniver leapt. It pinioned Mycul to the ground. Saliva dripped around him and the putrid smell of decaying blood made him feel faint. The creature's talons emerged and it bent to rip out his throat. The sword pushed the contents of the creature's gut over Mycul's body.

"No further!" he shouted, thinking he would also be sliced open. He took a knife and dismembered the carcass. He thrust his hand into the warm gelatinous mass and searched until he also found a cube.

"Just yours to go then Sartesh, now there's a creature who won't mind tunnels!"

"Thanks for that thought," Sartesh said as he gathered everything up and unfastened the horses. The others quickly followed.

"What we could do with is an automobile. Adee life was filled by them, they'd travel hundreds of miles in a day."

"I've had a thought, Sartesh," Mycul said going over to the fissile layers of oil shale. He sniffed them.

Sartesh dismounted, he crossed toward Mycul and put his hand on the youth's shoulder. "You're thinking will it burn."

"Yes. If the layer is nearly horizontal and near the surface. It's possible the columns of smoke will hide our escape and hamper the soldier's progress?" Mycul took a flint and struck it against its plate. The spark didn't take.

Tahoola hovered nervously by the quarry entrance. "Hurry," she hissed.

Sartesh pulled clumps of hay from beneath a bush. Mycul tried again and the hay ignited, then they held this against the rock. Black smoke rose and a putrid smell pervaded the quarry. The glow spread through the layer and the earth above started to heat up. Sartesh and Mycul hurried away. The column of smoke rose and became denser; it spread outwards creating a thick barrier. As the land rose, they could clearly see soldiers tackling the blaze and a further group mounting their own horses and heading towards the travellers. Mycul and friends galloped over the rich grasslands of the valley, seeing marsh plants taking over from bushes and grasses. The hooves created deeper impressions in the path.

"We should dismount," Tahoola said. She did so and carefully felt the ground, then put her ear to it. "I think it's hollow."

"But the path is clear."

"So it appears but we need to be careful and the horses need a rest."

They all agreed and travelled several miles on foot as the land rose and the soil became a moist peat in which nothing but heather grew. The landscape looked dark, brooding and unnatural. They found a slight dip in the land and decided to follow the stream up to its source. At the summit the view of the mountains was inspiring, their jagged pinnacles barren and snow-capped.

"Let's walk straight for them," Mycul suggested mounting his horse.

Sartesh held out his hand then rested his lips on his index finger. He surveyed the land and shook his head.

"This is a moor top marsh; see how the peat is saturated?" He picked up a handful and squeezed out the water. "We need a path or we'll be lost forever, if not sucked under," he headed northeast alone. He vanished from sight. Mycul and Tahoola followed him, stopping just in time to find Sartesh was up to his neck in waterlogged peat. "I was hoping you might be able to get me out."

"We'll try," said Mycul, running back to the horse for a rope. He threw the end and together Tahoola and Mycul heaved Sartesh in. Sartesh arrived on more solid ground cold and his skin tanned by black peat.

"You've lost your tattoos but on the plus side, you're alive," Mycul said.

"And bloody cold! But at least I know how to pick our way through this terrain now."

"Good because our pursuers are only an hour or so behind us," Tahoola noted.

Mycul prodded Sartesh in the ribs and pointed. They all looked to the north. The woman wore a grey fur trimmed basque which extended over a warrior's skirt but this itself was short and revealed her slender legs. She beckoned the party forward.

"Do we have a choice?" Sartesh asked.

"No. I'm sure I've seen her before at the Ornithon, her name is Alleyya." Mycul's eyes had widened and sparkled with desire.

"The last beautiful woman I met was the Protector, I wouldn't follow her very far," Sartesh suggested.

"There has to be a reason for this," Tahoola said and moved toward her. The party followed but the girl mysteriously stayed ahead of them, all the time beckoning them on the path toward the mountains.

They followed despite their misgivings. The land around was flat but bisected by ridges of drier ground over impenetrable marsh. As the rain eased, flies emerged and gathered around their heads. They concentrated on the nose, ears and eyes becoming a nuisance, landing to suck up salt and blood. Sartesh covered himself and used a vest as an impromptu fly swat.

Still the lady remained ahead of them. They glimpsed her attire, the fine embroidered flowers around her hem, the jewellery made from miniature skulls. Mycul in a burst of energy ran forward. The lady looked back smiled and was magically ahead once more.

"She's not real. At least she's not really here," Sartesh suggested. "It is some image generated by technology from the Adee."

"Or magic?" Tahoola suggested.

Sartesh gave her a look and continued swatting the flies gathering around him again. "This is a problem to be figured out, not a mystery, we must be scientific and not engage in fantasy."

"That's alright for you to say, you're the only one able to do something about these dratted flies!" Tahoola looked ahead to Mycul. "He has been captivated."

Sartesh saw how far he was beyond them and no amount of shouting would bring him back.

Chapter 12: The Perdisher Revolt

"Welcome to my lair," the woman said extending a hand which Mycul accepted then noticed the rings decorated with bones, "I am the Necromancer's daughter, Alleyya."

"I am Mycul Zas and these are my friends, Tahoola and Sartesh."

The lady smiled. She was more radiantly beautiful in reality. Her porcelain skin was enhanced by makeup. The kohl around her eyes contrasted with the brilliance of her amethyst irises.

"Thanks for steering us through the marshes, we would undoubtedly have been drowned in some pool or bitten to death by flies," Mycul said.

"Yes, that's why I brought you here to the kingdom underground. Welcome to the caves of Perdish." Alleyya poured liquid into waiting chalices. She took one herself. "I give you a toast: the Perdishers."

"The Perdishers."

"What is this place?" Sartesh asked.

"Follow," she beckoned them along a corridor lit by phosphorescence emanating from the walls.

Mycul swallowed the contents of his chalice quickly and fearing he'd be left, ran after the group and Alleyya.

The walls of the corridor were totally smooth as though they had been hewn from rock and melted to create a seal of glass. Sartesh looked closely and saw the radiant stars of crystalline decay which showed the glass was of antiquity. The corridor ended at a balcony. Beneath them and stretching far to the south was an agglomeration of buildings composed of the same glass and emitting a green glow. The architecture was solid, functional and lacking charm, unlike the graceful towers and domes of Faires. "My mother wants to meet you all; she wants to know of your plans and work out how the chapters of the Ornithon's predictions knit together," Alleyya said.

"Is she the one in control of everything?" Mycul asked. "The Protector of Faires said if the future is pre-determined then someone must be in control?"

"She will answer your questions if she can, but first you must wash and change into clothes fit to meet the Necromancer."

"She sounds much less frightening described as your mother," Mycul said.

For the first time the lady smiled, then she moved close to Mycul and placed a kiss on his cheek. Sartesh put his hand over his eyes and sighed.

Tahoola went up to the woman and stood next to her, they were of similar stature. Both looked at Mycul, then at each other and laughed.

"I hate it when women do that," Mycul said.

"I'd love to see you in that sort of outfit, Tahoola." Sartesh said to change the subject then realised the implication and his cheeks reddened.

"And you will," Alleyya replied. She then showed Mycul and Sartesh to a room richly furnished with satins of deepest burgundy. There was a simple bath lined with black tiles that shimmered with stars. Sartesh ran the hot water and sniffed at the jars lining a recess until he found one of a pleasant aroma. The crystals dissolved and the water foamed and steamed.

Sartesh stripped and entered, followed by Mycul. They lay back in the warm water and let the heat soak into their tired muscles.

"Did you ever find out about those," Mycul pointed to the nipples Sartesh possessed but he did not.

"We left a bit too quickly," Sartesh replied.

"You need to take that Mennedic thing off."

"My beard? For each year of being a warrior I can add a plait, althoughTahoola was right that it was too long. This would make me forty!"

Mycul flicked his face with water and the two wrestled until both emerged gasping for breath and laughing. "Remember one thing Mycul, no one does anything for free."

"You're wrong there, Sartesh, people do the strangest things for love."

"Precisely what I mean, don't let that be you," Sartesh said emerging from the bath. He dried himself and peeled away the beard before proceeding to shave. He pulled on the clothes spread out on a large circular bed. Black trousers of the softest cloth, a white shirt over which he wore a gold and black hauberk of leather etched with a design of a dragon swallowing its own tail.

"I feel like wearing jewellery!" Out of various concealed places, Sartesh pinned gold studs and rings into his ear, then he placed the purple and gold rings the Protector had given him on his right hand. Finally, he secreted a gun in a concealed pocket inside the hauberk.

"You look fantastic. Showy but fantastic," Mycul said. The clothes placed on a second bed for Mycul were the equal of Sartesh's, except their design was picked out in silver.

"Here," Sartesh thrust his hand deep into his bag and pulled out a ring. "I give you this Mycul. It is made from the purest of materials the Adee could synthesise."

Sartesh placed it gently over the younger man's finger. Mycul accepted it and turned his hand around to examine the ring. "It has a design etched into it written in Adee, I don't know what it means. Perhaps one day you will find out." Sartesh opened the door and gestured before leading the way to their audience with the Necromancer.

They met up with Alleyya and Tahoola on the corridor. Tahoola wore a sable lined skirt that ended half way up her thighs and a basque of pure grey satin, lined again with fur.

"You look beautiful," Sartesh said.

Tahoola acknowledged the compliment, "and you both look engagingly handsome."

Alleyya beckoned them to follow her. The buildings were all similar and Mycul noted that to find your way you had to follow the colours of the lights on each street. The largest building stood at the end of a crowded square. There were several market traders touting for business and a flow of happy looking citizens. They walked past guards dressed in severe uniforms and entered a large hall lit by torches and light emerging from lines in the ceiling.

Alleyya told them to wait as she approached a large throne set towards the back of the room. It was intricately carved with representations of subterranean beasts. Alleyya beckoned them forward. "Mother, our guests."

They each bowed. Mycul stood upright and came face to face with another beautiful woman. Her silver hair framed an almost youthful face except for the lines around her eyes. A high collar decorated with the face of a carniver, concealed her neck. "I am the Necromancer of Perdish," her voice echoed round the chamber. "All who see me must die."

Each of her guests cast their gaze to the floor.

"Sartesh Andrada, Keeper of the Seventh Law, you are welcome," she held out her hand and Sartesh dutifully kissed it. "Welcome Tahoola-gen, we have much need of you." Tahoola opened her mouth to speak but thought better of it. "Mycul Zas, you cannot judge a man by what he has not yet done but so far you have shown great bravery and compassion and for that you are also welcome."

Everyone stood in silence, taking in the strange décor of the room, part shrine, part study. In one corner was a box which looked like a sarcophagus. It was brown and possessed a window. The Necromancer stood; her dark flowing gown shimmered around her. "We will talk in private, if you would care to join me," she said and walked ahead into a small room lit by a roaring fire.

She removed several ceremonial items from her hair then sat. "Make yourselves comfortable," she said, her voice sounding thin in the poor acoustics. "I expected Sartesh as we found this waiting in ambush on our borders."

At the click of her fingers, a large object was carried in. Sartesh went pale. The veil was drawn back and the carniver burst into life, snarling and growling, throwing itself at the bars and pulling them apart with all its strength. "If we leave it here long enough, it will succeed in killing you, Sartesh."

"I'd rather not put that theory to the test, thank you your majesty."

The Necromancer snapped her fingers and the cage was veiled once more and the creature subdued. "I will have its cube removed and sent to you and then the carniver will be at peace."

"You called me gen, madam, why was that?"

"Ah! Tahoola, you've seen to the heart of the matter. Alleyya and I have had many discussions about this. She will assist you but she is needed as future necromancer and has many studies to complete. So I called you gen because I wish you to take the leadership of my army. It is small but they're brave fighters and they need to be taught the ways of the Protector's assassins."

"You are well informed," Tahoola said.

"I need to be, we are but a little place on the borders of Faires and Menne and Sartesh will turn us into Yderiphon if he succeeds."

Sartesh twisted the purple and gold rings on his fingers.

"I believe am the link between two parts of the prophecy, this is why I sent Alleyya to rescue you from the marsh," the Necromancer said. She removed a heavy necklace of metal carniver heads and placed it on the table. She also unstrapped the armour from beneath. "Do you know what this place is, Sartesh?"

Sartesh thought about the buildings and said, "I think it's a nuclear bunker from the time of the Adee."

She mocked him with applause. "The town was built to withstand great bombs but not the ravages of time. Sartesh has seen the changes to the glass of which Perdisher is made. It weakens and decays and then the walls collapse. We need to build a new city above ground.

That need is urgent but neither Faires nor Mennes will let us have land, so we will have to take it by force."

"I can train your army," Tahoola stated confidently.

"And I know how to get others to help," Mycul stated. "There is much dissent in Mennes and an opposition movement of sorts; all very secretive; but we could try to persuade them to help you, if it was reciprocated."

"You seem knowledgeable in the affairs of Mennes, for one who's never been there." the Necromancer span the Ornithon cube until its colours turned deeper than violet. She watched the images. "You travelled with Stazman Zem?"

"Yes, but he might have been killed when the spider creatures in a great forest trapped us."

The Necromancer span the cube again, this time stars twinkled through the blackness. "He is not dead, but he is in grave danger somewhere in Mennes. The image of a red and white castle haunts the scene. A dragon surmounts the tower. Someone is interfering with the lines of thought."

"The Protector?"

"No, someone with greater authority over the Ornithon. Their anger searches you out, Mycul. You must have upset some plans."

"I'd like to believe I have," he said.

A tray of drinks and plates of food and fruit were brought in by guards. Alleyya served her mother first then the guests.

"By your leave, madam, do you think Mycul and I should go to Mennes and…" Sartesh was interrupted.

"…Kill two birds with one stone? Yes," she sipped her drink then smiled, "but be careful what you wish for Sartesh Andrada, you may find your dreams come true and set you on the path to ruin."

"Isn't that everyone's fate no matter what part they play?"

The Necromancer avoided answering but continued, "Rest here a few days, then I will have you taken secretly to the border of Mennes to meet with Gorangoth the Golden."

Mycul remembered Nag-Nag's story of the giant and decided he would listen to the tale again and see if he could find any clues about passing safely into that country beyond the mountains.

Mycul also thought about Ra'an's talk in Pem and how she'd later betrayed them. He wondered if this information could be trusted. The most important thing was to rescue Stazman and help restore him to his inheritance. Perhaps that was the best hope of helping the Perdish as well.

"Ma'am," Sartesh wiped his lips with a silk napkin, "I'm intrigued. You said you were the link between two parts of a prophecy and yet..."

Again Sartesh was interrupted.

"...Do not ask it of me, young man, though be assured I will help you all I can."

Sartesh bowed.

"Mother, it is time for the adoration of skulls." Alleyya stood and offered the Necromancer her hand. The woman deferred to her. "It is a ritual of cleansing. Please make yourselves at home." They all stood as the two Perdisher left the room.

Sartesh sat down and began eating again. Tahoola poured a large goblet of wine. She turned the item round, observing the revenant carved into the design. After they had eaten their fill, Mycul stood and examined the murals on the wall. They depicted violent deaths and the release of souls. "Are we safe here?" He asked.

Tahoola stood, a little unsteadily but regained her balance. "I have heard that Voya—the Necromancer is a conduit between this life and the next. She can make the souls of the departed do her bidding."

A steward cut short their musings. "It is time for you to leave," he said firmly but politely and showed the guests to the door. "Goodnight." They followed the coloured lights back to their lodgings.

Mycul slept fitfully at first but when eventually he did sleep, Alleyya came to him in his dreams.

She kissed him again and he felt the moment of pleasure and woke with a start. Sartesh was nowhere to be seen. He wrapped himself in the sheets again before drifting back to sleep.

Chapter 13: The Midnight Garden

When Mycul woke the second time, he found that there was no difference in light and was disorientated. Sartesh was obviously an early riser and had taken the cubes to listen to Nag-Nag's story in another room. Mycul sponged himself down and found new clothes had been put out to wear. After dressing he decided to explore.

Mycul asked a guard for directions to the library and found it in an annex of the palace. He read various books on Mennes and its bloodthirsty history and also its language and culture. He wrote out a list of useful words to use and practised them.

"Come with me," a librarian said. She ushered him into a small room with a table and chair and beckoned him to sit. She produced a cube from the wall and spun it until the voice within could be heard. "This is how the Adee learned their words. Listen and you will hear Mennedic, repeat and practice."

Mycul thanked her and began his lesson, this time listening to the sound of the words and copying. After some time doing this, he began to hear the voices inside his head. Mycul felt a gentle touch on the back of his neck. He turned and for a moment held his breath. He couldn't speak. Alleyya smiled and let her finger repeat the journey along his shoulders until she stopped at his fringe and twisted a strand of his black hair. Mycul took hold of her fingers and kissed them.

"At last we meet in person," Alleyya said and took a step forward.

"It was you at the Ornithon?"

"Yes, indeed. I saw…."

"Hush… Mother and I are both aware of what you saw. I'm sorry we violated the defences and caused… well you escaped, that's the main thing." She beckoned him and he followed her out of the library and into the street.

She turned right and disappeared down an alley. Mycul forced himself to breathe. He felt lightheaded, his heart pounding at the thought his dreams might become reality. A hand reached out from the darkness and pulled him through a gateway. She placed her finger on his lips, then covered his eyes and led him into a place of byzantine scents.

"You may open your eyes now." Alleyya stood at the edge of a garden. The flowers were all as pale as moonlight but scented with such a narcotic mix of perfumes that Mycul thought he might burst from his body and fly.

"Do not fight the sensation, Mycul. It is my gift to you."

Mycul didn't know what to say. He mumbled, "I love you."

Alleyya smiled, "Well, let us see if that is true. Relax, let the scents take you."

Mycul breathed deeply. He felt Alleyya's grip slowly slacken as he floated above his body. He felt his soul fly through the midnight garden. Alleyya came close and their two souls entwined then danced in the air. Like butterflies, they sipped nectar from lilies and orchids until they glided to the ground and lay upon the obsidian grass. Fingers slid over delicate surfaces of skin. Mycul could do nothing but smile and Alleyya gently stroked his face and hair until he slept.

From a balcony overlooking the subterranean town, Sartesh observed the view. He held a glass of wine in his hand. "It is as you surmised Tahoola, Alleyya has enchanted him."

"It is an enchanting garden. Perhaps I might experience it one day, with its strange perfumes," Tahoola, said as she stood next to Sartesh. "There is something unspoken between us."

"I was thinking that," Sartesh replied and sat upon the balustrade.

Tahoola stepped forward and observed the drop. She raised an eyebrow.

"I wonder why there is no plural of sorry," she said and saw at once her words had found their mark.

"Nallor became a father to me after his own son was killed in an accident at the mine. In his grief, he turned to me for everything and made me what I am. Yet…" Sartesh thought long and hard before proceeding, "…I loved him dearly but I could not become Keeper of the Seventh Law until he had fallen from grace. The trick was not falling with him. You provided that."

"So you put yourself first?"

Sartesh nodded and Tahoola could see he was remorseful and that he had carried this burden of guilt for a long time.

"Look at my stub," she held her stump aloft. "This was my folly. I sought to change my life, to trap my gang members underground so I could escape them and start afresh. I didn't appreciate the effects of an explosion on the weakness between the rock types. I will always have their deaths on my conscience."

"Does Mycul know this?"

"He suspects. We none of us are perfect."

Sartesh turned and dangled his legs over the edge. "I'm pleased we have spoken, there must be nothing left unsaid which might poison trust when we part."

"Nothing?"

Sartesh smiled, "You wouldn't understand the type of man I am."

"You don't give me enough credit, you might be just the type of man I'm after, imperfect, unique. Can you see them in the garden?"

Sartesh nodded, he felt a pang of jealousy as Mycul stripped. The youth's flesh turned grey in the phosphorescent daylight of Perdisher, then his body vanished between the tall plants of the midnight garden.

"It was the way he looked at her and the light in her eyes. I hope this doesn't offend the Necromancer."

"I think it is part of Alleyya's plan."

Sartesh somersaulted off the balustrade and landed upright besides Tahoola.

"I always wanted to be a pirate. I don't understand how someone like me could ever become Emperor of Menne and married to you."

"Married to me?" Tahoola laughed.

"Mycul saw it clearly in the Ornithon."

"Standing next to each other perhaps?"

"No, he said our daughter was the Child, the one prophesised."

"I'm not at all religious, Sartesh Andrada and our daughter is never going to happen. I am my own woman. Soon you will go with Mycul into Mennes, whilst I remain here and train this army. As plans go, the Perdisher Revolt doesn't quite seem enough to topple Warmonger Lazlo but with the help of dissidents in Mennes, it stands more chance." Tahoola looked at herself in a mirror.

"Do not doubt yourself," Sartesh said.

"Even you must, at times," Tahoola replied. "Help from Mennes might create two fronts. The best trained troops always have the advantage but the strategy of gens is the *coup de grace*." Sartesh stood next to her and observed their reflection.

"I have the advantage," she turned him to face her, "I've read the strategies of Alexander, Julius Caesar and Napoleon. The Protector liked her assassins to be well educated."

"You'd do much better to study the landscape and the weather for both have won and lost more battles," Sartesh continued, "for my part, I have read how Octavian manoeuvred his way to power, and although he lived several thousand years ago, the quality of humanity hasn't changed." Sartesh briefly took Tahoola's hand and kissed it before vanishing into the deep shadows of the corridor.

_*_

"Genetics, the science of heredity. Our cells contain all the information to make us unique. Human cells contain 23 pairs of chromosomes according to the Adee but in the humans I have studied, there is something extra, a lengthening of a chromosome by additional genes. This means humans alive today are not exactly the same as the Adee. It's as if the virus used in those first experiments thousands of years ago mutated and infected everyone." The Necromancer replaced the genetic fingerprints.

Mycul stood in front of the Necromancer, not knowing what to expect. He had fallen in love with Alleyya: of that, at least, he was certain. He counted backwards in his head so as to not remember the details of her skin, her curves and her scent.

"You have chosen Alleyya but it is not certain she has chosen you. The path of a necromancer is unique, we are not made for just our own cares."

Mycul didn't know what to say, so he tried, "I have fallen in love with her."

The Necromancer smiled, "No Mycul, you have fallen under her spell and that is not the same. Alleyya will always be greater than you. A man is unnecessary really. Tahoola was born genetically identical to her sisters without sperm and egg in a process the Adee called cloning. Here in Perdish, we have no such technology. The next generation must be created," she said as her hand hovered over the skulls piled neatly before her. "I have divined from the bones of the ancestors what troubles you. You are free to go to Mennes whenever you want to," she said warming her hand on the brazier nearby.

"Free to go? But I love Alleyya, I want to spend my life with her," Mycul blurted.

The necromancer looked into the sockets of one skull, then picked up another and another. With each she seemed in a trance as though some silent communication was afoot. "I would never withhold my consent, so if Alleyya agrees…"

Mycul smiled then thought about the indefinite amount of time he would be away. He opened his mouth to complain but shut it tight as the necromancer brought out a knife.

"You must become a Perdisher, Mycul Zas. I will initiate you into the priesthood of our ancestors, so they can find your quality. Take off your shirt."

Mycul stood before the woman. He looked down as the blade moved toward his heart and away as he felt the blade twist upwards into his flesh. A moment of pain numbed as the blood flowed. This was collected in a silver vessel. Suddenly she produced a red-hot ring and plunged it onto the wound. The burn seared through him and the smell of flesh offended his senses. Mycul toppled backwards into a waiting chair. His blood was poured over the pile of skulls and appeared to vanish into the bones. Lights grew from within the crania until each eye socket was a source of luminosity. The voices that followed sounded like the chant of mordonts, and Mycul thought of his father.

Cevennes appeared and walked towards him and a woman of dark complexion but taller than his father also drew near. Soon the room was filled with people Mycul knew or suspected he knew, people who looked like him and yet were not.

"These are your ancestors, your mother and father. You never knew your mother yet she is held in high regard by those who have gone before. You rescued your father and set yourself on this course of events. Half of your genes are from your mother and half from your father. So it will be with the child to be born."

"Are these images real?"

"Real but fragile, the movement of your hand will destroy their presence."

Mycul stared at his mother, who had died over eighteen years ago. He could see the likeness, the fine nose, the slight point to her chin but above all the clearest blue eyes under her jet black hair. He could even hear the idiom of her speech repeated in his own.

The necromancer struggled and parted her hands. All the visitors vanished.

Mycul felt sad and stared at the point where his mother had stood. "I wanted to say something," he said trying, to comprehend what had happened, what aspects of science had caused the illusions but he could find no reason.

"That's why I asked them to leave. Next time when you understand more about us it will be different." The necromancer carefully placed each skull back in its niche.

"Is that box a sarcophagus?"

The Necromancer looked over her shoulder. "No, it is a stasis chamber given to me by the Adee."

Mycul began to ask another question.

The Necromancer held up her hand, "I am tired now and you have much to prepare before you go with Sartesh. Please leave me."

Mycul did as he was told. He found Alleyya waiting as he closed the door. "I knew she'd like you," she said.

"Do you like me?"

Alleyya smiled but did not answer the question. "Love moves equally in two directions. At the moment it is going only one way."

Mycul took a deep breath.

"You see I am an important person in Perdisher. Who I love will also be influential."

"I understand that but I feel bound to you. I am in love with you."

Alleyya smiled and kissed his cheek. "You are really good looking but I am not giving up anything for a man."

"I didn't ask you to. I'm giving up the sea to remain with you," Mycul said moving closer to Alleyya. She stepped back.

"Well, let us see what happens." Her fingers drew him closer until he could smell her rare and expensive fragrance.

-*-

Mycul entered the room with a dreamy expression on his face. "I'm in love with Alleyya," he said.

Sartesh looked at him. "Don't go upsetting the Necromancer, I was just getting comfortable here."

"No, I've talked with her and she has no objection to Alleyya and I becoming lovers."

Sartesh smiled but said nothing to shatter Mycul's dream. He busied himself packing his bag and ensuring the revolvers were working properly. The gun he kept at all times near his heart was also cleaned and checked.

"Do you know anything about genetics?" Mycul asked when he had sat down and sucked the juice from an orange.

"Only that the information which makes us what we are, is carried by the sperm and egg. Twenty-three chromosomes on each."

"Yes, the Necromancer said that. She also said we differ from Adee humans in some way."

"That's not surprising, thousands of years have elapsed. Even the natural course of evolution might have produced some change but with the advent of genetic modification... if only I'd had time to complete that experiment at the gold mine."

"Do you think we are the product of natural evolution?"

Sartesh wondered what Mycul had understood from their talks and his visit to Alleyya's mother.

"We are what we are and cannot be anything else. Perhaps we are all part of the genetic experiment but should we live the less because of it? Should the way we are born decide our position in society or feed our hopes?" Sartesh lifted the bag and checked the weight was evenly distributed.

122

Mycul lay on the bed and closed his eyes. His lips were still curved up in a smile. He sighed, "Whatever and whoever we are, all equal."

Sartesh watched him and saw the emerald ring he had given him was still in place. "We set off at first light tomorrow, if there's anything you would rather be doing…."

Mycul shot off the bed and ran down the corridor. Sartesh laughed. Slowly the laugh died as he realised he had never experienced such love or if he had, the memory was supressed. He packed Mycul's bag before going off to do his own research into the Perdisher.

Mycul found Alleyya in her rooms. She was reading and leapt to her feet when he was admitted to her presence. There was an uneasy moment before they embraced. They kissed and sat down next to each other without a word. Alleyya offered Mycul a drink, which he accepted. He offered her a gift. "I don't own much but this is the cube from a carniver. I believe we can use it to communicate across distances."

Alleyya accepted the gift. "We don't need to communicate. You'll always be here. I will carry your heart in my heart, and when yours fails, mine will beat for both."

Mycul smiled and kissed her again. "Sartesh is organising everything for our journey. I should be helping him but I think he understands."

"That is good of him. Remember nothing is given for free, Mycul." She picked up a comb and began running it through his hair until his long fringe fell either side of his face. Mycul turned and relaxed his head in Alleyya's lap. She placed her hand over his forehead and closed his eyes.

Mycul felt his memories running through her fingers. She paused at the Graken.

"Always the sea, there'll always be the sea between us."

"Our love can stand that."

"And Stazman Zem, he stands in your memories and the revenge you want on your uncle. Revenge is never a good thing, you should let go of that emotion if you can and you will be the better person for it," Alleyya said.

"I will try," Mycul closed his eyes. More memories surfaced, his father baling hay, and briefly his mother. Alleyya smiled as he laid next to her, knowing Mycul was totally under her spell. She would have to organize for him to be given the potion of forgetfulness before his journey.

Mycul took in his lover's perfumes and the shade of her irises, the contours of her face. Alleyya escorted him to the balcony and they watched the lights of Perdisher.

"I remember where I saw you now, it was at the Ornithon and your mother spoke to me."

"You remember it all?"

"I remember it all, good and bad."

"Was I part of the good?"

"Of course but the more I think about what I saw, the more it is open to interpretation… but I'm certain something dreadful happens to your mother."

Alleyya stopped what she was doing. "Describe the scene."

"There was a shot and the Necromancer fell, only she fell onto a pile of bodies whose eyes were open in surprise," Mycul said.

"I hope that never comes to pass. No one can know the future for certain."

"Unless our lives are in some way replayed."

"No," Alleyya said with confidence, "for us there are no contours in time. Our lives are too brief, so time plays us a linear game of beginnings and endings."

Mycul did not understand this. He looked down at the garden. "Shall we?"

Alleyya nodded. They remained together for many hours until the bell tolled for a new working day.

Time passed by in preparation for the journey ahead. Mycul knew they had to leave but found any excuse to delay until one day had become four.

Chapter 14: Gorangoth the Golden

Alleyya wore blue beads threaded through her hair and a short skirt layered over a longer one. She whispered to Sartesh and discreetly passed him a vial. "The potion of forgetfulness, use one drop in every drink," she said.

Sartesh discreetly hid the vessel.

"What was that about?" Mycul asked.

"Nothing," Sartesh lied.

Mycul kissed Alleyya.

Sartesh briefly embraced Tahoola. "We will all need good luck," he said. He nudged Mycul and both looked up to a balcony where the Necromancer stood. The men bowed then mounted their horses.

The Necromancer's voice carried far. "Do not be alarmed by your guide. He might not speak and once you get to the border of Great Menne, the spectre will vanish."

"Don't you just hate the idea of using ghosts as a guide?" Sartesh asked.

Mycul was under Alleyya's spell and could not take his eyes off her until they had left the town for a dark passageway. Sartesh fingered the phial he had been given. The potion of forgetfulness would need a while to take effect. Sartesh took a swig from a water bottle, poured a drop of the green liquid into the canteen and passed it to Mycul who drank deeply.

The revenant floated ahead of them, its tattered gown undulating with the motion. "I found out a lot yesterday about the Perdisher," Sartesh said when Mycul appeared to be less lost in memories of Alleyya. "The town is an Adee nuclear bunker. The people who hid there were the ancestors of the Perdisher." He saw Mycul was listening. "Yet they have the same genetics as you. Doesn't that tell you something?"

Mycul shrugged and looked back down the corridor.

"You are all descended from the Adee who sheltered in Perdish."

Mycul tried to comprehend what Sartesh was telling him but couldn't fathom it. "Very few humans survived the final holocaust," Sartesh said.

They followed the ghost towards a faint breath of chilled air. The light in the tunnel became more natural and the temperature dropped. The ghostly figure evaporated and Sartesh and Mycul emerged above a wide road in the heart of the mountains. A light smattering of snow coated the rocks around them. Sartesh unpacked a long coat from his bag and put it on. He then searched for gloves.

"Aren't you cold?" he asked Mycul.

"No," Mycul smiled and spurred his horse along the road.

The path rose slowly, cut into the contours of the mountain and following a bedding plane in the pure white rock. When this ran out the path cut up the flank of a tree lined slope until, with the summit in sight, it veered north and began a descent toward the next mountain. The path must be ancient as it was carved into the rock face and wide. Perhaps it had once been smooth enough for the transport of the Adee.

By late afternoon, the deep shadows of the mountains contained snow and frost that hadn't melted.

"Are you in love with Alleyya?" Sartesh asked.

Mycul smiled. "Yes," he said in a calm and sensible tone.

Sartesh breathed a sigh of relief that his companion was removed from her spell. He didn't have the heart to tell him that the midnight garden captivated with narcotic scents.

Mycul broke out a coat and gloves from his bag and shivered as he put them on. He wrapped a scarf around his neck. "Where will we sleep tonight?"

"Out in the open, under the stars. I have thick blankets to keep us warm."

"I don't think I remember what it's like being warm," Mycul said rubbing his hands together.

"It's the wererats we have to fear. We'll need time to light a fire," Sartesh said.

"Every Mennedic in this forsaken place will know our position if we do that. No fire!" Mycul said. He noticed his friend wore no jewellery and that his hair was slicked back.

The shadows became impenetrable and the sky above turned from azure through to midnight blue and was punctuated by many stars. The horses were tethered and they made camp sheltered from the north by a rock wall and the south by a stand of larch trees. In a gap created by two boulders, Sartesh prepared their shelter. He lashed branches together and threw a tarpaulin over as protection from any rain. Finally he put in their blankets.

They ate bread and cheese and watched the stars before pulling the blankets tight, each with the other man's body for warmth.

"I feel insignificant looking out on such a sky," Mycul said.

Sartesh took a while to reply. "There are as many stars in the sky as there are sperm inside a man. What is contained inside those cells is all we can ever leave behind."

"Surely you don't believe that?"

"It is a scientific truth but a tragedy nonetheless. Perhaps great books, carvings or buildings can remain, but look at the Adee and all they did. What is left? Material items decay whereas children should long outlive us and grow to pass some element of themselves to the next generation. You'd think such a whittling down of all that is good would make us pure."

"And how do you explain our differences?"

"I can't, not yet."

Mycul nestled his head against Sartesh's shoulder and shivered.

"A cold night alone on the mountain is no time for philosophy. I'll imagine Alleyya's arms around me and her kiss on my lips." Mycul yawned. Each other's warmth and the thick fleecy blankets kept them safe as the frost penetrated. Mycul's eyes closed and Sartesh watched the stars. Orion set in the south and a star moved quickly from north to south. Sartesh stood and took out a telescope. It was a craft. He just stopped himself from waving; Mycul wasn't yet ready for a confession of that magnitude.

Against the deep blue sky of dawn, the silhouettes of mountains became more pronounced. The planets Saturn and Mars shone brilliantly. Sartesh stood and walked a little way off to pee. He continued to stare out at the firmament until a shooting star flashed across the heavens. He was reminded of the night before and felt a pang of sadness.

When Mycul woke, the blankets were frozen in position around him. Sartesh handed his friend a cup of warm broth. "How did you do that without a fire?"

Sartesh showed the fuel tablets and the metal flask. "More Adee science?"

"Do give me credit for some of my own ideas," Sartesh said.

Mycul warmed his hands round the cup and sent hot breath dissipating in the morning air. Sartesh collected the horses and they walked with the blankets wrapped around them until the new day filled the east with pink and silver rays.

The road climbed again but this time it remained above the snowline and they could see it coil like a snake up the mountain beyond. As they rounded the corner, they caught a glimpse of a tower. From the next bend they could see it was built from a black rock and cruelly surmounted by spikes, from which flags appeared to flap in the morning breeze. Closer still, the companions could see these pennants were the skins of people preserved like hides and painted in the colours of their country.

"Gorangoth the Golden," Mycul said, "I don't suppose you have any ideas?"

"None," Sartesh replied. He fingered the cubes from the Ornithon and hoped what he would tell the giant might work.

The road climbed severely on the corners then flattened a little on the straight. The tower now soared above them, its shape a frightening imposition on the landscape.

"It's been built from the igneous rock lining the road."

"Geology, even up here, Sartesh?"

"Any time is a good time for geology, it distracts my thoughts," Sartesh added.

The final coil of road took them by the walls, their horses shied away from the skins which made a sighing sound in the breeze, as though their dead owners still suffered.

Sartesh touched the walls. They were smooth as glass.

"Obsidian," he said to Mycul.

"So it's left over from the Adee like Perdish?"

"In part perhaps. When you destroyed the Ornithon…"

"Technically it was the Graken who destroyed it," Mycul replied and then in a more serious vein added, "I wonder if they were right? That we should destroy everything left over from the Adee and really start again."

"To embrace everything we know and use it to our advantage has been my motto," Sartesh said. He looked up at the battlements.

The pair hurried beyond the castle and found the upper road cleared of snow and lined by piles of stones from rock falls. Even as they passed by pebbles rolled down and echoed. A peculiar smell like violets floated on the air. Sartesh fingered the cubes in his pocket. "Is there any chance of passing by unnoticed?"

Mycul looked around. "There's a sweet smell on the air," he said. Both men looked at each other as they felt the first vibration shimmer through the road. Rocks tumbled on the way ahead. "Does that answer your question?"

A second vibration was louder still and more rocks tumbled, blocking their way forward. Mycul touched Sartesh on the shoulder. He turned and he heard his friend swallow hard.

Gorangoth the Golden strode towards them. His armour glinted with gold and jewels and the horns on his helmet made him appear twelve foot tall. He carried a notched battle-axe which he began swinging to and fro. As he got closer they saw his grey beard was carefully plaited and held by gold rings. Mycul bowed before him.

"Good morning Gorangoth," he said, his voice shaking with fear.

Sartesh also bowed but did it in Mennedic fashion, crossing his arms onto opposing shoulders.

The smell of violets emanated from the giant. He stood still then knelt down in front of them.

"I am Gorangoth the Golden. No one passes into Menne without my consent."

"That is what we have come to ask you for," Mycul said a little more certain now. "I am Mycul Zas and this is my companion Sartesh Andrada. We are trying to find any opposition to Barser de Sotto's rule in Mennes and save our friend Stazman Zem."

"A noble quest but I am charged with keeping Mennes safe from those who would do her harm. Your lives are forfeit."

Sartesh stepped forward and held out the cubes from the Ornithon."

"Trinkets?" The giant laughed.

Mycul took one and placed one on his hand. He spun it round. The image of Nag-Nag Naroon appeared and his voice was clearly heard, *"Upon the purple mountain lives a man, whose ways are wondrous strange to me. Upon the purple mountain lives a man who guards the only path to Great Menne. Many have tried this route to fame and fortune but only I succeeded with the giant's consent. My purpose was unhindered for once you pass the route forever you are free."*

The giant stroked his beard. "This is subterfuge. I must let Nag-Nag through unhindered. I remember his stories well, he told them day and night until I tired and slept. Of course he took the opportunity and sneaked across the path whether I'd let him or not. Storytellers are all the same, cowards at heart."

"Are we free to go then?" Mycul asked.

"Well, yes. No! I need more time to think this through. Come into my castle and take ale and meat with me."

They had no choice but to follow at a run as the giant strode ahead. The doors to the tower closed with a finality and the lock and key which made them secure were too high for either man to reach.

Gorangoth hung the key from a gold ring in his beard. He threw logs on the fire and rang a bell. Servants appeared and set the table for a meal.

"Tell me about yourselves," the giant asked. "What desperate quest brings you to Great Menne?"

"It was as Mycul said. We want to rescue our friend Stazman Zem then find any opposition to Barser de Sotto and Warmanger Lazlo."

"What has Warmonger Lazlo done to deserve your enmity?"

"Nothing, but how can there be an Emperor in Menne if he still lives?"

"Our friend Stazman is Prince of Catherine," Mycul added.

The giant stroked his beard. He pulled off his gloves and helmet as the beer was served. Each was poured a quart of ale in a large tankard. The giant swigged his down in one. They drank more carefully. The giant observed his guests. "Place all your cubes upon the table."

Sartesh placed the one the necromancer had given him, and Nag-Nag's cube on the table. Mycul added his. The giant set each in motion.

"You have seen the Ornithon. Ah! Both of you have seen the Ornithon? Is it beautiful?" Gorangoth asked.

"It is like a lighthouse standing over a sea arch," Sartesh said before Mycul could admit what he had done.

"You are Keeper of the Seventh Law of the Adee, Sartesh. You are the friend of mordonts, Mycul Zas. You unlocked the secret of the Reach of Key and destroyed it." Gorangoth drank again, "But even this is not enough. I will kill you at dawn and skin your bodies as a warning to other adventurers." Gorangoth stood to leave the room.

"You will not kill us," Mycul said.

The giant turned and thumped his fist on the table. "No one tells me what to do!"

"I can!" Mycul shouted, "Both of us have some part to play in saving the Child, the one who will redeem us all."

"What part?" Gorangoth asked.

"That neither of us knows even though we have seen the Ornithon," Mycul said.

"And it has been destroyed, erasing that part of the future from us all."

"I'm sorry, yes. I caused that to happen after I had consulted it."

Gorangoth sat down again. "Then I am bound to you. I may not kill you and I may not let you go."

"Then come with us," Sartesh said, "and you will see what we say is true."

"I cannot leave this pass unguarded." Gorangoth chewed the meat off a leg of beef and took more ale. "The snow will close the pass soon and I will have four months to join your quest. I will do as you ask. I have not seen the city of Karlize for many a year. If you play me false, Sartesh Andrada, I will kill you and eat your flesh."

Sartesh smiled. "I only ever lie to myself," he said and drained the tankard of ale.

"So what do we do now?" Mycul asked later when the giant had fallen asleep, his beard draped over the edge of a large table.

"We kill him and run!"

"That's immoral, Sartesh."

"I was joking. But we're hardly relying on stealth with a twelve-foot giant following us everywhere."

"No, but he would be helpful in rescuing Stazman. And think on this, if we split up, who will he follow?"

Sartesh smiled. "Why you," he replied as if he had some secret plan.

Mycul spent an hour looking round the castle. It became apparent that several smaller rooms had been knocked into one much larger one and that an upper floor had been taken out to accommodate the giant. The walls were made from the glass the Adee used and windows set into the walls were lancet in design and possessed intricate carvings of beasts emerging from the walls as though they had been sealed into the structure of the growing building.

There were also signs of a feminine touch in wall hangings of unicorns and knights rescuing maidens. Mycul stopped a servant and asked. The woman shook her head and would not speak. She hurried off down the corridor and a door slammed. Mycul stood in silence.

Sartesh joined him. "You're wondering who she might be?"

"Yes."

"If you are a giant and do not know your own strength when drunk, it can be easy to kill a lady. He loved her without question but he was also insanely jealous of any man she talked to. Jealously is even more destructive than your revenge, Mycul," Sartesh warned.

Mycul's anger rose. He felt his cheeks burn. He felt the breath force through his nostrils."No one is perfect it seems or immune from mistakes. We just have to try and do our best or what are we?"

"And no one likes hearing the truth of their flaws," Mycul said.

"That's what friends are for."

Mycul placed his hand on Sartesh's shoulder. "Where do you think we should sleep?"

"Ask this gentleman carrying the sheets." They did and followed him up the narrow stairs to a room at the top.

A fire burnt in the grate and the room was warm. "This was our lady's favourite room. She loved the view," the servant said. "Will there be anything else?"

"A jug of ale?" Sartesh said, then added "and water to wash with?"

"The baths are down in the cellar, you are welcome anytime, just ring the bell." The servant reappeared a few minutes later with the ale and two tankards, saying, "Gorangoth has fallen asleep but the scarf dancers are waiting. Will you watch them?"

Sartesh shrugged his shoulders noncommittally but Mycul insisted that as guests, not watching the entertainment provided would be an insult. They both went downstairs to the great hall. Gorangoth was indeed asleep over the table. At the other end of the room, three men and three women waited. They were wound around with scarves of brilliant colours.

Musicians struck up a hypnotic rhythm on their instruments and the dance began. At first it was slow and the colours of the scarves were pure but relentlessly the pace picked up as more and more scarves were unravelled. Now the dancers were semi-naked and writhing as the colours mixed and patterns created by bodies were reflected in the colours and the shapes of the cloth. In the final moments the music reached a crescendo of noise and the dancers were revealed as fully naked except for the piercing in their navels from which the ends of the silks were fixed. The music and dance stopped suddenly. The dancers remained motionless on the floor panting and waiting.

Sartesh burst into applause and Mycul followed. "Bravo!" they cheered. The noise of the final few seconds roused Gorangoth. He farted and then waited to burp before rubbing his eyes.

"Ah! My dancers. You must perform for me!" he bellowed. No one dare argue.

The dance proceeded as before except that this time Mycul watched Sartesh as much as the performers, as he stared determinedly at one dancer. He smiled as the piece reached its erotic climax.

The giant beckoned Mycul over after the applause was finished and gold had been thrown. "Tell me, where are we bound for in Mennes? It is a big country, mountainous, and the passes aren't always available until April."

"I don't know, except the Necromancer gave one clue, she clearly saw a castle of white and red stone."

Gorangoth thought about this, he sat back in his chair and played his fingers against each other. "She gave no other clue?"

"She said it was surmounted by a dragon."

Again Gorangoth cupped his hands together, then blew across his fingers.

"In the literal sense or a banner?"

Mycul shrugged. "I don't know," he admitted and looked around the room. Sartesh had vanished. For a moment he was concerned and then he remembered the look and the light in his friend's eyes and smiled.

"I didn't see the image. This was reported to me by the Necromancer."

"We will have our work cut out. I will cause the snow to fall and close the pass. The only castle I know with a dragon above it is Warmonger Lazlo's in Karlize. Now how would your friend have got there?"

Mycul thought back. The image of Ra'an getting into the bath with them came to mind, he fought past this to her conversation about her sister Barser de Sotto. "If Ra'an was lying and she was working for her sister, removing the last male heir to Catherine would be logical."

"Yes, you said he was Prince of Catherine, now I understand, the brothers Zem are murdered and the fourth becomes the heir. The one sold into slavery years ago by Lazlo," Gorangoth laughed. "I told Lazlo evil was always returned nine-fold upon the perpetrator. Now I know I can help, for Catherine is a principality of Great Menne. Perhaps this small act will somehow set the real Emperor back on his throne."

"I thought Manhedreth was eaten at the coronation banquet of Lazlo?"

"He was indeed, but his son Sension was never discovered. Lazlo had a badly charred body strung up in the city for all to see but I wasn't convinced it was Sension. I didn't voice my doubts, that would have been fatal; even though I'm a giant, I'm not invincible. So I returned to guard my pass hoping Lazlo and all his cronies would be swept away."

"I understand." Mycul looked at the giant. He realised Gorangoth was yet another genetic experiment; the diversification of life by creating new human phenotypes. They drank some beer and a little later Sartesh appeared. His cheeks were flushed but otherwise he was immaculately dressed.

"Is there some of that left for me?"

Gorangoth laughed and the room vibrated. "You have a healthy appetite, sir."

"Not everyone sees it as healthy but it certainly is an appetite and needs sating like anyone else's!"

Mycul wasn't certain who was referring to what but kept his own counsel. He looked over the rim of his tankard at his friend. Sartesh saw and winked.

"The castle we head for is Warmonger Lazlo's in…"

"… Karlize," Mycul replied catching Sartesh off guard. "We all have our ways of finding things out, some use seduction and others use charm."

"I think you mean deduction?" Sartesh corrected.

Mycul broke into laughter at his own joke and Sartesh followed. Gorangoth related all he knew about the last surviving member of the Mennedic royal house.

"Sension was such a handsome prince, the type a lady might fall for in some tale. Tall and handsome, he was everything you might have expected: chivalrous, loyal and intelligent. He played the flute exceedingly well and used to charm the court with tunes he invented, or resurrected from the Adee. The world is a poorer place without his company," Gorangoth said then fell silent and drained his tankard.

"They say it is a curse, *may you live in interesting times*, but we only have the one occasion to live and maybe we should make our own lives as interesting as we can? To stretch the rules and…" Sartesh observed the servants by the door and stopped.

"What is it, Steward?" the giant asked.

"By your leave, sir. The dancers want permission to cross the pass into Menne."

Mycul put his finger to his lips and whispered to Sartesh. He nodded and Mycul repeated the idea to Gorangoth. The giant roared with laughter. "I'll pay them double. Bring their leader to me."

Chapter 15: Barser de Sotto

Mycul and Sartesh followed the party of dancers as their cart scraped and slid over the pass and entered the country of Menne. The landscape changed subtly. Here the mountains were formed from recumbent layers of sediment contorted to angles so severe gentle slopes ended at precipitous cliffs. The green valleys gave way to barren rock and scree before resuming the gentle incline.

Sartesh nursed a bad head and he looked rather unwell for most of the morning. Mycul fared a little better through greater restraint. Gorangoth was nowhere to be seen but Mycul opined that he watched everything they did. He had given both men a low-pitched whistle to blow if they needed his assistance or advice. The stem was decorated with a dragon coiled around the pipe, so that the sound emerged through the dragon's jaws.

The dancers were unrecognisable from the performers of last night. They were dressed in warm skins and hide coats that entirely concealed their athletic bodies. Mycul kept looking for the person who captured Sartesh's interest had but found no obvious candidates.

If uphill had caused the wheels of the cart to slip and slide, downhill required everyone to act as brakes. Smoke rose from the metal wheel rims as the wooden brake was applied and most of the friction converted the heat. The smell of burning pine assailed them. The troupe held onto ropes fastened to the back axle to further prevent the escape of the wagon.

It was a merciless descent that took layers of skin from Mycul's palms and caused him to swear more than once.

By mid-afternoon, the dancers were entering their next venue, an old hall with symmetric wings. The gravelled path was lined with grotesque statues of dragons devouring men or ripping them apart, their death agonies portrayed vividly. The owner obviously wanted to frighten all who approached. It had the desired effect on the company as they approached in silence. The great door to the building was possessed of metal hinges in the design of a dragon grasping the severed head of a knight. This last embellishment acted as a door knocker. "I think we get the message," Sartesh whispered.

A steward appeared and welcomed the leader of the troupe. They were ushered inside whilst servants unpacked the wagon. The hall was lined with wainscoting and the ceiling coloured in the purple and yellow flag of Yderiphon. Over the fireplace was yet another dragon, this time benign. Mycul nudged his friend.

"Did you see it wink?"

"What?"

"The dragon!" Their hushed conversation was interrupted by a steward.

"Her Highness, Barser de Sotto will greet you personally after dinner and before you dance," the steward said and walked down the line. "Mind, no slacking; her oubliette contains several dancers who disappointed her."

"Will Warmonger Lazlo be here?" the leader asked.

"That is none of your business. Her majesty has had men crucified for asking less."

The leader bowed and preparations were made. This allowed Mycul and Sartesh to slip away and search the castle. They each went their separate ways and planned to meet up later.

Upon reconvening, Mycul shook his head. He had found nothing concerning Stazman. Sartesh smiled and opened his hand. It was the charm from a pendant. "A trisos? So he is here!"

Sartesh held up his finger and pushed Mycul into a darkened corner. The servants passed by without noticing the men squeezed together in the recess. "No, he was brought here, then taken to Warmonger Lazlo in Karlize," Sartesh advised.

Mycul pushed him away. "They're gone now."

"Pity," Sartesh said, "I was beginning to enjoy that game."

"Yes, I could tell!" Mycul joked then realised he had said it too loudly. "So we'll have to leave as soon as it gets dark."

"No," Sartesh looked around. "These dancers go to Karlize. We must stick to our original plan. Besides anything else might alert Gorangoth. I want him on our side, not doubting us."

"And you can get better acquainted with your new friend?"

Sartesh touched the side of Mycul's cheek and smiled.

Mycul nodded and they returned to the room set aside for the dancers to prepare their performance. The choreographer was barking orders as they practised intricate moves. Mycul and Sartesh were instructed to operate the backdrops for the dances. It was a substantial frame with pulleys which rippled the cloth to make it appear more like the sea; a boat sailed through the waves using a windup mechanism.

Mycul stopped and watched the boat. He remembered the words of the Graken. "I don't suppose Karlize is a port?"

"It is, does that help?"

"Yes, it means I can speak with the Graken," Mycul said.

"Ah! The Graken. She'll be jealous when you tell her about Alleyya," Sartesh replied.

"I won't need to tell her, she can read my mind and might just feast on me instead."

"Just remember friendship and love should work two ways," Sartesh held out his hands as if expecting some comment. Mycul simply resumed his work.

After the meal, the troupe entered the great hall and Mycul and Sartesh took their positions behind the scenes. There was a speech to begin with, which afforded an opportunity for Mycul to look out at the guests of Barser de Sotto. The tall elegant woman looked familiar with her cropped black hair; she wore knee length boots decorated with silver garters that matched the silver skirt she wore over black leggings. When she smiled her ruby lips parted and Mycul saw the similarity, or perhaps it wasn't just similarity: she appeared identical to the Protector of Faires.

The first dance began. Mycul looked at Sartesh to see if he'd seen the same thing but he was sweating and operating the pulleys to create the effect. Mycul joined him in the work and Sartesh cast him a glance. The boat sailed the waves then returned laden with cargo. There was a round of applause and the troupe stood in silence before their bow.

"Encore!" Barser demanded and the company brought out the scarves as they had done last night. The rhythm built steadily towards its erotic climax. The audience sat in silence at the end. Applause when it came was slow and forced. Somehow the dancers had offended their hostess. Barser stood and gestured for her friends to lead off. Mycul fixed his eyes on her shapely legs.

"I won't tell Alleyya," Sartesh joked.

"Don't you see it?" Mycul was incredulous that Sartesh hadn't realised.

Sartesh clasped his friend on the shoulder. "They are clones and clones are created in batches of three; where is the other? We'll have to destroy them all."

"I don't think we'll have to worry, what I've got in mind will bring them to us."

"You want one big battle to save us all?"

"No, I'm going to set one against the other," Mycul said. "They each have their dreams of glory so it shouldn't be difficult."

"Jealousy amongst sisters, I hope your plan works. Something tells me they are in contact despite their bitter rivalries, using pieces of the Ornithon."

"I hope they are or we won't be able to set the seeds of doubt. One thing concerns me more and that is the Ornithon. What if it wasn't destroyed but is simply sitting at the bottom of the ocean?"

"I have news for you, Mycul, I don't believe that was the Ornithon. I think it was some outpost, a church which might be one of many connected to some central point. Why else would the cubes still work? If you'd destroyed the heart, the whole system would be dead."

Mycul placed the cube onto his hand and peered into it. The clouds lifted and a room emerged shimmering through the haze and behind the desk sat Nag- Nag Naroon. "Did you see that?"

"What? I was too busy folding ropes."

"The cube showed Nag-Nag Naroon."

Sartesh brought out two cubes, one from his dead carniver. He spun them on his hand. The voice emerged as if he stood next to them.

"Where is Gorangoth the Golden?" the male voice said before the clouds obscured the image.

"Fine and well," Sartesh replied to the fading image. He glanced at Mycul. "Are you sure Nag-Nag Naroon was killed? He looks very much alive to me." The image had been clear; both had seen it.

"I'm not certain any more. I remember what I saw at the Ornithon, it still makes me feel queasy," Mycul said.

"Well, now let's do something useful and find a way of hearing what Barser de Sotto is up to. She may also have news of Stazman."

Once the scenery was packed away, they forsook the meal provided and ventured down half lit corridors. This was not a palace with secret passageways but they discovered the servants had separate entrances to each room. Their stone stairs ended at a landing with a small table and one discreet fish eye in the door. All the rooms on the first floor were empty.

"It was a large party, they couldn't just vanish," Mycul said. He looked at the choice of three staircases ahead. "Left, right or centre?"

"I've always played left field," Sartesh joked and twisted the yellow and purple rings on his fingers. Mycul held up the green one he'd been given and smiled.

"I'll take the right," Mycul said mounting the stairs two at a time until he neared the top. He took off his shoes and silently gained the landing. Barser and her comrades were sitting round a table. There was a heated argument going on.

"I say execute him!"

"Yes, yes!" It was Barser who spoke. "That goes without saying but can he be useful first? Could he be released and persuaded to assassinate my husband?"

"With the right application of torture, I believe so, ma'am."

Mycul strained to hear what was going on. Then he felt his mouth drop open as Sartesh entered the room with a large tray of decanters and placed it on a side table. He bowed and quit the room. No one noticed him. Barser looked over at the drinks. "Who was that?"

"A servant, ma'am. You ordered the drinks for sunset."

Barser waved her hand but looked ill at ease.

"What are you doing?" A servant girl had taken the last couple of steps. She held a tray of glasses. Mycul gestured for her to put them down.

"Waiting for you," he said as he embraced the girl. "I saw you earlier. The steward said you'd be bringing the glasses."

The door opened on the loving couple.

"You're in the service of Barser de Sotto!" The man's anger subsided and he winked at Mycul before gesturing for the girl to enter. She did as instructed, but looked back at Mycul several times. He had half a mind to run away but knew such an act would raise the alarm straight away. Instead, he waited and the girl reappeared. He led her downstairs.

"I'm glad you're not with the dance troupe," she said. "Barser ordered the men killed."

"All of them?"

She nodded.

Mycul bit his lip and played the errant lover again. He saw Sartesh make it down the stairs and gestured for him to move. Eventually Mycul stopped kissing the girl.

"You should come to my room in an hour when you finish."

The girl laughed. "What sort of person do you think I am?"

"We won't find out if you don't come up and see me," Mycul said with all the charm he could muster. The woman skipped off down the corridor. Mycul felt for the gun hidden in his breast pocket. He gained confidence from knowing it was there.

The ground floor was alive with troops moving and dragging screaming men outside. Sartesh spoke from the shadows behind Mycul.

"Someone is suspicious, they've doubled the guard, so now would be a good time to think of a plan."

"You're the inventor!" Mycul looked around. "The best I can come up with is jumping from a first-floor window."

"We don't need to jump, we can use this to bring our friend." He raised the whistle and swung it on its thread, "I reckon twelve feet is tall enough to get us down safely."

"And then what?" Mycul asked.

"Run like hell!" He began trying the carved oak doors finding them bolted. The sounds of guards coming up the stairs made Sartesh desperate. He took out his gun and shot the lock; his shoulder completed the work.

Mycul blew the whistle. They opened the windows and looked down. "I'll give him thirty seconds then I'm going to jump."

"You'd never land uninjured from this height," Sartesh observed.

"Let's hope it doesn't come to that."

They both sat on the window ledge with their legs dangling. They felt the vibrations of Gorangoth striding towards them.

"Well, our spies are revealed!" Barser de Sotto stood in the doorway. "Guards!" She then sneered.

"My sisters wanted you both dead, it would be nice to send each one a head, although maybe she'd prefer some other part. I'd have a basket specially woven in the colours of Yderiphon, Sartesh Andrada."

"Which sister?" he asked.

Barser smiled. "I doubt either would lose any sleep but Ceelan expressly asked for my help."

"So even though you are raising an army against her, you'd do her this favour?"

"Indeed, I'm often misunderstood," Barser said.

"I can understand why!" Sartesh replied, "I wish you well! First you've got to catch us!"

Gorangoth lifted both men from their position. Barser ran to the window and looked out. "I'll get you both! I know what you're trying to do! I'll find you, and when I do, you're going to writhe in pain whilst you tell me how sorry you are!"

Gorangoth ran.

"Stop! Stop just beyond arrow range!" Sartesh jumped down. He watched the writhing agony of the dancers tortured by crucifixion. He took out a Mordocki revolver, aimed and shot each one of the men in turn. Guards were mounting horses when Gorangoth swept Sartesh up again. The giant ran until he gulped for air. He set them down and regained his breath.

"What did you find out?"

Sartesh straightened his clothes then said, "They're going to use Stazman Zem to assassinate Warmonger Lazlo, so Barser can become sole ruler in Menne."

"And she crucified every man in the dance troop for giving some offence," Mycul added.

Gorangoth thought about this. "Cruelty has its place in setting an example but Barser does such things for pleasure. In that I think she is not the same as Ceelan, though I wouldn't trust either." The three of them set off at a pace down the road to Karlize. Sartesh and Mycul had to run to keep up with the giant.

"Wait!" Sartesh put his ear the ground, "horses at a gallop. We must leave the road."

"What we need is a device to stop them in their tracks," Gorangoth said. He took out his sword and thrust it into the ground. The blade penetrated the rock to its hilt and caused boulders to fall. He quickly strode into the birches by the roadside and cut off slender branches. These he tossed to Sartesh and Mycul. "Whittle the ends and dig them into the ground, just by that steep bend."

The men began their work and Gorangoth took over digging the makeshift spears into the ground. He stood behind the trap waiting, sword in hand. The guards rounded the bend on a full gallop so they had no time to respond. Horses and riders were impaled on the slender stems as a screaming and writhing morass of bodies.

Gorangoth began to despatch the survivors. Mycul stayed his hand. "Save one, I want to get a message to Barser."

Gorangoth picked out the youngest and disarmed him. "There you go. Shall I play with him first?"

"No, Barser will do that when he gets to her castle." Mycul prised out several bloodstained spears and stood in front of the youth. "Tell Barser de Sotto that within a day her husband will know of her treachery."

The youth cried and begged to be freed of this errand. "You should kill me now, it would be kinder."

Sartesh whispered in Mycul's ear. Mycul nodded. He gestured the open road ahead of them.

"I've changed my mind, you are free to go. Your life should be in the gift of no one else."

The youth didn't wait to be asked again. He collected the nearest horse and spurred it onward. He stopped a little way down the road and turned. "I hope to repay your kindness one day."

Mycul shouted after him. "Then tell us your name."

"Orgin," was all they heard as he rounded the next bend at a gallop.

"You were right, Sartesh, confirming our destination would have been foolish."

"I'm not certain that letting him go wasn't equally foolish, he could now alert both Barser and Lazlo."

Gorangoth stroked his beard. "No, he'll save your life. Of that I'm certain." He erupted in laughter, "And I've never seen the Ornithon!" Gorangoth wiped his sword clean on the grass.

"Barser will already have told Warmonger Lazlo that she's uncovered a plot, it will be her gift to clear her name and one of her inner circle will be found guilty of treason and hurriedly executed. The conspiracy will be convenient."

"Being evil really does appear to be in the genes," Mycul said.

"Is it genetic or environmental?" Sartesh asked.

Mycul laughed. "Are you bringing the ethics of the Adee into play?"

"I might be, why?"

"I'm not certain their ethical code could survive thousands of years."

"Nor might it apply to cloning."

"Is that what they are? The Protector and Barser," Mycul asked.

"And Ra'an in all probability," Sartesh added.

"The question has to be, who is doing this?"

"And why?"

Gorangoth coughed. "You two are talking in riddles again."

"Fair point," Sartesh said and resumed the path downhill.

It was a long descent and the landscape opened into a wide fertile valley with a loud stream tumbling in its ravine. Sartesh looked back. The mountains loomed behind, snow-capped and menacing. Fir trees were replaced by plants that grew taller than Gorangoth. They encroached on the road making it difficult to see anything other than the next bend.

"Mutant plants," the giant said. "What were the Adee thinking when they started this?"

Mycul looked up and saw that they were walking through grasses; plants which normally might manage a foot high were now fifteen.

"And they spread. It's only the mountains which keep them out of your beloved Faires," Gorangoth said.

Sartesh cut one down and examined it more closely. The seeds were the size of his palm. "What we could do with is a really big herbivore," he joked.

The giant gave him a look and pointed at the large trunk which undulated across the road and grasped at the choice seed heads.

They walked on in silence but Sartesh kept looking back for a glimpse of the rest of the creature.

"It's the pollen," Sartesh said focussing on the path ahead. "It travels for miles and cross pollinates with similar species. That's the trouble with altering things; you start an unpredictable chain of events."

Gorangoth looked at him. "And does that science apply to us as well?"

"I believe it does. Between humans who aren't quite the humans of the Adee and the descendants of many genetic experiments. It looks random but there is a brain behind it all. For instance, faeries were adapted to replace extinct pollinators," Sartesh said then realised no one was listening. He ran to catch the giant up.

"Then how come our future is predicted by the Ornithon?" Gorangoth asked.

Sartesh thought about this. He had no answer except for the nagging suspicion that someone was trying to manipulate events for their own purpose.

"When we get to Karlize, I'm going into the city alone," Mycul said. "Sartesh can't because he's previously upset the Mordocki."

The giant looked around and raised an eyebrow.

"And you can't, Gorangoth, for the very obvious reason."

"I can and will!" he thundered. "I'll be a welcome guest at Lazlo's court, well, perhaps not welcome but tolerated and I can listen out for things. Report what I hear," he touched his nose with the very edge of his battle axe.

"And what you might say, if you drink too much!"

"There is too much at stake here for drink in that quantity."

Mycul wasn't going to argue with Gorangoth.

"I suppose I'll just hang around outside the city walls then?" Sartesh sounded hurt but then he thought about this. "Have either of you a piece of Mennedic gold?"

Gorangoth looked at him before withdrawing a ring from his beard. "I'll expect full repayment for leaving myself unkempt."

Mycul looked. There was so much gold threaded through the giant's beard he couldn't tell any difference.

"We will meet at the Inn of the Fifth Happiness on the third night," Gorangoth said and bellowed so loudly the corn around them rustled. A child tumbled onto the road, followed by a second. They both wore rags and had hollow cheeks and dull eyes. They knelt in supplication and whispered, "Food."

Gorangoth looked with pity on them. He saw their distended stomachs and ribs sticking through their skin. He passed each a thin strip of preserved beef from his pocket.

"What has happened here?" Mycul asked before unscrewing a canteen of water and letting them drink. They waited.

Eventually the girl said, "We were forced from our land to make way for a big landowner. They said they needed to get more food from the land for the invasion."

"Invasion?"

They each shook their heads, knowing no more. Gorangoth untied another gold trinket from his beard.

"Buy food," he ordered and patted each on the cheek and smiled.

Chapter 16: The Inn of the Fifth Happiness

The carnival atmosphere in the city permeated every street. The alleys were lit up with multi-coloured lanterns decorated with dragons, and vendors plied their trade from candy coloured carts: roast chestnuts, cinder toffee and baked apples. The concoction of sweet smells made Mycul feel hungry. He looked around and for a few paces walked backwards, until a burly man who threatened to draw his sword stopped him. Mycul bowed and apologised. The man stared at him and continued to do so until the crowds closed around him.

The masses were heading towards a large square in front of an imposing fort built from alternating red and white stones. From the turret, the flag of Mennes fluttered in the cool breeze. It possessed a contorted dragon.

"Water!" He heard the plea of a man and looked around, then he saw a woman hold a sponge up on a stick. The man was suspended inside a metal cage swinging from a lamp post. Mycul looked away in disgust and continued walking. All ornate lamps possessed cages within which bodies in various states of decay hung. Above the crowd vultures circled in the sky.

He tracked the woman who had shown charity. She didn't follow the crowd but struck off down an alley lined with various shops then entered a ginnel. Mycul felt his heart rate quicken. He took a breath and jumped round to see if there was an ambush.

The woman stood perfectly still. "If you have come to kill me, make it fast."

"Sorry to startle you, I just want information," Mycul said.

"You're not Mennedic."

"I come from Vold Nujun in the borderlands."

"What sort of information do you want?" the woman asked.

"The sort which could get both you and I hanging from one of those cages, if I'm not mistaken."

The woman pulled Mycul down the alleyway and unlocked a door. This opened onto a large courtyard replete with fruit trees and bushes. They entered a room that served as kitchen and dining area. The walls were hung with tapestries depicting the acts of kings and all gloriously stitched with purple and yellow flourishes.

"You believe in Yderiphon," Mycul remarked.

"Sh! You talk too loudly," the woman looked around the room. "That man in the cage is my husband. He was sentenced to hang and starve three days ago. His crime? A child said he spoke sedition about Warmonger Lazlo."

"And did he?" Mycul looked the woman in the eye.

"No, I was guilty of that," she said. The kitchen was basic but possessed pine surfaces all scrubbed clean. The woman poured hot tea into a cup and passed it to Mycul.

He looked at her round face and dark skin. Her eyes were warm like chalcedony.

"I followed you. I've been here three days and got no closer to finding out who the opposition to Warmonger Lazlo is."

"Well you've found one member."

"At last! My name is Mycul Zas."

"I am Meerla Melu and you are welcome here but I don't know how I can help you."

"Us. I'll ask my friends to visit."

"You'd better ask them to stay until after the curfew is lifted. And a word of advice, it's best for foreigners not to sign in to Inns, they can disappear." The woman ran a cloth across two plates and placed a quantity of cakes before him. Mycul smiled and ate them all. "You've been a long time on the road."

Mycul nodded and wiped his mouth. "We've come here to rescue one of our friends from the castle in the square."

The woman laughed. "You'd need a giant and a fool to get in there!"

Mycul wondered how Sartesh would react to being so described but he decided to trust the woman. "I have both in my friends, Gorangoth the Golden and Sartesh."

The woman looked at him and sat down opposite the visitor. "And who are you rescuing?"

Mycul thought about saying nothing but he had already given too much away. "Stazman Zem," he said.

The woman took a deep breath and cupped her long delicate fingers over her lips. She breathed out through them. "If only my husband were here. He used to work as a palace guard and knows the place intimately."

"Then Meerla, you'd better meet us at the Inn of the Fifth Happiness at dawn tomorrow."

"Are you going to rescue him? It isn't possible, I hardly dare believe," she managed to say before tears welled up and flowed down her cheeks.

"Ok, perhaps I should deliver rather than just promise," Mycul said and left the house. He retraced his steps through the courtyard garden and out into the narrow street.

Soon he rejoined the mêlée of people. He could just make out a military parade and heard the marching band play with its incessant beat of drums. The crowd were intent on watching the events but Mycul walked away from the scene and passed Meerla's husband hanging in his cage. The device swung gently.

There appeared to be no guards on the gate and the way was open, so Mycul slipped out of the city and took the road towards the Inn of the Fifth Happiness. The fields here had been ploughed ready for the spring sowing. Giant grasses had been cut down, and their stems burnt at the wayside. One or two bonfires still smouldered.

The Inn was about three miles from the city walls and had a large chestnut tree growing through the centre of its ramshackle buildings. The outside belied the inside, which was richly painted in burgundy, and a large dining room possessed an ornate brick fireplace with a fire roaring in its grate. Mycul sat at a table and immediately a barman came up to him. "Have you come a long way?"

"From Bretan," Mycul lied.

"You'll know your compatriot then," the man took out a pad and pencil. "What would you like?"

"A pint of your best ale and steak pie."

"Three shillings please," the man said and continued writing. He tore off a slip, placed it in front of Mycul and walked away. "Steak pie with all the trimmings," he shouted through a serving hatch then went behind the bar and pulled a pint of ale.

Mycul toyed with the paper then turned it over and looked around: *Sartesh was captured by Warmonger Lazlo yesterday. Take care: there is an informer here.*

The barman brought over the tankard of ale. He waited with his hand held out. Mycul passed several coins over. The barman spat.

"Faires coin, hardly worth the gold it's made from, but beggars can't be…" He placed it in his pocket.

The samy young man brought over the steak pie, potatoes and change. As he placed the food on the table he muttered, "They took Sartesh last night. He didn't argue, he said he'd be in good company in Lazlo's jail, a remark which earned him a beating."

"Could you give me a piece of parchment,a pen and some salt," Mycul said in a loud voice.

The barman brought all the items over and smiled. "I wish you every success with Gorangoth the Golden." He spat on the floor and walked back to his duties.

Mycul ate the meal and then cleared a space before composing a note for Gorangoth. When the barman returned, he asked, "Can I trust you with this?"

The barman smiled, "You could trust me with your life. Come to think of it, you have!" The man bent closer and added, "I won't rest until Sension is King of Mennes."

Mycul pulled the man down to an uncomfortable angle. "I expect discount, that pie was nothing but gristle!"

"You Bretans wouldn't know meat if you sucked on it!" the barman rejoined, playing the game. "Get out," he whispered, "now, whilst you still can."

Mycul realised his only chance to save both Sartesh and Stazman was the giant. First, he needed Gorangoth's strength to save a man's life.

Mycul walked out of the inn and took a lesser path towards the city. Mounted guards rode up to the inn, half-heartedly looked around and and finding nothing, returned the same way. Mycul realised he would have to go in disguise. He wondered how he might barter for clothes and surmised the giant's name was enough to persuade disaffected Menneans.

The path took Mycul over a turgid stream where algae grew across the surface. He pushed his hand under and withdrew a few drops of water which he used to cool his cheeks.

Later he passed a ramshackle farmhouse. A dog barked from the safety of a shady corner. Mycul ignore the dog until he heard a gruff voice growl, "We don't like strangers here."

"What happened to the famed Mennedic hospitality?"

"It died with the last king," the farmer said, leaning against a spade. He stared at the traveller. "Why aren't you using the main road?"

Mycul smiled, "Because I don't want to be arrested by Barser and Lazlo's troops."

"Got something against you, have they?"

Mycul placed his hand over the gun he'd been given. "Yes, I'm going to rescue the Prince of Catherine from the warmonger's dungeon."

The farmer laughed and slapped Mycul across the back. "Well you'll have time to share a quart of ale with me first."

Mycul agreed to one beer. "I won't be able to rescue my friend if I'm drunk!"

"You're not Mennedic," the farmer said as they sat at opposite sides of a scrubbed oak table. A fire burnt low in the grate and a cauldron of vegetable stew sent aromas in to the room.

"No I'm from Vold Nujun. I'm meeting Gorangoth the Golden in Karlize."

The farmer drank, all the while his eyes fixed on his guest.

"Do you know what might give me the edge? A Mennedic warrior uniform."

The farmer squinted and drank some more. "You haven't the build for it."

Mycul realised the farmer was right.

"My son used to work at the castle as a server. He's been conscripted. Everyone of age has been taken and trained for the Great War against Faires."

"Which war against Faires?"

"You haven't heard? We have got rid of Kings so tyrants can fight each other."

"Sisterly love," Mycul said.

"I don't follow." The farmer banged his tankard down and wiped foam from his mouth.

"Barser de Sotto is the sister of Ceelan, the Protector of Faires."

"So it has come to that! Still only one will be left to create Yderiphon."

"I very much doubt that Barser or Ceelan has the Yderiphon from legend in mind, but something more evil."

"They are both mutant."

Mycul smiled before drinking some ale. The farmer went to a cupboard and produced a blue and yellow liveried outfit. It smelt of lavender. "You must promise to bring it back."

"I'll leave my own clothes as down payment, if that's agreeable."

The farmer nodded.

The servers outfit fitted reasonably well: the sleeves were a little short but Mycul hitched them up to avoid this being noticed. Finally he placed the gun in a large pocket.

"We have become a nation in thrall to our children and when they grow up, they are taken away to train for battle. How many will come back to tend their ancestral farms?"

Mycul squeezed the man's shoulder. "I'm very grateful. I know how much these mean, so I'll return them as soon as possible," he said then walked out into the afternoon sunshine and squinted. He felt light headed from the drink. He waved and strode off down the lane towards the dark towers of Karlize.

The sound of singing could be heard from a great distance away. Mycul was grateful that the gates to the city stood open and so he passed through without being challenged. "Server!"

Mycul stopped and turned around.

"You should already be at the castle." The captain of the guard approached him. "Have you been skiving?"

"Me, sir?" Mycul sighed, trying his best at the accent. "It's like this sir, there's a girl…" Mycul pointed.

The guard laughed.

"I wondered why you looked flushed!" He slapped the lad on the back and walked back to the gatehouse. Mycul continued on his way.

The singing grew louder as he neared the main square. Thousands of voices joined in with *Zhedhelion barkbada uita,* the anthem of Yderiphon. He stood in the crowd and slowly worked his way to the front.

He watched as young men also dressed as servers walked in and out of the gate carrying loaves of bread and ale for the feast. He joined them and did several trips carrying the heavy unleavened bread but on the third return, he slipped into the shadows of the palace and watched.

He established were he was within the palace. Servers were taking materials throughout the building and so he joined one and struck up the conversation. "Have you seen the giant?" Mycul asked.

"Gorangoth, yes. He's asleep in the great hall. They've been trying to wake him for an hour now."

"Thanks!" Mycul returned down the stairs and entered the Great Hall. It was littered with the debris from a good party the night before.

"Thank goodness you're here," the steward handed Mycul a brush and gestured the stone floor.

Mycul began sweeping and took his route closer to the giant. Just as he was passing by he took the handle and jabbed it in the giant's privates. Gorangoth opened his eyes. He let out a gasp of pain then roared. "Who disturbed my sleep?" He banged his fists on the table as servants scattered and found the nearest door.

Mycul jumped up on the table. "I did!"

The giant rubbed his genitals. "Why I should…" he lifted Mycul down from the table and laid him on the floor. "I should crush you with one foot!" He roared. Mycul shook with fear but was mollified when the giant winked.

"Sartesh is captured and is here in the dungeon. However, before we rescue him, I need you to save a man incarcerated in a gibbet. He was a palace guard."

Gorangoth stroked his beard.

"He hangs from a lamppost nearby." Mycul drew a plan in the dust and crumbs on the table. "As far as I can tell, he is the only one alive, on the avenue towards the south gate."

"The one we came in on? And where shall I take him?"

"The Inn of the Fifth Happiness but trust no one there except the barman."

"I'll have to be fast, the Warmonger expects me at the Festival of Yderiphon tomorrow."

"Then tomorrow's today and last night must have sated your thirst!"

"You talk in riddles which hurt my head young Mycul."

"Just remember that Yderiphon can't be achieved by force, Gorangoth, and that's what Barser and her husband are planning, an invasion of Faires! Yderiphon was about freedom and equality under a purple flag with a yellow z."

"I'd be lying if I said I didn't know. Emissaries came a few weeks ago to ask for safe passage across the pass."

"Did you allow them?"

"My mission is to keep enemies out of Mennes. I had no grounds to refuse."

Mycul thought about the number of days it might take to get an army into Faires.

"There's to be a big speech at the festival," the giant continued. "Lazlo and Barser will stand together as the troops file out of the gate and march on Faires."

"But it's winter and your pass is closed."

"I fear that I am out of a job there. They will take great fire breathing cannon to melt the ice and snow and men will dig what cannot be melted."

"The surprise will be absolute. They'll overrun the whole country."

"Possibly, but there are your friends, and the opposition here. If we release Stazman and get him to Catherine in time," Gorangoth sounded hopeful.

"We could remove Catherine's troops from Lazlo's command. It might weaken his forces," Mycul said. He hit his fist in his open palm then bit on a knuckle as he thought. "We need an airplane."

Gorangoth looked perplexed.

"A flying carriage. An airship..."

151

"Or a Graken," Gorangoth suggested. "They've been known to swim the River Umbre."

"That's it! I'll take Stazman to Catherine and leave Sartesh here to meet with any opposition and start a revolt."

Mycul realised he had been getting excited and might have spoken too loudly. He looked around. He could see no one else. They had been alone since the giant had awoken. "As soon as it's dark, we start."

Mycul worked in the castle for another few hours, sweeping and taking messages. He understood the geography of the castle better after his shift but he had heard nothing about prisoners in the dungeon. A bell sounded at dusk and staff filed into a large hall for soup and bread. Mycul was surprised by how quiet everyone was.

"You're new here," a girl said.

"Yes, my first day. I signed on for the feast."

The girl looked him up and down. "You must be very poor; your uniform is so old it shows the king's crest, not the warmonger's."

Mycul looked down. He felt a wave of panic and took a deep breath. He forced a smile. "I hadn't realised when it was offered. I'll change it tonight."

"Do, or you'll getting a whipping, not a salary tomorrow."

It had been a foolish oversight and it knocked Mycul's confidence. He sought a quiet corner on his own to eat and gratefully broke the bread into the vegetable soup.

The doors burst open and a group of guards entered. Mycul recognised them as Mordocki. Their arms were tattooed with intricate runes like the ones on Sartesh's revolvers. Their tight black trousers revealed their shaved bodies and tattoos, just as Sartesh had effected in disguise. If anything, they stood even more proud. Mycul tried concentrating on his food. They were looking for someone. All the other servants were staring at the dark-skinned warriors. Mycul felt his hand stray towards the gun, but pulled it back in time. One warrior approached.

"Carrssne'ak, drame'ak hro."

Mycul had no knowledge of their language. The man repeated the phrase, only this time his face was right up against Mycul's. He saw his filed teeth and smelt the blood on his breath. The warrior lifted Mycul from his seat. "You are a spy!" He flung the youth to the floor.

Mycul had no time to pull out the gun as other warriors ran toward Mycul, and pinioned him. Their strength was tremendous. Two held his arms and another his legs as a fourth produced a knife. "I am going to start skinning you alive unless you reveal all, spy."

Mycul examined those holding him. One he realised was a woman. "This place isn't safe for you anymore!" she said.

"What vermin have we got here?" Gorangoth asked. "Skin the beast. Let's hear his screams," Gorangoth said and passed over a curved blade to the Mordocki. He started walking away. "Wait, is this the spy Warmonger Lazlo asked us to search for?"

"I believe so, Gorangoth," the lead warrior said. He stood and talked with the giant. He looked back a couple of times, the expression on his face changing from anticipation to resignation. "Warmonger Lazlo has ordered the youth detained with the others in the dungeon."

The giant took hold of Mycul and with a single blow knocked him out before trussing him over his shoulder.

"I will take this spy to the dungeons for our leader's pleasure. Do not worry, you will hear his death agonies soon, my friends."

One warrior squared up to Gorangoth. His tattoo of a dragon took up the whole of his torso and its tail vanished into the line of his trousers.

"Let us play with him first?" The man took out a blade so thin it was flexible.

"Warmonger Lazlo will want to do that himself. Didn't you see the badge, this man is a royalist. And you know how our leader likes to deal with them!"

The Mordocki warrior stood aside. "I never know which order is best, crucifixion, skinning, quartering, the triple death… I believe there are ways of keeping prisoners alive throughout the ordeal," he said.

"I know you are right, I have employed them in my own castle. You must have seen the skins of my enemies dyed and fluttering from the battlements?"

The warrior lost confidence and let Gorangoth past. The giant descended the spiral staircase with his load. Mycul groaned as they went from daylight to torchlight.

Ahead a large metallic door loomed. It was embossed with the instruments of torture held within and the chilling legend: *Your body is mine to finish* engraved over the arch. Gorangoth banged on the door once. The bell like sound reverberated before a central wheel turned left then right before the doors swung open. Gorangoth almost bent double and entered the large chamber.

Mycul groaned once more and his vision slowly came into focus. What he saw repulsed him. The walls were lined with cages but Sartesh was tied to a table in the centre of the room. Bruises of various colours extended over his body. He looked again and saw Stazman pinioned to the wall with a cruel spiked gag strapped over his head.

Gorangoth put Mycul down.

"Treat him gently, no marks. Lazlo wants him personally."

The jailer bowed and Gorangoth placed Mycul in a cell, turning the key and handing it to the jailer. The great door closed with a loud finality, which echoed into silence.

From this vantage point Mycul could observe everything going on in the circular room. He rubbed the side of his head, which felt tender and swollen. He wondered if he could trust the giant. Mycul panicked, feeling his pockets for the revolver. He felt the outline and counted the bullets through the cotton of his tunic. There were three remaining. He could easily kill the guards but there were no prisoners free to remove the keys.

He sat and looked at Sartesh who stared back and shook his head as if he was reading his thoughts. The table he was laying on possessed a mechanism bristling with knives.

The guard ran his whip along the bars. "Never make an enemy of Warmonger Lazlo." Mycul said nothing. The guard flicked the whip over a nearby prisoner. "Talk to me or feel pain, scum!"

"What would you like to hear?"

"A story," the guard said and pulled up a stool.

Mycul felt his pockets but realised he had left Nag-Nag's cubes at the farmer's house, with his clothes. "I'll tell you about the destruction of the Ornithon," Mycul said and began weaving the tale. Mycul's voice got quieter.

"I can't hear you," the guard said, cracking his whip.

"I need water," Mycul pleaded.

The guard stood and went over to a cistern. "It's not the cleanest but you won't be worrying about catching anything," the guard laughed.

Mycul had his back to the cell door.

"Here, you ungrateful swine!" The man's hand hovered through the bars. Mycul turned and shot the man through the head. He slipped to the ground, gargling and cursing from a growing pool of blood. Mycul collected the keys and fiddled with the lock.

Other guards had been alerted. He shot one in the leg. A third escaped towards the door. The shot echoed round the room. Mycul gained his freedom and bounded across the chamber. He brandished the gun at the one remaining guard and beckoned him back into the centre.

"Lower the platform and release Sartesh," Mycul ordered. The guard did as Mycul commanded then released the ropes with a knife. Mycul watched every move. Sartesh rolled over and sighed.

"Now release Prince Stazman."

"Prince Stazman. There are no royals left."

"Think again. This man is Prince of Catherine."

"Only one left to kill then. Never leave a job unfinished." The guard plucked a knife from the mechanism, and drew back to throw. A trisos landed in the man's skull. Its spikes flooded with blood. Sartesh, exhausted by the effort, lay back. The guard slowly fell to the floor and weakened as more blood erupted from the wound.

Mycul lowered the platform Stazman was attached to and unlocked the gag. They embraced. Stazman stretched and moved his arms and legs. "I'm grateful. I didn't think I'd ever get down from there."

Mycul returned to Sartesh. "You never disappoint, do you? I won't ask where you got it from."

Sartesh smiled. "Don't. But you're becoming a hard act to follow, Mycul."

Mycul supported his friend and Stazman brought over water. He drank deeply. Sartesh ran his fingers through Mycul's jet black hair.

"Thanks."

Stazman and Mycul lifted him to his feet and Sartesh took a few steps. He beckoned for them to leave him standing.

Stazman looked around the bodies and picked one of similar stature to Sartesh. He undressed him and passed over the clothes.

"No matter how much pain you are in, we have a lot to do tonight. There are others to rescue," Mycul said.

Sartesh nodded and gingerly dressed with Mycul's help. He then sat in a chair.

"How would you prove to the troops here that you are Prince of Catherine?"

"Prove it?" Stazman thought about this. "My father had a seal he used on all official documents and a crown made from finest gold and fashioned into oak leaves and acorns."

"Are they still in Catherine?"

"I haven't been there for many years. I would guess they would remain where Barser needs them to rule the kingdom."

"Then we go to Catherine tonight and must be back here by dawn for you to declare yourself and remove your troops from the invasion force."

"To Catherine and back by dawn?" Stazman was incredulous.

"I do not have my aeroplane," Sartesh said.

"No, but I have the Graken."

"Then we must try." As Mycul and Stazman made for the door, Sartesh stayed and prised open a cupboard. From it, he removed his belongings and another gun.

Mycul began twisting the wheel in the centre of the door. He tried left then right, then scratched his head and did the reverse. The door unlocked. Ahead the stairs swept upward in a great spiral.

"Go!" Sartesh shouted. "Don't worry about me, I'm going to be emperor here, even your Graken knows that."

"Meet us at the Inn of the Fifth Happiness before noon."

"I'll have had time to enjoy the other four by then," Sartesh joked.

Mycul saluted. He and Stazman ran up the stairs and out of sight. Sartesh turned and sat down on a step. His head lolled into his hands and he wiped away a tear before standing. Finally he took a swig of Calufras before slowly ascending the stairs.

Chapter 17: The Return of the Prince

Many of the inhabitants of Mennes were drunk, dancing or both. Mycul and Stazman were easily able to gain the safety of the square. Mycul looked back at the palace with unease.

"Sartesh will be fine," Stazman said. "He's a remarkable person," he continued, "though I don't know how he endured his torture."

"He plays the fool but don't be fooled by him."

"Also," Stazman smiled, "and I know you'll hate this but he loves you."

Mycul raised an eyebrow and didn't bother replying to something he'd suspected for a long time. "I'm assuming downhill to the port." He stood at the top of a narrow street with numerous cobbled steps. He placed his fingers on his shoulder where the marks of the Graken remained. He thought out his message and was taken aback by the strength of the answer. *I felt your presence getting closer to water and so I came because as you are bound to me, I am bound to you,* the Graken said.

"She is here and waiting!" The two of them ran down long cobbled alleys in which their footfall echoed. The passage became dark and menacing before an archway revealed sailing ships in the port. Mycul tapped Stazman on the shoulder and they made for a long jetty. Before they had reached the end, the Graken surfaced. Her skin shone silver and her head tossed back to emit a loud wail. She gnashed her teeth before placing her head low down.

You will have to ride without a saddle, she said.

"I'm sure you'll look after us," Mycul replied. Her head now touched the jetty and they climbed behind her horns. Stazman sat in front of Mycul and Mycul clung on to the creature's horns. The Graken plunged through the river. Stazman hung on grimly, ocassionally Mycul heard him curse at his discomfort but he held him in place, and spoke directly with his Graken.

We must get to Catherine and back by dawn. Can you swim that quickly?

There and back by the time the sun rises above the horizon. But it leaves you an hour at most to collect those trinkets.

The crown and seal of Catherine might be trinkets but they are the symbols of power which Stazman must use to stop the invasion. Besides, there is someone special who needs our aid.

157

You think of Alleyya in your dreams and in your waking. It's a good job Sartesh used the potion of forgetting on you.

Did he?

It was something he and Alleyya agreed, for your safety.

I thought I didn't love sufficiently.

No, Mycul Zas, you love well enough for a human, yet there are many who love you, although you spurn them.

I can only love Alleyya. There is some chemistry that binds us. I can see her now, her slender shoulders, her graceful thighs and the intricate pattern round the hem of her dress.

I see the image you create perfectly. She is a woman of rare beauty but you have been beguiled.

Probably but she is beautiful. Mycul was elated. He forgot himself and punched Stazman on the arm.

"Mycul, I've enough bruises from the dungeon!" He shifted forwards and held onto the Graken's horns again.

The Graken sounded sad. *I cannot take you to her. She is bound by the land and to the land all humans return, except you Mycul.* The creature slowed as the river became more meandering. Ahead Mycul could make out lights in various buildings and braziers of glowing coals atop watch towers.

Stazman turned and grinned.

"That's my home, that's the city I've not seen since I was twelve! It's too dark to make out the beautiful white turrets and the central mountain flattened by the Adee millennia ago and now a park full of rare trees. I tell you Catherine is a beautiful place but cold."

That worries me, the Graken said, *I cannot move by frozen water and the ice comes, I feel it at the edges of the bank. We must be fast,* she continued as she drew down her neck and let the men disembark.

"We will return promptly," Mycul said and bowed before turning and running off into the night following Stazman.

The gates to the city were closed. Stazman pulled Mycul round the base of a tower and waited in the shadows. The nearest windows were some twenty feet above them. Stazman moved out and threw a stone at the glass. It hit. He repeated this. A window opened and an elderly man appeared.

"Throw down the ladder, Inchon," Stazman ordered.

The old man leaned out further and peered into the darkness. "Are you Barser de Sotto's spies?"

"You'd better watch your mouth if you want to get any older. Throw down the ladder, it is I, Stazman Zem."

"How could that be true? He died six or seven years ago," the old man said as he peered into the darkness.

"I'll pull your beard if you don't throw down the ladder now."

Stazman's order worked. The rope ladder descended and Stazman climbed quickly. Half way up he turned and saluted Mycul, who followed.

By the time he climbed over the stone sill, the old man was on his knees and weeping. Stazman helped him back to his feet. "Your brothers are dead, Stazman. One poisoned, one garrotted and, well, the final body was never found. Your mother has kept faith, all these long years she's hoped."

"My mother?"

"Yes, she's been permitted to live. She has the second tallest tower, near the park. On fine days you might see her gardening or walking through the trees, no one knows her, it's been so long…" The old man didn't finish his sentence.

"We have very little time, Stazman," Mycul reminded him.

Stazman looked undecided. He took a deep breath, "Take us to her tower."

The old man put on a cloak and the group went out into the street. They followed a wide avenue upwards. It wound round the base of white towers until the cobbles were strewn with the remains of leaves blown into corners and left to rot.

"Here," the old man said. He knocked five times. "Visitors for Irana Zem."

The guard drew back the peephole. "The lady does not receive visitors," he said.

"On whose order?" Inchon asked.

"Whose order dictates everything in Catherine? The lady who must be obeyed."

"I am Irana's only surviving son," Stazman said moving into the light.

The guard sneered with contempt. "Do you know how many times I've heard that line? They've all visited the lady and then been executed. Go home boy, and keep your head."

"I cannot keep what is not mine but Catherine's."

The guard hesitated at this answer. "No, it's impossible," the guard said.

"Let me be the judge of that." The woman stood behind the guard. The guard bowed and opened the door. Stazman bounded past the guard shouting.

"Mother? Mother!" He embraced and kissed her.

Irana Zem suffered him a moment then pushed him away. Her scrutiny was severe but eventually her head shook and tears poured down her cheeks. Mycul noticed she was wearing black lace over a long black dress which revealed the contours of her body. Her face was lined with age and anguish. "Another imposter courtesy of Barser de Sotto?" Her voice waivered with confusion.

"I am Stazman," the youth said, also with tears in his eyes.

"How can you prove it?" The woman asked.

"I cannot," Stazman said with regret.

"Do not doubt him, lady. I rescued him from the Reach of Key and the dungeon of Warmonger Lazlo in Karlize."

"Who are you?"

"I am Mycul Zas," he said and bowed. "I saw Stazman in the images of the Ornithon. It is definitely the man you see here."

"The Ornithon? I have waited seven years for this moment. I thought I was deluding myself by keeping hope alive," she said and embraced her son.

Mycul looked around the room and wandered over to the window. He thought he saw the Graken move in the river.

"Lady, we need the seal of Catherine and the crown. Stazman must appear before his troops in Karlize at dawn or our plan is lost."

"Karlize by dawn, what magic is this?"

"I am a Graken rider, lady. The creature waits in the river but we must hurry. If the soldiers of Catherine march on Faires at dawn then we will have lost everything."

Irana took a key from the hem of her skirt and rolled back the rug. She inserted the key and opened a door, which revealed a strong box.

"This contains all you need."

She handed the container to Stazman. He opened it and his face lit up as the crown was withdrawn. The gold shimmered and the leaves and acorns nodded as though there was a slight breeze. Underneath was the seal. Stazman gently placed them back in the box. "You must come with us," he said. "The change of air will do you good."

"And ride a Graken?"

"That we must do to get back to Karlize by dawn," Mycul said.

"I'll slow you down," the lady warned.

"But the troops will know you much better than I and your acceptance of me will help win them over. Any fool can wear a crown but only a Prince commands authority. So yes, I think you being there will help. You'll be safe when the people realise that Barser de Sotto has been overthrown in Catherine."

Irana laughed, "We'll only be safe when Barser and her sister are dead."

"On that we can all agree," Mycul said.

They led Irana through the streets, her guard following, ever cautious, and preventing anyone from getting close. Finally, they crossed the fields to the river.

"We must swim quickly, my friend," Mycul shouted at his Graken and helped Irana to sit behind Cyrene's horns. Stazman and Mycul crowded in behind her.

Do not worry Mycul, the tide is with us and we'll reach Karlize by dawn! The Graken set off, gracefully paddling downstream and trying not to jerk her head. *I have never carried royalty before.*

"Aren't all people made equal?" Mycul asked. The Graken did not reply.

Mycul did not realise he had spoken out loud, so he was surprised when Stazman spoke. "No. We are not all equal, some of us have titles which place us higher than our peers."

Mycul was dumb-founded. "How can you say such a thing?" He felt as though he couldn't swallow and had to force himself to breathe deeply. He had a moment of doubt but it was too late, he had cast the die. Within the hour Stazman would be Prince of Catherine or he would be dead.

He hoped the people of Catherine weren't having one tyrant replaced by a youthful pretender to the title. His instinct was to stop the Graken and prevent Stazman but too much depended on this course of action. He remembered his own death by Stazman's sword.

No good can come from this, he thought.

How can we know the consequences of our actions? Perhaps some we can predict with greater accuracy than others but we cannot truly know, the Graken said.

"Then why destroy the Ornithon?" Mycul asked his Graken.

Because it is being manipulated by someone for their own ends.

Is? I thought we destroyed it?

So did I at first, but it appears the place you went to was just an outpost? The central section is far away and beyond my powers of thought to reach.

Sartesh believes the same as you. Mycul bit his lip. He was concerned about leaving his friend in Karlize. Mycul looked into the distance for a sign of the city.

The Graken almost purred. *Do not worry about Sartesh Andrada. Even when you think all is lost, he'll return. Sartesh is the future king and in his service you will be the greatest Admiral in all Yderiphon.*

Yderiphon. How do you know all this with such certainty?

161

To a human like you, time is linear. To a human like me time has all the contours of a mountain and greater beauty.

You cannot be human?

Is to be human possessed only in how we look?

But if you are that would mean you are a genetic experiment as well, Mycul said. Slowly the idea took hold.

Indeed, we all are created for a purpose.

You aren't going to get religious on me are you?

The Graken laughed. *Mycul Zas. The purpose of any living thing is to reproduce. To pass on the genes whether naturally or unnaturally acquired.* The Graken swam into Karlize just as the first rays of light broke across the horizon. She lowered her neck and allowed the passengers to disembark.

Goodbye and thanks, Mycul said.

Soon, young Mycul, the sea will welcome you, Cyrene queen of the Graken said. She swam out into the estuary, turned and howled at the land so that people opened shutters to see her glide away and submerge.

Horses were waiting and a figure cloaked in grey sat in the saddle of the third. Sartesh slipped the stirrups and slid off as Mycul ran up and embraced him with, "I'm so pleased to see you."

"So am I," said Sartesh. "I failed to count properly, who is the lady?"

"Irana Zem."

"Will she help us?"

"She will help her son," Mycul whispered.

"I'm not certain that's the same thing," Sartesh muttered back, then announced, "I am honoured." He introduced himself. He swung up on the horse then spurred her to a trot before kicking her flanks to a canter. The others followed, with Irana mounted behind her son.

There was a great clamour within the city and many people and troops were preparing and getting into formation. The contingent from Catherine lined the side streets leading up from the square. The heads of the cavalry almost touched bay windows jutting out into every street.

"Take me to your general," Sartesh ordered.

"We are busy," the decumen replied.

"You'll be dead if you don't take me to the general." Sartesh was in no mood for delay. The man looked up at the travellers; he seemed to recognise the woman and gave a slight bow. He walked up past the troops as the group followed on horseback. The shops were beginning to open, spilling the perfumes from their wares.

"General, you have guests," the decumen announced as he saluted a man sitting at a campaign desk.. He returned the way he had come.

"My lady Irana, what brings you here?" The gen stood and bowed.

"Palacre-gen, may I introduce my son, Prince Stazman of Catherine," Irana stated with authority. Stazman dismounted and strode up to the general.

"I thought he was lost," Palacre said, stunned.

"I was lost, but thanks to Mycul Zas, I am found and returned to my birthright, though I realise my older brothers would have had a greater claim, had they lived."

Palacre-gen thought about the consequences of seeing this young man. "Survival gives you the greater right. Do you fight with us?"

"No, we are not going to fight Faires. Let sister kill sister. We have a more noble battle ahead. We will be a free people and start Yderiphon," Stazman said.

Mycul felt the hairs on the back of his neck bristle; the word conjured up so many possibilities.

"Yderiphon?" the gen asked. "So you will have us fight Barser de Sotto and Lazlo at one go?"

"Yes but not here, not now. We will withdraw and return to Catherine. It is time a Zem sat on the throne, it's too long since my father was butchered."

The gen allowed himself to smile. "She will kill you of course."

"She will try, no doubt, but not until she has defeated her sister. We will tackle the victor, who will be tired and much reduced."

"Battle-hardened and buoyed by victory is also a possibility," Palacre said.

"The important thing, Palacre-gen, is will you abandon this battle as a serf of Lazlo? For one in which we will, however briefly, be the free people of Catherine?"

Irana stared at the gen and tried to read what was going on in his mind. "We have been friends and allies for twenty-five years and even after my husband was killed you stood by me."

"I've seen the tragedy of your sons. Is this one greater?"

"Lesser in stature and greater in his friends," she said with cunning.

"Then we will leave by the southern gate before heading off west toward our beloved country."

"I will prepare a letter for Warmonger Lazlo," Stazman said. "I have the seal and the crown."

"When we get to the Inn of the Fifth Happiness, you can address your subjects and hear their reaction. I do not know whether Barser and Lazlo will let us go without a fight but our troops are almost equal in numbers." Palacre-gen withdrew his sword, bowed, and held it out to Stazman.

As if by instinct or some distant memory, Stazman lifted the sword and bringing it down on Palacre-gen's shoulder said, "Arise Lord of Catherine, first of the gen, Palacre Iron Fist, Palacre the Counsellor."

"The troops have little will for the fight in Faires and it would only take a good speech to win them over. They'll be glad to go home. However, you must assure them you are equal to the task of removing Barser De Sotto," Palacre said, leaping onto his horse. He then turned to the troops and began issuing orders.

Stazman looked pale as though the enormity of the task had dawned on him. He turned toward his horse, but mother leant down and whispered something. Stazman straightened, and pivoted back to the gen. "Palacre-gen, do you have a horse appropriate for my mother?"

He whistled and barked orders to a decumen. The man returned with a dappled grey pony, saddled and ready. The gen helped Irana down from her horse and even gave her a boot up onto her new mount. Stazman mounted his horse.

"We will follow you, Prince Stazman," Mycul said putting his doubts to one side and allowing himself a moment of pride. His friend was installed as prince and now they stood a chance of being successful against Lazlo and his wife. "I will follow you all the way back to Alleyya."

"Alleyya?"

"The love of my life, the Necromancer's daughter, she is so beautiful," Mycul said, and saw the expression on Stazman's face change.

"Once we are in possession of Catherine, we might consider supporting another state."

Irana trotted to Mycul's side and smiled. "It is the first lesson I ever taught him. Always give the appearance of saying *yes* without actually doing so."

Mycul fell back and his horse shook out its mane. Sartesh joined him, and Mycul peered pointedly at him. "You've made a remarkable recovery."

"A good bath and a draft of arnica laced with morphine."

"I won't ask."

"No, don't, then I won't have to lie," Sartesh said and placed an arm on Mycul's near shoulder. "I'm made of sterner stuff than you might think and my friendship is not conditional, unlike some."

Mycul nodded. He held up the emerald ring Sartesh had given him. Sartesh showed him the purple and yellow of his own. "Are you up to a battle?" Mycul asked.

"I am. I feel we might have support from some sections of Mennes."

"You mean you contacted the opposition?" Mycul was impressed.

"I mean they contacted me. There are many who hate Lazlo and still more who despise Barser but more importantly, they share a vision of Yderiphon. Zhedhelion barkbarda uita!"

The soldiers nearby repeated the expression, and then those further away picked it up in greater numbers. Soon the whole army of Catherine marched and repeated *Zhedhelion barkbada uita!*

Sartesh and Mycul smiled but when Stazman turned they saw his face was clenched in anger. He spurred his horse forward and quickened the marching pace, his mother following him. The flags were unfurled as they passed through the gateway: the white flag of Catherine with its oak tree rising through a crown, and the purple flag of Yderiphon with its yellow Z reversed.

The column headed down the road. Various outriders delivered messages and Palacre-gen received a rolled parchment. He read it and passed this over to Stazman, who read it and turned to Mycul.

"The gen is summoned to a command meeting and celebrations. Lazlo expects a reply, we will have to act now."

"You are the prince," Mycul said.

"But you are my friend, my rescuer. Can you not think of a plan?"

Mycul shrugged his shoulders, and Sartesh came to his rescue. "Send out an order to surround the inn. The ground is a little higher than the encompassing fields and with a low winter sun rising behind the mountains, those approaching will have the sun in their eyes."

Stazman looked at Sartesh, "What gives you the right to tell me what to do?"

Sartesh for a moment flashed anger in his eyes but he maintained equilibrium. "Everyone has a future. I'd like yours to be outliving this day," he said.

Stazman consulted with his mother, then Palacre-gen, before ordering a decumen to inform all cohorts of the plan. The column bore right, leaving the main swathe of troops marching into the distance. Outriders kicked their horses into action and galloped down the line.

The soldiers of Catherine approached the Inn and surrounded it. Palacre-gen positioned the various sections. They all waited. The dust from thousands of feet and hooves settled. The smells of latrines lingered as people took advantage of the lull in marching.

Further dust was kicked into the sky when fifty cavalry swung up the hill. Mycul recognised the lead rider as Barser and the bearded man behind was finely dressed in midnight blue silks over his armour. "Warmonger Lazlo," Palacre-gen said. "We have the full complement of Mennes."

"Good morning gen, is there a problem?" Barser asked. She brought her horse to a standstill and jumped down.

"I've received orders from my leader," he said.

"I am your leader!" Barser did not sound happy.

"Catherine," continued the gen, "is a principality and when the heir to the throne returned you took second place."

Barser's face reddened in anger. "Second place! Explain yourself Palacre, or I'll have you…"

"What he means Barser de Sotto, is that I am returned," Stazman stated.

"And who are you pretty boy?"

"Stazman Zem, Prince of Catherine. I have broken our alliance. I do not think killing your sister is in the best interests of my country."

"Then you are not thinking at all."

"And who is the orchestrator of this plan?" demanded Lazlo.

"It is my own plan," Stazman said.

"Is it? Then you are badly advised by Sartesh Andrada and Mycul Zas," Barser said flatly.

"You are doing us an injustice, Barser de Sotto. We would be your allies and secure your northern border."

"I need troops to fight my sister, not vultures waiting to pick over the spoils."

Stazman smiled, "A vulture is an odd analogy as they so readily circle the skies above Karlize."

Barser drew her sword. Thousands of troops did likewise. She replaced the blade in its sheath. She smiled.

Lazlo pushed his horse forward. "Either you join our crusade or you are our enemy."

"Why, Warmonger Lazlo, my brother, I will not invade Faires." Stazman stood tall in his saddle. "Nor will I invade Mennes whatever the outcome of your campaign."

"I never forget a slight."

"You may not but then neither do I," Stazman replied.

Lazlo drew his horse closer. "Remember it was I who roasted your father alive and had choice cuts served at my coronation banquet alongside the despised Manhedreth. I will devise something altogether more lingering for you, boy."

"Remember it was you who sold me into slavery and I have a keen memory for revenge," Stazman said, and turned away.

Lazlo pushed down his visor, turned his horse and in a fraction of a second drew his sword. Sartesh had his own foil stop the blade within an inch of the Prince's neck. A second blade swept through the air severing the head of Stazman's horse and causing him to tumble in the muddy field. He got up in ungainly fashion and shouted abuse at the Warmonger. The dictator galloped from the field laughing. His wife joined him.

"Get up. Can't you see how you have lost your dignity?" Irana Zem wheeled round her horse.

A decuman dismounted and offered the prince his horse. Stazman brushed himself down and regained some decorum.

"They still look intent on invading Faires," Mycul said, noting the troop movement ahead.

The gen thought about this before answering. "They have the advantage of surprise. We are merely players on the side lines now. We have a month to prepare our response."

"I have another plan, Palacre-gen. Every successful prince needs a wife and I intend to use my son in a game of marriage."

"Marriage! I'll never be persuaded of that!"

"A month is a long time in war and politics," Irana Zem said. "Give out the orders, we start our march home after a meal."

The leaders of Catherine discussed how best to organise the movement of so many. They gave orders for their baggage train to be brought into the army's protection.

Sartesh and Mycul took advantage of their discussions to enter the inn. "I've not eaten in a while," Mycul said and sat down. "I'll have pie and ale."

The man serving them was the same who had warned Mycul.

"I'm glad to see you and your friend safely back here. What strange events. This morning a giant arrives carrying a cage, in the company of two others, one being a physician. Now an army waits at the door."

"Is the giant still here?"

"Yes, sleeping in a back room. The others tend the man released from his cage."

"Good," Mycul said. "We'll eat, and then join them."

Sartesh tapped the server on the shoulder. "Could you return that box I entrusted you with?"

The barman nodded and pushed a nearby table aside; then lifted a floorboard. He reached into a space beneath the floorboard, and a box was pulled out; this was placed next to Sartesh. He patted it with a smile.

"We must find a balloon or airship to take us back to Perdisher." Sartesh said.

"Perdisher?"

"Yes, there's no place for us in Catherine. We need to unite the opposition and overthrow Lazlo." Sartesh looked outside at the resting army.

"That reminds me," Mycul said. "You drugged me so I'd forget Alleyya!"

"A necessary evil and a decoction provided by that very same lover. A man thinking with his cock is no good in an emergency," Sartesh said and laughed. "I wanted your full attention."

"Don't do it again, please."

Sartesh nodded. "Well, perhaps you could arrange not to be beguiled by the necromancer's daughter?"

Mycul thought about his beloved Alleyya and his eyes glazed over. She appeared to be walking towards him, her short skirt revealing her slender thighs and long legs. She smiled and beckoned.

Sartesh spun a cube on the table. "Talk to her," he said.

Mycul picked up the cube and walked to an empty corner. Sartesh saw the light emanate from the cube's facets and heard the love in Mycul's voice.

Chapter 18 Night Flight to Perdisher

"Alleyya."

"Mycul." The couple stared at each other through the cubes of the Ornithon for a long time. Alleyya's cheeks were flushed and her hazel eyes shone like jewels emanating from her flawless skin.

"You look tired and dirty," she chided. "Is everyone safe?"

"Yes, Sartesh is here with me and we rescued Stazman," Mycul said, and floundered. "But…"

"But he's not the man you thought?" Alleyya helped.

"I don't think I am a good judge of character."

"There's only one character I want you to be a good judge of and that's your own. I am happy if you have done your best."

Mycul thought about this and swept the hair from his face. "I couldn't have done any better."

"When will you be back?" Alleyya asked.

"Sartesh has talked about finding an airship, otherwise we'll follow the army at a safe distance."

"Army?"

"Lazlo is invading Faires. Barser de Sotto is determined to oust her sister and create Yderiphon."

"Then we have a chance," she said, and moved her head slightly, revealing some of the fine ornaments which kept her hair in place.

"I can't trust Sartesh," Mycul whispered.

"Can't trust him, why not?"

"He drugged me, so I'd forget you."

Alleyya smiled. "Silly, I asked him to; I didn't want you losing concentration. You men are all the same when it comes to love. The brain stops working." Her laugh resounded round the room she was in. "There is something about your naive innocence which makes me want to love you."

"I love you too."

The cube turned opaque and darkened, the clouds gathered, and Alleyya was gone. A voice could be heard saying: "Remember the Ornithon."

Sartesh listened from across the room. On hearing the voice he wandered over and slid into the seat next to Mycul. "Do you recognise the voice?" he asked him.

"If I didn't know better, I'd say it was Nag-Nag Naroon but I saw him die. It was horrible, the flesh was stripped from his body by ants."

Sartesh thought about this. The food and drink arrived.

"By the way, have you ever seen an airship here?" Sartesh asked.

"A dirigible?"

"That would do. Where might we find such a thing?"

"Well, as a kid I used to watch them take off from the banks of the Umbre. There's a large field at the back of the fort. I'm afraid I remember nothing more."

"That must be where we met earlier. Thanks, that's a start," Sartesh said. The two men tucked into their meal. They ate in silence.

"Would you eat before your prince?" Stazman stood in the doorway, supporting his mother on his arm. Palacre-gen was behind, flanked by decumen.

"Sit and be our guests," Mycul said.

"And would you not observe the decorum of our rank and stand in our presence?" Stazman asked.

Sartesh shot a glance across the table, then smiled and continued eating. Mycul looked at his friend then Stazman, uncertain how to proceed. The decumen took up positions.

"Sirs, you will observe the etiquette of their rank," a decuman ordered.

Sartesh began opening the box of Mordocki revolvers. Mycul stayed his hand. He shook his head. Mycul stood, "My apologies. It's been a long day."

Sartesh also stood and gave a respectful nod. Stazman was satisfied with this show and the royal party sat down. Sartesh and Mycul returned to their meal.

"We couldn't take on the whole army of Catherine," Mycul said.

"I'm too angry to speak," Sartesh replied. He stared at Stazman.

"The food smells good," Stazman said.

"It is," Mycul agreed, eating heartily. For the first time, Mycul could imagine how they might end up killing each other.

"There's one thing I haven't been able to work out, Prince Stazman, and that's how you got away from the mutant spiders."

"It's quite simple, Ra'an de Sotto saved me from them," Stazman said. "We were both captured on the road here."

"Dreadful, what happened to her?"

"I don't know but I will find out, she proved herself a true friend."

Mycul desisted from reminding him she had double-crossed them on Pem and had likely done the same again. Mycul shovelled a final fork full of food into his mouth, pushed his plate away and leaned back.

"This is really important, Prince Stazman," Mycul said. "Lazlo will be back to stage a counter coup, or an assassin will finish you off. I'd put my money on the latter but if everyone thought you were to marry Ra'an, it might give you some time."

"Mother said something similar earlier."

"We both wish you well in Catherine! Remember all these people had a nice life under Barser de Sotto. You have to make things even better; I'd start by bribing the army. An extra bit of pay does wonders for loyalty."

"Have you been reading Caesar's campaigns in Gaul?" Sartesh asked.

"I wish you both well," Stazman said. "We are leaving for Catherine within the hour. If you observe due decorum, you will always be welcome guests."

"You will always have my friendship," Mycul said and passed Stazman an Ornithon cube. "Spin it and we can talk."

Stazman seemed genuinely surprised to be given such a thing. He looked into its opaque surfaces then placed the object in his pocket.

"Until the final battle," Stazman said.

"Our final victory," Mycul raised his tankard, then stood and gave a bow. Sartesh stood but did not bow.

"Have the meal brought to the royal tent!" With the order, Stazman stood and left the inn. Mycul stared at the doorway for some time before taking a deep breath.

Irana and Palacre whispered over goblets of wine before following Stazman out of the building.

"Please protect us from those who think themselves better than other people," Sartesh said.

"That's good, coming from a future king!" Mycul joked.

Sartesh scrunched up Mycul's hair and they both laughed.

"He'll let you down," Sartesh said.

"He'll be the death of me," Mycul replied remembering the images he'd seen in the Ornithon. "Let's see how our new friend fares."

They went into the back room and found Meerla and the physician still tending her husband. He was sat upright and clean.

"Is he able to talk?" Mycul asked.

"He's drunk water and a little gruel, but he is still traumatised by his ordeal." Meerla fussed around her husband.

"Do any of you know where I might steal an airship?"

Meerla shook her head, "I've seen one occasionally."

"Likewise," the doctor said, "we'd love to get our hands on one."

The husband beckoned Mycul closer. He whispered a name and an address. The effort exhausted him.

"And what should your friends do whilst you are gone?"

"Prepare for a battle. We need to overthrow what remains of Lazlo's guard. When he returns the warmonger must find the gates of Karlize barred and bolted."

Meerla looked at the doctor. "We'd be delighted to arrange that."

"My thanks, Meerla and best wishes to you all. I will send messengers when we have everything in place. It would be good to have troops from Mennes supporting our cause in the coming battle."

"There is something else Mennes can do," Sartesh interjected. "I need Nofa Flows dammed."

Everyone looked incredulous.

"If I can do the calculations, an army crossing Nofa Flows would be inconvenienced by a flood and it might even wash the bridges away. It would give us time."

"Zhedhelion Barkbada Uita!" Meerla said. "All are equal under the sun."

Mycul thought about the plan but made no comment. "I suppose someone must awaken the giant!"

He left the room and joined Sartesh in the corridor. The two of them went to the only other door off the corridor, and knocked. There was no answer. Mycul turned the handle and entered. Gorangoth was sleeping across two beds and must have entered the room via patio doors.

"Gorangoth!" Mycul shouted and rocked his shoulders.

The giant shuddered and roused himself.

"You drank too much again!" Mycul sat in a chair at the bedside. "You missed Stazman being accepted as Prince of Catherine, and their army marching home."

"I did not miss it, I chose to sleep through it! There is a difference! You forget I was awake most of the night on your errands. Carrying a cage with a grown man through the streets is quite an exertion, even for a giant!"

"I'm grateful for your help. I've come to tell you we think we've found an airship. If we can raise her…"

"We'll be able to do that, you know flying is my hobby!" Sartesh boasted.

"And you need my help?" The giant sat up as best as the dimensions would allow.

"I'm certain you can help keep the Mordocki at bay. But I doubt we could take you with us to Perdisher," Sartesh said doing a calculation of his mass.

"My feet stay firmly on the ground!" the giant announced.

"With Meerla's help you could gather some opposition and hold the palace guards off."

The giant stretched and farted. "You must look after Mycul Zas, he's going to be very important in the days ahead."

"I know there is someone he feels has a greater importance," Sartesh said and watched Mycul colour.

"Love is a splendid and dangerous thing," Gorangoth said with remorse. "I'll be there for you, now let me wash and dress."

-*-

The afternoon saw cloud descending and a fine cold drizzle slowly turned to sleet. The walk back to the city was unpleasant and the two men easily passed the guard without drawing any attention to themselves. They continued through the suburbs, taking the narrow streets to avoid the palace. They arrived at the address given and knocked. The door opened a fraction.

"Melu sent us," Mycul said.

Sartesh looked back up the alley. They had not been followed. The two men entered the house. It was not unlike Meerla's with an enclosed courtyard of fruit bushes and a large kitchen on the side.

"You had Melu rescued by Gorangoth. I thank you both," the man said.

"We need help to liberate an airship. We need to get to Perdisher before Mennes does battle with Faires."

"So our time is limited. But tell me, who will lead Mennes when Lazlo and Barser are memories?"

Mycul thought briefly; his answer was swift. "Gorangoth the Golden."

"A good choice, but he'll never accept. He'll go back to his beloved pass and remember his beautiful wife."

"Then you'll have to choose someone," Sartesh said. "There must be many worthy people amongst your ranks."

"Perhaps so," the man said. He put on a cloak. "And indeed there is yourself, Sartesh Andrada."

"How do you know my name?"

"You aren't the only one to talk to mordonts. Follow me but keep many paces behind so as not to arouse the Mordocki."

173

The men ventured out into the sleet. A chill descended, with the night. Always their path was downhill. The streets became narrower and the puddles between the cobbles deepened. Water cascaded from broken gutters. Sartesh shivered. Mycul had forgotten how much this must be a trial to a man who had survived torture. Sartesh took sips of morphine when he thought no one was looking, so he knew his friend was still in pain.

Their guide pointed with two fingers and pulled back into the shadows. Ahead of them was a large building with enormous sliding doors. It opened out onto a field.

"This is the place." Sartesh put down his pack and unlatched the box. The Mordocki revolvers were holstered in the ornate gold buckled belt he wore. A third gun was secreted in a breast pocket. "Best being prepared, I'm too tired to argue with Mordocki warriors."

Mycul slid back one door and revealed four guards playing cards. They immediately leapt to the defence of the airship inside. They drew their swords and charged.

"Sorry guys!" Sartesh said. With both guns he aimed for their legs and shot. The guards tumbled and screamed. The pair ran for the airship and Mycul circled it, cutting the retaining ropes.

Sartesh clambered aboard and stabbed the remaining guard who had leapt to stop him, tumbling his body from the side before starting the engines. The craft was designed like a small ship suspended beneath a lozenge shaped, gas filled balloon. The noise and smoke was tremendous as the two sets of propellers spluttered into life.

The ship hovered and Sartesh inched the vehicle forward. The field was filling with people. Mycul saw Gorangoth swing a war hammer and despatch several Mordocki. There were also Menneans who were brandishing swords for the first time in many years. Despite their danger, Mycul felt a moment of pride. The fight–back had begun and the airship slowly reached the door.

"Get in, Mycul!" The ship was already five feet off the ground and Mycul had to run and jump, his fingers curling round the edge. Sartesh grabbed his back and pulled him in. Both men landed on the deck. Mycul pulled Sartesh up and he pumped more gas into the balloon of the airship. It rose further.

"Until the final battle, Gorangoth! Don't forget Nofa Flows!" Mycul shouted.

"Now for the bad news," Sartesh said. "To gain height you must pump in gas, here. To steer, turn this: it moves like a ship's wheel. Wake me when we reach the mountains. I'm completely whacked!"

Sartesh found a comfortable corner and packed up a sail as a bed. He was asleep within seconds.

The airship chugged along. Westward, mountains stood, impenetrable and the sky behind them turned deepest blue and became littered with stars. Solitary birds flew alongside before wheeling off to fish in the Umbre estuary below. Mycul steered by the river until it was a silver thread disappearing into the vast ocean. The mountains loomed to the right, with their snow-capped peaks.

Mycul watched his breath tumble in clouds as he breathed out. His fingers felt cold and he looked around for another jacket but found nothing. Sartesh slept soundly.

Slowly the ground rose under the craft and the tips of great larch trees were only be a few feet below. Mycul made the airship rise and he felt the air chill further. He started to shiver. The appearance of a slender moon above the horizon cast the ground into shadows until he could no longer tell earth from sky.

He imagined Alleyya waiting somewhere in the subterranean passages of Perdisher. How many hours of flight might that be? He thrust his fingers into opposing sleeves and used his forearms to steer the ship. He felt particles of ice rest inside his nose and a second bout of shivering took him. He looked back at Sartesh. He had perhaps been asleep three hours but Mycul knew he could not go on.

"Sartesh!" he shouted then quickly prodded him. Sartesh slept deeply. His body was warm inside the layers of sail. Mycul looked around. He found a pennant with the dragon of Faires coiling through the red flag. This he folded and draped around his shoulders.

For a while his temperature recovered but as they travelled south along the range, the mountains grew taller and Mycul again had to gain height. The anchor scraped over the snowfields.

Eventually there was no more gas left to pump. Mycul looked around at the barren landscape. Hills rose in each direction and so he turned the ship to port and flew over the featureless scene. The mountains diminished and the temperature rose a little. Despite this Mycul was chilled to the bone: several fingers were numb and his toes pulsed unpleasantly.

"Sartesh! How about some help here?"

He heard Sartesh groan, then he stretched and rubbed his shoulders. Sartesh pulled the sails with him to the wheel.

"Are you in pain?"

"Even my pains have pains! Have I slept long?"

"Four hours, maybe five. I followed the river then turned south. I had to turn east over the plain. We're out of gas."

175

"That's bad. There's no other way of lifting this craft without throwing things overboard." Sartesh stared out at the stark landscape and back at the mountains in the distance lit by the setting moon.

"The good news is we're in Faires. The bad news is I don't know where but, if I'm not mistaken those are the lights of the advance guard of the Mennean army in the distance. That would put the Pass of Gorangoth about there, where the gap in the peaks is, and Perdisher…" Sartesh turned the airship and they headed towards the mountain.

All the time they were losing height. The sound of treetops brushing under the hull alerted them to their danger. Together they threw articles overboard to gain height but they were fighting a losing battle.

Sartesh released some of the remaining gas and the ship fell through the trees to a clearing. They landed with a jolt and the hull keeled over, disgorging them into the undergrowth. "We aren't going anywhere until dawn," Sartesh said, pulling out the sail and creating a warm shelter in which they both might sleep.

They woke long before dawn with the cold penetrating their bones. Sartesh winced in pain as he tried to move. "Do me a favour," he said, as he handed a small pot to his friend, "rub the cream gently into each bruise."

Sartesh stripped and Mycul tended each of the bruises. He was amazed at how they were fading. He rubbed his fingers down Sartesh's back to remove the last of the cream. He felt the ridges of scarring.

"What happened?" Mycul asked.

"An argument with a whip."

Mycul changed the subject. "I don't think I'd make a good nurse. I wouldn't make a good cartographer either, flying us past our destination. How far are we?" Mycul secured the lid of the salve.

"I'd reckon Perdisher is ten miles south east and the armies of Mennes another twenty west."

"But it all looked so close."

Sartesh collected a small amount of gas in a jar and tried to ignite it. "Good," he said, "it's helium rather than hydrogen. Lighting a fire under the wrong gas could prove fatal. Don't blame yourself, Mycul, the height and the clear night make distances deceptive. So let's get our flying boat back in the air."

"So it's a fire then?"

"Why don't you contact Alleyya via the Ornithon cube whilst I gather the wood? You can do the hard work stacking and lighting the fire."

Mycul studied the balloon. It was mostly still inflated and hovered above the boat. The boat cast on its side had wedged between two trees and this had prevented further damage during the night. Mycul spun the cube, the clouds lifted and revealed a room of midnight blue. Alleyya peered into his world. "I've been worried…"

"I'm fine. Sartesh thinks we're ten miles from you. Will you set some marker visible from the air?"

"Easily done, I can feel you are close but the army of Warmonger Lazlo is not far behind you. The Necromancer pulled the spirits of his ancestors from beyond the veil to warn him of Barser's treachery but the man was so drunk he thought them dreams and paid no heed to their words. Our own army has been well trained by Tahoola. She has found a purpose here and they will know the moves of assassins as well as any in Faires or Mennes," Alleyya said.

"And what of you?"

"I have almost completed my training as necromancer but it doesn't mean I don't want to feel my arms around you and smell your hair against my skin in the midnight garden."

Mycul smiled. He remembered the sensations and fragrances of that delightful place. He stammered something, stopped then nervously laughed at his body's reactions. "I must help Sartesh collect wood or we'll not meet today."

"Safe journey!" Alleyya blew him a kiss. Mycul stared at the cube long after her image had disappeared. He sighed and sank into a malaise.

"You've got it bad again," Sartesh poked him with a stick. "I've got some of that potion to forget her, if you want."

Mycul smiled and stood. "I don't believe I'll need that. I have a reason to get us there quickly." He brought back arms full of wood as Sartesh lit the fire and opened a large flap in the balloon. The most difficult job was pulling the boat free from the trees. To do this they needed to fill the balloon with hot air until it just lifted, then use the reduced friction to manoeuvre it into the clearing. Briefly the vessel was anchored before Sartesh jumped on board and stoked the fire.

"Well it's a one-way ticket. We'll either get there alive or be roasted mid-air by the fire we've created. It might even burn the boat!"

"Look for some marker, Alleyya won't let us down."

"And nor will I," Sartesh said, his eyes alive with a mischief Mycul hadn't seen in many a day.

"You are feeling better."

"Yes, I've turned a corner. Let's hope this airship can as well!"

Mycul smiled. The airship scraped along the ground and slowly gained height. At times the smoke was so intense their eyes watered and they leant over the sides for air. The ship itself started to smoulder and smoke. "Any ideas?" Mycul asked.

Sartesh shrugged. He lowered his trousers and pissed around the fire.

Mycul shook his head. "Sorry, I'm out of that sort of ammunition."

They struggled on for what seemed ages before Mycul shouted, "The flag of Yderiphon!" Around it a group of people were pointing and waving. "Get us down! Get us down."

Sartesh took out a Mordocki revolver and let off one shot. It penetrated the top and left a single hole then the silk ripped and the airship tumbled from the sky to a hard landing. The contraption skidded along the open ground until the group of people helped bring it to a stop. Mycul jumped out and ran into Alleyya's waiting arms. They embraced and kissed and Mycul forgot the world around.

Chapter 19: The Shattering Dome

Tahoola stood there with a broad smile on her face. Her cheeks had colour and her grey eyes sparkled. She had platted strands of her hair like Alleyya and affixed silver ties to hold it in place. "Did you miss me?" she asked Sartesh.

"I thought about you, but wouldn't have wanted you in Karlize," he said.

Something in his tone warned her that not everything had gone according to plan. She put her arm over his shoulder. "You need a good bath and some of my tender care."

"Don't go falling in love with me, Tahoola," Sartesh replied.

"Gen, Tahoola-gen," she corrected. "Don't worry, I know more than you're prepared to admit. Let's just say, I don't mind and leave it at that."

Sartesh gave her one of his looks but he couldn't disguise the fact he was intrigued. "Food, bath, sleep. Could I negotiate the order?"

"Your wish is my command, for one night only," Tahoola promised, leading him into the subterranean corridors. The ghosts guarding the entrance stood to attention in their wall niches and saluted as they passed.

"Is this the army you've been training?"

"The living and the dead, yes," Tahoola said, and inspected some of the revenants as she passed. "It was unsettling at first, due to the intense cold of their presence but as we drilled, I was amazed at how the dead keep their character. How they can smile and joke and cry, but the chill if they pass through you is startling."

"I hope there is something better than being a spectral soldier in store for my future. I'd like to think of Elysian Fields."

"And your friends?"

"Ah! Friends, there you have me, friends."

"Sartesh, I'm surprised, you have many friends."

"Perhaps in you and Mycul but from the past there is no one. It leaves me time to read books and build airplanes. My life has been dedicated to Adee technology."

"And that's why we're here and still alive. But I don't believe you." Tahoola stopped and gestured to one ghost. Sartesh bowed politely then stopped. His mouth fell open and he pointed. "Surely you are Nallor Dhze?"

"I was in life," the ghost said impassively.

"Remember, they see you only as well as you see them."

The ghost raised its fingers and touched Sartesh on the shoulder. Sartesh felt the chill run through him but he overcame his fear and bowed once more. The ghost saluted. Sartesh looked at Tahoola. She said nothing though her eyes betrayed the difficulty she had in keeping her emotions in check.

"Don't blame Tahoola," the ghost of Nallor said. "The orders came from Ceelan and if Tahoola hadn't carried them out painlessly my passing might have been more protracted."

"Can the dead be trusted?" Sartesh asked.

"More than the living," Nallor replied. "We have less to lose."

Tahoola bowed her head and walked down the corridor. Instead of going to their rooms she diverted towards the baths.

Tahoola chose the perfume for his ablutions. The scent at once relaxed him and eased the pain. The luxury of a room set in deepest burgundy and warmed by under floor heating was in stark contrast to how he'd spent previous nights. Sartesh stepped into the simple bath lined with black tiles, which shimmered with stars. He submerged himself and when he surfaced, Tahoola entered the water.

"Turn around," she ordered. "You have suffered greatly." Gently she massaged his back and shoulders with a salve. Sartesh stopped her, turned around, and gazed at her. He took in the contours of her slender body and the beauty of her curves. He smiled. Tahoola smiled. "It's alright, you don't need to say anything." They lay back in the water and just briefly their hands touched.

"Are we doing the right thing?" Sartesh asked.

"Us as a couple or us in this predicament?"

"The more general one."

"It's the right thing, these people are honest, decent and in need of a home where the sun shines. They cannot stay here. Only yesterday there was aloud crack and a three-storey building collapsed," Tahoola said.

"It's a fatal weakness in glass, no matter how hard. Eventually it crystallises and weakens."

"The science is of no benefit to those they buried. But science might provide the solution."

Sartesh lay back still further and let his body float to the surface, then he remembered who was with him and changed position again.

"You are not the first naked man I've seen. We assassins lead a sheltered life from the cloning tanks to adoptive parents and finally to the school run by elder assassins. We are all genetically identical but I developed some defect on falling in love with Nallor." Tahoola waited for Sartesh's reaction.

"And yet you are not identical. I detect the possibility of redemption in you. I could not believe Ceelan or Barser capable of any such change."

Tahoola ran her fingers through his soft sideburns then gently touched the tip of his nose. She stepped out of the bath, leaving a trail of water before collecting a towel and wrapping it around her. All the while Sartesh watched.

"You'll have to get out and get your own towel," Tahoola joked. She walked a few paces further, turned and waited.

Sartesh also got out of the bath, his body lithe and muscular with a slender waist and lower, his pubic hair fanned out like red dust set against the pale skin. Sartesh grabbed a towel and placed it strategically.

"So Sartesh Andrada, how did you find out you might become the once and future king of Mennes?"

"The Ornithon?"

Tahoola wagged her finger. "You might have found out much there, but not that."

"Three mordont ladies stopped me and made the prophecy." Sartesh took a towel to dry his hair.

Tahoola nodded. She replaced her clothes.

"How long were you and Ceelan lovers?" Sartesh asked as he pulled on his trousers and collected the rest of his clothes so he could follow the lady down the corridor.

"I might ask the same question!" Tahoola laughed, and let her hair fall around her shoulders.

-*-

A feast was laid out on the table. Mycul, Alleyya, Sartesh and Tahoola-gen stood and waited for the Necromancer. The lady arrived, her face pale and her hands trembling a little. Alleyya moved to offer support but she gently pushed her aside.

"Be seated, honoured guests." They all sat. The Necromancer wore a long and flowing skirt of midnight blue, decorated with silver skulls whose eyes were inset with diamonds.

"Mycul, what is the disposition of our enemies?"

"Some five thousand strong, including a thousand Mordocki. Stazman succeeded in stopping the soldiers of Catherine from joining, but they have gone home. Whilst Catherine will not fight for Lazlo we should not rely on their support."

"I thought…" the Necromancer paused. She picked up her fork and ate some of the stew. "All is not as it seems. I am uneasy. When Alleyya used the Ornithon cubes, someone was listening in. A man I think, but who?"

"Nag-Nag Naroon?" Mycul hypothesised. "I thought he died when the Ornithon was destroyed on Pem but as Sartesh says, the cubes still work, so there must be a more central place which links them. How might we find it?"

"If they used light to communicate, it travels in straight lines. Two or more cubes in use might plot the light source back to its core."

"But we never see anything when they are used," Alleyya said.

"No, I think we need total darkness and some chalk dust," said Sartesh.

"That experiment will have to wait, at least until tomorrow. Tonight should be a time for reuniting friends," the Necromancer said, raising her goblet and saluting Alleyya and Mycul.

Everyone else followed suit. The Necromancer pulled grapes from a bunch. Sartesh could see something was troubling her. She kept looking at Alleyya but the couple were engrossed in each other, hardly even needing to speak.

After an hour of eating and drinking, the Necromancer stood. Everyone stood also and bowed and she left the room.

Sartesh quickly pushed in his chair and followed her. He walked a respectful distance behind the leader of the Perdisher. At the entrance to her apartments she whispered to the guard and Sartesh was able to pass without being questioned. Her rooms were well lit. He saw a large desk on which skulls were placed in patterns. The walls contained niches each with a skull and a light burning behind it. The Necromancer smiled.

"You saw my concern."

"I was worried, your concern is for Alleyya."

"Yes, my daughter. It's ironic, a necromancer who is afraid of death. What are you afraid of, Sartesh?"

"People finding out the truth."

"There is no cure for that except to live out in the open under the full glare of the sun. Shall I cast your future? The ancestors speak more clearly than the Ornithon."

"Another version of what is to come?"

"Who can tell?" She picked up a skull and stared into the sockets. A warm glow emanated through the cranium. She repeated this until several skulls sent out this strange colour into the room. Sartesh felt light headed. She approached him and with her dagger took a single drop of blood and let it land in a tube attached to her belt. He recognised the Adee technology.

The Necromancer blew out the lamps in turn. An old woman appeared from nowhere. She walked with the aid of a staff. "Sartesh Andrada, keeper of the Seventh Law, I salute you." The woman walked towards him then vanished as she passed through him. He shuddered. "I wanted to know if we can save Alleyya?"

The Necromancer put a finger to her lip. He saw at once she wore the gold and purple rings of Yderiphon on her fingers. He looked at his own.

He saw a man, not the ghost from earlier: Nallor Dhze, his old master. He thought of Tahoola. The image became a nightmare vision then slowly returned to Nallor's form. "All hail the Emperor of Menne."

The final spectre was a mordont, a huge creature whose horns were white and curled down past the man's ears. The bovine face struggled with the human words, "All hail the once and future king."

The Necromancer looked up and the image was gone. A slender young man appeared. "That's not supposed to happen." The Necromancer whispered and closed her eyes. She intoned words but the ghostly form remained.

"I am the one you must cast away to regain the crown."

Sartesh looked at the phantom. It could not be older than sixteen and didn't have the same appearance as the others. It approached Sartesh, and the hand which touched his shoulder seemed real. He saw the Necromancer bite her hand in fear.

"Do not be alarmed lady," the youth said, "for I am the man the prophets spoke of. You must find me, Sartesh. Only you can release me."

"Sension?" Sartesh asked.

"Sension, Manhedreth's son," the figure said. "You must release me, Sartesh."

"Release you and cast you away?"

"That is your choice, Sartesh. Do the right thing or become Emperor of Menne a second time," the youth said.

The skull's light faded and the room became dark. The Necromancer waited before striking a match and relighting the lamps. "The past and future collide in you, Sartesh." She stared at the screen set into the tube.

"I don't see anything," he said.

183

"Look!" She showed Sartesh the screen and he saw a series of lines. "These are the genes extracted from the sample I took."

Sartesh looked at the arrangement, and counted twenty-three pairs.

"It's missing the extra length of chromosome. You are pure Adee human. Do you know what that means?"

Sartesh shook his head.

"It means you are not descended from those who sheltered in this dome." She sat on her throne. "No wonder past and future collide in you and the Ornithon wants you to be Emperor of Menne. There is a perverse logic at work, a storyteller's mind."

"An alternative answer is possible," Sartesh said. He stood and examined the stasis chamber. The Necromancer followed his gaze. "Mars?"

Sartesh nodded. "It is possible."

The Necromancer shook her finger. "Then the storyteller was not devoured by ants but nanobots, parts of the Ornithon. If that is true he is a construct." She arched her fingers in front of her face. "I have wondered if each cube we possess is part of something greater."

"That is something I hadn't considered." Sartesh bowed and left the room.

He returned to his apartment and found himself alone, so he walked out onto the balcony. He felt lightheaded with tiredness. Below in the midnight garden, he saw Mycul making passionate love to Alleyya. He took a deep breath of the scents and returned to the bed. He fell upon it and slept.

Mycul picked a slender stem of grass and ran its point along the contours of Alleyya's body. He felt liberated, exhausted and lightheaded from the scent of the deep purple blooms around them. He lay next to her, experiencing a moment of happiness. She rolled on top of him and caressed his skin with her tongue. He felt every undulation as she gently aroused him once more.

"I love you so much."

"How much?" Alleyya teased and twisted a lock of his black hair around her finger. She gently kissed it.

"I cannot imagine you living above ground in the sunlight," Mycul said. "Your skin would burn too easily."

"You think me weak, Mycul. I am not. We will live above ground."

Mycul heard the sea in his mind and the whisper of the Graken's voice.

"What is it, my love?" Alleyya propped herself upright.

"I thought I heard the sea."

"The Graken. I understand you are bound to that creature and must return to her. You must lead our navy to victory and install the rightful emperor of Menne."

"But I don't believe in emperors and kings. I believe everyone is born equal. We should tell our children this simple truth. I could not fight unless I believed victory would help assure this."

"Oh! Mycul, next you will say people should have equal wealth whatever their status," Alleyya's joke fell on a contemplative silence. "Oh! You do think that."

"Well, sort of. It doesn't sound practical but it does sound fair."

"Mycul, you're such an idealist!" She kissed him passionately and all discussion ended.

In the morning they took a long bath in the warmth of the burgundy room before dressing. Once out in the corridor they found many people running around.

"What is happening?" Alleyya asked.

"The Mordocki are coming!" a servant cried and ran with her valuables into another corridor. A bell of low timbre sounded through the city.

"We must part," Alleyya said. She ran off one way, stopping only once to look back. Mycul went to his room. He found Sartesh asleep and roused him. "Sartesh! The Mordocki are approaching!"

Sartesh jumped out of bed then realised the pain he was in. He stood momentarily, shook his head and took a few drops of tincture from his bag. Both men dressed for battle. Sartesh checked all the guns were working and passed one back to Mycul. He placed the revolvers in their holsters and removed all his jewellery except the rings of Yderiphon.

Sword, daggers, and bullets were quickly acquired and the two men joined the flow of soldiers to the square.

Tahoola-gen stood on the steps impassively watching her troops line up in formation. The air was filled with the smell of fear. The Necromancer appeared with Alleyya. Both were prepared in leather armour for the battle ahead.

"How far away are they, Tahoola-gen?"

"Two miles at most, their pace has been relentless. Our position has been betrayed by someone," Tahoola said and passed orders to her decumen.

"We should fight here," the Necromancer said. "They'll never be able to take the entry corridors."

"But we are also trapped here. They could starve us out in weeks," Tahoola-gen replied.

Mycul looked up at the great glassy dome which protected the Perdisher from the world above.

Sartesh followed his gaze. "Oh! That would be dangerous," Sartesh said.

"But possible. I'm assuming you can climb to the surface of the dome?" Mycul pointed upwards.

"While I have strength. I'm sure Alleyya can show us the way but…"

"Tahoola-gen, can you get your troops to solid ground? I mean with rock beneath?" Mycul asked.

"Yes," she pointed the direction. "I believe we'd have the sun in our eyes though. That's not tactically good."

"Is it sunny?" Mycul asked.

The Necromancer raised the skull to her eyes. "Yes."

"I have an idea," Tahoola spoke to a messenger, who quickly ran to the decumen. "I have asked each man to polish the inside of his shield until it reflects every part of their face. We will outshine the sun before we fight."

"And we will destroy the dome as the Mordocki cross. They will be swallowed by the ground."

"Is that not a Pyrrhic victory?" the Necromancer asked.

"It will ensure we live to fight another day. It will ensure the Perdisher survive," Alleyya said.

"You'll still have your city but it will be open to the light." Mycul saw the Necromancer's indecision.

"So be it. I'll order the midnight garden lifted to the safety of complete darkness." The Necromancer began issuing commands to her decumen.

"So that just leaves one problem," Mycul said.

Everyone looked at Sartesh. He raised his hands. He gestured that he had no idea, then he smiled. "Bring me sulphur, saltpetre and charcoal and as much rope as you can find. Young Mycul, we need bronze or steel buckets, and cotton to make a fuse."

"Then we are all set. We all know what we are about to do." The Necromancer hit the step with her staff and snakes emerged from the ground. "We fight, we fight bravely against the Mordocki and our strength will increase with each blow we strike!"

She moved to the top of the steps. The bell sounded once more. Everyone fell silent. "People of Perdisher. We have always been free and after today we will have secured our freedom forever and the land above ground to go with it!" There were loud cheers which echoed round the dome. The army started to file out down the north corridors.

Tahoola-gen marched by with all her weapons about her. She gave a nervous wink before turning her back.

"Alleyya," Mycul said, tears rising, "I'll always love you."

"I'll always be with you, Mycul." They kissed then parted. Mycul looked back once as the Necromancer and her daughter joined Tahoola and marched from the city. Alleyya turned and briefly their eyes met.

"I imagine we have about fifteen minutes to sort this out," Sartesh said. Servants brought pots of the chemicals Sartesh had asked for and copper buckets. He made a saturated solution of some of the saltpetre and soaked cotton rags in this before drying them. Carefully he prepared the mixture then filled the pots provided. He twisted the cotton fuses and embedded them in the powder. He looked up and found Mycul half way up the wall.

Mycul looked down on Sartesh who was still busy preparing some explosive. He took a deep breath and remembered his success would help the Perdisher to survive on the surface. As he neared the glass dome he could feel the vibrations of people moving overhead.

"How will we know?" Mycul shouted down.

"You'll hear the Mordocki battle songs and drums."

Mycul threw down a rope. He looked around for somewhere to place the devices. The obsidian roof was carefully fused to the bedrock but the builders had provided a ledge for water to drain.

Mycul hauled up a bucket. It was heavy. He wondered what it was made from until he saw the verdigris etching the design. He wedged this first bucket in place. The second one seemed heavier still but by luck he managed to place this hard by. Sartesh signalled that a third was ready.

Mycul pulled with all his might. The bucket swung and powder cascaded below. It became stuck a few feet below him. A final tug and the bucket rose quickly, almost overbalancing him. He moved round the dome. A fourth and fifth bucket were placed before Mycul took out the tinder box and waited. Vibrations grew. He touched the roof and felt them flow through him: the beat of many drums, voices crying, "Chu ba, chu ba," punctuating the drumming.

He lit the first fuse and the second. He climbed to the other side and lit the third, fourth and fifth.

"I hope you've given me enough time!" he shouted to Sartesh, who presented a rude gesture as an answer.

"Hurry in case I miscalculated!"

187

Mycul slipped and slid down the rope. He looked up and saw the fuses near the pots. He looked down. He looked up again and in panic let the rope slide through his fingers. He screamed in pain, let go and fell. He landed on a thick bed of cotton, the wind knocked from him, and he panicked again.

"Take a deep breath," Sartesh reassured. "It will come back."

Before he regained his breath, Sartesh slapped saltpetre on his hands, then water, before pulling him into the nearest corridor. There was a pathetic thud. Sartesh held his hand over his eyes and sighed.

"You tried your best," Mycul whispered, leaning against the wall and gasping.

"I did my best!" There was another dull thud followed by an almighty explosion. Silence followed then the shattering of glass and the screams of soldiers falling to their death.

"We must go, before shards of glass cut through us," Sartesh advised.

Mycul nodded. They ran, following the path the Perdisher had taken earlier. They arrived in daylight and squinted until their eyes adjusted. The sound of battle raged. They turned and saw the Perdisher surrounded by a wall of braying Mordocki. The shine on their shields had the desired effect: the Mordocki were confused and kept using a hand to shield their eyes.

"It didn't work!"

"It did, you saw and heard! But they are fearsome fighters and we have perhaps killed half their number. What shall we do?"

"Fight our way in towards them!" Mycul ran forwards brandishing his sword. Sartesh pulled out the revolvers and followed, covering his young friend's back. Suddenly mordonts appeared beside them, bellowing with anger. They were armed as the Protector intended, a powerful army with tridents and axes.

"We waited for you, Mycul Zas," Leeman said, still restored. "We will always serve you." He bowed a little, took out a sword and joined him in fighting the Mordocki warriors.

Mycul was amazed by the noise of battle and his nostrils filled with its smell. As the spearhead of mordonts and humans pushed through, the Mordocki parted and fell over each other in retreat from beasts and their battle axes. They scythed a path towards the beleaguered Perdisher and were soon able to join them on the hill. The shield wall was reinstated and the Perdisher fought with renewed vigour.

The Mordocki warriors drove themselves onto the defenders' spears and still cut their way to the soldiers. Alleyya set off arrow after arrow into the mass of the invading force along with her compatriots. The dead on both sides littered the ground but the Perdisher were now able to push forward using their shields as protection.

They moved down the hill and the Mordocki ranks broke. The remaining warriors were pushed over the edge of the glass dome and fell to their deaths. Perhaps fifty warriors remained who lost heart, turned and ran. The Perdisher were victorious and a great cheer went through the ranks.

Mycul lifted his sword and hollered with the others before running to Alleyya and sweeping her up into a grand embrace.

Chapter 20: The Passing of the Mordocki

The victory had been achieved at great cost. A quarter of the Perdisher ranks were dead or injured. "We were betrayed," Alleyya said with tears in her eyes. "Someone brought them here."

"Us," Mycul admitted. "Our airship could be seen for miles around."

Alleyya thought about this, then held Mycul's shoulders. "No, do not blame yourself, if the Mordocki had seen the airship they would have been here yesterday. No, there is some connection which eludes me."

"The Ornithon?" Mycul surveyed the scene of carnage. "We used the cubes to speak yesterday, perhaps someone was listening in."

Sartesh overheard the last sentence. "If I can think of a way of using the cubes to find the source of the Ornithon's power then surely someone else could use them to find our position."

"But who?" Mycul pushed his sword into its sheath.

"Someone who wants Barser de Sotto to have the advantage?"

"We need to find out *who* and quickly." Mycul took Alleyya by the arm and they left the battlefield.

Sartesh was alone on the rise, surrounded by mutilated bodies and hearing the moans of the injured. He put his hands to his ears before deciding to help with any wounded.

In the dusk, one wounded soldier looked like another until he found a Mordocki warrior. The man had a tattoo of a trisos on his chest and arm. His leg was transfixed by a spear, and broken. He'd lost a lot of blood. Sartesh's first instinct was to run him through but something about his demeanour stopped him. "You're of high rank?"

The man looked at Sartesh with anger but said nothing.

"Honour," Sartesh said.

"I know you," the man said, his voice weakened by loss of blood and pain. "You stole those revolvers from us after a girl accused you. It wasn't true of course, you were framed. So now you fight for the Perdisher, for the evil lady who eats brains."

"I've never seen her do that, though she does divine from skulls," Sartesh looked for other injured soldiers. He pulled a sword from the heart of a woman. She had been dead a while as no blood flowed and material on the blade was congealed. The sword was inset with opals whose iridescence was unique. He studied the writing down the blade.

"Zhedhalion Barkbada Uita," he repeated. "The battle cry of Yderiphon."

The man shifted then groaned in pain. "Please don't torture me, be kind, just one blow through the heart."

Sartesh handed him the sword. "You can do it yourself if that's how you feel. You need not die," he said. "You could help us all solve the mystery of the Ornithon and indeed help create that very country shown on your sword."

"You mock me."

"No, I offer you a chance," Sartesh said.

"The Necromancer will have all her prisoners crucified. I will die with honour with the Mordocki." The officer stroked the hilt of his sword as though it meant a great deal to him.

Sartesh saw the affection, not for the weapon but the giver of the gift.

"They must have been special?"

"My father served Manhedreth at the Battle of Tolepo. The sword was returned as a gift by Lazlo, along with my father's head."

"Yet you still serve Lazlo."

The soldier grimaced in pain as he tried to sit up. "Are you going to help me?"

"Not without a name, I need some information to ensure you live," Sartesh said.

"I could give you any name."

"You could but I suspect I can guess. I've met your brother."

"My brother? All of them are dead."

"Not Stazman. My friend Mycul rescued him from slavery. Stazman is now Prince of Catherine."

The man groaned and appeared to be in mental as well as physical torment. "Poablo Zem."

Sartesh helped the man upright and he hobbled a few paces.

Tahoola joined them. "I see you are showing the enemy mercy. He is the only Mordocki still alive."

"Ah! He isn't Mordocki, though it's difficult to tell," Sartesh said.

"Who is he?" Tahoola asked. She looked at the warrior and saw he wore a shield over his torso. Apart from this he only wore the battle trousers of a warrior. "Do you have a name?"

Sartesh smiled and gestured for the man to introduce himself.

"Poablo Zem."

Tahoola took a closer look and walked round him. He had the same chalcedony eyes as his brother but his hair was darker and he wore the trochbar filial of a warrior in his second year.

"Explain your name. I have very little time and no patience!" She pulled a trisos from behind the man's shield and a curved blade from his ankle.

Sartesh swallowed. "Were you about to kill me?"

"I might have done so if you upset me," Poablo said.

"That serves me right for being nice." Sartesh felt his stomach knot in response to his stupidity. Tahoola-gen wheeled the device until its blades shone.

"You are an assassin." The man recoiled in pain as a spasm jarred along his leg.

"I was, now I'm Tahoola-gen in charge of the Necromancer's army. Your answer please."

"I am the third son of Irana Zem. I thought safety was best found by hiding in plain sight, so I enrolled in Warmonger Lazlo's body guard."

"It is a strange world we find ourselves in, Sartesh. Take him to the healers with my blessing and tell them nothing of whom they are treating."

"What is there to tell, gen?"

"You are the rightful heir to Catherine, not Stazman. If he finds out you'll have a knife in your back. For your own safety, I suggest a pseudonym."

Tahoola left and her entourage of decumen followed. Sartesh struggled to get Poablo to the tent of the healers. Inside there was a smell of stale blood and faeces.

"Heaven forbid, am I to die in this place?"

"No," said Sartesh, "you aren't to die at all! You have my word on that!"

Sartesh whispered to the healer, who nodded, and immediately began to tend the warrior. As he screamed in pain, Sartesh left.

-*-

Inside the dome, moonlight could be seen for the first time. The protective roof had shattered across half of its length; the rest remained substantially intact. The streets were littered with the bodies of Mordocki, whose blood seeped into the gutters and made the paths treacherous. The Necromancer's rooms were still beneath roof. Mycul walked round to the midnight garden. He gripped Alleyya's hand as he saw that any remaining plants were wilting. Too much daylight had killed them.

"We have the specimens to plant it anew," Alleyya said. "First I need to go and clean up. Then I need a drink to take away the taste of death."

Mycul was silent. He thought about the bitter scene of victory: nothing would ever be the same. Alleyya stood in the doorway to her rooms. "I want to be alone," she said.

Mycul nodded and walked back to the room he shared. He threw himself on his bed. When he closed his eyes he saw his sword cut through bodies and his victims fall away. He thought he might cry but took deep breaths and finally rose and stood on the balcony. He took a glass of wine but the taste was sour, so he poured it onto the remains of the garden below.

There was a loud knock at the door.

"Come in!"

The door opened and the unmistakeable outline of a mordont appeared. Leeman still had a human face but the horns were beginning to protrude from the sides of his skull. "Didn't you bring any Calufras?" Mycul asked.

"Sometimes being a mordont is the lesser of the two evils."

"Thank you for your timely intervention, Leeman. Would you be willing to stay and help us further? It'll mean you losing your…"

"Humanity?" Leeman came into the room and stood on the balcony next to Mycul. "I'll leave being human to those of you who are human."

"Sometimes we are the worst examples."

Leeman patted Mycul on the shoulder. "What happens next?"

"The answer to the question, how did you find us?"

"That's simple; the Ornithon cubes in Deidar Mela. An unkempt man spoke to me." Leeman looked at himself in the mirror, turned to observe his profile then touched the points of his horns. "It is time I accepted who I am whatever the consequences."

"I think it's time my friend did his experiment and we found the source of the Ornithon's power," Mycul said, remembering what Sartesh had talked of.

-*-

Sartesh worked on his theory for two days. He insisted on being alone. Mycul busied himself repairing the airship which had brought them to Perdisher. The fabric of the boat and the silk were easily put right but inflating the balloon and finding fuel for the engine proved much more difficult.

Mycul knocked at the door to the room Sartesh had sequestered as a lab. "Sorry to disturb you but I wanted your advice," Mycul said. He took in the various objects his friend had collected, glass prisms and blocks, coloured filters and devices for measuring angles. "It seems our stolen airship was filled with a gas which cannot now be replaced. The Perdisher only know one gas lighter than air, and that's hydrogen. Will it do?"

Sartesh beckoned him over to a test tube. He placed a small piece of iron in it and poured a clear liquid over the top. The metal fizzed. Sartesh produced a lighted splint and gently fed it into the top of the tube. There was a loud pop which made Mycul jump.

"There's your answer," Sartesh said.

"That was no answer," Mycul replied. He tried the test for himself and gained better results.

"Hydrogen is explosive. The airship was filled with helium, a light inert gas but, if I remember correctly, it's difficult to produce without fractional distillation. Hydrogen on the other hand should be easy to produce in quantity but we'll need a large store of it."

"Or a way of making it on board?"

"Yes, that might be the better answer." Sartesh sketched a container with a tap and pipe feeding into the balloon. "You might try this."

"How are you doing?"

"In a word, nothing. If these cubes use light then I can't detect it."

"Our plans rely on you," Mycul said. He picked up a prism and observed the spectrum of light produced. "By the way, have you seen Poablo?

"Why ask me?"

Mycul smiled. "He seems more genuine than his younger brother."

Sartesh looked at Mycul, "What do you mean?

Mycul whispered into his friend's ear.

"It doesn't matter if he is or isn't," Sartesh changed the subject. "We will need to get the people of Catherine to believe he is the older brother with a better claim. However, I would give Stazman a chance: I think he'll persuade his gens to join our side."

"You have more faith than I do. I'll leave you for the shadows outside. The Perdisher are fascinated by them."

"What did you say?"

"The Perdisher, they're fascinated by the shadows."

"That's it!" Sartesh clicked his fingers. "If I cannot see the light, look for the shadows." He busied himself with some new development and didn't notice Mycul leave the room.

The next day, Sartesh set up his experiment in the Necromancer's room. She sat on her throne and looked on dispassionately. The cube was placed on the centre of a circular device marked to every tenth of a degree round a great circle. A lens was positioned due north and a clockwork mechanism slowly paced it round the circle until it returned to its original point.

"It looks good," Tahoola said, "But what does it do?"

"Black light cannot be seen but its shadow can. The circle is sensitive to it and the trace shows up briefly and can be recorded. As the lens moves round the perimeter it will pick up the black light and concentrate it. Now all we need to do is connect the cube. Who shall we talk to?"

Mycul scratched his head.

The Necromancer stood. "Let's see if our sister shows a greater friendship now she's in the line of fire. Talk to the Protector of Faires."

Mycul hesitated but saw the expression on the Necromancer's face. He spun the cube.

"Ah! The insignificant one. Indeed I'm honoured, you are all there. How fares the Perdisher Revolt?"

"We have survived the first onslaught thanks to your Keeper," the Necromancer said. "And you?"

"Sister, my troops fall back and lead Barser into a trap. I have but to click my fingers and the snare pulls closed."

"Can we assist you?" the Necromancer smiled, her eyes lit with inner radiance.

"I'll allow your conceit. Keep the land you inhabit if you can pull off your revolt. It will create a second front and no army can withstand that." The Protector of Faires was dressed in deep purple scattered with diamonds which glittered in the sunlight. Her short black hair was decorated with a net of diamonds as well, as if she expected important guests.

"Sartesh, there might be a way of you re-joining me as Keeper of the Seventh Law. Would you be interested?"

"I'd like to keep my options open," Sartesh said, hushing Tahoola's concerns.

"Then talk to me in private sometime soon." The Protector gestured with her hand in an exaggerated fashion then blew Sartesh a kiss.

Tahoola's face tightened in jealously. The cube stopped spinning and fell to rest.

"Well," the Necromancer said, "it seems I'll have to watch you." She swept back to her chair and picked up one of the Mordocki skulls. Everyone looked at the blank paper. Slowly a line revealed itself. Sartesh took a pencil and ruler and marked its position.

"Which way is Faires Argenta?"

"East by south east." Alleyya said.

Sartesh calculated the direction of the line. "This is a degree beyond due south."

The Necromancer banged her fists on the throne. "I should have known. The Desert of Assiez and the old Adee capital! I have maps and sketches. It is a dangerous and desolate place. Alleyya may not go nor Tahoola, I need them here to prepare the army."

Tahoola looked at Alleyya. "It is true, there is much to be done."

"I cannot leave mother at such a time. There is too much to do, you understand, Mycul?"

Mycul nodded. He felt as though he had been manoeuvred into a course he did not desire.

Alleyya stroked his cheek then suggested, "We should have that victory feast tonight so that our friends can leave tomorrow and solve the mystery of the Ornithon."

"I agree with Alleyya, your majesty," Tahoola said. "There is much to do in training our soldiers."

"There were others who helped," Mycul looked around the room, "and I'd like them to attend any feast."

"You mean the mordonts." The Necromancer thought about this prospect. She tapped the skull of the Mordocki warrior. "You are right of course and Leeman will be able to help when you reach the ruins. Mordonts are genetically modified to withstand radiation, you are not. Do not remain near the ruins more than two hours."

-*-

Mycul expected a grand affair with many people in attendance. The people were well dressed: the decumen in their uniforms of purple leather over yellow shirts and trousers. The leaders of the Pedisher council were placed at the head of the table; Mycul and his friends including the remaining mordonts who had set out from the Reach of Key sat furthest away from the Necromancer. Only Leeman dressed as a human, and sat next to Mycul.

There was one other present, Poablo Zem, who stood with his leg encased in plaster, crutches resting against a chair. He wore the borrowed clothes of a decumen and looked uncomfortable.

A servant dimmed the firebrands and the room darkened. Slowly lights from various skulls began glowing. These were the heads of vanquished enemies, detached after battle. Coloured vapours emerged from their mouths and their bodies reformed as ghosts in front of their skulls. A bright light shone from above and the Necromancer began intoning ancient words. The ghosts slowly migrated towards the light, looked back once and vanished.

"I now possess the souls of the vanquished. They will return to do our bidding in the battles to come."

There was polite applause and the Necromancer sat on her richly carved chair. She wore a large lion broach in front of her high collar, such that her neck could not move. Her hair was richly decorated with skulls whose diamond eyes sparkled as she talked.

Mycul watched Sartesh engage Poablo in conversation. Tahoola observed him as well. Alleyya spoke to Leeman, asking how he'd become a mordont. Mycul half listened but was more interested in the body language of the people round the table.

"Have you ever flown before?" Alleyya asked.

The mordont nodded; he was having trouble with words again. He took a sip of wine and smiled.

"I will never again be fully human, there will always be something of the mordont about me. If I drink, the animal takes over.If I take Calufras I look as I was before my capture but I never feel as I was before."

"That will only come when your soul is released from your body," Alleyya noted, "though I hope that won't happen for many years."

"mordonts do not live for long. That was not our purpose; we were bred to serve the Protector as soldiers. One day she will have us fulfil that role and humans will be subservient."

The idea disturbed Alleyya. She turned to Mycul. "Did you see mordonts taking over in the Ornithon?"

"No, but it appears the Ornithon is only telling the truth from one perspective: a plot conjured by a storyteller like Nag-Nag Naroon. I think that is why Sartesh struggles with the predicted future for him."

"And yet it is well known by others who've seen the future, including mother."

Mycul had no answer. He changed the subject. "Will you miss me?"

"No," she said. "What do you think?" Alleyya's impish laughter filled the room. Mycul let the layers of her hair fall through his fingers. He stopped at a slide formed into a skull.

"I forget that one day you will be a Necromancer too."

"There's good and bad in us all, a necromancer is no different to anyone else. The source of our power is neutral and can be used for any purpose," she said pointedly.

Mycul poured a small amount of wine into her cup and then into his own.

"A toast to us!" He raised his goblet.

197

The portions were small but the courses many and by the time the bell sounded for the middle of night, Mycul was full and lightheaded from drink.

A herald announced the presence of a messenger. The woman bowed and passed a note to the Necromancer. Alleyya's mother stood and without a word left the room. Her guests accepted this and continued chatting. Later, tables were pushed back and a dance floor revealed. Mycul and Alleyya rose with other guests but before they had completed the first round they were summoned to the Necromancer.

The Necromancer sat brooding in her throne. She passed over the note. Alleyya read it and passed it to Mycul. "I'm sorry." she held his arm.

Mycul looked at the words. He felt anger rise within. "He's betrayed me! Stazman Zem has betrayed me!" he shouted.

"He has let us all down, Mycul," the Necromancer said. "He will sit in Catherine and see who wins this battle and then decide to shake hands with the winner. It is an old diplomatic trick."

"So it seems I head towards the end the Ornithon predicted."

"What was that?" Alleyya asked with concern.

"Stazman and I die on each other's swords at the height of battle."

Alleyya supported herself; she went pale and looked as though she might faint.

"At sea? On land?"

"Land I believe," Mycul replied supporting his lover. "It wasn't what I wanted to see."

"Then you have a vested interest in destroying the Ornithon forever. It will never blight another life," the Necromancer said and clicked her fingers. "We must return to the banquet and honour our guests."

The joy of the proceedings had evaporated for Mycul. He turned his goblet round and didn't drink. When he thought of Stazman, he gritted his teeth and clenched the goblet tighter. Alleyya's hand touched his. He was momentarily distracted.

"Don't do this on your last night with me for a while. Tomorrow you'll see nothing but sand and I'll be just a memory."

"You'll never be just a memory to me," Mycul said. "But you're right about tonight. I knew Stazman would betray us. I'm not certain why this note confirming it has made me so angry."

Alleyya combed her fingers through his hair and kissed him. "Because you expected better of him, after all you rescued him from a life of slavery," she said then changed the subject. "Let's dance again."

The couple took themselves off and enjoyed the rhythms and exertion. They returned flushed to their places where Sartesh joined them.

"Does take-off at dawn sound ok?" Sartesh sat opposite the couple.

"How about midday?" Mycul asked.

"Let's split the difference. There'll be a headwind so we'll make slow progress at first. Plenty of time for you to wave and blow kisses!" He slapped Mycul on the knee and laughed.

"I think he's had a lot to drink," said Alleyya.

Sartesh wove between the guests and made for Tahoola. He kissed her on the cheek before pulling up a chair and sitting by her. He raised his glass to his friends and gave a silent toast. A little later, he helped Poablo rise from his seat. When Mycul looked again both men were gone.

The room was quieter. Tahoola was in conversation with an official but managed a discreet wave as Mycul escorted Alleyya from the room. He had plans for the night; plans that Alleyya's smile showed would be reciprocated.

Chapter 21: The Desert of Assiez

The airship was working. The propellers moved so quickly their blades appeared to go backwards. The oblong balloon was now fully inflated, flying the flag of Yderiphon and the pennant of Perdisher from the rear.

"You've done a great job, Sartesh!" Tahoola held his face and kissed him fully on the lips.

"So have you," he said. "You've trained the Perdisher army well."

"Don't go changing sides because of a beautiful woman," she chided playfully, "I'm always here. Hurry and return, if only so we have more men to fight for us!"

Alleyya had released Mycul for a moment but still held an arm at his waist. Her cheeks were flushed and they both possessed dark rings under their eyes. Mycul was reluctant to let her go and even more reluctant to get back into the craft.

Leeman had already taken the plunge and was standing on the deck, looking at the people assembled below. The other mordonts stood at a distance waiting. Sartesh climbed up the rope ladder. A deep horn bellowed and scattered birds into the air.

"Hurry back before the ice creeps into our world, Mycul," Alleyya shouted above the engine noise.

"I'll hurry back, don't you worry."

He went over to the Necromancer and held her hands. Her fingers were chilled. He stood for a moment looking into her eyes and seeing an older version of Alleyya.

"I'll send you the disposition of any troops on a daily basis and you can plot them on the map of Faires."

She nodded. The crowd watched in silence as Mycul climbed the ladder and disappeared into the boat. He looked around at the provisions of water and food he had ordered and the arms stowed aboard. Sartesh released the anchors and the ship rose slowly. "You've done a fantastic job. I never thought this bird would fly again!"

Leeman peered over the edge at the ground getting further away. "How high did you say?"

"A thousand feet or so. Out of the reach of arrows and bullets," Sartesh said.

"A thousand?" He sat cross legged on the seat at the centre of the ship and waited.

To the west the snow-capped mountains loomed and to the east the landscape appeared even flatter in comparison. The air was crisp and cold and before many minutes everyone on board had put on a quilted coat. They proceeded due south, following a lodestone compass. The clouds built from the east and the light became dull. The temperature dropped still further.

Sartesh pumped more hydrogen into the balloon and took them higher still, skirting the base of clouds. Mycul handed out protective glasses and gloves to ward off the cold. Later they took a simple meal of bread and cheese.

Sartesh steered and talked with Leeman, trying to take his mind off the boredom of flight. Mycul watched the ground below and looked for troop movements. "Look! There's another airship in the skies," he shouted. Following the line of his finger, they saw a large brown dirigible hovering over the troops lined below them.

"Is it a battle formation?" Sartesh asked.

"No, it's Warmonger Lazlo's troops drilling and training. See the red flags?"

Mycul sketched positions and estimated numbers. He spun the Ornithon cube and reported to the Necromancer.

The landscape became more wooded and rivers meandered across the fertile valley. The brown dirigible was following them but didn't seem to be gaining ground.

A third airship appeared ahead. It flew out of the sun and was much faster. Sartesh took out a telescope. "It's technically advanced. Like my plane it has ailerons for manoeuvring, yet that hollow above the gondola suggests it's a hot air balloon. It can't be, not at that speed."

"You mightn't have noticed but *not at that speed* is closing in on us!" Mycul said.

"If we can't win the race we could try to out manoeuvre them!" Sartesh put the airship into a steep dive. The engines of the third airship droned overhead.

"Tactically bad!" Mycul shouted. A bomb of some description detonated a few yards to their port. The shock waved rocked the gondola.

Sartesh revved the engines and pulled the airship upwards. It almost reached forty-five degrees before the engines laboured and Sartesh was forced to level. They were back on an equal height with their opponents. Arrows flew around them. The balloon was hit. "Oh!

That's bad," Sartesh observed, as the craft slowly deflated and sank. "Leeman, can you attach us to our enemy?"

"I'll try!" Leeman swung the cast iron anchor as though it was straw. It rose through the air and caught on the undercarriage of the dirigible. The craft jolted and lost stability.

"Pull! Both of you pull!" Sartesh kept control of the steering as Mycul and Leeman brought the airships together. A flaming arrow pinioned in the deck and another burst the silk. The hydrogen ignited with an intense yellow flame. Now both craft began ditching.

"Perhaps we should board our enemy?" Mycul suggested.

"Good idea!" Sartesh reached for his revolvers. He shot two assassins firing arrows from the rear of the gondola. Mycul climbed the rope between the two craft and jumped on board. There was a scream and the sound of sword clashing with sword, finally a single gunshot and silence.

The airship fell to the level of their own. Leeman grabbed onto a rail by his fingers before using his immense strength to haul himself aboard. Sartesh caught hold of a rope and swung over. He landed gracefully on the rear deck and remained crouched whilst he took everything in.

"Is it secure?"

"Yes! And we have a rare prize," Mycul shouted from within.

"Leeman, help me cut lose our airship or we'll be burned to death!"

The two hacked at the ropes but the anchor was still attached to the undercarriage and holding the burning airship below them. Flames began to scorch the acquired dirigible.

"Sartesh, you hold this ship steady. Leeman, tie that rope securely round my leg. I'm going to climb down." Mycul clenched a dagger between his teeth and slipped over the edge. The airship travelled on and Sartesh kept good control until there was a jolt. The craft pitched forward then rose. The engines laboured and Sartesh brought the craft back to an even keel.

"I've got him!" Leeman shouted. The airship which had brought them safely from Karlize fell in flames. It landed on a group of white tents with red flags. There was a large explosion and debris shot out into the surrounding woodland.

"Bravo!" a female voice called, hands clapping. "I hadn't expected to meet so soon."

Sartesh smiled. "Why, hello, my lady Protector of Faires."

She approached Sartesh and ran her finger along his gun. "I could murder a good man."

"Ah! But what about a bad one like me?" Sartesh said.

The Protector cocked her head. "I assume you're going to kill me."

"That wasn't part of the plan," Mycul said. "In fact you weren't part of the plan at all. Now you're here, you should join us as we destroy the Ornithon."

"I thought you'd already done that." The Protector removed her hat and half veil. Her short dark hair emerged, perfectly coiffured. Her earrings shone with a variety of different coloured diamonds.

"So did I, but it seems we were deceived by Nag-Nag Naroon."

"The storyteller?"

"The same; we thought he died but now we're not so sure."

"Not a lot to go on. You do realise the Ornithon is worth much more intact than as rubble?" The Protector was playing games again.

"But our lives will be free of its influence."

"Ah! Yes; but the influence is from whoever controls the Ornithon, not the device itself, I thought a clever man like yourself might know that." She gracefully sat on a chair in the control room. "Of course I might be a great candidate for controlling the Ornithon."

Sartesh raised an eyebrow.

Leeman picked up the bodies of the assassins and threw them over the balustrade. Mycul watched the Protector flinch. He thought she might still have some essence of humanity left, something to redeem.

Sartesh played with the controls until he was satisfied he knew everything function. Only then did he lock them on a course due south.

"There's nothing but desert that way, Sartesh." The Protector took a glass from the cabinet next to her and poured a blue drink. It perfectly matched her eyes and dress.

"The ruins of Undon are across the desert," Sartesh replied.

Mycul looked at the Protector and wondered if she really was different to Barser when they had identical genes. He walked out onto the rear balcony and saw the other airship was a long way off and hovering over the remains of the Mennedic camp. Mycul pulled up a table and spun the cube. He reported to Alleyya with all the information.

"Will you join me for a drink, Sartesh?" Ceelan asked.

Sartesh sat next to her and poured a glass of the blue liquid. He sipped it and savoured the taste.

"It will be poisoned," Mycul said.

"Mycul Zas, what a low opinion you have of me!" Ceelan watched him through the cut glass facets. "True I was going to have you cut up alive but," her hand opened and threw away the gesture, "I need someone to fly this contraption. You see I thought I was safe, lording it above everyone but I didn't reckon on an airborne assault. I'll build that into my next design."

"Your design? I'm impressed," Sartesh was interested now. "We should talk about flying objects, you know I've recreated a…."

The Protector smiled. "Recreated an airplane? Yes. I remember how you rescued Mycul. Only one man could have done that," she said playing some sort of game.

Sartesh smiled. "Is that praise?" He returned to the controls to check the air speed and heading. They were approaching another bank of cloud. When they emerged the fields of Faires had been replaced by a wilderness of contorted plants. Trees stood stripped of their leaves and bark. The scene was one of desolation. Mycul realised he was looking down on acres of mutant plants. The trails of large creatures criss-crossed the terrain and just once Mycul thought he saw the trunk of an elephant emerge from its grazing.

"It might take all day to reach the ruins of Undon," the Protector said. "There is food on board, if anyone would like to cook. Of course I'm not dressed for it."

Mycul smiled, enjoying the moment, "If you want to eat, you'll have to cook."

Sartesh took a deep breath and adjusted the course heading. Leeman busied himself searching every drawer and cupboard, making a stockpile of weapons near Mycul. He then turned his attention to the Protector. He pulled her upright and frisked her. He took out a trisos from a concealed pocket and a revolver. The Protector slapped the mordont. "No man touches my flesh without my permission."

"I am sorry. I merely wished to live," Leeman enunciated the words strangely as though fighting instinct.

Sartesh held his hand out for the gun. Its exquisitely inlaid handle was decorated with nacre and tortoiseshell. The barrel rolled freely and the chamber contained six bullets.

"Well maintained," he said and pocketed the weapon.

"I worry about you, Sartesh. Real men are supposed to like swords and knives and close combat, the taste of blood, the smell of battle. You don't. Your attitude seems to be one of why get your hands dirty if you can use a gun."

"No one, woman or man likes combat," Mycul said. "It is a last resort."

The Protector clapped her hands mockingly. "But what you don't know about Sartesh is that he loves other men. Don't you, my Keeper of the Seventh Law?" Ceelan ran her fingers teasingly round the contours of his face. As she touched the dimple in his chin, he restrained her fingers. Sartesh looked straight ahead.

"Some men, some women. Is that a crime?"

"It is in Faires my darling, that's why you were whipped and exiled from Bretan. Didn't you think about those scars, Mycul? You must have seen them?" She returned her attention to Sartesh, walking around him. "Your Uncle Morgin had the whole thing recorded by the Keeper and of course, he passed that useful information to me."

"Well, so now everyone knows," Sartesh said and checked the compass heading again, only this time his hand shook a little as he did so.

Mycul stepped forward. "The quality of someone is not determined by who they fall in love with." He took Sartesh by the shoulders and kissed him fully on the lips.

"Very noble," the Protector laughed. "And there was that accident at the gold mine," she said carelessly, "but he's already told you about that unsavoury event."

"I have spoken to Nallor's ghost. He didn't lay any blame with Sartesh."

"Bravo! I see we are all going to get along famously, now we know each other."

Sartesh gritted his teeth and steered forward. He looked up briefly. "And of course you loved Tahoola. I presume that's why she's still alive?"

"Ah! A woman has no past, Sartesh. We are creatures of the present." Ceelan walked up to her Keeper and without warning, kissed him. "Last time you enjoyed it," she said bitterly before returning to her seat.

The sun set behind the mountains and still the craft continued south. The vegetation had given way to karst landscape: limestone denuded of soil. The geology interested Sartesh. He took out a notebook and sketched rock formations.

The moon rose and Venus appeared close to the horizon. The sky darkened by degrees yet still the craft flew. It wasn't until the last rays of light emptied from the sky that Sartesh ordered the anchors weighed. He went to the galley and prepared a simple meal.

They sat in silence and ate slowly as darkness enveloped them and strange sounds echoed through the night. Claws could be heard scuttling on rock. Mycul leaned over the balcony and shone a torch. Scorpions moved out from the circle of light. He came back into the room. "It's getting cold," he said. "Do you have any blankets?"

The Protector indicated the drawers. Mycul passed out the contents.

"Sartesh, will you take first watch?" Sartesh nodded, grateful for the opportunity to be alone. He poured a small measure of the Protector's liqueur and went out onto the balcony dressed in the royal blue coat of an assassin. He pulled up the collar and shivered.

The Protector joined him. "You have a good, loyal friend in Mycul. I thought it might turn him against you. It was worth a try."

"You interest me," Sartesh said. "A woman alone with supreme power and yet it can't always have been so. There must have been friends, lovers…"

"You were one."

Sartesh raised his glass then sipped.

"In private you may call me Ceelan still. You're right, there were friends and lovers and some who were both. My route to power is littered with the remains of those who thought themselves more useful or important than they really were. With each one I killed, a part of me died but in the end bereavement made me stronger."

Sartesh said nothing.

"And you started off alone, Sartesh Andrada. You prefer to work alone and now find you are part of a team. You'll have to decide whether you can be honest with them or not: and for everyone who accepts you another will not."

"I've known that all my life. I've fought prejudice on two fronts, looking like a Mennedic and also being…"

"Ah! You were nearly honest enough to say it." The Protector looked out into the darkness. She listened to the knock of chitinous exoskeletons against rock.

Sartesh put his finger to his lip. He cocked his head to one side. Slowly he backed away from the balcony and picked up a sword from the pile of assassin's weapons.

A claw suddenly grabbed Ceelan and her body was bent backwards over the rail. The stinger jabbed forward but Sartesh's blade severed it before the poison dart penetrated. The creature screamed but Ceelan remained strangely calm as she struggled against its fierce grip.

Mycul joined Sartesh and together they tried to prise open the claws but the scorpion backed down the rope dragging its prize. Leeman joined Mycul and using a sword as a lever broke the arthropod's grip. Ceelan fell but the mordont caught her hand. Sartesh charged at the creature's eye and it fell and split open. The pincers and legs thrashed, then others of its kind began devouring the meat.

Ceelan was grappled back onto the deck, her clothes ripped and her stomach bleeding. Mycul poured a large quantity of the sweet liqueur, which he offered her. Ceelan gulped it in one before returning to her room and locking the door.

-*-

Mycul watched the first rays of light of a new day. The Protector emerged wearing a lilac battle dress and thigh length brown boots. She had combed a pink colour through her hair. "Well insignificant one, what's today's plan?" She walked stiffly, her injuries still causing some discomfort.

"To find the Ornithon and leave here before we are all eaten by those creatures or killed by radiation." He tapped the dial; it remained stubbornly fixed in the upper reaches of orange.

Ceelan touched his wrist. "Thank you."

Mycul raised an eyebrow. "It's okay."

"The trouble with radiation," Ceelan said, "is it's invisible. The effects might be fast if the dose is high or long term. We'll only know when the inevitable happens."

"The Adee must have known…"

"They did, they were warned but everything was done for profit. The Adee weren't concerned about consequences for the next generation."

"I suppose that's obvious as they're no longer around. Everything they dreamed of has been swept away."

Ceelan smiled. "Not quite everything. We have perhaps twenty-four hours to get back to safe levels of radiation."

"Then we'd better get started."

For a moment, Ceelan's eyes betrayed anxiety.

Sartesh stripped and washed before putting on a clean jumper. It was of powder blue, assassin issue rather than his customary white, and he checked the mirror, turning from side to side. They cast off and soon the airship gained height. The terrain below them was pitted and great holes appeared where some long-forgotten building once stood, the remains having subsided. Some of the desert was composed of lines where automobiles might once have run.

The Protector took more interest in her surroundings. "This must be all that remains of Undon." The outline of streets could be discerned under the sand and occasionally walls jutted at angles through the dunes.

"It doesn't look much like an Adee city," Mycul said, "at least not the ones you showed me pictures of, Sartesh."

"Those pictures were photographs the Adee took and we are lucky they survived. What you see is all that remains after thousands of years:

207

a dangerous warren of mines and tunnels and only one intact building."

"How would you know there is one intact building?" The Protector seemed very keen to know an answer.

Sartesh smiled, "I am your Keeper of the Seventh Law."

"What is that grotesque place?" Mycul pointed. "It is concealed and yet the only building standing. Those were Nag-Nag's words at the Reach of Key."

A great river flowed through the landscape. Emerging from its north bank was a keep. The four faces of a clock eternally stuck at one minute past six were set into an ornate tower. A landing strip built from rubble was next to this; yet more rubble formed the banks, which kept the waterway hemmed in. A shattered complex emerged from the river, which looked incongruous and appeared to be associated with the tower.

The remains of the city were quiet. The Protector took out a telescope and surveyed the ruins; the others also observed from the edge of the gondola. "We'll only know if it's safe once we step on the ground." Ceelan shivered with disgust, remembering the claws. Sartesh closed off the gas valve to the balloon and opened a flap. The airship descended.

"Leeman, can you stand guard, whilst we three find the Ornithon?" Mycul dropped the anchor and as they landed, he jumped down. He carefully observed the sand. It remained still, leaving only his footprints. Sartesh joined him and filled sandbags for ballast. These he passed to Leeman.

At first, they walked round three sides of the building from which the tower, rising straight from the ground, must have once been part. Its ornate façade was preserved in the same glassy material from which Perdisher was composed. There appeared to be no entrance. The fourth side was blocked by pieces of ornately carved debris, and the flow of the river.

From out of the river, a great grey tube emerged and was secured to the tower. The group searched. The sand swirled in the breeze and formed little dunes of debris. They sat and waited.

"This is useless!" Mycul finally exclaimed, and took out his sword. He tapped the ground with its tip. After several minutes, he hit metal rather than stone.

Together they cleared the dust and found a door inserted into the ground, engraved with figures. It had no handle and no means of opening it. Mycul sat down but Sartesh circled the door looking at the figures set in it. "It is a mathematical puzzle," he said. "Lend me your sword and I'll try the answer."

"Take care; if it's like my last encounter with the Ornithon, there'll be death traps, or those ants."

Sartesh began pushing the numbered blocks. "One, three, six, ten, fifteen, twenty-one." With a clunk, something within the door unbolted, and the panel itself shot sideways, revealing many steps. Each one had a word etched upon it in.

Sartesh looked at these and scratched his head. He picked up a stone and dropped it on the word *All*. Nothing happened. He tried *equal* on the second step. A bolt thundered across the passage and embedded into the rock of the far wall.

He smiled.

"*All are created equal under the sun*. If I remember my Adee."

"Wait," the Protector intervened, "sun or son? The Adee ate the son of god in places called 'church'. There's one easy way to find out."

"Yes, you stand on *son* and I'll stand on *sun*!" Sartesh said.

The Protector dropped a stone onto *son*. A series of darts flew across the steps and hit the far wall before falling. She took the steps and demanded Mycul and Sartesh follow.

"Not that religious then!" She disappeared into the dark but as she walked, a strange light emanated from the walls, its colour turning from cerise to violet. A lot of rubble was scattered across the steps.

Mycul looked up and saw the ceiling was in disrepair. He held his finger to his lips. The path went on for several yards before they reached the staircase of the tower. This was no high-tech place. The stairs were created from stone and the workings of a great clock hung silent in the centre.

They took the steps slowly and looked for clues on the way. The Protector paused to take in the view through a broken pane in the glass, and signalled for them to go ahead. The ethereal violet glow returned when they reached the level of the clock.

A door stood wedged open. A dog barked a few times then returned to its bed. "Welcome, friends," Nag-Nag said, shaking each person's hand. "I bet you're surprised!"

"We thought we had seen you killed by ants," Mycul said.

"They weren't ants, they were nanobots and it wasn't me but a hologram. That's why you had those cubes, they power the image and relay messages. You see, everything's possible when you know the future."

"So you know what's going to happen now?" Mycul said as Sartesh wandered round the room gazing at the wall made from pure glass and looking for the almost invisible circuitry.

"Oh! Yes, Faires will lose the battle of Salleppo, and the Keeper of the First Law, Gurdon, will replace Ceelan as Protector. It is he who makes Sartesh ruler of Mennes according to the calculations."

The Protector emerged from the stairs. "If I am replaced as Protector you have given me an advantage."

Nag-Nag looked at the woman as though he had seen a ghost. He set the Ornithon in motion and watched events unfold. Sartesh shielded his eyes but Mycul and Ceelan watched the story. "Oh dear," Nag-Nag said, "it's come to..." He was cut-off mid-sentence. The Protector had taken a dart from her ring and embedded it in Nag-Nag's neck.

"It's a slow acting poison, Nag-Nag, slow and painful. You'll beg me for the antidote before you're through, and I'll give it to you when you've explained everything."

Nag-Nag collapsed on the floor and writhed in agony. He convulsed and contorted. Even his pores started to bleed. "Never! No one will ever know my secret."

"What are you doing?" Mycul demanded.

"Interrogating the prisoner. We don't have time for social niceties. If he wants to live he'll tell us."

"And if he doesn't want to live?"

"Then he'll die," the Protector said and lifted the antidote as though she might pour the liquid away.

"No! I was at least in part human. A genetic experiment like you all but I can send out solid holograms of myself. There is only one person not genetically modified here. That is you, Sartesh."

"You mean I'm the only human?"

"You are pure Adee human, Sartesh." Sartesh and Mycul lifted Nag-Nag to the control panel. He began manipulating the device.

The Protector handed over the vial of antidote.

"Who do you work for?" Ceelan asked.

Nag-Nag swigged the contents of the tube then pointed above.

"God? Don't give me that, old man. We live in an age of reason," Ceelan said and turned away.

"No, Ceelan the Magnificent. Those above are not Gods but..." The storyteller sighed. "It is time you found out everything." Nag-Nag pulled back a dusty curtain. "I have kept these in good order. Stand on the pads and you will see."

210

Sartesh did as asked; the other two were more reluctant. "They are transport tubes," Sartesh explained. "Not the most comfortable ride but safe, usually."

"How do you know this?"

"I just do. Trust me. The stasis chamber you saw possesses one."

Ceelan and Mycul took their places. The anti-gravity device swirled around them, and everything became green. A noise like a hurricane enveloped them.

Mycul felt energy build around him and for a moment there was no sensation of moving. When it began, Mycul felt he was being flattened into the floor. He felt the muscles in his face and body pushed then released as though he might be floating.

The feeling of motion was intense as they were swept towards their destination. His focus returned to the glass floor with a rotating blue marble rolling away below. Sartesh lay on the floor, tears rolling down his face. "What is it? Have they hurt you?" Ceelan placed a reassuring hand on his shoulder.

"No. Don't you understand?" He pointed at the large ball resplendent in blue and the greens and browns of land broken by wisps of cloud. "That is our planet, our Earth."

"An illusion, surely?" Ceelan said but there was doubt in her question. She knelt down and observed the motion. "That is Faires, if I'm not mistaken. The promontory to the city marks it out."

"And those are the mountains of Catherine and the Umbre."

"They are watching us," Mycul said. "Sartesh, are we on a vehicle in space?"

"Yes. Yes indeed. I wanted to tell you but without the evidence of your own senses you would never have believed me."

A door opened and a glass screen slid across the room. An older woman entered the vestibule. "Sartesh, how are you?" She placed her hand on the glass and Sartesh mirrored this. He smiled.

"How are you?"

"I am fine. We are fine. The colony thrives but what have you found out for us?"

Sartesh shook his head. "I have not found a cure."

"A cure?" Mycul asked.

Sartesh looked at the woman, who nodded. "We are the Adee," Sartesh said.

"What my son means to say is we are the exiled Adee. We lived too long on Mars, subject to Mar's bacteria and viruses. Now we find we die within a few days of landing on Earth. Any who survive succumb to brittle bones. Earth's gravity is greater than ours is. All we want is to find a way back."

"You mean mordonts and their kin are all your work?"

The woman paled.

"No, they are the work of successive tyrants who hijacked our laboratories." She looked pointedly at Ceelan.

"And the Ornithon?" Mycul asked.

The woman became thoughtful. "You cannot destroy it," she said.

"I think we can," Ceelan said.

"It is the link to our computers, so to destroy it severs all communication with us."

"Your point is?" Ceelan became imperious.

"It only tells you what you want to know. It doesn't foretell the future. It superimposes your desires, fears and makes the image real. A dream machine. It is a side effect of the communication devices."

"The cubes?"

"The cubes."

"So no one is manipulating events via the Ornithon?" Mycul was finding the information difficult to take in.

"No. People see the future it offers and embrace it, or else they are revolted by it and fight hard to see it doesn't happen."

"I've visited the Ornithon several times and on each occasion it has shown me some things the same, and others different," Ceelan remarked.

The lady on the other side walked to the window. "That's because different things were on your mind. Below is your reality. Only the Earth can shape our futures," she sighed. "It looks so beautiful. I suppose eventually humanity will be just another extinct species preserved in the fossil record."

Ceelan walked up to the glass screen. Her breath steamed up the partition.

"Why might we become extinct?"

"There were ten billion people on Earth when the Mars colonies were founded by the Adee, now there are less than one million, and your genetics are diverging from ours because of the high radiation levels."

"How many Adee are left?"

"Alive? Seven hundred, and several thousand in stasis waiting for the cure."

Ceelan turned her attention to the rolling planet. Mycul joined her and they looked down in silence. Sartesh went to speak but the woman the other side put her finger to her lips and shook her head. "Is that true?"

"Sartesh, how long have you been my son?"

"Twenty-five years but it's only a bond of genetics. Your genes and father's were united artificially. I've met you barely a handful of times."

"Well: genetics means a lot to me," the woman said.

"So much that you'd experiment on your own genes?"

"I'd do anything to find a cure except listen to that John the Annunciator we just exiled to Earth."

"You did what?" Sartesh so forcefully, both Mycul and Ceelan turned to listen. "Don't you think the Earth is tired of factions and religions? My friends have done well without them."

"You don't have any friends on Earth."

Ceelan approached. She smiled. "There you are wrong. Perhaps it is time you sent us back to the surface."

"Can't we have a few more minutes watching?" Mycul asked, his eyes bright with enthusiasm.

"Go back to Mars, mother, and leave us all to our lives, free from interference."

"Well let's see how long it takes before you beg me to return and rescue you." With these words, she pressed a button, coils of gravity captured them, and the return began: the feeling of floating, acceleration and finally a compression in which the body was rendered paralysed. The green coils intensified and the noise subsided.

Nag-Nag sat bolt upright at the control panel.

"Your antidote, what was it, Ceelan?"

"Extract of Calufras," Ceelan replied.

"Calufras? You have killed me."

"No old man, Calufras preserves, even Leeman returned to human after using it. Once he stopped…"

"Calufras supresses DNA replication and reverses change. I have few genes, being partly light." Nanobots poured out of every one of Nag-Nag's orifices. "It comes from Mars. They think I'm an intruder now." He could no longer talk, though he tried. Nanobots crawled from his mouth and eyes. They accumulated on the walls and floors of the room.

"He isn't real," Mycul said, astonished.

"Then he won't mind being destroyed." Sartesh primed a grenade and threw it towards the body. Mycul drew Sartesh out of the room, onto the stairs. He pushed closed the cast iron doors and heard the mechanism lock. The force of the explosion pushed the doors open again. Millions of nanobots emerged.

Sartesh and Mycul ran down the stairs leaving bombs primed on each landing. They caught up with the Protector then overtook her; she looked behind then ran with renewed vigour. At the bottom of the steps, they stopped and reversed the sequences of words before running across the courtyard.

"Cast off!" Mycul shouted to Leeman. They climbed aboard as nanobots emerged from every hole in the ground. Leeman cut the ropes and the anchors fell into the seething mass.

The area was alive with creatures, which immediately began climbing on each other in their effort to reach the airship. Sartesh revved the engines until they screeched. One ladder of nanobots touched the craft. Mycul took out his sword but Leeman stayed his hand.

"Know your enemy." He scooped a jar through the air and trapped several of the Ornithon creatures. Quickly he screwed the lid in place. The airship lifted and the towers of nanobots faltered and collapsed.

"Is that the end of the Ornithon?" Sartesh asked.

"No, but the bombs we planted have worked!" Mycul watched as the glass shattered and exploded. The tower itself erupted smoke then collapsed upon itself in a cloud of dust. Brick tumbled over brick and as the dust settled it appeared there was little left of the structure.

"I fear you are wrong, Mycul," the Protector said. "Those nanobots will slowly repair and recreate."

How can you be so sure?"

"Look!" The captured nanobots were reproducing and recreating a wall inside the jar. "Soon that jar will be too small for them."

As they watched, they saw the first layers of the tower being rebuilt.

"They will never stop until it is completed," Mycul said. He threw the jar overboard.

Sartesh took a heading due north and turned the craft. "It seems I've got a lot of reading to do."

"Did you know Calufras would kill Nag-Nag?" Mycul asked.

"No, I thought it was a universal cure and now we know why, don't we Sartesh?" Ceelan said.

Sartesh gave the thumbs up sign and continued to fly the craft.

"Hah. We are now on same side, Mycul. Not only is Sartesh different, he's an alien."

"You've always known the truth," Sartesh said. He checked his calculations as he set the dials for the return journey. "Perhaps you'd be safer in your room until we get back. I wouldn't like any more accidents."

"Fatal accidents are invariably successful for me when considering enemies. You've taken many liberties, Sartesh. Be careful not to overdo them or you will become one of my statistics." Ceelan didn't wait but took herself to her room and closed the door firmly behind her.

Mycul came over. "I'd rather have her where I can see what she's up to. And there again, perhaps the same applies to you."

Chapter 22: The Protector of Faires

The smoke from fires could be seen at a great distance. It curled and ran west towards the mountains. The snow covering the ground showed every movement of the armies with clarity. Mennes was camped on the Bretan side of Nofa Flows and Faires on the eastern bank. Each was building pontoon bridges to reach the other shore. As the airship gained on their positions, they could see that the fires were intended to dispose of bodies. Soldiers looked up from their chores and some pointed.

"I have a bad feeling about this," Mycul said.

"You know what will happen if you keep me here?" Ceelan said.

"Yes, you'll be deposed. Gurdon will step into the breach and we'll all return heroes."

"And I…" The Protector had lost a little of her confidence seeing the funeral pyres.

"I might leave you on the Reach of Key with a detachment of mordonts to protect your every move. It would have a certain poetic justice. I might visit on occasion." Mycul tried to sound sincere.

"Very kind of you but there's still one good fight left in me." Ceelan went back into her room.

"We can't put her down without being captured by her assassins. We're in a difficult position," Sartesh said.

Leeman looked over the edge. He pointed. "Mycul!"

Mycul ran to the balustrade and looked down. He saw the army of Faires had many carnivers arranged in the front line. Behind them lines of mordonts waited with their double-edged battle axes.

"I don't think they need our help," Mycul stated.

"I'm pleased," Sartesh said. "We might need the Protector."

It was impossible to know which side might have the advantage but it was obvious the natural boundary of Nofa Flows had prevented a battle. Sartesh looked along the line of the river. "I wonder if Gorangoth had the opportunity to dam the river in Mennes?"

"That would only delay the battle," Mycul observed.

"In Mennes the valley was once a glacial lake and Nofa Flows travels through a gorge. Yes, it would delay the battle but it would give us a few days to get to Karlize."

"Three, possibly four," Mycul said. He took out the Ornithon cubes and spun them. They stayed opaque and the dark clouds swirled within. Mycul peered into the shadowy mists of the cube but received no answer. Sartesh took up the cubes and studied them. He took out the ones in his possession and placed them on the table. He appeared deep in thought.

"Is everyone up for a voyage?" Mycul asked. He placed his fingers on his shoulder and sang out for the Graken. Her voice returned, quietened by distance.

My sisters and I are waiting for you, Mycul Zas. Ask for us when you get to your ships and we will draw them to Karlize in record time. You will have your army!

My thanks, replied Mycul and sat in a chair. He frowned; then snapped his fingers. He stood and looked at the charts.

His attention was later drawn to the wide bay developing on the horizon and the causeway busy with traffic. The highest building in the city was the Protector's palace in Faires Argenta. The pennants flew from the towers and the buildings looked clean under the crisp, winter sun with their scattering of snow.

The Protector appeared. She was now wearing a white fur coat and matching hat and her jewellery was set with moonstones but she still walked stiffly as she recovered from her encounter with the arthropod.

"My city looks beautiful from up here." Her chin was raised. "There's a much faster airship in the port buildings if you'd care to steal another," she added calculatingly. "We're heading for the ships, then. I suppose you'll need me to get you on board and take you to Karlize. What a dreadful name for a city, I don't know why my sister chose it for a base."

"We are still on the same side, apparently," Mycul said.

The Protector smiled and slowly took a brass object out of her pocket. Mycul saw Sartesh reach for his gun. The Protector smiled once more. "Men are so easy to fool," she said. "Usually they think with their cocks. You, Mycul can be different. You're able to hold a stratagem. It's as if you're connected to others in some way."

Mycul took the telescope she held out and surveyed the ships at anchor.

"They are graceful and functional," Ceelan said with a note of pride.

"They are beautiful. Which is your flagship?"

"Why, the Windseeker with its sails painted black and gold. It appeals to the melodramatic in me."

The ship was well proportioned and possessed a deck of cannons and harpoons. The ship's head was carved as a mordont pointing the way forward and at the rear flew pennants of Faires and Yderiphon.

Sartesh landed the craft on the beach and had it secured. "Could I trouble you to have it refuelled, Ma'am?" Sartesh asked of Ceelan as he helped her down from the craft.

"Going somewhere in a hurry?" she asked as she set foot on Faires and everyone around bowed.

"It's best to have a contingency plan," Sartesh said and stretched. Movement on the ground felt odd after flight.

"Very well." The Protector whispered in an assassin's ear and then walked gracefully to the jetty where the fleet was at anchor. Soldiers ran to greet her then bowed. "Prepare the fleet; we sail for Karlize with the next tide!"

The four were piped on board the Windseeker. The captain appeared flustered but managed to bow and give his welcome with dignity.

"We cannot summon the Graken, lady," he said, "so I'm not certain we can move with the next tide."

Mycul held his shoulder and thought out to the Graken. Her voice replied inside his head, *Mycul Zas, welcome back to your home. Lesser of the three yet greater. My sisters and I are here to do your bidding.*

Will you pull these ships to Karlize? asked Mycul.

Yes, there and back again. Do not worry. The battle will not start until the bridges across Nofa Flows are complete. In that, Nag-Nag Naroon was mistaken. It remains to be seen if destroying the Ornithon undoes his influence or simply delays it. Perhaps delay will be enough. Sartesh gave your giant a well thought out stratagem. He has dammed Nofa Flows in the foothills of Mennes and at dawn tomorrow the waters will be released and hopefully all the pontoon bridges will be damaged or destroyed.

Did you know the Ornithon builds itself anew? The device cannot be destroyed, Mycul thought.

Everything can be destroyed, Mycul. First you must know its secret.

It appears I have more work to do. Mycul turned back to the deck after his communication with the Graken.

"So that is your secret, you are a Graken herder! I should have realised sooner," the Protector said and pulled her coat about her. "We'll cast off with the next tide!" She took herself off to her quarters.

Mycul whispered in the captain's ear. He nodded. A cabin girl escorted them to a room. It was at the rear of the ship with a small window. There were chairs and a table and hooks on each wall, from which hammocks might swing. Sartesh emptied his pockets and put down the Mordocki revolvers. He stroked the richly inlaid surfaces before throwing himself into a seat and putting his feet up on the table. He promptly began cleaning and servicing the guns.

Leeman paced the room. The human was struggling against the encroaching animal. His face had distorted further, his nose widening and jawline thickening. The horns had become more pronounced during the flight across the desert and the man was almost as Mycul recalled him when he first met him on the Reach of Key.

There was the sound of many feet on deck as the sailors prepared for the voyage.

"I'd better go on deck and make sure no assassins creep on board." Sartesh put his feet down and picked up a revolver.

"Don't worry; they're already here disguised as crew. The secret will be finding them before they try to kill us. The Graken will help: she can hear everything said on board."

"Everything?"

"Yes, Sartesh, everything!" Mycul nudged him. He put on a waterproof coat and went out onto the deck. The place was a hive of activity. His thoughts turned to the Graken. *I'm glad you are here to keep watch on my back.*

I will always be here for you. One day the feel of spume flecking along my body and the cold wind running across my skin will be irresistible. Can you smell the salt spray?

Mycul nodded, he knew it was true. *By the same token, you must feel my love for Alleyya and the way I miss her touch, her caress, her kiss.*

I have been many years on this planet and seen all this and more. If I could save you from what is to come, I would, but it's not in my power. The Graken hung her head and pulled the boat northwards.

Mycul wondered what she knew that he didn't; but one could have too much knowledge of the future.

He shook the captain by the hand and asked him when it would be convenient to study the charts around Karlize. "When you hear the third bell, I'll be in my cabin," promised the captain. He returned to his sextant and resumed instructing the junior officers who surrounded him.

Mycul looked up to the stowed sails and heard the sounds of the sea, the rigging creaking, cloth flapping and the hull cutting through encroaching waves despite the ship being at anchor.

Behind was a scene that made the hairs on Mycul's neck stand up. The ships of the fleet were at anchor with their black sails stowed and purple pennants of Faires flying behind them. It was a sight he fell in love with. He leaned against the port rail and watched the flotilla in the harbour at Faires. The biggest ships of the fleet would be pulled by Graken. Even now he heard their chatter about the state of the water and the brief lives of their riders.

We are hopeless gossips, his Graken said surfacing. *My sisters and I are searching the oceans for the only male of our generation.*

When all this is over, I'll bring Alleyya and we'll search together. I've always wanted to be an explorer. I visited a craft in space and looked down at the vast expanse of oceans. When I was a child I lay on the grass at home on many a night, imagining what it was like to walk on the face of the Moon and look back at the Earth. Sartesh told me the Adee had done just such a thing. I thought he was spinning a story but now I know it was true.

It is good to have you back at sea, Mycul. I have missed you.

Mycul smiled. He looked at the slender neck of the creature who had pulled ships for him, with her ears swept back as she ploughed through the waves. Mycul spoke to the Graken. *If you can look out for Sartesh, please do.*

I always do. I could not have it said that I lost the twice-crowned Emperor of Menne on my ship.

Why do you always sound as though you know much more than I do?

The Graken didn't reply. The answer was obvious.

As soon as Mycul entered the cabin, he hung up his waterproof. Sartesh was so engrossed in charts for Mennes' capital, he jumped when Mycul touched his shoujlder. "Working hard?" Mycul asked.

"Look at the depth contours." Sartesh indicated the area on the map, and together they considered the deep water channel which ran past the city. Mycul realised the channel was too narrow for a fleet: only one ship at a time would be able to command the route, if unopposed. It would be foolhardy and open each ship to ambush.

"You see the difficulty?" Sartesh looked up and smiled.

"Yes." Mycul thought about how they might fire on Karlize. "It doesn't look well defended, but the geology has made them complacent."

"Your ships can't get close enough to fire, except one at a time as they pass the city. What you need is a ploy using shallow-drafted boats."

Mycul drew up a chair and played with the compass. "Ah!" He looked at the layout of the port and the way culverts drained into it. "We could load pitch onto the lifeboats and row them into port. The sailors ignite their cargo, then slip over board and swim back."

"A bit of a suicide mission but it would create mayhem and destroy some of the surrounding buildings. In the confusion one ship might get through and fire on the city unscathed."

Mycul nodded.

"We'll put it to the captains this evening. I've asked the Protector to invite them to join us for supper."

"It sounds civilised."

"It will be. You won't be on board. I've work for you to do, if you'll agree. A secret mission."

Sartesh was intrigued. He picked up a notebook. "Go on."

"Whilst the Protector is dining, I want you to break into her cabin and find her Ornithon cubes and the seal to Faires. Use the seal to impress these orders, without reading them."

Sartesh looked at the folded parchment he was given. He turned it over in his fingers, looking for some clue. Finally he placed it in his breast pocket.

"Without reading them? A lot of trust is involved in that."

"Trust is the issue. It appears there's history between you and the Protector of Faires," Mycul said.

"A little too much perhaps?"

"Well, she is going to hate you after today."

"Is that wise, making an enemy of her?" Sartesh looked at his finger nails and avoided eye contact.

"I'm not, not yet. Just you."

"Ah!" Sartesh realised the implications. "Divide and rule. And where am I going?"

"The Highlands of Catherine."

Sartesh smiled, "The remaining two pieces of Ornithon cubes. That makes sense but I need to be back here for this battle."

"There will be others."

"But will we be on the same side, Mycul?" Sartesh moved close to his friend.

"I doubt I'll be alive, but if I am, you will know what to do."

Sartesh touched Mycul's hair then turned and walked away. He paused by the door. "Never doubt me, Mycul."

"I never would," Mycul said. "Safe journey."

Sartesh nodded and left the room. The air on deck was cool and the badly-stowed sails flapped in the breeze. He looked at the airship docked not far away and watched for any guards protecting the anchors.

Chapter 23: A Matter of Trust

Mycul left Sartesh alone in the cabin; he leaned against the closed door and took a deep breath. Of course, he knew he could trust him but temptation was there. The plan needed stealth. The evidence must be absolute and his vengeance swift because that person had murdered his father and set these events in motion. The death of his father hung over him. Mycul realised that to manipulate events it wasn't enough to tell people what might happen, you had to make certain the right people were in the right place to influence outcomes.

Sartesh took out the paper and unfolded it once. He then placed his hand firmly over it. It was a matter of trust and he could not betray Mycul, yet he felt he should know. It dawned on him that the test, for surely it was a test, was concerned with the Ornithon and that knowing what the letter contained would place him in great danger. Not knowing might help fulfil his destiny. Two choices and each would have consequences.

Sartesh drew out his idea in dust scattering the floor. It was impossible, no one could predict with accuracy the outcome of such choices. Even with the best of predictions there must be an element of doubt, a road not taken. Sartesh pondered and applied logic to the problem. The more he thought, the greater the realisation that the Ornithon could influence the future but could not be guaranteed to get it right all the time. His biological mother was correct. Sartesh was reassured that he was in charge of his own destiny and that if he was, the same applied to everyone.

-*-

Ceelan, the Protector of Faires, made a grand entrance onto the deck. Two assassins waited behind her. Mycul and the captain of the Windseeker moved into position and all stood awaiting the salute from each captain as they came aboard.

Ceelan was still dressed in thigh-high leather boots but now she also wore the uniform of an admiral with fine gold brocade and epaulettes. For once she wore no other jewellery. "Mycul Zas, you appear to have helped me change the course of history. As a Graken herder, you need status in my fleet. I therefore raise you to the rank of Commodore of Faires."

Mycul bowed and Ceelan placed a large medal of rank around his neck. Polite applause followed as she kissed him on the cheek. He felt a moment of pride then looked around at the faces of the experienced captains. He realised he had much to learn about the sea, the Graken and the way of ships.

The procession began: each captain was introduced to Mycul, who bowed, receiving a bow in return. He knew none of the people present and felt out of place.

Smile, the Graken said. *Sartesh is safe below. See him through my eyes. He is a rare friend. He has not read the letter, although he was tempted.*

Mycul saw Sartesh melt the wax and apply the Protector's seal to the orders. He was now searching for her Ornithon key.

His vision returned to the deck and the captains lined up before him. They shared tanned complexions and a variety of beards to conceal the damage salt and sun had wreaked upon their faces. They appeared fixated on Mycul's medal and waited for an announcement, as if they'd seen all this before. The captain of the Windseeker whispered to Mycul, "It takes much to impress these men."

The Protector moved in to the centre of the assembly.

"Fellow officers, it gives me great pleasure to introduce Commodore Mycul Zas to you all. He is no ordinary man but a Graken Herder. He can speak with them all. Beyond that, I can vouch for his bravery."

She beckoned Mycul forward. They waited. There was an awkward silence. He realised a speech was required.

"I thank the Protector of Faires for her confidence but you should know that a commodore can only be as good as the captains in his team. I hope one day we will all see Yderiphon."

For a moment, Ceelan's face froze. Mycul almost heard the sharp intake of breath. He bowed and stepped back into line. The Protector managed a false smile.

"Let us go down to my cabin and start our work," she ordered as she led the party to her room.

Mycul, the Graken said, *Sartesh is still within and two assassins guard the door!*

Mycul desperately searched for a reason to delay. He could find none.

He has left all you require on the desk.

The party was already at the cabin door.

Has he escaped? Mycul asked.

I do not know. I was distracted by the thoughts of an assassin.

223

Mycul sighed. The door was flung open for Ceelan. She entered and he followed closely, sliding to the desk to snatch the letter. The Ornithon key was nowhere to be seen. The room was empty: Sartesh had hidden well.

Ceelan looked uneasy and her eyes darted quickly around the room. She went over to the window and peered out. Something had made her suspicious. "Where is Sartesh?"

Mycul looked her in the eye. "I'm assuming our cabin."

Ceelan went to the door. "Kindly ask Sartesh to attend on us," she ordered, with not a hint of kindness in her voice.

Mycul swallowed hard and looked around. He saw the diagram etched in dust on the floor. He felt a knot tighten in his stomach as he gently wiped one foot across the markings.

"Well gentlemen, before I leave you to organise and lead our armies against the infidel Barser de Sotto, I have but one command. You must follow the orders of Commodore Mycul Zas and bring Mennes' dissident army to join us on Salleppo's fields. Come by way of Nofa Flows as far as is safe. On the fields, we will make such a battle that the fate of nations will be decided, and who knows, perhaps I will rule Yderiphon thereafter."

The captains' whispering was interrupted by a knock at the door.

"Enter, Sartesh." Ceelan ordered, but as the door swung open it was not Sartesh but an assassin who waiting.

"I'm sorry Ma'am. We've searched the ship. He is nowhere to be found."

Mycul felt his face drop in anguish. He looked around the room once more. If Sartesh was still in here there was going to be a lot of trouble.

Ceelan waved the assassin away. "I know where to find him." She moved to her desk and unlocked a drawer. A large black box was placed on the polished mahogany surface. This too was unlocked and the lid opened. Ceelan slammed it closed as she realized the cubes were gone. Her face went red.

"Gentlemen, let us retire to the dining room to discuss Commodore Zas' plans to reach Karlize by sea," she said and dismissed them all. The door was locked firmly behind them.

Mycul was swept along by inquisitive captains and had no time to consult the Graken. Glasses of a blue liqueur were being served as they walked into the room and a toast was made to the sea. "Well Mycul Zas, a Graken herder," said one of the captains, "My grandfather spoke of such a man who rose to be a captain, but you have bettered that."

"It appears I have."

"And your plans to collect Mennedics?" another asked.

"And your plans to attack Karlize by sea?" queried a third.

"We'll speak of that later," Mycul said.

"And Yderiphon?"

"Yes, Faires and Mennes united as one country once more. A union of like-minded people all equal under the law."

"That's some prediction," the captain of the Windseeker sighed and appeared dreamy eyed at the prospect.

"It will happen and you are all part of the plan now," Mycul vowed. A glass of wine was passed to him but he put it down and walked to the window. He heard a low vibrating sound and watched an airship take off. He threw open the window and saw Sartesh waving from the gondola.

What is going on? he thought to the Graken.

Sartesh is leaving. He made out a second set of orders to fly to Catherine. It must concern the Ornithon, as soon as he found the Protector's cubes he laughed. He held it up to show me.

The Protector will know by now, Mycul suggested.

Yes, I can feel her anger!

What did he find?

A pattern, an answer. The cubes lock together. Now he needs the other six pieces.

"Are you alright, Commodore?" asked one of the captains. "Should we await the Protector?"

"We must," Mycul replied, watching the airship disappear into the darkening skies. He really did think he was onto something. Mycul knew that the other pieces of the Ornithon were with Barser de Sotto and her husband, and in Catherine with Stazman. Sartesh faced a long, cold and dangerous journey to bring those pieces together. He felt the letter in his pocket. Sartesh would make a good thief… if he survived.

"Perhaps you are tired?" the captain of the Windseeker suggested.

"No, I am running through the strategy in my head one more time. Pull out the charts and I will outline my idea, then we will at least be in agreement when the Protector arrives."

"Dissent never looks good. Some would use that to set captain against captain."

Mycul nodded. He looked around the room. There was a buzz of conversation but every so often someone would stop and stare at him. If he caught their eye the person would quickly look away. Tables were brought together and charts unrolled across the polished mahogany. Mycul toured the tables once then set his finger down on Karlize.

"He can read at least!" a man blurted out. The captain realised wha he'd said and bowed in apology. Mycul smiled.

"I can read and I can navigate by star and compass. And after the fashion of the Adee, I can use longitude and latitude to calculate position, though I like someone to double check my maths!" He hac everyone's attention. "Now I propose sailing only one ship past the city walls but before this happens I want sailors to row barges of pitch and explosives to the walls and detonate them."

"That is suicide!" There was a murmuring amongst the officers present.

"Possibly, however if we choose sailors who can swim and pinpoin our attack on the storm drains, I believe we'll achieve results. The sailors should make for this point where the giant Gorangoth and his friends will be waiting. They'll be well cared for."

There was a lukewarm response to the plan. The officer who'c spoken out previously pointed at the map. "If I might suggest a variation?" He ran his finger along a narrow isthmus. "It should be possible to hoist cannon into barges and land them here. It is a shor journey to Karlize and the batteries could be arranged on the hil beyond the Inn of the Fifth Happiness. If nothing else it will divide their forces."

"I like the way you think!" Mycul slapped the man on his shoulder "That deserves my gratitude and reward if it is successful."

The captain smiled, bowed and received polite applause from others.

"I will always reward initiative. Within our conclave you must allow yourselves to speak freely," Mycul said.

"Even of Yderiphon?" the captain of the Windseeker asked.

"Even of Yderiphon, my friend," Mycul replied just as the Protecto barged through the door. Ceelan's eyes were wide with anger and he could see she struggled to contain her emotions.

"Mycul Zas, a word if I may."

Mycul walked over and bowed. The other officers murmured behind him.

"Your friend has stolen two pieces of the Ornithon and used the great seal of Faires to forge orders. In doing so he has signed his own death warrant."

Mycul looked her in the eye. "He must have a reason. He wouldn' do it otherwise." He could feel the other officers staring.

"Are you certain he didn't confide in you?"

"He mentioned something about the Ornithon. I'm afraid I didn' take much notice with the captains arriving on board. By the time saw him steal your airship it was too late. Do you think he has betrayed us? Perhaps he is working for that woman we met." Mycul pointed upwards.

Ceelan examined Mycul, walking around him once, then jabbing him with the pommel of her knife. The room was hushed.

"If I thought you had anything to do with this, I'd string you up from the yardarm!" She combed her hair with her free hand. "Still, one man on his own is vulnerable."

"He looked to be on his own. Certainly Leeman is here still to guard me."

"A mordont! Creatures so removed from humans they hardly figure on our scale." The general murmuring of conversation resumed.

Mycul remembered his father. He was sorely tempted to tell Ceelan that she was mistaken but bit his tongue and deferred to her wisdom.

"When I expanded the Adee's genetic experiments, I wanted to create an army composed of invincible creatures but I got these unmanageable beings."

Mycul looked at her. "How many labs have you got?"

Ceelan smiled, "Always one more than you think."

"The mordonts showed great courage in battle against the Mordocki, fighting their way into the heart of our enemy's lines. They put fear into our foes. I doubt we would have won..."

"Then you have witnessed their potential but intelligence is not in them."

"That's it!" Mycul walked over to the window and traced a line with his finger. "His father had been turned into a mordont, brave and strong, with beautiful horns which curved around his ears. He didn't want to be cured. He didn't want to find Calufras with father and me."

"Sartesh's father? But Pregule Andrada was always a mordont. He was born to it. Thirty generations of pure bred mordont."

"But how?" The words emerged before Mycul had time to think.

Ceelan laughed. "So, Sartesh is the product of a union between mordont and human."

Mycul didn't divulge the fact that his DNA tested as a pure Adee human. That was a conundrum and he didn't have the time to devote to it now. He hoped Sartesh could find a way.

"Well, young Mycul, I know you're hiding something from me but there will be time for interrogation after the battle."

"I'm always available!" Mycul replied.

"Touché!" The Protector kissed him lightly on the cheek. "You see we're on the same side now. Funny, isn't it? Of course it's a blessing and a curse. Just remember, I am determined to keep hold of power.

It's a fix and I'm an addict. Without power I become Ceelan Devoit once more and I couldn't allow that, could I? No one, not you or Sartesh or any of your followers will prevent me from becoming the Empress of Yderiphon!"

"A noble aspiration," Mycul bowed.

"Oh! Mycul, you obviously don't know me at all." Ceelan made for the door, which was opened by an assassin. The assassin announced Ceelan was going to the battlefront. She held open the door then followed Ceelan out. As the door clicked closed, Mycul sighed.

"You're no good at lying," the captain of the Windseeker said, coming to stand near. "It is a skill you need to develop if you're to keep your head."

The others laughed. Mycul lifted the corners of his mouth fractionally. He heard many footsteps on deck and saw through the Graken's eyes that Ceelan and twelve assassins had disembarked the ship and walked into the darkness.

It was a long night with the captains, discussing the voyage, provisions and strategies.

Just after first light, the fleet set sail on the ebb tide. A south-westerly helped them gain speed on their journey north. The Graken pulled the ships, and the sails were left stowed on their masts.

Leeman approached Mycul. He found it difficult to mouth the human words and a long bray emerged from his throat. Mycul patted his shoulder in solidarity. The mordont's hand covered his. "I'll find you Calufras again."

Leeman shook his head and the words emerged indistinctly, "This time I will remain mordont."

"It's your decision, Leeman." Mycul took readings and an accurate time from a clock. He worked through the calculations and plotted a cross on the chart clipped in place behind the wheel. The sailor adjusted the heading and followed the compass at 315 degrees. All day and night the Graken pulled the ships. The sisters spoke of the song of the whales and their strange notes which punctuated the oceans. The moon set and the decks fell quiet.

Dawn emerged slashed with angry reds and pinks spreading across the cloud-ripped horizon. The coastline was more mountainous and a great gap marked the mouth of the estuary of the Umbre. Mycul felt a wave of excitement turn into a knot of nerves churning in his stomach. Everyone was depending on his plan. He looked up at the Graken.

You can only do your best, she said.

You must be tired after your work, replied Mycul.

The Graken flexed her slender neck, almost unseating her rider. *We will leave you soon. Take care, Mycul.*

And you, he thought, with something akin to love for the great beast.

Together the Graken released their ships and turned. Their riders slipped into the churning waves and were collected and set on board each ship by their Graken's tails. The fleet slowed as sails were unfurled. One ship broke away as agreed in the plan, making for the sandy peninsula. The rest of the fleet turned into the estuary.

A bell sounded and all the men appeared on deck. Mycul stood on the poop deck and addressed them. "Today we will collect the dissident army of Mennes. Their numbers will swell our ranks. Remember, whatever your enmity, these are our friends who share the common aim of killing Warmonger Lazlo and Barser de Sotto. Mennes will be free once more; a land where all are equal. Perhaps one day we will all enjoy such freedom!"

There was silence as Mycul looked around the assembly. He caught the captain of the Windseeker's smile. He began applauding. Others joined in and quickly the sound grew to a crescendo of whooping and cheering.

He bowed, feeling pride glow within, which was slowly replaced by apprehension. Again he looked round the people who now stared expectantly at him. He wondered how many would not survive the night. Whether they lived or died depended on his plan. The realisation made him tremble. Leeman placed a hand on his shoulder, and smiled.

The fleet entered the Umbre and began taking up positions. The Windseeker pushed toward Karlize and fireboats were prepared with tar, saltpetre and sulphur. Slowly they were lowered into the water.

Mycul shimmied down the rope and took charge of one of the fireboats. He placed the oars in the rowlocks and heaved against the tide. At first he seemed to make little progress but when the first arrow whizzed overhead he realised how close he was.

The walls loomed out of the mist and Mycul rowed with every bit of his strength until his muscles ached. He reached the culvert. He set fire to the boat and slipped overboard. Several other ships had reached their target and yet more floated back out to sea, their cargo unspent and oarsmen dead.

Arrows pierced the water and Mycul dived until the pressure on his ears forced him to swallow. He swam, his arms pulling through the water, then surfaced to gasp for air. His sword weighed him down and he submerged, his muscles burning despite the cold.

A hand reached down and pulled. He found himself starring at the plaited beard of Gorangoth. His shield was held against stray arrows.

The giant threw him onto the strand and in a stride was next to him. He dragged him to safety.

"Get those sodden clothes off and wear these."

Mycul shivered and his teeth chattered. The giant ripped the wet garments from his body. He placed his fur cloak around Mycul's shoulders. A bundle of clothes was tossed at Mycul's feet.

"Welcome back to Mennes!" boomed the giant. Producing a flask, he took a sip for himself before offering the liquid to his friend. Mycul took a swig. He felt rejuvenating warmth emanate from his stomach and flow round his body. He struggled into the garments, which clung to his wet form.

"Thanks. Good to see you again," Mycul said, his teeth still chattering.

The giant turned and waded back into the water, pulling out more sailors. He called over his shoulders, "That was a brilliant plan. It distracted the Mordocki and gave us something to see our enemy by."

Cannon fire continued as ships sailed by Karlize. The walls began to crumble, their great stones tumbling into the river. Later, Gorangoth came and stood beside Mycul.

"I don't like death or destruction," he said to Gorangoth.

"You wouldn't be human if you did," Gorangoth replied. "We have many people to help you fight but once we've secured the city, I must take a few and release the dam built in your absence."

"You have completed it? Well done, Gorangoth."

The giant held up his shield and staved off stray arrows. "Let's move from here."

The rebels sheltered in the ruins of warehouses which fronted the dock as the sound of cannon fire continued relentlessly. The air was thick with dust and the smell of sulfur. Occasional screams took long to fade into silence. The walls of Karlize facing the river were almost rubble and through the air Mycul thought he saw something.

"Look!"

Gorangoth placed his battle-axe on the ground.

"They are surrendering. The Mordocki are surrendering." Mycul felt a moment of joy, tempered by all he saw around him. "It is a sad day for great warriors but a good day for us," Mycul said and punched the air.

"You should be proud, your stratagem has worked," Gorangoth congratulated him, then strode over to the Mordocki leader who had stumbled from the rubble.

The man knelt and held up his sword. Gorangoth accepted it. He whispered something then swung the blade, cutting the man almost in two. More warriors knelt in surrender. The giant dispatched them similarly.

"Gorangoth! We need the Mordocki."

The giant turned round, a look of incomprehension on his face.

"This is the beginning of Yderiphon. Beginnings should be good. If it is the wish of the Mordocki to die rather than accept defeat, so be it. But give them the choice," Mycul ordered. He shouted over the noise of cannon so the Mordocki could hear. "If you want to follow us, we have news of Sension, youngest son of Manhedreth. Even now a search is ongoing."

"Is that true?" the giant asked, staring into Mycul's bloodshot eyes.

"Yes."

"A good lie is sometimes worth a hundred truths," the giant said disbelievingly.

"Sension is alive," Mycul reiterated.

Gorangoth stroked his beard, yanked out his flask, and took another sip of the liquid. The fires burned furiously and the walls were little more than smouldering piles of rubble. The giant lifted another sailor from the water but this one was dead, her heart transfixed by an arrow. He gently pushed the carcass out to sea.

"We must go and help in the city. We'll need to find arms, amass the troops together, and organise cohorts to search the ruins." The giant strode ahead but stopped suddenly. He turned back. "I did remember to tell you Sartesh was here yesterday, or was it the day before? He took a piece of the Ornithon from Warmonger Lazlo's rooms and before he got in that flying machine of his, he said something strange. He said, tell Mycul to build with the Ornithon cubes."

Mycul fell silent. The giant broke into a run and soon Mycul was alone with the Mennedic freedom fighters. After a pause he, and the rebels loyal to him, followed the giant's footsteps.

Other Mordocki warriors had formed a phalanx in front of the palace. Their bodies were sweating and their clan tattoos contorted on their muscular torsos as they prepared for the last stand. Flames rose through the palace and glass shattered. The giant stood before them. He growled and shouted abuse. They returned the insults. Mycul stood at the giant's side.

"Move to safety, little one," Gorangoth said. Mycul waved his hand in a curious gesture as the flames flickered through the building. Gorangoth understood. Reluctantly he lowered his axe and took one pace back, leaving the space to Mycul.

"You are brave warriors and you need not die here," Mycul addressed them.

The Mordocki cackled and threw insults. Mycul ignored them and took a pace forward. He unfolded a purple flag and held it up for all to see. The reversed 'z' in gold was clear.

"I offer you a place in Yderiphon if you join us. The old order has passed away and Prince Sension is waiting to be found and reunited with you. For the present he has declared Sartesh Andrada Emperor in his stead."

"Who is this Sartesh Andrada?" queried a decuman, stepping forward. His sword was curved and possessed cruel phalanges designed to inflict pain.

"The once and future Emperor. The Ornithon has predicted it."

The decumen snarled and showed his filed teeth. "The once and future Emperor! You talk in riddles."

"He speaks the truth!" the giant called out. Do you think I, Gorangoth the Golden would betray my country? My heart and blood is in the soil of Mennes. My heart and soul belongs to Yderiphon. Zhedhelion Barkbada Uita!"

"Zhedhelion Barkbada Uita!" the Mennedics chanted.

"Zhedhelion Barkbada Uita!" the Mordocki replied until all had joined in.

"If we are not to fight we should put out the fires then join the ships for Faires," the giant shouted.

"We should all go to Faires to fight with the free people against Barser de Sotto, for who is she?" Mycul asked.

"The person who pays us," the Mordocki decuman replied.

"Sartesh Andrada will pay you in gold," Mycul promised then hoped there was enough in Mennes to do this. It was a minor consideration.

"Take me to some high point and I will give the signal to break off the attack." Mycul passed the flag to the decuman.

"You trust me with this mission. Why shouldn't I kill you?"

"Because I have spoken with Prince Sension through the Ornithon cubes," explained Mycul, producing a cube from his pocket and showing it to the officer.

The decuman bowed. Holding the flag, he climbed the perimeter walls. He found a point facing the port and unfurled the flag of Yderiphon. Cannon fire soon stopped and there was cheering from the ships.

The Windseeker hove to in the deep water and ropes were cast onto the dock. A gangplank was lowered and the captain ran ashore to embrace him, then stood to one side and lifted Mycul's arm in triumph.

The crew broke into song and a hornpipe began. Over the melee of happy voices, Mycul asked the captain for his name. He whispered it in Mycul's ear, each syllable separate: "Desela Volta."

"Well, Desela, we must collect our precious cargo and be away on the next tide. A night and a day to Nofa Flows."

"And another night, as I fear as the wind is against us."

"Desela," Mycul studied him carefully before handing him the sealed envelope. "These are secret orders from Ceelan. Open them if I am killed or incapacitated and follow them without question."

Desela checked the seal, holding the envelope to the light. He nodded.

"If Gorangoth's dams work, that might give us enough time," Mycul said, more in hope than expectation. "Even Ceelan would await full strength before attacking, surely?"

Desela spread his hands. Perhaps it was too much to fathom the mind of the Protector of Faires.

Chapter 24: Assassin

Sartesh threw open the window of the gondola and waved at Mycul. He had been seen. The orders were safe in his breast pocket but not knowing what they contained ate into his thoughts. He had the engines running but found the distribution of devices difficult to figure out. He suspected the Protector was reading Adee manuals for her own advantage: in this she she and Sartesh were alike.

The odometer and altimeter were set under watch glasses behind the ship's wheel. There were several buttons, one of which turned on a huge spotlight: Sartesh quickly extinguished it. He pressed another and thought nothing had happened. Slowly he realised he was listening to music; a flute played a languorous tune, which reminded him of a sultry evening. He listened as he manoeuvred the craft over the roofs and domes of Faires and headed west.

After several minutes, Sartesh put the airship on autopilot. He tapped the speedometer: they were apparently travelling at fifty-six miles every hour. He did a rough calculation and realised he would be in Catherine in a day and a half, all being well.

He sat in the Protector's gilded chair and took out the Ornithon cubes. For a second time he began stacking them together, looking for clues. The cubes could be built into something like a pyramid. There were several gaps. Two cubes resided with Mycul, two with Barser and he hoped the remainder were possessed by Stazman. He left the construction on the table and wondered what the design achieved.

Sartesh peered down. Occasionally he saw lights from some house or inn but otherwise the landscape was difficult to make out. A moon rose and Sartesh looked once more for markers. Nofa Flows glinted like a silver necklace and in the distance he could see the campfires of many troops.

The flat, fertile valley was replaced by an undulating landscape which set Sartesh's heart racing. He recognised the village where he grew up. One day he would return for retribution.

He programmed the craft to rise to a thousand feet and as forests became denser, he turned on the spotlight and slowed the craft. He pulled the chair up to the window and watched whilst attempting to solve the problem of finding Stazman in Catherine. Which building? Which room? He smiled, picked off a cube from the construction and spun it.

"Ah! Sartesh!"

"Ra'an I presume. How delightful." The communication troubled Sartesh as it meant the Ornithon must now be being rebuilt. "How go preparations for battle?"

"I believe they are progressing well for both sides," Ra'an looked behind her and whilst she was distracted, Sartesh poured powder into the black light stream. He calculated the bearing.

"How is Stazman?" Sartesh asked her.

"Imperious! You wouldn't believe how power has changed him - not for the better," Ra'an said. "I have him locked in with me."

"I'm sure it's nothing you can't handle."

"Indeed," she smiled. "But what caused you to contact us, as if I couldn't guess?" Ra'an arched her fingers over her nose and waited.

"We need extra troops," Sartesh lied, and sat back in the chair.

"Why would you ask me, and not Mycul?"

"Or the Protector?" Sartesh was enjoying thinking through the strategy as the airship edged ever closer to the city. He looked at the size and shape of the room and judged it to be in a circular tower. "Mycul thought I might be better able to persuade Stazman."

"Persuade or entice?" Ra'an's face darkened. "Knowing your reputation, I would never allow him anywhere near you."

Sartesh smiled and played his fingers over his lips. "Well, it was worth a try. Surely you can't blame me for attempting to enlist your support."

Ra'an relaxed a little. "No, inferior creatures like yourself need reminding of their place."

Sartesh realised he had heard that line before, from Ceelan. Her clone in Catherine perhaps differed only in eye colour and style of hair but certainly not in her ability to seek opportunity and win. That desire he could empathise with. Sartesh was wondering how to end the conversation when Ra'an unexpectedly broke off. The cubes became opaque once more.

The long and tedious journey resumed: all day he drew lists and calculated. He stopped the craft when darkness fell and the mountains of Catherine loomed. He waited for dawn.

Sartesh had the direction and possible design of the room he was seeking. As the moon set and the sky brightened, he could see the mountains of Catherine, snow-capped and shimmering pink with the rising sun.

The River Umbre curved towards the city and Sartesh spied a recess low in the rising cliffs where he might stow an airship for a few hours. He manoeuvred the craft and let the gas escape quickly.

Jumping down, he anchored the dirigible before climbing the rope back to the gondola and reinflating the balloon. Shimmying down the rope again, he secured several more anchors. He looked back at the craft. He wished he wasn't working alone.

Sartesh Andrada, a voice said within his thoughts. *My daughters attend you.* He turned around and observed two small Graken awaiting his instruction.

I thank you Cyrene, queen of the seas.

He soon sat astride the back of the larger Graken and together they neared the city.

"Would you mind waiting? I believe a quick escape might be necessary."

"Your every order, Sartesh Andrada," they said in unison. "Cyrene was following your thoughts from the Windseeker."

"I'm pleased someone had the foresight." He bowed once after regaining dry land. The creatures dived out of sight.

As he approached the city walls, he noticed all the circular towers flew pennants. A solitary guard patrolled the barbican. He waited; soon an opportunity arose for Sartesh to smuggle himself through the gates. A cart carrying vegetables slowed as it negotiated the ramp towards the gate. Leaping aboard, Sartesh quickly hid himself under layers of cabbages, until he was safely inside.

Once beyond view of the guard, he slipped off and melted into the shadows. For several minutes, he watched people pass by. Guards going off duty walked up hill towards a park where winter trees stood. He toured the perimeter of the park and found that the only way in was guarded by a man and a woman in fetching uniforms of yellow and purple.

He fired a tranquiliser dart at the woman. She felt the shot, stood for a moment, tottered then fell into a faint. The second guard looked around unsettled. Seeing no immediate threat, he checked her pulse and breathing before unlocking the door and pulling her inside. Sartesh struck with a second dart and walked over, pulling both out of the way, locking the door behind him. Sartesh took the steps up to the trees.

At the top he nearly collided with an older woman dressed in black lace over a black dress. Sartesh bowed and apologised.

"Don't I know you?" the lady asked.

Sartesh stopped and smiled.

The lady recollected. "You are the friend of Mycul Zas who helped rescue my son."

Sartesh gave a gesture of supplication. "My apologies, Lady Irana. I have come to talk to Stazman."

Irana Zem laughed grimly, then she glared. "No one sees Stazman except Ra'an de Sotto," she spat. "That lady is weaving spells around my son, so if there's anything you can do to bring him into my presence I would be indebted to you."

Sartesh bowed again. "I'll try. We have a great need of Stazman or I would not risk coming here."

"I walk alone every morning. I sleep little since the loss of my three elder sons." The lady started to walk away.

"Two," Sartesh whispered. "Poablo is still alive; he broke his leg at the Battle of the Perdisher dome. He had been hiding from his enemies disguised as a Mordocki warrior."

Irana turned, her worried face brightened. "Can I trust you?"

"It isn't wise to but I wouldn't have you grieve unnecessarily."

Irana stepped back and grabbed Sartesh's arm. She searched his face and smiled. "He is alive and you love him."

"Is it so obvious?" Sartesh asked.

"To a mother, yes."

"I would take you to him but for the battle."

"Battle?"

"Barser de Sotto has invaded Faires and Ceelan waits at Nofa Flows."

"And my son does nothing?" Irana's face reddened, but she took a deep breath to recover her composure.

"That's why I want to speak to him," Sartesh drew back a little into trees as a guard came near.

"He will see no one. Ra'an ensures only she has contact with Palacre-gen and the decumen of the army. I am tolerated, so long as I don't get in the way."

"Can you take me to his room?"

"I will point it out and then you are on your own."

Sartesh followed as the woman led him across a lawn and up the spiral staircase of a tower. She stopped at the second floor and pointed to an oak door. Guards stood either side. Sartesh loaded a dart and fired. He quickly repeated the act.

"Now all you need is the key!" Irana moved back into the shadows.

Sartesh rattled a skeleton key and moved over to the door. After a little time, there was a click. Irana joined him and followed him through the door. The room was sparsely furnished but looked similar to the one he'd seen in the cubes. Sartesh walked to the central desk. The Ornithon cubes were still on the green inlay. He stretched out his hand. The trisos landed by his fingernails. Sartesh closed his fingers and lifted the cubes.

"I'm pleased to meet you, Ra'an."

"Guards!"

Irana Zem held up her hand. "He is my guest."

"Then you should have the pleasure of killing him," Ra'an said offering a pistol to the woman.

Irana smiled, took aim at Sartesh, but pivoted as she squeezed the trigger. A bullet penetrated Ra'an's heart.

"What have you done?" she whispered. Blood pumped from the wound. She briefly held herself upright at the desk, then cocked her head to one side. She collapsed.

"Thank you," Sartesh said. "I have the cubes I came for but feel I may have outstayed my welcome."

Irana pointed with her other hand. Stazman stood there, his face pale. "You've put on weight," Sartesh said. "You look the part of a prince."

"These past few weeks I have been reduced to Ra'an's slave."

"And now you are free, could you see your way to helping the Perdisher in Karlize?"

"Everything is possible." He looked at the body of the fallen Ra'an, walked past it and embraced his mother.

"I'll leave the family reunions to you," said Sartesh.

"Sartesh, if you go back to the gardens and turn left, the path winds down to the river."

Sartesh nodded. "I am in your debt."

"No," Irana added, "I am in yours. And send him my love."

"Of course," Sartesh said. He took in the scene then ran. He did not stop until he had reached the banks of the river and the safety of the young Graken.

Chapter 25: The Battle of Salleppo

There was a dreadful silence. The fleet sailed up Nofa Flows as far as Crilce. No beasts grazed the fields and no birds flew. The world was too silent, an unnatural void into which hopes and fears drained.

Each ship's company lined up for the march: behind them were the Mennedics and, distributed between the companies, the Mordocki. Mycul loved their ostentatious show of warriorhood, women and men with tattooed torsos proclaiming their affiliations and lucky jinn. Despite his admiration, he worried about their loyalty and deployed them in groups of twenty. If they were sincere, their bravery would give everyone heart. If they were traitors then their numbers were small in each century.

Four multi-coloured airships hovered above the battle lines. Mycul stopped Leeman and pointed. He hoped Sartesh would return soon with the fifth. A great field of tents blocked their way but over to the left the army of Faires ranged along the banks of Nofa Flows. Someone had deployed them with skill.

Mycul marched to the cohort nearest the Protector's tent. Swords were being sharpened on wheels and sparks cascaded; soldiers cleaned out their musket barrels and oiled them ready to take lead shot. There were no horses in this area, just men and women running up and down the lines carrying orders and equipment.

Mycul reached the banks of Nofa Flows. He looked along its length. The debris from previous bridges lined the strand on both sides, but already a pontoon bridge stretched halfway across. In addition, soldiers built under the cover of a great shield.

"The battle will not be today," someone remarked. Mycul turned. Ceelan was dressed in leathers, complete with holster and sword. Her hair had been dyed. "It will happen, the Ornithon predicted this," Ceelan smiled.

"But we destroyed it."

"Weakened perhaps, but destroyed: no." Ceelan patted his cheek. "We'll have to see. How many people have you brought to my army?"

"Two hundred Mordocki and two thousand Mennedics."

"That is excellent news, you've done well. Thank you." The Protector turned back and issued orders regarding deployment. She then addressed further remarks to Mycul. "Strange things have happened. Yesterday a torrent of water came down from the mountains and tore through their camp nearest the river. Tents and equipment were washed away and the bridges all but ddestroyed."

"Gorangoth did well," Mycul replied. "That was to delay battle until we arrived."

"Gorangoth the giant? I thought him a legend." Ceelan read a document. She scrawled a note in reply and sent the messenger back up the line. "Will your mordont fight with us?"

"I believe he's his own person. Perhaps you should ask him."

"Ask a mordont?"

"If you want his help, you will have to ask."

Ceelan appeared uncomfortable with this. She looked around at her assassins who tried not to betray their feelings.

"We are all genetically modified humans, Ceelan. You are a clone; I possess the Ornithon link gene. The only pure human is Sartesh."

"Pure?" She laughed. "One day I'll let you read his file. But," she held up her hand, a gesture Mycul knew well meant 'do not interrupt'. "Expedience is the better part of valour. So Leeman, will you fight with us?"

Leeman struggled to speak: the sounds that emerged were a cross between *yes* and a braying sound.

Mycul was genuinely surprised when Ceelan said, "Thank you." For a moment, she looked out at the far bank. Smoke from many campfires distorted their view of the enemy encampment. This, no doubt, was deliberate.

"I assume you will fight with the Perdisher?"

"Are the Perdisher here already?" asked Mycul.

"Yes, Tahoola has made an excellent gen. Her troops are well trained and disciplined. Mine might walk away if Gurdon gave the order." She smiled. "I underestimated him. I won't make the same mistake twice."

Ceelan twirled the black stone on her pendant. Instantly, Mycul saw stars twinkling in a void. He stared then closed his eyes but still saw the stars. When he opened them, the light had changed.

A shock wave emanated from somewhere distant. Vibrations filled the air and a deep and malevolent noise charged the air and then rushed by like as a gale. Trees were uprooted and tents felled. The waters of Nofa Flows gathered and parted with the earthquake.

He heard the voice of the Graken faintly.

The armies ran towards each other in a great frenzy. The killing began. The tumultuous sound poisoned his ears with screams and cries.

He ran to the lines and pushed his way north. He was surprised Gorangoth had made it to the battle. He must have run all the way. Nonetheless he wielded his battle-axe in great scything motions. Ahead, a phalanx of well-disciplined Perdisher pushed into the enemy lines. Mycul fell in at the rear of them and readied his sword. The forward momentum halted as lead soldiers fell or were crushed by the sheer weight of the enemy surging forward.

He thought he heard Tahoola's voice exhort them to greater efforts but the soldiers' strength was spent and they fell back, tripping over the bodies of their comrades, breaking formation. This left everyone to the mercy of Lazlo's Mennedic soldiers bearing down for the final push. Mycul summoned several Perdisher to reform, saving the line so that wave after wave of the enemy broke against their shields.

Tahoola stood on a slight rise and directed events, her sword poised ready in her left hand. The right sported a series of foils, which looked lethal.

Mycul spotted Alleyya. He felt he could not breathe. A mix of concern and fear mingled with love caused him to be distracted and, had he not regained his senses, he would have been run through on a Mennedic spear. He fought his way out and ran up the hill. Tahoola raised her sword, then lowered it and shouted.

"Mycul! You are safely returned."

"I am!"

"Now is no time for reunions." Alleyya parried a blow.

"It isn't! But fight next to me." Mycul unsheathed his sword and skimmed a trisos into the opposing ranks

Alleyya looked at him.

"Sartesh taught you?"

Mycul nodded, dodged a blow and blocked another. In the distance, he saw Barser de Sotto. He pulled a revolver from its holster and took aim. The noise startled those around him and Barser somersaulted to safety, vanishing into the melee before Mycul could shoot again. Momentarily distracted, Mycul was unaware of the Mordocki soldier sprinting towards him. Alleyya instinctively blocked the blow, enabling Mycul to run him through with his sword.

"Keep your wits!" Alleyya spat and moved away.

Tahoola had deployed her mordonts to charge the line of Mennedics ranged against them in the west. Mycul saw Leeman scythe a battle-axe before him and others moved to take advantage of his progress. The Mennedic lines broke and a retreat began.

Tahoola and her decumen crossed the spongy Nofa Flows riverbed and Mycul followed them with his sword held high, ready for further fighting. He fought next to Tahoola as they cut into the heart of the Mennedic army but again the sheer weight of numbers pressed in around them.

Mycul could see it was difficult for her to swing her sword because of the melee. His heartbeat pounded in his ears. The Mennedic's repeated rallies tried to push Faires' soldiers from the western shore but the troops fought without stopping. Airships hovering overhead began to off-load its cargo of bombs on the retreating Mennedics. It was a cruel twist of warfare to re-invent such Adee tactics.

Barser had reserves and just as the Mennedics gave up, her carnivers leapt into the fray. Their teeth ripped into the bodies of any from Faires who were in their way: soldiers were torn apart in their fever for blood. Alleyya collected a group of archers and fired from a vantage point. They began picking off the creatures; many arrows were required to pierce their flesh and weaken them before swords finished the work.

A breeze from the north carried a roar and tumultuous cascade as the river returned to its course. The rolling and spuming waves seemed to possess faces and their power swept all in their path to their death. Many of the carnivers were too intent on killing to break off and run. Their bodies rolled and churned with the water, unable to escape the raging currents. The Mennedic forces were now divided and diminished.

The press of bodies cleared but Mycul had to step over the dead and dying to keep up with Tahoola. A trisos skimmed past and embedded itself in her shoulder. It was a glancing blow and Tahoola was able to pull it out. It was then she noticed the sticky slime coating the surface and let the object drop.

The trisos had come from a group of Mordocki. Who were they protecting? Tahoola shouted to Mycul and pointed. She screamed at the decumen to change direction.

The hand-to-hand fighting was fierce with several Faires officers falling before they reached their prize.

"So it has come to this, sister," Barser shouted to Tahoola. Immediately, Mycul saw the resemblance. She held her sword ready. The fourth clone: it was Tahoola! Her grey features enabled her to be differentiated from Barser.

242

"It has indeed!" Tahoola nodded, expecting Barser to attack at that moment. She thrust with the sword and cut into her enemy's leg. Barser swore but returned to the fight more determined.

Barser savagely swung her sword and came towards them. She engaged Tahoola who parried and countered but was dealt a blow from one of the Mordocki guarding their leader. Tahoola slumped to the ground leaving Barser to complete the execution.

Mycul saw her danger and thrust his sword up and through Barser's shoulder. The woman screamed. Alleyya blocked an assassin's knife meant for Mycul before Tahoola jumped up and lunged with her sword, severing the tyrant's windpipe. Her blood spurted onto the ground and ran towards the river. Alleyya swung her sword and decapitated Barser, holding up the grisly trophy. Soldiers around saw their leader fall and began to drop their weapons.

The sounds of battle ebbed as soldiers of all ranks turned and fled. Alleyya took a couple of steps before realising the folly of following. The Necromancer arrived.

"Will you take prisoners?" she asked.

Tahoola looked to Mycul. "Not the highest ranks. Behead them here on this field," he commanded.

"In this we concur," Tahoola replied.

The Necromancer nodded. "Ceelan has a spectacle she'd like us all to witness." The lady turned and gestured towards the river bank.

A man knelt in front of Ceelan, his hair matted with blood and his cloak stained from the fighting. Assassins stood with arrows drawn.

Ceelan smiled. "It was worth every death to see you humbled before me, Warmonger Lazlo."

"Will you show mercy, Madam?"

The Protector placed a hand under his chin and lifted his face into the sunlight.

"I will," she nodded. Her assassins lifted the warmonger to his feet, stripped him and dragged him off to a tree.

"Enjoy yourselves, ladies," she hissed. "But slowly; death should be a long-endured journey." She turned her back. The sound of arrows filled the air. At first there were screams which faded to whimpers and finally to silence. Ceelan did not look back.

"Mycul," she ordered, "I'd like you to see this."

Mycul ran to catch up with the Protector. Her path from the battlefield took her by a curious sight. Gordun, the Keeper of the First Law lay frozen in what seemed like shock, as though he hadn't expected the bullet which penetrated his forehead and must have killed him instantly.

Ceelan paused. "Poor man, one more casualty of battle."

"It must have been a stray bullet," Mycul said.

Ceelan smiled. "Yes, it must have been."

"I doubt anyone could prove where it came from."

"No, but I could," she said. "All my enemies will be dead soon."

"The desire of us all, Ma'am." Mycul hoped he did not sound too fawning.

"How does it feel to have won the battle and lost the war, insignificant one?"

Mycul looked around the battlefield. "A necessary evil. When you get rid of enemies, you have no friends."

Ceelan looked at Mycul, smiling. "You are learning."

"I have a good teacher and role model."

"Perhaps you'll join me in a celebratory glass of liqueur?" The Protector waited beside her tent whilst Mycul lifted a flap of fabric and held it in place. Ceelan entered. It was opulently furnished, with a throne in centre.

"Tomorrow I shall be crowned Empress of Yderiphon."

"My hope is you are crowned Empress of the World."

Ceelan looked carefully at Mycul. "Let's not get carried away, just yet."

Ceelan poured her blue liqueur into two glasses. Mycul savoured the taste. He had long ago realised Ceelan would be the final adversary.

"Why did you send Sartesh away?" she asked.

"He is determined on another course. How could I prevent him?"

"Some might think you sent him to Catherine to murder Ra'an de Sotto."

"It would have certain benefits to all of us."

"Yes, it would clear the opposition. However, I don't like people acting on their own initiative, Mycul. It makes things unpredictable."

"As I say, I know nothing of Sartesh's plans."

Ceelan smiled. She obviously knew more than he. This reminded Mycul about the Ornithon cubes. They were still with Barser! He bowed, made his excuses and left the tent. He broke into a run, desperate to reach the body before looters.

Gasping for air as he returned to the knoll where Barser's severed head had been wiped clean and impaled on a long spear. He looked up into her clouded eyes and then scanned nearby for her body. Once located, he rifled through her pockets until his fingers touched the pair of cubes.

He took them out and held them in his hands. They were black but glowed with starlight, just as Ceelan's jewellery had. Curiously, one piece possessed a hole that looked as though a key might fit in it. Mycul understood in that moment.

He looked around the battlefield and felt sadness at the loss of so many lives. He looked at the cubes again.

In the distance he saw Alleyya waving from the Necromancer's tent. He strode over and kissed her. "Thank you; you saved my life when I overstretched my abilities."

"How could I not?" Alleyya said. She held his hands tightly in hers. "Not everyone made it through the battle." She pointed inside the tent, at the body of the mordont laid out on an obsidian table. Mycul went over and closed Leeman's eyes. "He was faithful to the end. He chose to be who he was and not hide behind the disguise of Calufras."

"Indeed. "He showed we are all equally human, whatever our genetic make-up." Mycul felt hot tears rise and Alleyya comforted him. When he had composed himself, he said, "Tomorrow we will crown Ceelan Empress of Yderiphon."

"Tomorrow maybe, but putting a crown on someone's head doesn't make them capable of ruling." Alleyya took Mycul's arm and they returned to the door.

As the sun descended fierce and red behind the mountains, great pyres were built, bodies piled upon them and set alight. The smoke added to the heavy atmosphere and choked the soldiers with its acrid taste. Survivors of all ranks stood in silence and offered up prayers.

Later as Venus appeared in the darkening sky and embers guttered into the air, Mycul stood alone. He felt something was missing. Alleyya had already retired to bed. He had run his hands over her skin then knelt and placed his ear to her ribs, feeling the warmth of her breasts, listening to her heartbeat. It had given him a moment of happiness to counter his developing dread.

"Well Mycul Zas, you should be congratulated. You have altered history." The voice was faint and familiar. Mycul looked around. A great many campfires were lit but he could see no one near him. "You remember me?"

In a moment of inspiration he took out the cubes. "Nag-Nag Naroon!"

"Indeed. The Ornithon restores itself."

"Then you will know what has happened." Mycul cupped the cubes in his palms.

"That's not fair. It seems only you, Sartesh and Stazman possess the cubes now. I believe your friend has a plan."

"If he does, he didn't tell me. Is your tower in Undon rebuilt?"

"I'm not in Undon. I'm travelling north to return the future to a correct path."

"Ah! A correct future, if only there could be one."

"There is if the Adee are ever to return to Earth."

Mycul thought about the Adee. "They have exiled a man to Earth called John the Annunciator."

"He will die quickly or become mordont. Either way his ideas will fade," Nag-Nag said.

"Is that what the Ornithon wants? The echo of this idea about a child…"

Nag- Nag momentarily revealed himself as possessed of half a face with nanobots actively rebuilding his features. The image reminded Mycul of his father. The storyteller faded. Nag-Nag had disclosed something of his intentions, although he suspected Nag-Nag was not telling the whole truth.

As Mycul returned to the Necromancer's tent he heard another voice in the cubes. "Mycul, I have all but two cubes. A final key needed."

"Sartesh. Return quickly. Nag-Nag is nearly restored," Mycul implored.

"I need the final cubes and key."

"I have the cubes and will hold the key in my hand."

"What do you mean?" Sartesh sounded concerned.

"The Protector knows our plan and my part in it. She means to murder us all, just as I saw in the Ornithon."

"In that case, inform the Necromancer and use the stasis chamber," Sarteh said. The voice faded.

Inside the Necromancer's tent, Mycul hid the cubes in the most recent skull, the newly prepared head of Barser, skin and sinew removed. He walked around the tent as lights appeared in skulls. Shades and ghosts walked towards him. He saw his father, his mother and finally Leeman. "Lesser of the three yet greater," they chanted in unison. "Beware Ceelan."

Hands clapped once. "Be gone!" the Necromancer ordered. She studied Mycul, "What did you do?"

"I put the Ornithon cubes back in Barser's skull, for safe keeping then I saw lights…"

The Necromancer held out her hand and caught his shoulder. She looked into his eyes. "You are near death. They call you over. I am sorry."

"Sartesh asked me to use the stasis chamber. Does that make any sense?"

The Necromancer thought about this. "Yes it does. You must tell Alleyya as I fear I also will not survive tomorrow. Ironic, isn't it? A necromancer who fears her own death."

Mycul realised what she was telling him. "Living is a dangerous game and if we are to have freedom for ourselves and our children, some must be sacrificed. I do this by my own free will."

The Necromancer kissed him lightly on the cheek, "You are an inspiration, Mycul."

Chapter 26: The Empress of Yderiphon

"Not again!" Alleyya heaved over a large bowl.

"I was the same with you. It will pass," the Necromancer said, and smoothed her daughter's brow. "But not soon enough to attend the coronation of Ceelan." The Necromancer moved away and drifted aimlessly through the room. She picked up a head. Two cubes fell out. She studied them idly, beyond caring, rolling them on the desk like dice.

Mycul picked them up and fitted them together. "This is the answer."

"Ornithon cubes? They do not answer our dilemma." The Necromancer trailed her finger over skulls she had long used in her rituals. "We are no longer following the path of the Ornithon. The Adee were controlling events so they could live once more on Earth. Destroying a central Ornithon has removed their influence."

"It is strange to think of free will factoring into predictions of the future," Mycul said. He heard Alleyya spew again and looked on with concern. "Are you ill?"

The Necromancer spoke up. "Mycul: you are to be a father!"

Mycul stood with his mouth open. He felt his legs shake and his throat went dry. "A father?" he whispered.

"This began at dawn and I realised I had missed my cycle," Alleyya croaked, then sipped water. "I feel so foolish fighting yesterday. I could have endangered a new life."

"But you saved mine!" Mycul ran up to Alleyya as though he might lift and swing her but changed his mind and settled for an embrace. As they separated, they both were crying tears of joy. "Then you know how important it is to keep you safe from now on," Mycul ordered and looked to Tahoola.

"Yes, I will be Alleyya's guard from now on," Tahoola confirmed.

The mood of elation was replaced by the reality of their position. Mycul remembered what he wanted to say. "I want you to listen very carefully. I have no evidence for what I am about to say but I want you, Alleyya and all the Perdisher to leave here now and find somewhere you can withstand a siege. I suspect Ceelan will try to murder us all." The silence in the room could have meant many things.

The Necromancer caressed the skull of Barser de Sotto. She closed her eyes but said nothing. "When I consulted the Ornithon, I saw Tahoola and Sartesh looking after our daughter."

"Did you witness my death?" Alleyya asked.

"Perhaps. This is why I feel unsettled," Mycul added.

Alleyya trembled and was sick once more. "I'm going nowhere."

"You are all leaving, so Ceelan can try to murder me," Mycul announced. He thought he managed to say this calmly.

Alleyya trembled and her mother steadied her. "Here, drink this. It will help you feel better," the Necromancer said. Alleyya sipped from the cup.

"Do you have the stasis box I saw all those weeks ago?" Mycul asked.

"It will avail you of nothing if she does not use poison. You will take Calufras and Alleyya will later give two drops of foxglove extract." The Necromancer sighed.

"There is a great risk. Too great a risk. If you suspect Ceelan will murder us all, why not just come away with us?" Alleyya said, her hand trembling round the cup.

"Because I am a Graken herder and Commodore of the fleet and I must ensure that you, Tahoola, and everyone else is safe. If I am not at the coronation, Ceelan will suspect what is happening."

The Necromancer thought about this. She poured hot water over some herbs; the aroma of ginger filled the tent. "Then it is time the Perdisher had a fleet. There must be Mennedic vessels we could acquire?"

"Some captains from Faires will be loyal, for a while at least. I have these orders," Mycul said and passed papers over.

"This is Ceelan's seal." Tahoola was incredulous.

"I had Sartesh forge orders. They say the fleet must take the Perdisher to Karlize as Menne will be your new home."

"This was a well thought out stratagem, Mycul," Tahoola said. She smiled and moved to look out of the tent. She pointed her finger in caution just as an assassin arrived. The woman stood in the doorway and waited. The Necromancer nodded.

"The instructions concerning the crowning of Her Magnificence, Ceelan, as Empress of Yderiphon," the assassin said, thrusting out a letter.

The Necromancer it round for all to read.

"I've been asked to await your reply."

The Necromancer smiled, falsely. "The Protector does the Perdisher great honour." She sat at her desk and dipped the nib of a pen in ink.

A reply was composed and the assassin dismissed with it. "So the ceremony will be here tomorrow at dawn with assassins as the guard of honour in the throne room," the Necromancer confirmed.

"And with the massed army of Faires waiting outside," Tahoola concluded.

The Necromancer stood and paced the room. She took a deep breath. "I will attend tomorrow. I am ordering you to follow Mycul's plan. It would look odd if Mycul and I didn't attend but Alleyya could be many miles away by the end of the ceremony."

"My ships are on Nofa Flows near Crilce, Tahoola. You must protect Alleyya and ensure the safety of all the Perdisher." There was a long silence whilst the implications of the strategy sunk in.

Alleyya sipped the ginger tea her mother had prepared. "Why Mennes?" she asked.

"Gorangoth has influence in Karlize and he will protect you, particularly if he thinks your child is *the* Child. Sartesh might become Emperor of Menne. Also on your journey Cyrene will look out for you all. Finally, it will make me feel happier."

"But Ceelan will bring her army to the capital."

"Undoubtedly she will. Winter will close the pass and Gorangoth will hold it thereafter and that gives us several months to prepare," Mycul replied. He picked up the tyrant's skull, flipped it over and examined the cranial cavity before replacing it on the desk.

"Mennes it is then." Mycul passed the cubes to Alleyya. "Give these to Sartesh when he returns."

"Yes, but I wish you would do that," Alleyya murmured.

"And you know I'll be in stasis relying on Sartesh to find a cure."

Alleyya nodded. Then she raised her brows. "You sent him to Catherine to steal the remaining two Ornithon cubes."

"Yes, I did and I hope he has killed Ra'an de Sotto. I figured it might give us time so we can decide how to destroy the Ornithon and end its influence forever."

A second assassin entered the tent. She bowed slightly. She whispered to the Necromancer who paparphrased the conversation as the assassin exited.

"There is a rehearsal for the coronation now, a run through for the guards and readers. I am needed, apparently." The Necromancer attended to her appearance, picked up Barser's skull, and left.

Mycul stood. "I have some preparations. I need to speak to Gorangoth," Mycul said. He hardly dared to look at Alleyya in case his emotions broke. She took a step forward, noticing his black hair was unkempt and his blue eyes less bright. She reached out and straightened the lions' head pendant at his neck.

"Ceelan has requested the Necromancer summon the souls of the dead to witness the crowning and pay homage," Tahoola-gen surmised. "I have a sense of foreboding I didn't feel before the battle."

"I heard from Nag-Nag Naroon. He is being restored, so I am guessing the Ornithon is also being restored. I believe several of us should have died at the Battle and he now is seeking to restore the programme as best he can," Mycul managed to say without his voice waivering.

"Why?" Tahoola walked up to Mycul.

"It was devised by the Adee. They want to return to Earth but can't without succumbing to disease, so they need genetic experiments to continue until a cure is found. They have made some dreadful pact with Ceelan."

"Ceelan is still conducting experiments?" Tahoola asked. "The genetics laboratory on the Reach of Key was destroyed." She paused. "You know, all assassins are clones. Indeed I am a clone."

"You may resemble Ceelan's assassins but you are our friend and have proven yourself many times. You have risen above them!" Alleyya stated.

"Alleyya is right, but so are you, Tahoola. She must have another place where clones are fabricated," Mycul said.

"I have no recollection," Tahoola admitted.

"The task at hand is staying alive. Ceelan must be thwarted in her plans."

"The banks of the river are strewn with her enemies. Gurdon, other Keepers of the seven laws, several assassins and council members. I suspect a coup has taken place." Tahoola looked at her friends.

Mycul swallowed, "You mean Leeman was killed by our own side?"

"I didn't want to tell you, Mycul," Alleyya said. She possessed more colour.

Mycul went over to her and placed his arm around her shoulder. "Tahoola, will you go with Alleyya to Mennes?"

"Alleyya's safety is paramount. I will take her to the Windseeker."

"I will ask the Graken to pull you to the city of Mennes."

Alleyya held out her hand. Mycul kissed her cheek. "I hope after you administer the drug I'll be resurrected from the stasis chamber." The room fell silent except for the flapping of the tent and the sound of a breeze in the trees beyond. "You must go to Karlize no matter what happens and I will attend the coronation knowing you are safe."

"We will do as you say but who will put you in the stasis chamber if it becomes necessary?"

"Gorangoth," Mycul said.

"At least he can be relied on. I will pack mother's sacred objects and send them ahead to the Windseeker. She will only need only the skull of Barser de Sotto to summon all the legions of dead."

Mycul left the tent and sought the giant. He found Gorangoth supping ale from a tankard.

"Hello!" Mycul shouted.

The giant lifted his tankard. "A great victory!"

"I was impressed with the speed of your journey from the dam."

Gorangoth raised his tankard again and smiled. "I have seen nothing of Sartesh."

"He'll be back soon. He's stealing a few items and solving another of our problems. There is one we have overlooked, however."

The giant wiped his beard, "Ceelan."

"I want you to ensure I am placed in the stasis chamber if I am killed."

"You have a plan?"

"Maybe, but I'll need you to be single minded and determined to live. Make certain you wear armour," Mycul instructed.

"Armour?" the giant asked. Then he nodded. "Have no worries on that score!"

Mycul patted the giant on the shoulder and left him to his drink.

-*-

It was cold in the grey pre-dawn light. Mycul had cleaned himself and wore his commodore's uniform. He carried no weapons as he knew everyone would all be searched. Rims of salmon pink and red edged the clouds.

The imperial crown of Mennes had been brought out on a velvet cushion and placed on an ornate table in front of a wooden throne. The crown was a simple set of gold bands. The back panel of the throne possessed an intricately carved reversed Z metamorphosing into a swan. In the back corner the stasis chamber had been placed.

Gorangoth had washed and stood in all his finery by the door. He looked tired; dark rings under his eyes told of too much drink and too little sleep.

Mycul waited as the room filled with the great and good of Faires and Mennes. Last to enter were the Protector of Faires and the Necromancer. Ceelan provided a contrast to the subdued colours of everyone else. Her dress was long and decorated with gold thread and ornaments and she wore the most elegant of hats over her short hair.

Mycul looked at the balcony. Assassins stood at every vantage point. Gorangoth banged a staff on the floor. Golden light emanated along fissures created by the blow.

"I call Ceelan Devoit to become Empress of Yderiphon!" Gorangoth exclaimed.

Ceelan bowed. She walked gracefully to the table.

"Does anyone here know of any just reason why Ceelan Devoit should not be proclaimed Empress of Yderiphon?" Gorangoth's voice reverberated. There was silence.

The Necromancer stepped forward. "We are here to give thanks for the great victory of all people at the Battle of Salleppo on the banks of Nofa Flows. Good has triumphed over evil at great cost to us all. Our first task is to honour all who died and see their souls released into the next life."

Mycul watched as the Necromancer intoned and light was sucked from the marquee. Wisps of ether formed and became the bodies of the departed. For a few seconds their human forms faced the assembly, then bowed and dissipated. The procession lasted a long time. Mycul wanted to leave; he felt the knot tighten in his stomach watching Barser de Sotto and Warmonger Lazlo appear together. He wondered if he had done the right thing, taken the right side. Leeman walked towards Ceelan and uttered a deep growl. The Protector managed to stay calm.

"I am Ceelan Devoit and as foretold by the Ornithon, I accept the crown of Faires and Mennes. The two countries are now united as one in Yderiphon."

Gorangoth moved forward, removed her hat and placed it on the table before picking up the crown and placing it on her head. The giant knelt before her. Everyone in the room bowed before Ceelan.

"All Hail the Empress of Yderiphon. All Hail! Long Life! Wisdom!" The assembly fell silent after the chant.

"This is my first act as Empress," she said, and gave a signal. "Keep the faith, my people and remember you saw the dawn of Yderiphon." A moment of calm gave way to whispering, abruptly brought to an end by a single arrow.

One woman was hit. People gasped, then more arrows flew. The air hissed with them. Screaming and panic followed, with more of the congregation killed in the aisles, and as they climbed over chairs. Ceelan smiled. "Behold my new order!"

Mycul ran toward her.

Gorangoth looked bewildered. He stepped forward a few paces and placed himself near the Necromancer.

"Don't forget the stasis chamber," Mycul mouthed, barely nodding to the corner behind the Necromancer.

Gorangoth nodded. He picked up his staff but was powerless to attack all of the assassins or defend the audience.

"Ah! Mycul. You have decided."

Mycul nodded.

"One last kiss as I promised."

Mycul accepted.

Ceelan's lips caressed his, her tongue found his. He felt something dissolve on his tongue. As Ceelan's hands gripped his shoulders, his fingers curled round her obsidian pendant filled with its flickering stars. She let go. Mycul felt faint, yet the pendant slipped from Ceelan's neck. The room swirled and blurred.

"Poison?"

Ceelan nodded.

"Your insignificant life is ended with a kiss," Ceelan whispered as her fingers caressed his cheek. As Mycul fell, he saw Ceelan produce a pistol.

The Necromancer stood before her. A bullet was fired. "You can join the dead you so enjoy conjuring!" Ceelan snarled, then stepped over the dying woman. Assassins cruelly dispatched the guests until the very fabric of the tent was dyed with blood and screams had subsided leaving quivering flesh and a stench of iron.

Ceelan surveyed all. The hem of her dress was splattered with blood. Finally she stretched out her arms and laughed heartily. "Behold, my new order!"

"Gorangoth, remember, whilst there is still time…" Mycul felt pain surge through him and became unconscious.

Chapter 27 Yderiphon Begins

The Windseeker cast anchor and sailors prepared the oars. Alleyya stood behind the wheel searching the banks. Tahoola stood next to her. The boat progressed slowly along Nofa Flows, taking the meanders and navigating the deepest passage. "They have been too long." Alleyya fingered the vial containing the antidote her mother had prepared that morning.

"What's that in the sky?"

"An airship, if I'm not mistaken," Tahoola said picking up a telescope and observing the object's progress. "Ceelan's."

"Well I didn't think escape would be that easy."

"Any more speed, Desela?"

"The day promises little wind and the river is too shallow for a Graken. The people pulling our oars are working hard."

Tahoola looked back towards the encampment. Smoke was rising from the marquee. Alleyya sat on a chair and caressed her stomach.

"Something has happened. I feel it."

Tahoola kept observing the bank. Tall grasses swayed and were being trampled. She felt her throat dry. "Archers to the deck!" A whistle sounded and many people took to the railings of the ship. Arrows rested poised in taut bows whilst the archers cast nervous glances toward the unknown.

Tahoola watched the grasses swaying then saw Gorangoth carrying a large box. He was running, and red from the exertion. "Stand down! Heave to the bank!" Tahoola pointed and a gangplank was lowered. The giant clambered on board and carefully put down his burden. "Mycul requested I do this."

"What has happened?" Alleyya asked.

The giant waved his hand. He was out of breath and sat on the deck next to the stasis chamber. A large tankard of beer was brought. He gulped it down and wiped his face. "Ceelan ordered all the guests at the coronation killed. It was dreadful carnage." He looked at Alleyya, recognising her. "I am sorry for your loss."

"No!" Alleyya's cry became a howl of grief.

Tahoola comforted her. "You must save Mycul. Give him the antidote."

Alleyya's tear stained face turned to the stasis chamber. She keyed in a code and the glass slid open. Mycul lay on his back, his skin pale but warm. Alleyya opened his mouth and poured in drops of the foxglove essence. There was no response.

"What did the Necromancer tell you to do?" Tahoola asked.

"Three drops and if nothing happened three drops more."

Tahoola placed her ear to Mycul's lips. She persuaded herself the faintest of breath stirred. She took the vial and administered three more drops. Nothing happened.

The sound of engines grew. The airship was upon them. Tahoola ordered the defence of the ship and prepared her soldiers. An anchor descended. It caught hold of the railings.

"Hello below!"

"Sartesh!" Tahoola waved with relief. The man swung down on a rope and landed perfectly on the deck.

"Did they teach you that in a circus?" Tahoola asked.

"Give me some credit," Sartesh said and ran over to the stasis chamber.

He hit Mycul over the heart and started pumping his hands on his chest. He breathed into Mycul's mouth, then pushed the air back out of his lungs. He breathed into his mouth once more.

Mycul moved, smiled and looked at Sartesh. "Voya," he said and his eyes closed.

"I have restarted his heart but he needs Deidar Mela for a full recovery. I need to close the stasis chamber, Alleyya."

Alleyya walked over, her finger stroked Mycul's cheek. She opened his hand and took the Protector's necklace. "You'll need this," she said and handed the obsidian jewel to Sartesh.

Alleyya paled and sat down again.

"He succeeded," Sartesh concluded and went over to Alleyya. "Don't worry, he'll be restored, I promise."

"Gorangoth, would you mind holding this a moment?" Sartesh climbed up to the airship, and returned minutes later carrying a large cube. "Alleyya, could I have the two cubes you were given?"

Alleyya fumbled in her pockets and found them. Sartesh built the remaining side of the Ornithon cube then took the pendant from Gorangoth and inserted the key.

"No!" Nag-Nag revealed himself from amongst the crew. He drew a gun. Sartesh ignored him. There was a simple click and a moment of stillness before the cubes rotated and fell away, as black light swept from the box out towards the horizons. Thunder could be heard in the distance and the ship felt as though it were rising as air molecules around them crackled with static.

Nag-Nag faded as the bullet fired. His reality dissolved taking the gun and bullet with it. Lines of darkness reflected as intense white beams, returning and engulfing the cubes. They melted and dripped onto the deck before their dust was blown away. Sartesh looked around; nothing remained of the Ornithon cubes.

"I feel a weight has lifted from me," Alleyya announced.

"That sense of foreboding has gone." Tahoola looked into the stasis chamber. "Seal it up. Let us see if we can revive Mycul in the place of healing."

Alleyya nodded.

"But first we need somewhere we can defend, a place with food, water and a good vantage point."

"I have the very place," Sartesh replied, "Karlize. A few more miles and the Graken will pull us, if I can remember her song."

Sartesh keyed in numbers on the stasis chamber and the glass slid into place. A fog accumulated within and the glass panel misted over with ice so Mycul's features could no longer be seen.

"I have lived with this device and always assumed it was needed for mother." Alleyya turned away, bent with grief.

"I don't suppose you want to tell us about the technology, Sartesh?" Desela asked. "A few captains think as I do and are loyal to me. So Karlize is possible and of course you have the forged orders."

Sartesh smiled and shook his head. "I'll tell you later, although you won't believe me. We must get to safety. Gorangoth, can we rely on your help at Karlize?"

"Yes. We will make Mennes a fortress against Ceelan. Never again will it be conquered by land or sea."

Sartesh stood and took a deep breath. He placed his fingers on his shoulder and sang the notes. The Graken surfaced, her great fins visible in the shallow water. She sniffed at the stasis box. Her saliva dripped onto the deck.

He is not dead, I can hear his dreams.

I thank you for confirming what I thought. I will use all my expertise to return him to you and the sea, Sartesh thought in reply.

You do me a great honour. You do not need to call me, Sartesh Andrada. I am yours to command.

I thank you for your help in heaving us to Karlize?

There and back again if necessary, the Graken said and took hold of the anchor in her teeth and began pulling.

257

The floodplains beside Nofa Flows grew larger and flatter and wild vegetation climbed and strangled the trees. Fields which showed signs of recent cultivation were being taken over by the mutant plants cascading across the soil and choking all other life. The river straightened and widened as they reached Faires Argenta.

The slender causeway of the city came in to sight along with the great sea walls. Above these, the buildings of the palace could be seen with their pennants flying.

Looking behind Sartesh counted the ships of the fleet following them as the open sea beckoned. It was as he feared; only ships carrying the Perdisher followed, others made for the port. Ceelan would never stop until all opposition was removed. Just like her sisters she had been genetically programmed to rule. She had no other purpose, which could be both a strength and a weakness.

Tahoola stood next to him. "A victory and a defeat."

Sartesh placed his arm around her. "No: a victory which is all ours and now there is only one enemy to defeat."

"Just the one? Are you sure?" Tahoola flashed a smile before returning to Alleyya. "Who is Voya?"

Alleyya pointed at her stomach and the life within. "I hope the world she is born to is a better place."

"It will be," Tahoola said, "because we are alive and united. Friendship and love. That is all that counts."

Other novels, novellas and short story collections available from Stairwell Books

Carol's Christmas	N.E. David
Feria	N.E. David
A Day at the Races	N.E. David
Running With Butterflies	John Walford
Foul Play	P J Quinn
Poison Pen	P J Quinn
Wine Dark, Sea Blue	A.L. Michael
Skydive	Andrew Brown
Close Disharmony	P J Quinn
When the Crow Cries	Maxine Ridge
The Geology of Desire	Clint Wastling
Homelands	Shaunna Harper
Border 7	Pauline Kirk
Tales from a Prairie Journal	Rita Jerram
Here in the Cull Valley	John Wheatcroft
How to be a Man	Alan Smith
A Multitude of Things	David Clegg
Know Thyself	Lance Clarke
Thinking of You Always	Lewis Hill
Rapeseed	Alwyn Marriage
A Shadow in My Life	Rita Jerram

For further information please contact rose@stairwellbooks.com

www.stairwellbooks.co.uk
@stairwellbooks